Crystal Grave

Crystal Grave

Daniel Fanning

Dedication

Thank you, mother. Thank you, father.
Thank you, Lord.
And thank you, reader. More than anything else, I wrote this in the hope
that people would read it.

Table of Contents

Chapter 1

Jasto needed to win, but once again he wasn't strong enough.

He still tried, getting his shield up just in time to stop Epha's gray quarterstaff. The blow sent a shudder down his arm, and as he went to counter she slapped down his baton, a verdant green with lines of white, and brought her staff around to strike at his shoulder.

He threw himself back just in time to avoid the blow, then planted his foot and lunged, thrusting his baton out like a rapier. It forced Epha to take a step back, but unlike Jasto she had far more control over the motion. Coming to a halt just outside the reach of his thrust, Epha brought her quarterstaff down right on his forearm, sending a painful shock through it. As he reeled back from that blow she closed in, feinting high to take his shield out of position before sweeping her staff low and into the meat of his calf.

Even with his sparring armor on, Jasto felt a shudder pass through his leg and nearly went to a knee as he stumbled back. His forearm and the other places Epha had whacked him were still numb, and he knew the veteran knight was just getting started.

She didn't bother following his retreat, instead spinning her quarterstaff idly as Jasto recovered. In her sparring armor Epha looked more like a living crystal than a person, the photothyst that formed it a smoky gray translucent enough to reveal glowing gold filaments. But despite that facade and the faceless protective grid wrapped around her head, disdain radiated off her.

Dad spoke up, distressed by the way the battle was going. "Sir Suncage, I understand that my son spoke out of turn and insulted your—"

Regardless of her age and growing irritation, Epha spoke clearly and didn't drop the formal dialect that older knights seemed to prefer as she cut Dad off. "Mr. Chaston, I may not be putting your son through my usual trial, but do not mistake that for a lack of standards. The Palace he wishes to enter is a dangerous place."

She gestured to it, and Jasto couldn't help but follow her hand. The Palace loomed behind Epha, the size of a baseball diamond but hexagonal and made entirely of deep blue photothyst. Some called the physics-breaking material 'starcrystal' or 'hardlight,' but Jasto made a point of only using the scientific term even in his head.

With little concern for what anyone called its building materials, the Palace had spent years growing over the rock of the ravine, forming hexagonal irregularities wherever the ground was too rough. Like all photothyst it was threaded with filaments, the thin veins within the crystal that made it a tangible solid.

But while filaments glowed in the photothyst of a fully human knight, shining white in Jasto's case and gold in Epha's, those of the Palace drank the light instead. Even within the ravine's shade it was shrouded by an unnatural amount of darkness, an undeniable sign that the knight forming it had been corrupted.

"Though our bargain remains intact, your son is nonetheless about to undertake a serious challenge," Epha continued. "If this is the best he can muster, I may need to delay his entry until I have trained him further." Jasto felt her gaze flick back down to him. "Especially considering his…records at the Valor Academy."

Indignation spiked. "You would bring the Academy up, wouldn't you? Honorable Sir Suncage?" Jasto taunted between breaths. "It makes sense, the both of you have your heads so far up—"

"*Jasto Chaston,*" Dad said, and he froze. "Your concern is reasonable, Sir Suncage, but if my son is exhausted and injured before even entering, how will he be able to defend himself at all?"

"Are you exhausted, Jasto?" the veteran crystal knight asked. "Or too injured to continue?"

He grit his teeth, feeling the beginnings of bruises under his own photothyst armor. Of course he could still fight. He just wasn't strong enough to win, something which burned even more because he'd come here to fix that.

And here he was anyway, stonewalled from getting stronger *because* he was weak.

But he didn't need to respond, because Dad was on the ball. "It's because my son has the will of a warrior that he will keep fighting, even when too injured for a later battle," he said. "What kind of crystal knight would concede before giving their best?"

Epha tilted her head. The old knight was more than capable of telling Dad to go screw himself, and if she did his father had no leverage, no way to force her to play ball. But for all that strength, Epha was still bound up in those invisible strings called 'expectations.' And with a few words, Dad had gotten a grip on them and yanked.

Jasto had sworn to himself that he'd never end up in those strings, so despite the fact that he was bruising under his armor and this mess was all his fault to begin with, he still grinned as Epha hesitated.

A moment later Dad got what he'd been aiming for: a handicap for Jasto. "Very well. Does one of your mercenaries have a timer?" Epha asked.

The sparring match paused as Dad turned to the masked and gun-carrying retinue he'd hired to ask, and Jasto had a moment to catch his breath.

And to think about the mistake that had started this fight, because as triumphant as he'd felt just now it had been completely avoidable.

Everything had been going perfectly just minutes ago, thanks to Dad's help. After three days of tense talks Epha had reluctantly agreed to let Jasto and his mercenaries enter this Palace, and to help them kill the corrupted knight within. Most importantly, she had given her word that the fallen knight's Crest would go to Jasto, after the kill. It had all been in motion, the strength that would secure Jasto's independence almost within his grasp. They'd been within sprinting distance of the Palace.

And Jasto hadn't even been worried about himself, when he'd asked if it was safe to be this close. But only a few mercenaries would be staying behind with Dad as he and Epha entered the Palace. Jasto was going after this Crest for his own sake, at the end of the day, so he'd wanted to make sure his father would be alright.

But Epha had responded like the question itself was stupid. "A Palace in a latent state only poses a threat to those who enter its territory," she'd said. "And its territory goes no further than the photothyst forming it does. You may not have spent long at the Valor Academy, Jasto, but I am certain you were at least taught that."

He'd crossed his arms. "I also learned about the stats Palaces show for remaining in latent states over time. For fun I even calculated the trend line formula: a horizontal asymptote approaching zero. You remember what that means, old woman?"

"Numbers are numbers," Epha dismissed. "This Palace is the home of a hero, and she is beyond your amateur calculations."

"This Palace, just like every Palace, is the home of a *corrupted* knight," Jasto had countered. "Hero or not, she gave in and that means she will go active. And since that could happen any time, you can excuse me for being a little worried about the safety of my…"

He'd stopped talking when he'd seen the look on his father's face, but it had been too late by then. Jasto was supposed to be calm, Dad had been telling him to focus on that for years, but instead he'd made almost as big of a mistake as he could. The kind of error Dad had been warning him about right from the start, and it had put this entire mission—his mission—in jeopardy.

"I believe ninety seconds will be sufficient," Epha said, jolting him out of the recollection. One of the mercenaries had separated from the pack, masked and tapping at a rugged watch on his wrist. Meanwhile Epha looked down at her quarterstaff.

A burst of bright golden filaments shot from its tip in rigid lines, then grew dimmer as they projected gray photothyst to form a spearhead atop the weapon. Epha turned and thrust down at the rock of the ravine, the exotic material easily carving a horizontal line through it as she moved.

"Ninety seconds," she repeated. "That is how long you will have to push me past this line, Jasto." She dismissed the spearhead from her staff, its projected photothyst vanishing from existence first and the golden filaments that had formed it right after. "I will defend myself as you try to do so," she continued, taking a spot a few feet in front of the line and holding her staff forward in a basic guard. "However, I will not advance forward. I will only stand my ground or retreat, until the ninety seconds have finished. They will begin on your mark."

Jasto focused on his breathing as he thought the challenge through. There was no denying that Dad had just given him a significant advantage, especially with how much Epha seemed to enjoy closing in.

But could he do it? Jasto was younger, and a little faster. But she'd read him consistently from the moment the fight started, and towered above him in terms of experience with duels like these. The doubts piled up.

But all Jasto had to do was think about the Valor Academy, and they scattered like ash. That school had tried to shape him, the same way it had shaped Epha and all the knights like her, but it had failed. He'd chosen expulsion and a branding with squire-errant status over letting that school keep him from his family another day.

He wouldn't choose to give up now.

Jasto stood straight, squared himself up behind his shield, and put all his focus on Epha.

"Start!" he yelled, and rushed forward.

Epha shifted her grip on her staff as Jasto charged, sliding both hands down to hold it more like a spear, and nearly jabbed him in the neck as he came in. Jasto just managed to get his baton up, pushing it aside, and as he went in for a shield punch with his other hand Epha did step back.

It wasn't over yet, and she brought her staff back around in a swing that Jasto had to defend from, but he felt his confidence surge. It was possible. He pushed forward doggedly, taking some hits and having to stumble back at times, but every step Epha took back she couldn't recover and they were starting to pile up.

"Forty-five seconds," the mercenary called. Epha shifted her grip back and began to defend with both ends of her staff, which meant the hits came in faster but with less force. Throwing caution to the wind, Jasto let himself take one of those lighter blows on his thigh, then pushed down on the staff with his shield and twisted to crack his baton into the old knight's side.

"Thirty seconds."

Epha felt that one, Jasto could tell, but it was just as obvious she was used to working through pain. It still forced her back another step, but even as she made space for herself she was swinging again and Jasto would have been kneecapped if he hadn't retreated.

However, that gave him an opportunity. He'd tried a straight-on lunge just after retreating earlier, and Epha had responded by stepping just out of reach of it and striking him on the arm. Jasto went for it again, making the preparatory motions obvious.

But unlike last time, Jasto would turn his lunge into a full-on charge. It would push Epha back further, and she was close enough to the line now that a tackle would take her over. It might not have been a graceful move, or in line with any of the teaching Jasto had been put through, but he wasn't the type to care.

His baton extended outward like an emerald lance, and he followed behind it with his shield pressed close to his body, ready to step forward again right as he completed the lunge.

But then it all went south as Epha twisted, letting the baton skid off her armor, and abandoned her quarterstaff to catch Jasto by the wrist.

He didn't see how but he was faceplanting into the ground a moment later, his arm trapped behind his back in a painful lock. The line was just in front of him.

But now he was closer to it than Epha was.

"T-twenty seconds," the mercenary said, caught off guard by the display. Jasto struggled against the pin, but his lack of experience with brawls only became more obvious as Epha shifted positions to keep him down.

"You said we were sparring!" he yelled as his face pressed against the protective grid of his helmet.

"And I told no lie," Epha replied. "This is a part of sparring as well. And I have not advanced a step, as I said."

"Ten seconds."

Should Jasto use his Lanterns? No, he knew Epha had him beaten there and it was against the terms she'd set at the start of this spar. But he had to do something. He tried to roll himself over to get out of the lock, but Epha moved her legs to block him from doing so.

"Seven. Six."

Jasto yelled wordlessly, and did his best to stand, but the pain in his shoulder forced him to stop. Too little. Too late.

Too weak, once again.

"Five—"

That was when an interloper arrived.

BeepBeepBeep. BeepBeepBeep. BeepBeepBeep.

Epha's grip relaxed and Jasto was up in an instant, whirling around to throw his shoulder at Epha's torso with everything he had. But right before she kicked out at him, sending him sprawling before he could complete the motion, he heard something unexpected.

"Stop the timer!" Epha yelled, and the mercenary obeyed. It hadn't been his watch that had made the beeping noise.

That was coming from some rugged electronic device strapped to her wrist, which she had dismissed her armor to reveal. Epha's face was still hidden by her armor, but the way her posture had shifted was strange. Like she was both irritated and relieved by the device going off.

"What is that?" Dad asked, trying to make sense of the strange chain of events. If Epha hadn't stopped the timer she would have won, Jasto was forced to admit. He resolved immediately to add grappling work to his training.

"That was a perimeter breach," Epha said after a moment, tapping the device and making it go quiet. She dismissed her sparring helmet a second later to reveal weathered skin, a compact military bun that mixed bronze hair with gray, and deep brown eyes like layered sedimentary rock, filled with history. "It seems you are not the only Crestbearer attempting to bypass my trial today, young Chaston."

Dad looked at Jasto immediately, warning him against fanning any flames, but this time he kept calm. Controlling your future started with controlling yourself, after all.

"Is it an issue?" Jasto asked, keeping his tone cool as he picked himself up from the hard stone of the ravine.

"None of the previous ones were. It simply means there will be a delay while I attend to this unchivalrous individual. And I will have to test you again, of course, to confirm your safety." Epha glanced to the side, her mind already shifting gears to the upcoming fight. "Since you insist on doubting Sir Seafall's ability to remain latent, your group may go back up the ravine to wait at my residence. I will meet you there after I—"

BeepBeepBeep. BeepBeepBeep.

Epha was faster to shut off her device's alarm this time, and she did so with a frown at its readout. "Strange. The same site?"

BeepBeepBeep.

Epha did something else to the device, presumably muting it. She stared at its display for a moment longer, and Jasto didn't like the way her eyes were starting to shift. They'd been resigned since her acceptance of Dad's terms, even in the midst of his argument with her, but now...

Epha rose to her feet, the frown on her face becoming a small smile. "It seems that there is one more knight wishing to undertake my trial, Mr. Chaston," she said. "Our agreement is on hold."

15

"What?!" Jasto stalked right up to the old knight, the aches in his body temporarily muted by indignation and the hypocrisy he was witnessing. "That's not what we talked about. You gave us your word!"

"I also gave my word that I would test all comers to this Palace to discern their worthiness," Epha said coolly. "Yet I broke that by accepting your father's agreement without you passing my usual trial. My lack of integrity did not seem to bother you then."

"So much for being honorable. You're only keeping your promises when it's convenient," Jasto scorned, and Epha's eyes narrowed. "But you're way too used to dictating terms, Suncage, so you must have forgotten: Dad hasn't fulfilled his side of the bargain yet. And if you think we will after getting snubbed like this, you're going senile."

"Let me assure you of something, young Chaston," Epha said. Jasto had been about to tell her to walk back her words, but he froze at the weight in Epha's voice, the years of her combat experience suddenly making themselves apparent. Immediately he was certain that she'd been holding back during their spar.

"I may not have always acted honorably," Epha continued. "But I have adhered to the duties placed before me all my life. And I continue to do so now. As for our agreement…I knew you might take offence and end it." There was a quick shiver of grief across the old knight's face, but she mastered it.

"I made the dutiful choice regardless."

Jasto almost took a step back in dismay. That agreement had been Dad's trump card. If she was willing to discard it…

"Sir Suncage, I don't understand," his father said, which was rarely true but was one of his favorite conversation leads. "Didn't you say that this person caused a perimeter breach? Wouldn't that mean they're attempting to ignore your trial?"

It was a good question, Jasto thought as he straightened up. Many had tried to go straight to Seafall Palace without fulfilling Epha's conditions in the years since she'd first announced them. None had escaped the detection of her security grid, or her subsequent response.

"If not for the nature of this breach, I would agree," Epha explained, looking past Jasto. "However, I leave one layer of motion sensors obviously visible around the edge of my receiving area to distract from the rest of my detection systems. This individual has triggered the same one repeatedly…" she looked down at her wrist,

16

"...and is continuing to do so. It is approximately an hour past the time when I would normally check for candidates, so I suspect they are proverbially knocking on my door."

"I see. May I ask what happens if they win?"

Epha smiled slightly. "Then they may enter Seafall Palace with my blessing. Should they fail to emerge after a day, I will assume Sir Seafall has felled them."

"And if they do not pass your trial?"

"Ah, the true question. Then our agreement resumes. It will also resume if they die in the Palace."

Jasto breathed out in relief, making sure he wasn't too loud. It was a good thing his face was still concealed, otherwise he'd be an open book to Epha. His easily readable feelings had directly caused at least a third of his troubles at the Valor Academy, there was no need for them to make this worse.

Dad considered Epha's words behind him. "Very well," he eventually said. "Should you resume your agreement with us, Sir Suncage, we will also resume our side of it."

The old knight glanced at Jasto with a raised eyebrow and, after a moment, he made himself nod. It felt deeply wrong to him that they weren't at least demanding a renegotiation after Epha had snubbed them, but he'd accepted long ago that Dad knew situations like this better than he did. He'd try to figure it out later.

"I respect your decision," Epha said. "Now, young Chaston, since you insist on doubting Sir Seafall's restraint your group may wait at my residence. Take your leave and see to your injuries, I will notify you when the business is done."

Jasto watched her turn towards one of the ravine cliffs. The Palace was large enough that it blocked easy passage through the ravine but Epha had been here a while, and had carved plenty of staircases into the rock to circumvent that during her time. The old knight was headed for one of them now, which would presumably take her towards the trial candidate.

Through sheer luck, he'd been given a second chance by the arrival of this trial candidate. And he ached all over, which modern medical tech would be able to do something about even in the short reprieve he'd gotten. But even knowing that Jasto felt something…weird in his gut.

Why did going back seem like a mistake?

Part of it was worry that this interloper would pass, of course. Epha's standard trial went beyond the 'combat certification' she'd demanded of Jasto, involving both potentially lethal fighting and loosely defined tests of character. This stranger's rigidity with the rules, the fact that they'd waited an entire hour before even slightly breaching them, was definitely something Epha would approve of.

But Jasto made himself set that worry aside. It was a concern, yes, but even those who passed Epha's trial still had to actually enter Seafall Palace and come back out. No one had managed that besides Epha herself, one of the reasons why both Dad and Jasto wanted to leverage her help. Still, even with that fear put to the side the gut feeling still lingered.

Jasto couldn't put his finger on what was causing it. He knew he wasn't concerned about Epha's survival, even though her trial involved combat. He'd seen plenty of videos of her fighting seriously, against knights far more dangerous than he was, and still winning with little trouble. And despite how thoroughly he'd pored over that footage, hoping for an advantage in case the worst happened, he'd still lost this sparring match by a large margin.

That was it, Jasto realized. Across all the footage he'd managed to compile of Epha repelling and occasionally killing the knights that came for this Palace, there was still something he didn't know about her fighting style. Something major.

And now he finally had the chance to figure it out.

"Actually, we'll go with you," Jasto said before the opportunity slipped. Epha and Dad both stopped, turning from the different directions they'd been heading in to look at him in total surprise. "We'll go with you, to see this trial candidate," Jasto repeated. "We won't interfere, but you struck a deal with us. We should be there."

Epha looked astounded for a moment, but quickly brought her expression under control. "No," she said flatly. "I have never needed accompaniment for my trials, and they are better as a one-to-one affair. Besides, this candidate has followed my rules to the letter." *Unlike some people*, she did not have to say. "I will not disgrace that by intimidating them with the presence of a third party."

"We won't be coming to intimidate, just to observe," Jasto pressed. "It's a trial, right? Wouldn't having a third party help, to assure fairness?"

"A neutral third party, perhaps," Epha said. "But you are far from neutral, young Chaston. And I have already made my decision."

Dreck, this was going nowhere. Jasto bit his lip, frustrated again by Epha's obstinacy, and turned to look back at his father.

Despite the protective grid over his face, Dad still met his eyes. With how important running the trial was to her and how much Jasto had already riled Epha, he knew his father would think it best to just go back and wait. He really wished they had some kind of secret code to communicate right then, so he could convey how important it was to persuade her. But all he could do was look, and hope the message got through.

As always, Dad's expression was hard to read. His tan but slightly gaunt features barely moved as he considered Jasto, Epha, and all the other puzzle pieces that formed the scenario in front of him.

"Sir Suncage, it was a major surprise to me when a Crest chose my son," he said after a moment. "Though I did serve as a military logistician, before losing that post in the Crystal Ascension, I have never experienced live combat like Jasto. It has been…difficult to determine the best way to instruct him, after the Valor Academy, and due to that I believe I've fallen short in several ways."

Jasto didn't flinch from the words. Regardless of the actual amount of honesty within the statement, Dad had said it because he knew Epha would believe it. And watching his father trick the old, expectation-bound knight was well worth a little shame.

Dad looked at Epha then, his shadowed eyes forming a mask as he twisted the truth into a useful shape behind them. His voice took on a pleading and very believable tone. "I think seeing this trial, seeing an honorable interaction between two Crestbearers, it might give my son some valuable guidance. We can leave our mercenaries behind so there's no foul play, too. Please…"

It obviously was true that Jasto had issues with the crystal knights, though he doubted Epha understood the full extent of them. And his father actually had, right from the moment Jasto was picked by a Crest, encouraged him to go with the flow and become an upstanding crystal knight. That had surprised Jasto at first, considering that Dad had lost his job because of the crystal knights, but Vikor Chaston was the type who refused to waste an opportunity no matter where it came from.

Because of that, when Jasto had been kicked from the Academy early with incomplete training, the black mark of squire-errant status, and only a vague explanation of why, there had been…tension.

So in a way, Dad's request was completely genuine. Jasto looked back at Epha to see sympathy welling up in her eyes, though she did her best to hide it by frowning and glancing down at the device on her wrist. "You chose to uphold your side of the agreement, even when I slighted you, Mr. Chaston," she said after a moment. "With that in mind, I will allow this."

She turned to resume her walk. "But you will leave your mercenaries behind."

Jasto let himself breathe out, but he still felt stuck in place. Even though he'd gotten what he wanted, now Dad would be coming along with zero mercenary protection. If the combat part of the trial got out of control…

There was a tap on the back of his shoulder, and he twitched before quickly dismissing his armor and following Dad after Epha. The two of them trailed the knight at a distance as she dissipated the rest of her sparring armor, revealing tan desert clothing, and reclaimed the black tabard she'd tossed aside for the sparring match. It was meant for proper fights rather than lessons, she'd said. At a word from Dad the mercenaries remained behind, while he and Jasto followed Epha up a staircase built to circumvent the Palace.

"That was an overextension," Dad said, all pleading gone from his tone, and Jasto swallowed. "I provided the explanation that I did to Epha so she wouldn't grow suspicious at your insistence. But I know you did this for Plan B."

"We have to learn how she fights, in case she turns on us," Jasto protested quietly. "You know it's possible, with how much she cares about Sir Seafall."

"Who I told you not to mention," Dad noted.

"Yeah, and I shouldn't have. But she just put an agreement we spent three days working on hold, on a whim. She's obviously unstable, Dad."

"Then you should not have pushed her for no gain," Dad replied firmly. "You already know how Sir Suncage fights, from both the videos you compiled online and the sparring match just now. What else is there to learn?"

"That's the thing," Jasto said. "I looked over those videos again—"

"Again?"

At least four more times, actually, but Dad already thought he was pushing himself too hard. "And when I did, I realized there was no clear visual of Epha using her Crest ability, in any of them. If we can get a clear look at it now…"

Dad thought for a moment. He was no warrior, despite working in military logistics, but even he knew that a knight's Crest ability could majorly change how they fought. "There would be some merit to that," he conceded. "But if this falls to a last-moment betrayal it has already left our control, Jasto. Also, Sir Suncage paused our agreement because she was never eager about it to begin with, and found an unexpected alternative. Not because she is unstable."

"Isn't that worse?" Jasto asked.

"Only while Sir Suncage dislikes us," Dad replied. "I said we'd be willing to resume our agreement after this to begin dealing with that. It was an 'honorable action' in her mind." He gestured towards Epha's back as he spoke. "In fact, we were permitted to view this trial because I did that. Instead of gambling on a fight with Sir Suncage, it would be far better to earn her approval."

Jasto knew his Dad was good at handling people, to the point where it became unnerving. That was one of the reasons the Chaston family had landed on their feet, even after being upended by the Crystal Ascension. He knew on some level that his father was being just as logical as he always was this time, too.

But hearing one of his own parents tell him the same thing the Valor Academy had tried to, to just grind himself down so someone else would call him honorable, had him spitting out words faster than he could stop himself.

"No way I'm playing the puppet just to get approval from that—"
It was too late, Jasto thought as he managed to clamp his mouth shut. Stopping himself early might have been better than nothing, but from the

expression on Dad's face he was seriously considering giving the whole mission up.

Jasto couldn't leave empty-handed after all this. His eyes went down and he rubbed at the racing stripes shaved into his sideburns, one wide and one narrow. He'd gotten both the stripes and the nervous tic at the Valor Academy, thinking the former would make people leave him alone. He'd been right, to some extent. Maybe he could convince Dad he was right about this, too.

"I know that she could keep her word," Jasto said. "And that there probably are good odds of it. It could be that I'm preparing for something that never happens." They reached one of the carved staircases, and Jasto stepped onto it.

"But 'probably' isn't enough, not when I can still do more. I don't get to choose if the worst happens, but I do get to choose if I'm ready for it. So, shouldn't I do all I can to be ready?" Jasto hoped Dad would agree, and not just for the immediate gains. He'd been pushing hard to claim a Crest, from the moment he'd been expelled, all to prepare for what he considered the worst.

His father looked at him for a long moment as they walked. "The problem is not your reasoning," he eventually said. "Neither is risking your life inside this Palace. You are my son but also your own person."

Here it comes, Jasto thought, his jaw tightening involuntarily.

"The problem is the instability you've picked up. You've already lost a valuable opportunity at the Valor Academy because of it."

"I *told* you, that wasn't my fault."

"Yes. You did tell me that," Dad replied, his voice stony, and Jasto looked away.

He…had gotten into a fight, that was true. And the fight had moved its way through the halls of the Valor Academy, very publicly. And it had ended with him crashing into a meeting between the Academy faculty and several of Andalon's senators before he was restrained. The angry senators had demanded Jasto's complete expulsion from the Academy in response, against the faculty's wishes.

Jasto hadn't had any kind of grand design at the start of that mess. He'd just been off-balance enough to let an insult become a shouting match, then an awkward brawl. But once the fight had started, he'd realized he had an opportunity, maybe his only opportunity, to get out.

He'd told Dad it was all unintentional, a partial lie, but his father had been treating it like a complete one. And that hurt, even though Jasto had no right to complain.

When it became clear that Jasto wasn't going to say anything, Dad spoke up again.

"Is your outrage against the crystal knights on my behalf? If so, it's misplaced." Dad made no further mention of how he'd challenged the lie, something Jasto was both thankful for and resentful of. "Being forced out of public service and living in hiding for a year or so out of safety was unpleasant, yes, but it is also in the past and dealt with. My work record made shifting to the private sector more than manageable. I am well past anger, son."

So where is all this coming from? was the unspoken question there. One that they'd both danced around, maybe for too long.

"It's not really about anger," Jasto eventually said. "I mean, yeah, I feel it. But it's not *why* I got…less stable."

He almost killed his next words before they left his mouth, but took a moment and then forced them out anyway. "I'm weak, Dad. That's what I learned at the Academy, why I…had to leave. And it's why I need the Seafall Crest, to cover that weakness."

Dad tilted his head. "Unless I've been badly misinformed, the Valor Academy is the best possible place to hone your skills as a Crestbearer."

"Not that kind of weakness," Jasto said, silently cursing his vague wording. "I mean on the inside. I could feel that place changing me."

Dad's background had created some stigma, given the history between crystal knights and the military, but the real problem was more insidious than that. Jasto had been starting to feel the teachings of the Valor Academy, the lectures on morality and proper ways of acting, sinking into his head like water into a paper towel. Some of those ideas might have been good, even righteous, but that hadn't mattered when they were supplanting Jasto himself.

"And you were concerned," Dad said slowly, "That these changes you felt would be irrevocable? That the Valor Academy would shape you permanently?"

"I know you don't get it." Jasto's eyes went down, because he'd known that for a while now. There was something different about Dad's

23

head, making the things that took root in other people's minds just slide off of his. And Jasto had admired it all his life, the way it let him navigate through groups and acquire favors so easily, but it meant there were some things his father couldn't understand.

"I'm sorry I'm so weak, Dad," Jasto said, his voice thin. "But I've gotta work around that weakness, not pretend it doesn't exist."

"You're no longer in the Academy," Dad said. "And after the way you left, it's unlikely you'll ever return. If that environment was the issue, then the only problem now is recovering from it. This...reckless endeavor is therefore unnecessary."

And there was the disconnect. "It's not something that could just happen at the Valor Academy, Dad. I could still get...influenced, even if I don't want to, as long as someone could force me to listen like they did." Jasto noticed his hands had clenched up, and made them relax. "That's what I learned there: that all it takes is the right kind of environment, and I'll crack. And I'm a Crestbearer, too, so I can't just keep my head down and hope no one bothers with me."

Dad's lower lip twitched a millimeter, his version of a wince. Jasto had been told that by Dad himself, during one of their talks on politics back before even the Crystal Ascension had happened. He hadn't understood why Crestbearers were required to serve in the military once they became adults, or why so many other restrictions were placed on them.

He'd gotten a clear and dispassionate explanation. Crestbearers were needed for the Drone War, for one, but more importantly they were extreme individual threats. Just one could do the same damage as a coordinated group of terrorists before being put down. But that illuminated the other side of the equation: a Crestbearer would be put down eventually, because they were just one person and couldn't fight forever. In a way that made them easier to deal with than a militant group, as long as they didn't get corrupted. That balance of power and weakness made it necessary for any government to make Crestbearer-specific restrictions, and even the Round Table reflected that: attendance of the Valor Academy was mandatory under them, and crystal knights were only allowed to do military work in the public sector.

Dad had put it simply back then: Crestbearers were glass cannons, too dangerous to ignore but too fragile to be untouchable.

That was Jasto's reality.

"I don't like it, that I need to be stronger just to stay as…me," Jasto said, picking up the conversation once more. "I shouldn't need it. But I do. And yeah, I shouldn't be so aggressive towards Epha. It's just, she's exactly what I'm afraid I'll get stuck as."

Epha Varison Suncage had been lauded when she'd first announced the trials she would hold over this Palace. How noble, people had said, that she would give up everything and live like a hermit for years on end, just to make sure her dead friend's Crest ended up in worthy hands. Those strings called honor and duty existed only in people's heads, but they'd bound Epha so tightly that she'd given the last years of her life to this.

And that was why Jasto didn't feel too bad about how they'd leveraged her. Vikor Chaston, even stripped of his military administration position, was still a master at accumulating favors. Epha's Seafall Trial might be a point of pride for many Andalonians, a symbol of knightly spirit, but the rest of her family had been put on the ropes financially by time, bad luck, and the damaged state of Andalon. Squatting out here guarding the Palace, Epha hadn't been able to do much for them. Dad hadn't just offered to set her family up with good futures.

He'd also offered the same for the remaining kin of Sir Ralica Seafall, the knight responsible for this sapphire Palace.

They were past it now, descending the staircase Epha had carved on the other side of the large hexagonal structure. The ravine continued onward, gradually leveling upwards to a small hollow just below ground level, and within it they could see a glimmering, humanoid silhouette next to a photothyst sword planted in the rock. The crystal knight waved, but didn't move from where they were.

Up ahead, Epha waved back.

Jasto let out a quiet, shivering breath. It had been a relief to tell the truth, after dancing around it for so long, but Dad's silence was ratcheting his tension back up one notch at a time. Would he end it? Would he order Jasto to go back home?

"You resent what you went through, and resent Sir Suncage for embodying that experience," Dad eventually said. "But bitterness is a useless emotion; all it can do is blind you. In the way she lashes out at

25

any who question Sir Seafall, Sir Suncage herself is a good example of that."

Once again Jasto heard the part Dad hadn't said. *And as much as you loathe her, the two of you have that in common.* It stung, because it was true.

"Y-yeah," he managed. "Sorry, Dad."

His father nodded. "Your reasons for wanting to witness this trial are logical. Your desire to gain security by strengthening your Crest holds merit. But if you ruin your best opportunities before getting to seize them, being right means very little. Can you keep yourself under control?"

Jasto breathed in, then out. It didn't help. "I can try to," he said honestly.

"Then it's time to do so, son. Before your anger kills you."

Dad turned to continue towards the pending trial. The mission was still on. Assuming, at least, that Jasto hadn't ruined it by antagonizing Epha.

He stood in silence for a moment, trying to master the shame he felt, then followed his father onwards.

Chapter 2

"Sir Epha Varison Suncage, hail!"

There was something strange about the crystal knight that had been waiting for them, but Jasto wasn't sure what. She was decked out in a cyan tabard and orange photothyst armor threaded with blood-red filaments up to her neck, and all that was normal. Her face wasn't anything too strange either: rounded, bearing freckled skin and wide blue eyes. Even the slight smirk she wore made sense, for someone with the guts to take on the challenges a knight like Epha would put forward.

But the way her hands sat at her sides, open but unnaturally still, was something Jasto recognized. Something was making this knight tense, and she was trying to hide it.

"Hail, knight!" Epha called back. "I would hear your name and your business." Jasto resisted rolling his eyes at the coy statement. They all knew why she was here.

"I am Sir Nilis Fenlin Truesword!" the knight called out regardless, revealing a flash of snow-white teeth. "And I'm here for the Seafall Trial."

"Is that so," Epha replied, lowering her voice now that they were closer. Just like she'd said, the small hollow was ringed with simplistic, weather-resistant sensors screwed onto metal stakes poking out of the stone. Jasto squinted, directing his gaze away from the obvious, and noticed a thin, almost invisible sensor wire just past the more prominent stakes. He was sure Epha had more.

"You've arrived at a difficult time, Sir Truesword," Epha said, tapping at the security interface on her wrist. "I have found an…appropriate candidate, and thus the Trial is no longer being held. I came here as a courtesy, due to your politeness in waiting, but you will need to leave now."

Jasto stiffened. Had Epha come to her senses? He should say something too, to back up—

"Do not react," Dad whispered forcefully. Jasto only just managed to prevent himself from stepping forward, wobbling for a moment before he steadied himself.

Up ahead, Nilis was frowning. "And if I don't want to leave?"

"Is that what you are choosing, Sir Truesword? I would hear an answer from you, not a question."

The frown deepened. Nilis' hands remained motionless at her sides, but she flicked a quick glance at the sword by her side, made of orange photothyst like her armor. Jasto kept himself as still as possible.

"If you would go back on your publicly given word," Nilis began slowly, "And would do so without even offering some kind of notice in advance…then I would seek resolution from you, Sir Suncage. Because this can't be ignored."

Suddenly Jasto was very glad he hadn't drawn any attention to himself. That phrasing, 'resolving that which cannot be ignored,' was the traditional way a crystal knight declared their intentions to duel someone. If Epha said 'then conflict will fashion the path forward' or some variation of it, she'd be accepting the duel.

The old knight let the moment hang, her posture stiff and upright. Then she spoke up, and Jasto heard the smile in her voice.

"Excellent answer, Sir Truesword. You have completed the first step of this trial."

This time Jasto couldn't hold back an eye-roll, despite Dad's instructions. Of course Epha was like that. Half of the Valor Academy's instructors were the exact same way, seemingly obsessed with hidden trials and trick answers that students were expected to uncover from vague clues and nudges. They'd almost seemed allergic to the kind of straightforward teaching that Jasto worked best with.

"Don't be disdainful. She wasn't just testing Sir Truesword with that," Dad whispered again.

Jasto frowned. "That's why you told me not to move?" he whispered back. He got a nod in response, and grimaced at himself. Was he going to stay in control or not? The strongest Crest in the world wouldn't help him if he couldn't manage that.

Up ahead, Epha was explaining herself to Nilis. "Those who hear a rejection from me and immediately resort to violence, or who only pretend to accept and try to sneak in at night, are too driven by impulse," she said. "While those who simply accept and walk away lack an appropriate level of conviction. You attempted to press forward with your goals, but did so in a regimented manner. Now, Sir Truesword, are you ready for the next trial?"

"I am."

"Very well. It is straightforward: a duel, with the conditions set in advance by me."

Jasto nodded to himself. He'd known some portion of the trial would involve combat, from the video footage he'd gathered online. This was what he'd come to see.

"As the challenger, you have the right to modify one of my conditions before we start," Epha continued. That explained a lot about why the duels he'd seen recordings of had looked so different. It had been hard to parse anything from them in the first place, with the anti-recording measures Epha kept active around her ravine.

"Alright, let's hear those terms," Nilis said, rolling her neck a little. Her hands remained motionless, despite her seeming ease, and Jasto watched her carefully.

Epha nodded. "They are: Death or yielding, no time limit, no Lantern limit, all photothyst projections allowed, all Crest abilities allowed," she said briskly. "The boundaries of the duel will be the crater west of us, and leaving once the duel begins is an automatic yield."

Jasto flicked a glance in the direction she'd pointed and his eyes narrowed. That crater was completely open ground, with nowhere to hide. And despite Epha's comment about dealing with things in a regimented way, her duel terms were about as close to unregulated combat as it got. Crestbearers could get stronger by absorbing the Crest of a corrupted knight, but had to wait years between absorptions to avoid becoming corrupted themselves. The other, faster way they could empower their Crests was by killing drones, and Epha had killed many during the War.

Under her rules, she'd be able to bring all of that raw power to bear.

Nilis gave her answer almost immediately: "I'm changing the number of Lanterns. We each get one, that's it."

"Very well, one Lantern," Epha replied. "Do you have any objections to these conditions?" Nilis shook her head. "Then please follow me."

Epha turned and began to walk briskly to the west. Nilis plucked her sword from the ground and followed. Dad, meanwhile, had the slightest hint of a frown on his face as he watched them leave. Though

29

not a fighter himself, he still knew that having more Lanterns could easily tip a duel between knights. Epha had just given up a sizable advantage by limiting herself to one.

"I wouldn't worry about Suncage losing," he told his father. "However Truesword was trained, there's no way she has more combat experience than that old-timer. Especially not in one-on-one duels." The past raids attempted on this Palace had seen to that.

Dad started walking, and Jasto matched his pace as he turned towards his son with a slightly raised eyebrow. "Interesting. I did not expect you to speak positively of Sir Suncage, Jasto."

"She's a tool, yeah, but she's also one of the deadliest crystal knights alive," Jasto replied. "They're both true."

Dad nodded in approval of the objectivity, kindling some warmth in Jasto's chest, and they both sped up a little.

"Dad," Jasto said in a quieter tone as they walked. "Something's up with that Truesword."

"You noticed as well?" There was an eagerness to his father's tone. "She didn't relax at all during that exchange. Not when she passed the first trial, not when Sir Suncage accepted her modification of the duel terms. Some nervousness would be understandable, but for it to remain this constant? Sir Truesword is hiding something. Something that puts her in danger."

Jasto knew his father was a little different from other people, when it came to emotions. His mother had explained it to him at a young age, and made sure he understood that his Dad did care for him. It was still a little unnerving, the way 'human puzzles' got a much stronger reaction out of his father than anything else seemed to.

"Maybe she's on the run?" Jasto suggested. "Fleeing some crime, only accepting this challenge to get away from it?"

"Hmm. Possibly, but then why wait so long before disturbing the alarms? A criminal on the run would be too nervous for politeness, in most cases. And Sir Truesword is doing an admirable job of hiding her nerves." Dad put a hand to his clean-shaven chin. "Watch her closely, son. Sir Suncage may be stronger, but she is a known quantity. Sir Truesword is not."

"You don't have to call them 'Sir' all the time, Dad. They can't make you do it."

"Yet they expect me to do so, and because of that playing along gives me an advantage. Now as I said…"

"Right, I'll keep an eye on her."

The crater Epha had indicated earlier wasn't far. It was an old scar of the Drone War, maybe twelve meters wide, but due to the old knight's cleaning it looked smooth. It was like a giant, flat-bottomed bowl had been taken and pressed into the earth, then lifted straight back up. Though they were clear of the ravine now, Jasto could still see the spot where the Palace waited thanks to the shadows gathered above it.

"The Crystal Star is overhead. A good omen for a duel," Nilis commented, and Jasto moved his attention back to her with a frown. Would someone like her really be the superstitious type?

"An omen, perhaps," Epha said. "Though after all I have seen, it is difficult to consider the Star a sign of 'good' things."

Nilis had nothing to say to that, whether or not she was actually superstitious. Some Andalonians thought of the source of all Crests as a positive, of course. But Epha had seen some of her friends corrupted by their Crests, and had probably put a few of them down herself during the Drone War.

Jasto's own feelings on the Crystal Star were more mixed. He took a second to confirm that Dad was watching Nilis, then gave it a quick glance.

Though telescope imagery could reveal the complex, faceted fractals that formed that strange satellite, at this distance the Star only looked like a tiny piece of glitter someone had stuck in the sky. The photothyst forming it was red today, a shade similar to Nilis' filaments. Like the Pandora Gate that had sent the drones down to earth, it had been made by an AI free of its human-imposed restraints.

Both the Gate and the Star had the means to wipe humanity out— they'd made that quite clear by eating every other satellite in orbit, along with all the missiles that had been sent to kill them. Neither had done so, but that wasn't why Jasto had mixed feelings about the Star.

It was the source of Crests, yes, and with no Crests he never would have become a Crestbearer, or had to deal with the problems that involved. But the Crests had been needed for the Drone War, and it had been the choice of people, not the Star, to think of Crestbearers as somehow elevated. That hadn't been the case before the Crystal

31

Ascension, and the Ascension itself had only succeeded thanks to support from key Crestless officials.

At the same time, Jasto wasn't about to ignore the fact that the Star had no love for humanity. It chose Crestbearers without their consent, just as Jasto had been chosen, and the fact that they could get corrupted was a clear sign that it saw them all as pawns. It might have been people playing the game, but the Crystal Star had made the rules. They'd both had a hand in this struggle for strength he now had to go through.

"Sir Suncage, I need to ask," Nilis began as they reached the edge of the crater. She pointed an armored finger back at Jasto and his father. "Who are those two? Are they part of the trial somehow? I was under the impression you conducted the whole thing yourself."

Epha turned to look back as she answered Nilis' question. "They are guests, coincidentally here at the same time as your trial, and will not interfere." She stared right at Jasto as she said the last part, and he resisted the urge to glare back. The old knight was probably testing him again. "Young Chaston, armor both yourself and your father."

"Oh, you're a Crestbearer?" Nilis squinted at Jasto, folding her arms over her cyan tabard. "Sir Suncage's squire, I'm guessing. What's your name?"

Dreck, the worst possible assumption and the worst possible question at the same time. "Jasto Chaston," he answered flatly, ignoring his father's stare. "And I'm not her squire. Just a guest like she said."

Nilis paused. "...And what's your Crest name? An introduction's not complete without it."

Then Epha dumped gasoline on the fire. "Come to think of it, you still have not revealed that to me," she said, thoughtful. "It's rare to find a knight, especially a young one, who will not give their Crest name at the first opportunity."

Everyone was looking at him now, and he could practically hear what Dad was thinking as he stared. *It's expected for crystal knights and squires to take up a Crest name, Jasto, and I've been bugging you to do so for months now. Bitterness is useless. Just tell them the one your brother came up with.*

"I'm still new to my Crest," he said instead, deflecting rather than giving a direct answer. He was certain Dad picked up on that, and from the flicker in Epha's eyes she did too.

Nilis didn't seem to, but that didn't make her response any better. "Your problem is that you've got the process backwards, kid. You don't pick a name to make yourself stand out. You do things that stand out, and then your Crest name gets recognized because of that."

With her unasked-for and completely off-target lecture dispensed, Nilis turned back to Epha and dismissed Jasto from her mind.

A hand was on his shoulder immediately, and he turned to frown at his father as Nilis continued her conversation with Epha up ahead. "I wasn't going to do anything," he insisted.

"I saw your face, Jasto," Dad replied, and he grimaced. For all that they shared straight dark hair and brown eyes, Jasto's face was the polar opposite of Dad's in terms of expressiveness. The full lips he'd gotten from Mom and his broad-eyed, almost incandescent gaze made hiding his emotions a conscious effort at all times.

"I still wasn't going to attack her or anything," Jasto protested. He just didn't want to concede any part of himself to the traditions that had built up around the crystal knights, and that definitely included his name. His irritation with the whole thing was made even worse by how everyone expected him to just take one up already.

"Better safe," Dad murmured as the two knights confirmed the fine details of their duel. "Especially since it's a sticking point for you. Now, that armor?"

"Right." Jasto stepped to the left a little so he had room to work, reaching out to a spot at the edge of his mind.

A visitor had been sitting there for the past three years. His Crest, like all Crests, hid its true nature behind a mental image plucked from Jasto's head. For him that image was a cloudless night sky, filled with stars and four blinking satellites. It was his Diagram, the control panel for the powers he'd been made to carry.

Jasto focused on the stars first, sticking out a mental stylus and drawing a loop that connected three of them. More loops quickly followed, interlinked with each other until he had a patch that was large enough. Jasto took a second to confirm that their structure was solid. Then he pushed out with his mind, creating a mental ripple of will.

The ripple was answered by a wave. For an instant the illusion of the Diagram dropped to leave nothing comprehensible, just a feeling that something much larger and somehow more *real* than Jasto had laid a finger on his head. That immense mental presence brushed past his thoughts, and without stopping it fulfilled the command he'd made.

In the real world, harsh white filaments emerged from Jasto's collarbone with a tingle to spread up his neck and down his torso. Then the glow bled out of them to take physical form, as rings of photothyst projected in a rich emerald green. The material settled onto his skin, feeling more like cool, polished stone than the solidified energy it was.

Just moments ago, that energy had been stored within the Crystal Star itself. All Crests were connected to that insane satellite, just like every drone was connected to the Pandora Gate.

Jasto extended the chainmail down his body and more filaments rose from his skin for it, the projections set so they overlapped with each other and linked up as they formed. The Diagram maintained itself this time, and the feeling of the Star passing over his mind was muted. He was still a little below average in terms of projecting speed, he knew, but that was acceptable. He'd needed to make that sacrifice in order to properly train for his...more unique fighting style.

The plate armor layer was next. Jasto didn't need to do any kind of interlocking pattern for it like the chainmail demanded, just a series of basic geometric shapes he'd long since memorized. Each plate formed with a localized tingle, translucent enough to hide the chainmail beneath itself while still revealing the white filaments it contained. He'd made this same arrangement of plates more times than he could count, and not once had the filament patterns within them ever repeated.

That fact continually bothered Jasto, but right now he had to put it aside. He delayed making himself a helmet, since he wanted a clear field of view to create Dad's armor. His father's arms were already out in preparation, so Jasto put a hand on one of his shoulders and green chainmail began to spread out from it, like a timelapse of grass covering bare dirt. He moved his other hand from part to part on his father's body, adding the larger plates one at a time. Each one he linked to the chainmail with thin supporting lines along the edges. Even so, it would all dissipate into nothing the moment he took his hand off of Dad's shoulder.

To deal with that he'd use his Lanterns, the levitating drones every Crestbearer could produce and command. They were machines, slim octahedrons the length of his hand and the color of glass, but because of his Crest Jasto could feel them like disembodied fingertips.

He called them up. In reality two of his Lanterns rose from belt sheaths and nestled themselves against Dad's armor, where he locked them in place with projections. In his Diagram, two of the satellites moved slightly in the sky.

Jasto lifted his hand. The filament glow in his father's armor reoriented, so that it was emanating from the Lanterns now, and only the left calf plate dissipated. He clicked his tongue and quickly reformed it, making sure to connect it properly this time, then straightened up.

Ahead of him Epha and Nilis finished their discussion, and the photothyst armor around Nilis' hand dissolved so she could shake with the old knight. She backed up, and both knights bowed to each other before walking stiffly down into the crater.

Jasto saw Nilis reform her dissipated gauntlet, then flex her hand a few times. She wasn't keeping it still anymore, but why? If anything, the moment right before a duel with Epha Suncage was the perfect time to be tense.

"Come to the edge, young Chaston," Epha called. "Since you are here, calling this duel is your responsibility."

"Alright." Jasto started to walk forward and saw his father beginning to follow. For a second he thought about asking him to stay back, but dismissed the idea. Dad would be able to keep a close read on things, and he was probably too interested in observing Nilis for Jasto to talk him out of it..

Instead he had him stop for a moment, and commanded the Lanterns in his armor to exert a lifting force that made the whole suit lighter. He quickly instructed Dad to only take small steps, otherwise he might trip, and they proceeded.

Epha and Nilis waited at opposite sides of the crater below them. Fortunately, Jasto knew what they expected of him; he might not have spent a long time at the Valor Academy, but duelling ceremonies were one of the first things they taught.

"Challenger, state your name," he called, projecting his voice.

"Nilis Fenlin Truesword!"

"Defender, state your name."

"Epha Varison Suncage." Nilis' voice had been louder, but Epha's was possibly more assured.

"Challenger and defender, you have agreed to duel under these terms: Death or yielding, no time limit, Lantern limit of one, all photothyst projections allowed, all Crest abilities allowed," Jasto continued. "Turn away from your opponent." Both knights did so. "If either side wishes to withdraw, they may do so now."

Jasto went quiet, and began counting to 60 in his head. It was ridiculous that most Crestbearers had been calling themselves 'crystal knights' even before the Ascension formalized it, and kept a tradition of dueling to go along with the label. That said, this part of their formal rites was something he did appreciate. A sizable number of duels ended right here, with both combatants deciding their grievance wasn't really that important and just walking away from the fight.

That wasn't the case this time, of course. "About-face," Jasto called a minute later. "The duel's on, people. Get ready."

Everyone present flicked a glance at him—he was supposed to say 'The duel will proceed, arm and armor yourselves' instead of that—but he didn't react. It was worth it to remind Epha that she was the one slighting him with this trial. Jasto might not have been strong enough to overturn this arrangement, but he wouldn't pretend to be happy about it either.

Nilis shrugged when he didn't say anything else and raised her hand. The photothyst sword she'd had from the beginning slapped into it, guided by its Lantern, and with quick projections became a long, wide-guarded claymore. Her five other Lanterns came up to hover at chest level, and for each she projected a flechette. Flechettes were sharp triangular wedges a little shorter than arming swords, meant to be flown around with their Lantern cores instead of being wielded by hand, and once she'd made them Nilis flew each out to the edge of the crater where they were driven into the stone. With six in total, Nilis had either absorbed the Crest of a particularly weak corrupted knight or had beaten just one or two drones during her career. Jasto, having done neither, only had the four Lanterns he'd started with.

Epha, still unarmored, began her preparations by changing that. She took her tabard by the shoulders and raised it up, giving herself space to make projections beneath it, and in an instant she was enveloped by bright, golden filaments.

They resolved into projections one layer at a time. First was a thick and woven coat of gray photothyst cloth, only possible to sustain because of its direct contact with Epha. Next was a sheet of hexmail, made of small hexagonal scales that were a cut above the chainmail Jasto could make for defense.

The projections ended with the sturdy, rounded plates of cavalier armor, threaded with overlapping filaments so that the whole suit seemed to have been carved directly out of a mineral deposit. Epha's face had remained impassive through it all, even though she must have been feeling the Star's presence, and finally it disappeared behind an equally impassive helmet, one whose only weakness was small crosses over each eye.

Epha let her tabard settle over the armor, shifted her feet to project the soles of her photothyst boots, then shook out her hands and lifted one of them up. For a moment nothing happened. Then Jasto ducked as a glassy blur shot over his head and towards her hand. More flechettes followed in staggered intervals, joined by the Lanterns that floated up from her waist.

"That's her perimeter!" Jasto realized. "She's got her security systems, but she also leaves flechettes around the ravine." That gave her an early-response system to anyone who tried to approach the Palace. No wonder people only made it in with her permission.

One of Epha's *sixteen* Lanterns floated up to her hand, and she projected a gray halberd to encase it. With quick, economical projections she turned the other unhoused Lanterns into flechettes, then planted them outside the crater opposite of Nilis'. For all the distaste Jasto had for the old knight, he could admit he looked at her with jealousy right then. Epha, with her strong Crest and the years of skill she'd had with it, had held Seafall Palace on her own terms for years. Many knights had tried to usurp that choice, and she'd beaten them all.

One day, Jasto would be able to protect his own independence just as fiercely.

Nilis settled into a stance as her helmet formed, orange photothyst with a v-shaped eye slit and a tail of exposed red filaments hanging from the back. Her claymore went up, held in two hands over her head. Epha held her halberd more like a spear, point forward between herself and her opponent.

It was time, and despite himself Jasto found his heart rate increasing. "Challenger!" he called.

"Ready!" Nilis yelled, tightening her grip on her blade. "Defender!"

"Ready!" Epha didn't move at all, already settled in her stance.

"Knights at the ready...lay on!"

The battle almost ended in seconds.

Nilis rushed forward, Epha advanced at a calmer pace. And just a few steps in, Nilis brought her sword down and released it. It glowed with red light and, moved by its Lantern, shot straight through the air towards Epha.

She slapped it aside with practiced ease but Nilis was right behind it, another claymore projection forming in her hands as she brought it around—

—But like she'd been expecting it, Epha didn't try to bring her halberd back in line. Instead she took a hand off the length of it, darted forward to grab one of Nilis' wrists as the swing came in, and rammed a knee into the knight's side.

It didn't hit squarely, the collision had happened too fast for that, but Nilis still staggered past Epha clutching at her torso armor as the old knight turned, grabbed her halberd with two hands once again, and swung a wide horizontal chop at the knight. Nilis threw herself out of range and Jasto thought Epha would pursue but she didn't. Instead she circled to keep both Nilis and her claymore within her view, not wanting to risk getting ambushed by the latter.

"I expected the fast opening just from your posture," Epha informed her opponent. "You limited our Shard numbers for this duel, Sir Truesword, so you should aim to exploit that through your melee skills. Live up to that name you chose."

Nilis just grumbled something Jasto didn't hear and took a hand off her projected claymore. Her other sword slapped back into it after a moment, but in a reverse grip. Jasto briefly wondered if the knight was really stupid enough to try swinging her claymore that way, but then Nilis cocked her arm back and threw it like a spear, the momentum of her throw added to the propelling force of the Lantern within. Apparently she didn't like Epha's advice.

But as she'd prepared to throw her sword Epha had changed her stance, widening it and placing her halberd flat across one shoulder. Jasto saw that she'd flipped her halberd so the long hook stuck out instead of the blade just in time for the old knight to pivot, step forward, and bring her gray weapon around with devastating force.

The spike on the halberd punched straight through orange photothyst, snapping the blade in two just above the grip, and now it was Epha's turn to rush forward as the two halves of the claymore skipped across the ground behind her. Nilis had been rushing in behind her thrown claymore but was now forced to backpedal, giving ground and turning a halberd thrust to the side as Epha came in.

But even though she was on the defensive, Nilis wasn't out. The lower half of her broken claymore, the piece that still held a Lantern and thus hadn't dissipated, suddenly lifted off the ground and shot towards the two knights. Somehow Epha sensed it coming and broke off, circling to the side to avoid an ambush from the flying weapon, and the moment it was back in Nilis' hands she'd reprojected the broken half of the blade and discarded her Lanternless one.

She took a step or two back as Epha resumed her assault, but then solidified her stance as the Lantern in her claymore started to glow bright red at the edges. The glow spread to the edge of the weapon, and Nilis swung at Epha.

This time when their weapons clashed, the sword cut through the haft of the halberd like it was paper.

Epha jerked back, escaping with only a score mark across her tabard and chest plate, and kept her composure as Nilis started to fight more aggressively. Projecting photothyst and making Lanterns were the most obvious things a Crest could do, but they also carried abilities that were unique to each knight and dependent on the presence of Lanterns. Now Jasto knew why Nilis was calling herself 'Truesword,' but he was losing hope of seeing Epha's Crest ability too.

Because despite deploying her Crest ability while Epha hadn't done the same, Nilis was having trouble making any gains. The old knight had only given ground for moments before guiding the severed head of her halberd back into place through its Lantern. Then the tide had shifted as she'd repaired her weapon with a flash-projection and switched over to simple, rapid thrusts. Her halberd brightened intermittently as she triggered its Lantern in short bursts, economically pulling the weapon back from its thrusts before Nilis could damage it, and the fight quickly evened out. Then, only a few exchanges later, Nilis was forced to take a step back and Epha used the small window to repair her armor as well.

Nilis must have been getting frustrated, because when Epha's next thrust came in, a little slower than the previous ones, she actually grabbed the halberd just below its head. She started to tug Epha in, apparently more confident in a brawl than the fight they'd been having, and the glow on her projected claymore dissipated. Jasto sucked his teeth, knowing a mistake had just been made.

Epha leaned into the pull, and vividly colored sparks flew from the collision of armor on armor. The old knight was already leaning in, snaking a hand past the grip of Nilis' claymore to grab her wrist. Immediately she twisted it, levering her forearm against the claymore's grip to try and break her opponent's grip, but she couldn't fully commit to the motion with Nilis still tugging on her halberd. The two knights struggled almost like insects for a few moments, seemingly locked in that close grip, and then several things happened in rapid succession.

First, Epha let go of her halberd as it blazed gold. Then, the halberd was jerked sideways by its Lantern and towed Nilis' arm with it, pulling the knight out of position and simultaneously breaking her grip on her claymore.

Finally, with her newly open hand Epha reached under the flaps of her tabard and pulled something loose. A dagger, Jasto realized, one that she'd projected as part of her armor so it didn't dissipate. A trick she'd had ready and hidden since the beginning. It came up in a reverse grip, bearing three sides that narrowed into a triangular killing point and no crossguard, and plunged straight down for Nilis' neck.

The knight panicked and lurched back, not escaping Epha's grip but moving enough that the dagger bounced off her chest plate instead of piercing the collarbone. Epha didn't seem to mind, and moved with the backstep to slip a leg behind Nilis. Immediately she shifted her weight forward and took them both to the ground, just as easily as she had with Jasto, and thrust at Nilis once again.

Had she been aiming to kill the knight from the start? The way Epha was stabbing now seemed almost hysterical, one arm helping to pin Nilis as the other went up and down wildly, each attempted stab deflected but not by much. Nilis cried out, and as the strikes continued the Lantern in her dropped claymore suddenly glowed. It came off the ground, and shot between the two knights just in time to catch Epha's latest stab.

Immediately the old knight's hysteria seemed to vanish. She seized the grip of the claymore and reared back, placing a knee on top of Nilis and pushing herself to her feet smoothly. A filament was already working its way free of the photothyst on her hand, glowing a brighter gold than those inside her armor as it burrowed through the stolen claymore for the Lantern set in its crossguard.

This, Jasto knew, was the main reason crystal knights had been so necessary during the Drone War. The destructive power a knight had was something, yes, but it was their ability to hack into and instantly kill the sturdy, regenerating drones sent by the Pandora Gate that had made them so essential.

And that hacking worked on Lanterns too. Jasto saw a single golden filament, running all the way from Epha's chest down her arm and into the claymore, make its connection to the Lantern.

"By my command," she declared. Golden light flashed, and a moment later the claymore dissolved in her hands as the Lantern fell, its glassy surface now cracked and leaking cloudy smoke.

Nilis scrambled to her feet across from Epha a moment later, her face still hidden but anger clear just from the way she stood, the way her hands twitched. "There is no shame in yielding," Epha told her calmly.

"You...you tried to kill me!" Nilis spluttered.

There wasn't a hint of guilt in Epha's posture. "I *succeeded* at forcing you to lose a Lantern," she corrected, circling to the right a little. The move brought her closer to where Dad was, so Jasto left the midpoint he'd started the duel from to stand between him and the fight in case it left the crater.

"Besides," Epha continued. "You understood what you would be stepping into when you came here, no? Honorable as your approach was, you came to claim the life and Crest of Sir Ralica Seafall, a hero and my dearest friend. Did you truly believe you wouldn't need to risk your own life?"

Nilis reacted to the words, but not how Jasto had expected. She appeared to shudder for a moment more but then her posture straightened, going from an angry stance to something more appropriate for a trained fighter, and she projected a new claymore into her hands.

Jasto had seen that before, how some people could get so angry that they looped back to a state of eerie control.

"The life of Ralica Seafall?" Nilis asked, her tone now stable. "That is rich, Suncage."

"Watch yourself," Epha warned, securing the dagger at her waist as her halberd snapped back into her hand.

"Why? You should know even better than me, you senile disgrace: Crest corruption doesn't come undone. Ever."

"*Yield*, Nilis. While you still can."

Instead the knight shook her head mockingly. "You know that Seafall is going to stay that way forever. You know that she's in misery, but you don't end it. Instead you *draw it out*." She settled into a defensive stance, ready for a frontal assault. "Some friend you turned out to be, Suncage."

Epha didn't answer with words.

In dead silence she rushed forward, chomping down on the bait Nilis had laid, and their weapons made contact at a furious speed. Epha's thrusts were fast, controlled despite her anger, and as Nilis was forced to give ground Jasto wondered if she'd made a mistake provoking the old knight. As Epha began to herd her around the edge of the crater, leaving a tear in her cyan tabard with one particularly close swing, he decided she had.

Nilis' sharpening ability was gone with her Lantern, but even so the orange-plated knight got her dreck together. She kept one hand on the grip of her claymore but raised the other to grasp its blade and, using the leverage of her grip, shoved Epha's next thrust aside. She attempted to follow up with a pommel strike but Epha was already stepping back and bringing her halberd around for a wide chop. The exchange that followed was more even, but it was still clear which knight was being pressured by the clash.

"How is she keeping that up?" Jasto murmured to himself. He'd watched footage of Epha commanding all sixteen of her Lanterns at once in battle. But somehow, the intensity of her attacks with one halberd here seemed to surpass that.

The exchange came to a halt as quickly as it started. Epha swung her halberd down like an executioner's axe, Nilis managing to lean just to the side of the blow with her sword already over her own head for a similar swing. For a moment Jasto thought the old knight had overcommitted, bringing the head of her weapon too low to block her opponent's follow-up.

But then, as Nilis' sword descended, Epha reversed her halberd and intercepted the strike with the butt of the polearm. The claymore jerked sideways, one of Nilis' hands leaving it, and Epha shoulder-checked her without hesitation.

Then, before Nilis could recover, Epha swung her halberd out and around, taking one hand off of it as she did. A wicked centrifugal force built up in the weapon, its head flaring with golden light as Epha augmented the swing even further with her Lantern. If a blow like that hit the right spot, it would kill.

Epha pivoted, and the halberd head whipped around and down like a meteor. Orange plate fractured, went flying, and Nilis dropped to one knee with a scream. Epha jerked her weapon loose from the other knight's shoulder, the gray and gold of it now tipped with blood, and stepped back coolly.

Only…there was something wrong. Jasto frowned as Epha stood before her opponent, his eyes on the head of the halberd. It was barely red. Had a blow like that really drawn so little blood? And while Nilis was obviously bleeding, and had put a hand to her injured shoulder, the bleeding was strangely shallow. Epha stepped back casually as the injured knight made a wild swing at the air.

"What did you do, Truesword?" she asked. "Even Ralica wouldn't have been able to lift her arm after a blow like that."

Nilis had indeed lifted her injured arm, and was trying to use her claymore as a prop to steady herself. Since the sword was so long, though, it was a struggle.

And more than that, even though the knight's face was still hidden, Jasto thought that the way she hunched forward spoke of panic. The control Nilis had briefly shown was in tatters, replaced by the nerves she'd shown before the start of this duel, and Dad leaned forward with interest as he made the same realization.

"The suspicion of Sir Suncage," he murmured. "That's what Nilis is afraid of. Her secret is in danger of being revealed…"

Jasto took in his father's words, looked at the hole in Nilis' armor, and once again registered how little she was bleeding. It all clicked together in a single moment.

"That's why you already had your armor on," he said out loud, and everyone turned to him in surprise. "That's why you wore it and your tabard right from the start. To hide your other protective gear."

If he had any doubts about his guess, they evaporated as Nilis froze in place.

"I haven't done—" the knight tried, but a swarm of gray blurs descended on her. Each of Epha's flechettes had ripped itself from the ground at her command and zipped across the crater to stab at Nilis' shoulder armor like a pack of rabid, mechanized crows. The knight swung her sword wildly, and Jasto saw some of her Lanterns at the edge of the crater light up and shoot in random directions as she panicked, but although Nilis managed to mangle one of the flechettes with a lucky swing her damaged pauldron and the armor beneath was torn off a moment later. The flechettes dispersed and Jasto caught a glimpse of glossy, form-fitting metal, torn open over the shoulder and lightly stained by blood.

"You wore non-photothyst armor into this duel? And kept it hidden?" Epha's voice was accusatory, and her flechettes drew back to hover in a menacing arch above her.

"It...wasn't in the terms not to," Nilis tried, taking a step back. As she did the body armor Epha had exposed caught the light, shining black and gray in evenly notched stripes.

Jasto squinted. He'd seen that before. Somewhere...

"It is a given," Epha said. "The codes for a formal duel are clear: Non-Crest armaments must be declared, and both combatants must consent to their use."

"I thought this was a trial," Nilis said. "You won't go back on your word, Sir Suncage. Will you?"

"You attempted to deceive me from the start by acting in bad faith. If you wished to trap me in my own rules, you should have followed them as well," Epha replied, not a speck of doubt in her words.

"How did you get that?" Jasto asked, almost without meaning to. The back-and-forth between the two knights paused.

"That armor, Truesword," he asked again. "How did you get it?"

She stiffened a little. "I purchased it. Obviously."

"No, you couldn't have," Jasto replied, the pieces starting to align. He hadn't realized it when he'd first spoken, but this was his opportunity. His chance to break this trial. "I recognize that striping. It's vythex weave, isn't it? The latest carbon fiber composite from Bastion Solutions, designed to protect against photothyst specifically."

The crater became even quieter. Epha slowly turned back towards Nilis, pure menace filling the movement.

"They've shown it at security conferences, which is where I saw it, but it hasn't hit the market yet," Jasto said, delivering the final touch. "The only way you could get it is if you worked for them."

"Nilis Truesword," Epha said, her voice frigid. "Did you lie to me, when you claimed to be a crystal knight?"

"You can't be taking his word over mine. You said he was just an observer!" Nilis protested, and Jasto flinched as she sent a glare at him.

"I'll pull up the video right now if you want," he managed to say, but didn't get any further before one of Epha's flechettes slammed into the ground like a judge's gavel.

"I asked you a question, Sir Truesword," Epha said, drawing the flechette back up. "Are you a mercenary Crestbearer, rather than a knight? Did you abandon your responsibility to Andalon, and whore yourself out to the private sector?"

"I...," Nilis managed as Jasto leaned back instinctively. Apparently the old knight had spared him her real venom.

He supposed it made sense, given how traditionalist Epha was. The restrictions on Crest use to nothing but public sector work had been rock-solid since the Crystal Ascension, with only the slightest relaxations coming years after the Drone War. It was still mostly illegal for Nilis to be working for Bastion Solutions as a Crestbearer, in fact. Only the lingering damage of the Drone War, the Palaces that still plagued Andalon, and the limited resources of the Round Table prevented them from properly enforcing those rules.

Though from the way things were looking, Epha was about to handle Nilis for them.

"Speak, Nilis. No mercenary is permitted to take this trial. Did you deceive me?" Epha asked. She knew the answer. They all knew the answer. But Epha was still insisting that Nilis either admit it, or lie once again.

Maybe that was what she considered honorable, but to Jasto it almost seemed sadistic.

And it was definitely getting to Nilis. She shuddered once with her whole body, and flicked another white-hot glare at Jasto.

He tensed and looked down instinctively. Jasto had spoken up without really stopping to think, aiming to take the opportunity he'd seen before it slipped away forever, but now what he'd done was sinking in. He hadn't just ruined Nilis' chance of getting the Seafall Crest with his words, he'd put her life in direct danger. Epha was more than willing to kill those who violated her trial. And Jasto had done all that to someone who basically wanted the same thing as him, to claim this Crest without having to conform to someone else's definition of honor.

"Look her in the eyes, son." Jasto blinked, turned to see his father watching him with a steady gaze through the eyes of his helmet. His tone was calm, but insistent.

"A choice like this needs to be seen all the way through, once it is made. So look her in the eyes."

Jasto managed to nod, then turned back and forced himself to meet Nilis' burning blue eyes. His hands trembled, but he shut them into fists. He wanted to look away, to take it easy on himself, but giving in at the Valor Academy would have been the easy way too.

Other thoughts rose up as the moment seemed to slow down. *We both gave up on the easy way to come here,* he realized. *We both took risks for this. I don't want you dead, honestly.*

But I'm not stopping until I'm free.

Maybe Nilis read some of that from his posture, maybe not. Either way, the mercenary Crestbearer's gaze snapped back to Epha, her open hand flexing like a claw.

"I will not wait—"

"—By the fucking Pandora Gate! Of course I am," Nilis sighed raggedly, the facade of a daring knight completely gone. "A monkey with half its brain left could've figured out I'm a merc-Crest by now. And you can't?"

"Then you have cheated me, disgraced Andalon, and sought to turn the last remnant of Sir Seafall to a disgusting, selfish purpose," Epha said flatly, the insult sliding off her. "But you have at least admitted the truth." She pointed her halberd across the crater. "As such, you may turn and leave with your life. Immediately, Nilis Fenlin."

If Jasto hadn't looked Nilis in the eyes, he might have felt some guilty relief right then. He might have let himself think that Nilis could live now, or at least that it wouldn't be his fault if she still chose to fight and die.

But those words wouldn't have stopped him, and now he knew they wouldn't stop her. "...Selfish..." Nilis said slowly. "Really, Suncage? You want to talk about selfishness?"

"Dad, we need to leave," Jasto whispered.

"Agreed. Slowly, without drawing her attention..."

"Even before you figured me out, all I had to do was mention Ralica and you tried to cripple me," Nilis continued. Her free hand was grasping the front of her helmet. She didn't seem to be fully aware of that. "I wore my vythex here because I figured you were unstable enough to snap, and I was right. Because this trial's got nothing to do with honor or character. Your friend died and you can't let go. That's it."

Her hand tightened on the helmet's visor. The cracks already within it, put there by Epha's assault, started to creak beneath her fingers. Jasto reflexively stepped in front of Dad, because this was worse than he'd thought. He knew that anger, that hazy feeling that everything was wrong and everyone but you refused to see it. He'd felt it too, right before getting himself expelled from the Valor Academy.

"And you want to talk about selfishness, Epha?!" Nilis yelled, tearing the front of her visor free. Beneath it, her blue eyes were wild and manic. "At least I didn't build a monument to it!"

Epha shifted her stance, preparing for combat. "Leave," she commanded, her voice tight.

"No, I don't think so," Nilis snarled. Her flechettes came free of the ground with a scraping noise, moving to hover around her left shoulder like a cloak, but they were trembling like the rest of her body. Jasto cursed how open this space was. There was nothing to hide behind.

"I'm not the disgrace, Epha. You are, because you made...all this..."

Nilis coughed suddenly, and tiny bits of something solid sprayed across the ground before her. Bits of something orange and glimmering, with faint red accents. Dread surged through Jasto. He'd been too focused on what Nilis was saying, so he'd missed the warning signs. The way her filaments were starting to glow in a pulsing, rhythmic way, almost like a heartbeat.

"Dad, get down!"

"But I'll tear it all…to piecee*EEEES*…"

There was no time to retreat so Jasto tackled his father to the ground, the Crystal Star thumping against the back of his mind as he made his armor as thick as possible. A dull red glow flared behind them, then bled into a light-drinking black.

In the next instant, something the size of a giant's hand slammed into Jasto and it was all he could do to keep his grip on Dad as they went flying.

Chapter 3

They were tumbling through the air and he had no idea which way was up, everything was moving too fast but he was projecting as much photothyst as he could, and he needed to get under Dad so he could take the impact. For a moment he tried to slow his fall with his Lanterns, but they used Jasto as a sort of anchor and couldn't carry any weight unless he had a stable position himself…

Then his panic was cut short as he suddenly stopped falling, far sooner than he should have.

Jasto was too confused to form words for a moment, only able to gape at the bed of gray-and-gold wedges that had caught him and Dad midair. Epha's flechettes dropped to the ground at a brisk pace and scattered a foot above it, leaving Jasto and his improvised photothyst casing to thunk into the rock as Dad groaned from the impact.

Jasto dismissed the casing and was above him in moments. "Are you okay?!" he yelled, his voice choked with panic. "Dad! Are you bleeding?! I need to get this armor—"

"—Fine," his father wheezed, rolling onto his back. "Will be…fine. Just need. Time."

"Dreck, why didn't I get a first-aid kit from one of the mercenaries?" Jasto moaned. "We have to—"

He stopped his turn towards the way they'd come as Dad laid a hand on his head. "Look," he got out, turning his son's face back towards the crater.

Long, bony spires of orange photothyst, all at least as wide across as his chest, had shot out from it. It was one of those that had knocked them away. The irregular columns all jutted out from a single point, now wreathed in a shadowy fog that only ever meant one thing.

"Crest corruption," Jasto murmured. Every time a Crestbearer used their Crest, they opened a link between themselves and the Crystal Star. Lose control and open too big of a link, try to project too much photothyst or create too many Lanterns, and the Star would make it permanent. Nilis' Crest was merged more deeply with her body and

49

mind now, no longer confined to just a Diagram in one corner. Wielding her, as much as she wielded it.

And the only way to break that dangerous connection was death.

"You'll see it now," Dad got out. "Epha. Her ability, in case we need plan B. You'll see it. Go."

A weird shiver of guilt went through Jasto's whole body. If he hadn't insisted on this…

He paused only to nod and adjust his father's position on the ground a little, then he was up and darting back towards the barebones roots of what would eventually become a Palace. Dad was far enough away from it that he felt safe doing so, not to mention Epha was here.

As he ran, a burst of golden light flared before the sea urchin-shaped cluster of photothyst. Jasto altered his trajectory a little to head towards it, shedding his cracked extra plate layers and quickly re-projecting them with flashes of white light. His skin tingled like it was asleep, but every Crestbearer learned how to work through that early on.

He came up on Epha to find the old knight was also reconfiguring her armor. Both the rounded, force-deflecting plates and the hexagonal mail she'd formed were dissipating, replaced by a single layer of basic chainmail and perforated, flared-out plates over her joints and vitals. Her helmet changed too, the cross-shaped eyeholes replaced with a wide visor of translucent photothyst as the whole structure of it thickened and smoothed out.

Now Epha looked more like an armored motorcyclist than a traditional knight, and Jasto found himself bothered by it. He'd never seen Epha use this arrangement in any videos.

And there were similarities between it and Jasto's preferred armor form.

Epha put a hand up as he stared. "Get out of here, young Chaston." Behind her in the crystalline core of the Palace, where all the columns converged, dark silhouettes twisted like unhatched tadpoles. "I will deal with this. Take your father and leave *immediately*."

"Palaces always spawn knaves. I can't let any stragglers you miss hurt Dad." That was true, even if it wasn't the only reason he was here. Before Epha could speak further, Jasto opened his palm to project the axe shape he usually favored. It was familiar and simple enough, one-handed with a heavy, bearded head, but still required a moment of concentration to form.

His Diagram flickered as he made the projection, the inhuman intelligence of the Crystal Star briefly revealing itself, and when the sky reformed it was larger, closer to the rest of his mind. Jasto took that for the warning it was, and left his other hand empty for his preferred weapon.

Epha spoke with an irritated voice. "As a crystal knight, I cannot let a novice with incomplete training anywhere near a threat of this magnitude—"

Jasto was sure he would have snapped at that under normal circumstances. Epha was about as devoted as it got to the Valor Academy's ideals, and he'd never liked being talked down to. But Dad hadn't been supposed to get injured at all during this trip, and even after the blow he'd taken he'd still put their mission first. Jasto's mission, if he was honest with himself.

So instead of arguing with the old knight, he distracted her. "The knaves are hatching," he warned Epha, pointing towards the Palace core with his axe.

She spun back around to face it and several of her Lanterns shed their flechettes to enter her armor, where they could augment the strength of her movements. Jasto had actually called it a little early but that was intentional, and he stepped back to make sure he had a clear view of the coming fight.

If he was honest, Jasto also stepped back because he was a little nervous. He'd fought knaves before, fulfilling the public bounties available to all Crestbearers regardless of status. But those had been stragglers separated from their Palaces. Minor threats like that had been the most danger Dad had been willing to allow him near, before. Now he'd be facing freshly made ones near their Palace.

One of the dark shapes wriggled close to the edge of the Palace, and he watched it carefully. Its back half was a tail of dense muscle tissue, corded with black filaments. At the front half that muscle puckered around a familiar pyramid of dark glass. Corruption didn't just change the Crestbearer, it changed their Lanterns. Made them capable of different things.

The other knave cores gathered at the edge of the Palace, and filaments rose from its surface around each in roughly humanoid outlines. Shadows bled from them to take on orange photothyst forms, an inversion of a regular projection, and one by one the cores swam forward into their waiting bodies. The first knave jerked like a puppet coming alive, then tore itself loose from the Palace to fall.

It broke stone on impact, then pushed itself up with a wicked serrated sword growing straight out of its hand. The knave looked more like a rough drawing than a human, asymmetrical and formed from sharp planes that made it clear there was nothing inside it but filaments and a core. Only the head seemed to have been designed with some care, shaped vaguely like a knight's helmet with dense filaments forming a visor shape. Three more knaves, similarly structured, dropped to the ground behind it.

Jasto thought he heard Epha sigh. "Keep your distance, young Chaston!" she commanded, then turned to attack the knaves. Dust pounded up as she rushed forward, her flechettes descending.

The first few seconds of the attack were no contest at all. It wasn't that any of the knaves were bad fighters. In fact, they would fight with a skill level close to that of their creator, Nilis.

Epha was just done holding back.

She rushed to the leftmost knave as her flechettes shot across the sky at diagonal angles. To Jasto's surprise, they aimed at the other knaves and left Epha to strike at her opponent alone.

Or so it appeared. The knave Epha faced raised its sword only to get stabbed from behind by a flechette, and it tried for a thrust instead only for Epha to knock the tip aside, then bring her halberd around in a chop augmented by the Lanterns in both her armor and her weapon.

The corrupted Lantern in the knave's chest cracked, spewing dark blood over the crater as it toppled. Epha hadn't slowed down.

Not only that, Jasto realized. She'd kept the rest of her flechettes harassing the other knaves while her own attention was on just one. The mental control needed for that was…impressive. And beyond Jasto, he was forced to admit.

The second knave pushed Epha's halberd down to pin it, only for two flechettes to pierce its core from behind, and as the last pair rushed in Epha actually dropped her halberd. She thrust her hands forward to seize each knave by the neck as flechettes pinned their legs and sword arms. Then she stepped forward, and with a maneuver that was half wrestling and half flechette control slammed both into the ground. Jasto saw golden filaments invade their bodies and make contact with the Lanterns they held.

"By my command."

As Epha spoke both of the knaves went dead, their photothyst breaking into inert, uneven chunks that left the now-smoking organic cores within to flop to the ground.

"So...annoying."

The voice echoed out from the Palace core, sounding like it had been digitized and then stripped of anything human. As it did the Palace itself reacted, sprouting tumor-like clumps of photothyst blades as black filaments rose from the structure as a whole, stirring in an invisible wind.

Jasto took a step back. Those filaments couldn't get through photothyst as fast as uncorrupted ones, he knew. But if they did, and if they reached your Crest, your mind joined the fallen knight in corruption. As a crystal thrall.

Epha hadn't moved. Her eyes were back on the core, and her flechettes returned to her as the bottom of it cracked open. Scraps of vythex weave dropped from the opening, hitting the ground with metallic pings one by one. Then an orange shape fell, this one humanoid and far more properly proportional than the knaves but still horrifying, and was followed by the remnants of a cyan tabard.

The sword was what caught Jasto's attention first. It was the same length as the blade Nilis had wielded a moment ago but far wider, almost reminding him of a construction beam. Organic, off-white cords ran through its length, forming a ropy bundle along the center that thinned out into tinier threads at the edge.

They were nerves, he realized after a second.

The rest of the corrupted knight wasn't any less grotesque. Some parts of its tall and strangely thin photothyst body were opaque, but the limbs were translucent and hosted bundles of pink muscle tissue wrapped in corrupted filaments. Each joint he could see was capped by a spike, and the black filaments now stretching from the helmet in a tail were as long as arms and curled as if they were alive.

The worst detail was the horizontal visor on the helmet. It was wider now, with a thin layer of nearly transparent photothyst set just inside it. Behind that, the visor was packed with blue eyes in widely varying sizes.

53

Several of them settled on Jasto, and he took a step back.

"*Were you really lecturing me on honor, Epha? Just to let a novice like that be this close to me?*"

"You will not get near him, corrupted." For emphasis, Epha flicked a line through the stone behind her with the point of her halberd. "You overreached, and thus your Crest consumed you. I would say that puts you in no position to lecture."

"*What a petty response.*" Nilis rose, now standing at least a foot taller than Epha. "*Especially from you. Regardless.*" A wicked photothyst finger, with a tiny piece of bone in its clawed tip, went up to point at Jasto.

"*Leave. You barely even qualify as a knight, and I will be busy. After Epha, Ralica will become my thrall too.*"

Epha bristled at that, but glanced back at Jasto. The finger didn't move.

He swallowed, every muscle in his body going tight. Why was it worse seeing a corrupted knight in person? He'd seen more grotesque ones on videos all the time. But Nilis was actually looking at him.

"C—Can't…" Jasto paused, forced down a shudder. "Can't let you…hurt Dad." It wasn't the whole truth, but it was true. His family was in danger, so he would not be weak.

Epha looked back, seeming to see that, and returned to facing the monster. "She will not get past me, young Chaston. Keep that shield up."

"*Your pride is about to claim another casualty,*" was all Nilis said. Then Jasto noticed the other dark shapes that had migrated out along the Palace columns, the movements that he'd been distracted from by the corrupted filaments and blade projections.

Crystal knaves burst out of the columns from too many directions as Nilis' sword flared with molten light, and they all charged Epha at once.

A gray-and-gold hurricane formed as the old knight set every Lantern she had to spin in a wild vortex, and Nilis halted in caution but the knaves just kept charging. Those that passed through the storm took a few hits but they were only glancing, and like the drones sent by the Pandora Gate they rearranged their remaining photothyst to compensate for any damage.

But the center of the charge was still foiled, and with augmented speed Epha swung out to the left side of the knaves. The move brought her closer to a bundle of waving corrupt filaments and Jasto panicked, but Epha trimmed them with a flechette before turning to re-engage her opponents.

She recalled her flechettes, all her opponents now inside her field of view, and the fight was on.

The knaves did their best to dogpile Epha, but that was a mistake. Several of her flechettes stayed in reserve above her head, and every time a knave got too aggressive she dropped them like hammers, knocking the attackers flat so they became obstacles to the rest. At the same time Epha herself continued to attack, steadily killing or disrupting knaves with every movement. One of the knaves reached out with the hand that wasn't melded to its sword, grabbing her halberd by the tip, but the old knight engaged her Lanterns and tugged it down to the ground. A reserve flechette dropped to pierce its core a second later, splattering dark blood across her tabard.

That was when Nilis joined the battle. As Epha disengaged from the dead knave and pivoted away, recalling several of her flechettes to cover the movement, she dashed towards the fight with speed boosted by her corrupted form. The knight's claymore snapped down, its molten edge carving through the shadowy air, and bisected one of Epha's flechettes just like that.

Jasto tensed. Crestbearers had to be cautious with their abilities, as overuse led to corruption. Nilis didn't have to hold back anymore, and one swipe from her sword would kill Epha flat-out.

The knaves changed tactics to support their master, some swinging out to make space for her while the others grabbed at Epha's flechettes and Nilis herself met the old knight head-on, her claymore coming in horizontally. Epha was ready, though, and her halberd glowed gold as she slapped the blade down with the haft of it, not touching the molten edge. It carved through the dirt instead, and two flechettes wedged themselves into Nilis' elbow to inhibit her movements as Epha herself swung around the corrupted knight, moving to keep both Nilis and her knaves within view as she'd done from the start.

"*No.*"

Nilis seized one of her knaves by the neck and threw it straight at Epha like it weighed no more than a dodgeball. The knave even pivoted in midair as it flew forward, swinging its sword to knock a flechette aside and colliding with Epha a moment later. She only just managed to activate her armor Lanterns in time, the photothyst around them blazing gold as they pushed forward, countering the force of the throw to keep her upright. The knave hit with a percussive crash and soon the rest were pressing in on Epha once again, doing their best to get behind her as Nilis circled the edges of the fight, waiting for something.

Jasto saw what when a flechette pierced one of her knaves a few inches to the side of its Lantern. The half-sentient photothyst thing lurched forward and swung its sword down at the flechette, carving into one of its edges. Trapping it, Jasto realized.

Nilis' molten sword thrust straight through both the knave and the flechette a moment later, killing another Lantern. Epha hissed, moving to reposition again as her flechettes did their best to cover the retreat, and immediately Nilis hurled another knave at her.

Jasto's hand clenched even tighter on his axe as he saw the way the knaves were beginning to move. Nilis was still hunting flechettes, her ponytail of corrupt filaments whipping behind her, but now Jasto wondered if even that was just to distract Epha from how she was starting to be pressed closer and closer to one of the Palace columns, where filaments the old knight hadn't had a chance to cut were waving eagerly around a clump of irregular blades.

He opened his mouth, then stopped. What if he drew the corrupted knight's attention by warning Epha?

But he still had to, didn't he? Even if Nilis really would let him leave, he still needed Epha. Needed her help to be more than just an easily suppressed four-Lantern Crestbearer. If he wanted to stand on his own feet and decide who he was, instead of being told by others, he needed power. That was the truth, in the world the Crystal Star had created.

And as backwards as Epha was, she'd been right about one thing: power was something you had to take risks for.

That didn't mean Jasto couldn't be cautious about it, though. Wary of overdrawing from his Crest, he quickly dipped into his Diagram and reforged just the photothyst around his feet from generic armor to his personal configuration. It had taken him months of practice to get the formation time down to just a few seconds, what with all the moving parts he had to fit together, but they'd been well worth it. He sent a Lantern into each of his much chunkier boots as soon as they were ready, stomped the prickling feeling out of his legs, then prepared to draw his preferred weapon. If Nilis came for him, he'd evade. Jasto just hoped he was fast enough.

"Epha, they're herding you towards the filaments!" he yelled.

Every knave froze for a split second, causing Epha to miss a kill she'd been setting up as Nilis' head snapped around to stare at Jasto with every single eye.

"There's a price for leaving the sidelines," she snarled.

"Face me!" Epha yelled, but Nilis brought her Palace to bear. Filaments burst from a Palace column near her in sharp lines indicating they were meant for a projection, and Epha was able to chop some down but then the knaves closed in on her once again. The old knight was forced to redirect her attention as the Palace went to work, its filaments oozing out shadow that became solid photothyst walls.

The old knight tried to barrel forward, nearly making it to a closing gap in the barricade, but one of the knaves stepped into the gap and merged itself with the wall just before she got there.

Two of Epha's flechettes shot over the barricade and zipped towards Nilis, but she cut the tip off of one and slapped the other aside disdainfully. Then the barricade finished blocking Epha's view, meaning she wouldn't be able to aim any more flechettes at Nilis. Even if she didn't need them for the knaves she was now trapped in close combat with.

It was just Jasto and a fully formed, murderous corrupted knight now. Nilis rushed forward without a moment's hesitation, her spiked photothyst sabatons jackhammering up and down as her sword blazed, but Jasto had been ready. His Lanterns were a part of him. and now he flexed the ones set in his boots like muscles. His Crest ability triggered.

White light flared, illuminating the squire-errant from below like he was on some kind of stage, and as Nilis brought her claymore down Jasto hunched and shot sideways.

The photothyst treads he'd added to his armor whirred as he cleared the sword swing, spinning rapidly thanks to the motive force from his Lanterns. That was Jasto's Crest ability: torque. His Lanterns could generate a massive amount of rotational force, and with the treads he'd built it was easy to clear Nilis' attack.

But Nilis freed her sword from the ground and was on Jasto again a moment later, moving unnaturally fast. He got back in motion, leaning forward like a skier as his treads navigated the uneven rock of this battlefield. Jasto had a wheel pattern too, but it wouldn't have worked here. His treads weren't the fastest or the easiest to turn with, but they still gave him more speed than he would've had on foot.

Speed he was needing every bit of. Nilis was taking him seriously, somehow nearly as fast on foot as he was on his treads, and her sword got closer to Jasto with every swing. He dodged another sudden cut, clocked a mostly even patch of ground, and twisted towards it as he reversed the torque of his wheels.

Sliding backwards along the open stretch of ground, wringing all the speed he could from his Lanterns, Jasto choked up on his axe with one hand and with the other drew his preferred weapon: a high-caliber handgun. Bracing the weapon with his axe hand, Jasto drew a bead and emptied the magazine as Nilis shouted in surprise.

The Mark XXI Redtail had been built for the Drone War, for enemies like Nilis, and Jasto had it loaded with explosive rounds. Chunks of photothyst shattered with each loud impact and Nilis stumbled, then put a hand up as Jasto continued to fire. Some of his shots breached the organs within her body, summoning trickles of discolored, viscous blood.

But none of the rounds reached the Crest. Photothyst was, as far as the scientists could tell, heavily resistant to any kind of force that came from mundane, non-photothyst materials. There was a reason mercenaries worked in groups even when they only expected a single knave.

Before Jasto could reload, Nilis shook herself and bullet fragments dropped from her wounds. She was charging again a moment later, but Jasto hadn't wasted the opportunity his Redtail had brought, regaining his composure and putting some distance between himself and the corrupted knight. All he had to do was maintain it until Epha got loose.

He faked going left, then pivoted on the tip of a toe and pushed his Lanterns hard to shoot right as Nilis charged the wrong way. Jasto turned again, heading towards the barricade Epha had been trapped in, but he'd been too predictable. He looked back in Nilis' direction to see a cauldron-sized rock headed straight for his face.

Jasto put his axe up a second before impact. There was a loud crash and he was sent backwards without it or his Redtail, tumbling to the ground but managing to right himself in a panic.

If he hadn't been armored with photothyst, that would've killed him.

Nilis' leg was still extended, damaged slightly from her efforts in tearing loose and kicking a boulder at Jasto. Blood trickled from her remaining bullet wounds for a moment, until corrupt filaments pulsed and the photothyst sealed, muscle tissue starting to reform beneath it.

"You could make a chainsaw, or an especially difficult shield with that ability. Instead you just hit and run. It's gutless."

Jasto was already making another axe and repairing his plate, a faint ozone smell filling his helmet from all the successive projections, but even so he couldn't stop a smirk from forming.

"I'm gutless?" he called, well past any insults to his fighting style after the Valor Academy. "If you'd left your vythex behind, you probably could've tricked Epha. But you were too scared to commit, coward." For all that the stars had aligned for it, Jasto had still taken a severe risk trying to get himself expelled from the Academy. The insults of someone who lacked that follow-through didn't mean much to him.

Nilis might have been corrupted, but that didn't make her immune to taunting. She rushed forward without another word at Jasto's insult, attacking furiously, but he was starting to get her rhythm now. In fact, in other circumstances he would have felt confident in going for a few axe cuts himself. He dodged the next few strikes easily despite Nilis' attempt at a surprise attack, confident he could hold out until Epha was back in it.

Or at least he was, until Nilis responded to his next dodge by whirling with one hand open and projecting a spiked photothyst chain out of it mid-swing.

Jasto's chest armor fractured as the chain whipped into him. That was the last thing he clearly perceived for at least four seconds, the pain of the impact clouding out his fall to the rocky ground and his eventual halt. At least one rib had been broken, Jasto was sure. He numbly started to pick himself up.

Nilis was already closing in, the chain that had hit Jasto trailing behind her as she ran forward. Jasto lurched back in a panic, putting his weight on his feet and spinning up his treads once again, but although he did start moving his balance on the uneven terrain was gone in seconds and he sprawled back onto the ground. If only he'd projected the rest of his usual armor. Without it he was dead.

Frantically, Jasto tried to bring his axe up only to remember he'd lost it in the fall, and as Nilis closed in he sent a desperate look to the orange barricade that had been formed around Epha.

Just in time to see the front of it melt.

A golden lance emerged from the dissolving barricade, and the only glimpse Jasto caught of what happened next was a linear blur of motion, golden light streaking across the ground and kicking up dirt as something blitzed past Nilis.

Her chain arm had vanished. Jasto hadn't seen how.

"I told you to face me, Truesword."

They both turned towards Epha Varison Suncage. She'd swapped her halberd for a massive lance, and Nilis's arm was impaled on it.

The lance was forged of gray photothyst, but threaded with so many glowing golden filaments that Jasto could barely tell. It was taller than the knight, angular, and at its base three Lanterns were nestled behind photothyst plates perforated by evenly spaced holes, each one filled by a steady stream of golden flame.

That had to be Epha's Crest ability: the power to make actual jets of fire from her Lanterns. The other plates on her armor, perforated similarly to her lance, were also glowing with fire like the doors of tiny furnaces. Jasto looked at them with new understanding. This altered armor form was built for the high speeds Epha could now move at.

The jets at the base of the lance suddenly shuttered, and the fire within went upwards instead to escape through thin channels along the shaft. Within moments Nilis' arm was dripping off the lance like candle wax, and the smell of burning meat filled the air as corrupted muscle tissue caught fire.

Nilis stuck out her stump and corrupted filaments uncoiled from it to begin projecting a new arm, muscle and all. Since there were organic components to make as well as photothyst, the process was slower. "*Interesting. Even in the videos of you fighting there was no sign you were capable of this. Were none of your other opponents worthy of this trick, Epha?*"

"Trick? Don't mistake me." Epha turned to face the corrupted knight, her jets tilting out to the sides to frame her like molten wings. Her gray armor shone in their light, her tabard stirred in the heat they gave off, and for a moment all Jasto could do was stare.

"This ability," she said, "is a weapon meant only for war. For the drones that once threatened to erase us all, and for the corrupted that need to be put down. You became active the moment your corruption started, Nilis. Not even a second was spent in latency."

She raised her lance, and the jets at the back rotated and primed. "So you will be put down right here, by my hand."

"*Try it, you sanctimonious bitch,*" Nilis snarled, and the shadows around her deepened as her joint spikes quickly tripled in length. Epha firmed up her stance, tucking her lance under one arm, and as one the streams of fire from her jets pulled together to point straight back. Jasto put a hand up just before they flared, saving himself some momentary blindness and still giving him a chance to see the following exchange.

Epha kicked up dust and rubble as she accelerated straight towards Nilis, curving her trajectory just a little as the corrupted knight tried to sidestep. Jasto was sure a single hit from that charge would give her more than enough time to take Nilis' Crest. Was the fight about to end so quickly?

Jasto got his answer when Nilis laughed and the spikes on her body began to glow molten orange, the same color as her seemingly unstoppable blade. Epha had already built up momentum, and couldn't bail out of the maneuver now without leaving herself vulnerable to a killing blow. The old knight was rushing straight into her death.

But apparently, Epha had seen the trick coming from the moment she'd started her charge. As Nilis planted her feet and raised her sword to turn aside Epha's lance, the curve of the knight's charge angled even wider. So wide that now she was off target, or rather would have been off target if she'd kept her lance in line.

But as she swept by the corrupted knight, Epha raised the length of it in a two-handed grip, venting fire from the long weapon, and swung it right for Nilis' face.

A metallic screech filled the air as the two pieces of photothyst collided, followed by Nilis screaming as she stumbled to a knee and swung wildly with her sword. Epha was already out of range. Blood steamed from Nilis' visor, the eyeballs within it boiling as the filaments supporting them turned to ash.

There was a thunk, and Jasto looked up to see Epha had driven her lance into the ground. The Lanterns within rushed out, flying into wide gray flechettes Epha formed as her lance dissipated, and the knight herself rolled her neck and opened a hand. Filaments uncoiled from it, not to project photothyst but to kill.

"*Get back here! Epha!*" Nilis yelled. Her eyes were still reforming.

The corrupted knight got her wish. Epha sent her flechettes forward first and followed them a moment later in a burst of fire, timing it so she arrived just after they did. The first two flechettes took Nilis in the shoulders, the spikes there doing some damage but not touching the Lantern within. They didn't manage to cut Nilis either, but Jasto was realizing they hadn't been meant to. Nilis fell back from the force of the impact and the third flechette landed on her to form a flat platform, nailed in place by the spikes piercing it. Then Epha tilted her jets and rose like a missile, thunking down hard into the landing pad she'd made for herself. Before Nilis could raise her pinned arms, grow her spikes further, or try anything else, the old knight thrust her handful of filaments downward.

"By…"

Nilis bucked but Epha held firm.

"My…"

Golden light flared against the shadows made by corrupt filaments.

"COMMAND!"

A shudder came from both Nilis' body, the improvised barricade she'd built, and the newly-formed Palace itself. Then there was a *crack* like a glacier had been dropped on solid stone.

The Palace began to break, long and jagged chunks falling from its ends. Thanks to their corruption they would take longer to dissolve than normal photothyst. As would Nilis' body, which had gone limp beneath Epha.

Jasto was careful not to look too closely at the pieces of it, especially the torso. The smell of blood and charred meat was already filling the air.

Then he remembered Dad, and turned without a word to accelerate towards him.

Jasto couldn't help but grimace as he did so, and not because of his broken rib. Epha was a master of Crestbearer combat, standing at the apex of the conventional methods taught by the Valor Academy. But when she'd started using her Crest ability, her fighting style had switched.

She'd revealed an entirely new set of unorthodox movements meant to take full advantage of her ability. The lighter armor, the jets, and the lance that went with them were custom as well, Jasto was certain of it. She would have needed to experiment for a long time to develop her gear and methods to that level, going against the grain with only herself as a guide.

Just like Jasto had, to create his own non-standard way of fighting.

Whatever discomfort he felt at the similarities between himself and Epha, especially given her traditionalist bent, was set aside the moment he came up to his father. Dad was where he'd been left, and sat up from the ground as comfortably as he could at Jasto's approach.

"I am fine," he said immediately. Jasto frowned a little at getting robbed of the chance to ask. "Some bruises, but nothing untreatable. From that newborn Palace dying I assume the corrupted knight is taken care of. Did you see Epha fight?"

Straight to business then. "I did...and we underestimated how much she's holding back." As quickly as he could Jasto explained the jet Lantern technique he'd seen, how Epha had used it to end Nilis in moments, and why that meant they had no chance of beating her if she turned on them.

"Anti-Crestbearer tactics rely on locking down the opponent first. Since Epha has those jets that'll be near impossible. She'll just close in before the mercs can finish breaking her armor, kill a few, then loop around and do it again. Even if that's the only way she can use her jets, it would be enough," Jasto finished. He looked down. "Plan B...won't work, with the mercenaries we have. Even with me helping, probably. Coming here was a waste." Dad had gotten injured for this, but Jasto was still too weak to even make it count.

Unperturbed by that, Vikor Chaston took in what his son had told him and made a rapid series of mental calculations. "Incorrect," he said, as firmly as if it was a fact. "We now know that we need plan A to work, and cannot consider other options."

"But that's…"

"It may not be the news you hoped for, but if we had moved forward without understanding our own bargaining position we would have paid for it."

That was true, of course, though this whole mess still felt like a loss. But before Jasto could say anything further, a wave of light washed over both him and his father from behind.

He turned and realized he'd been mistaken. It wasn't a wave of light, it was the darkness that had been emanating from Nilis' Palace retreating all at once. Even after a corrupted knight died, the darkness didn't go away until their Crest was extracted from their corpse. That meant…

Just as he'd thought, Epha trudged up to Jasto and Dad a few moments later carrying Nilis' Crest. Her helmet was off and the sides of her weathered face were marked by sweat, but that only held Jasto's attention for a moment.

His gaze quickly found its way to the orange, crystalline rectangle held loosely in Epha's left hand. It was a little larger than a smartphone, about as thick as a thumb. But its edges were crowded with complex, twisting embellishments, and its face was marked by an equally intricate symbol like a calligraphic star. The symbol was red, primarily, but a fourth of it had been drenched in light-eating black.

Seeing a dormant Crest always drew mixed feelings out of Jasto. He knew, from personal experience, that the symbols set within them only looked like flat markings. They were actually made of microscopic, tightly packed threads, and when an awakened Crest chose a host those threads would unfurl as it hovered towards its target, temporarily intangible until it made contact. Then they would slide beneath the skin of the collarbone and wind themselves through everything. Even the bones, even the blood vessels.

And especially the nervous system, where the filaments could be *felt* as they wove themselves into someone's entire being.

But as sickened as Jasto had been when his Crest selected him as its Bearer, he couldn't just think of them as strange and invasive

64

machines. He wouldn't be absorbing Nilis' Crest, of course, as he'd then
have to wait years before being able to absorb the stronger Seafall Crest
that he was here for. But in a post-Ascension world they were still
valuable, able to be exchanged to the Round Table for money or, better
yet, used as bargaining chips to gain valuable favors—

"—Your expedition will be delayed by a day, I'm afraid," Epha
told them in between breaths, and Jasto snapped his gaze back up. His
helmet was off, and she'd been watching him. Dreck. "Whenever
challengers come to plunder this place, and insist on continuing their
attempts to the death, I deliver their Crests to the Round Table for
redistribution." Though she didn't mention the monetary reward that
came along with that, Jasto now knew how she'd been able to maintain
her security grid all these years.

"It is one of the reasons the Table has allowed me to remain
undisturbed for so long," Epha continued, with a strange bitterness in her
voice. "The Crestbearers desperate enough to challenge me have often
lost their way in some manner or another, and their Crests better serve
Andalon in different hands."

Was that accusation in Epha's voice? Was she about to flip on
them, reject the deal Dad had made? Jasto discreetly pushed his thumb
into one of the chinks in his hand armor, putting his focus on that slightly
uncomfortable pressure. He'd learned long ago that doing this helped
him keep his mouth shut, and Dad was going to need no interruptions if
he had to turn the old knight around.

Jasto's father flicked a quick glance at him, then down at the
armor Jasto had made for him. Taking the hint, he dismissed it and
reclaimed his Lanterns, making it that much easier for his father to stand
and meet Epha's eyes.

"An important arrangement," Dad began. "Struck between two
parties that might not see eye to eye, but still know that there is a
common good to be attended to. Waiting a day is no trouble, Sir
Suncage. Would you prefer to redo Jasto's skill test tomorrow morning,
or in the afternoon?"

It might have seemed like bad form to mention the 'combat
certification' Epha had insisted on, but Jasto knew better. Dad had
already determined that Epha wasn't the type of person to forget about
something like that, so instead he was giving her a choice of having it

tomorrow morning or afternoon. The important thing there was ensuring that it happened tomorrow, which gave them time to plan. And by bringing it up himself, it would be easier for Dad to ensure Jasto got the same handicap as last time.

"The test is no longer necessary," Epha said, and Jasto's eyebrows went up. "Jasto showed sufficient skill and courage in choosing to face off with Nilis. But it would be best if you returned in the morning for our excursion." Her voice was still tired. Briefly Jasto wondered if he'd overestimated how dangerous she was, but quickly discarded that thought. For all that she was showing signs of exhaustion, she'd straightened her posture the moment the conversation had started and hadn't let it slip. Better safe than sorry, so he'd stick to assuming that plan A had to work.

"Very well," Dad said, his voice a little hesitant. From the look in Epha's eyes he must have thought there was going to be some hurdle, like Jasto had, but he didn't look the gift horse in the mouth. "In that case, we and our mercenaries will see you tomorrow, Sir Suncage."

"Ah, yes," Epha said. "On that note."

Jasto had been starting to turn away, but the way Epha said that had him pivoting back to face her fully.

"I was reminded of an important lesson today," Epha declared. "The only way to truly know something is to see it up close. Yet I have not truly known you yet, Jasto, and you have not truly known me or Sir Seafall. Tomorrow I will change that. I will escort you, young Chaston, and just you through Seafall Palace to claim the Crest. No one else."

Jasto almost opened his mouth, ready to rebuke the old knight for failing to keep a deal she herself had agreed to, but the pressure of his thumb against his finger stopped him. Dreck, that had been close. And if he hadn't known how shaky their bargaining position was, like Dad had mentioned earlier, he might have said something anyway.

It was rare for Dad to be off-balance, but this time he took longer than usual to draw himself up and give Epha an answer.

"That puts my son in danger," he began simply.

"Yes," Epha said. "It does."

Jasto blinked, and the old knight turned to him. "The gaining of power never comes without a risk," she said, echoing her earlier words to Nilis. "Those who do not take that risk themselves, and instead offload it to others, never truly respect the power they wield. That creates people like Nilis, who approach a fair trial with the intention of cheating and hold to no principles except the ones they are forced to. I will not pass Ralica's Crest on to such a person."

"And what respect do you have, for the risk you're pushing onto Jasto?" Dad asked, some actual emotion entering his tone.

"Enough to give him his opportunity, and to assist him in doing so. I have entered Seafall Palace more times than I can count, Mr. Chaston. I have come face-to-face with Ralica herself several times on those trips, and beaten her in single combat." Epha folded her arms. "Moreover, she remembers me as a friend and lowers her defenses for me. On several of my delves a single knave was the only obstacle I faced."

Ralica could *recognize* Epha? Jasto's mind whirled for a moment, but after some thought he realized it wasn't as insane as it sounded. Nilis, even though she'd entered corruption in an active state, had only attacked Jasto after he'd gotten involved in the fight. He'd heard of similar cases, pieces of a crystal knight's personality or habits being retained even after they were turned.

The really surprising part was that the Drone War had ended years ago. For Ralica to have maintained her rationality, and her desire not to hurt a friend, for that long…

"In truth, Vikor, your son may have been at greater risk with the mercenaries present," Epha continued. That was the first time she'd ever used Dad's first name. "Others have entered the Palace for their trials, but never more than one at a time. I suspect bringing too many people at once might lead to an…adverse reaction from Sir Seafall."

"And you didn't feel the need to mention that?" Jasto asked suddenly. Dreck, he was losing control. He pressed harder into the joint of his finger, photothyst starting to creak a little, and forced his expression back to neutrality.

"Yes, my apologies," Epha said, surprising him. "I had told myself that you were unlikely to believe me at all and that it was your own insistence on bringing mercenaries that might do you in, but that was a twisted notion. An old woman's spite." She glanced over her shoulder. "Truesword's folly reminded me that I must aim higher. You were removed from the Valor Academy too early to have a mentor,

Jasto, but this will be similar. You will earn not just a Crest here, but the wisdom to wield it properly."

"And if Sir Seafall does not play along?" Dad asked. "If corruption and time get the better of her?"

If...she has finally let go, failed to adhere to her duties and seek a proper end..." reluctance spread over Epha's face, but she held eye contact with Dad. "Then I will do what I should, end her regardless, and present the Seafall Crest to your son."

The weight behind those words crushed any idea of the conversation going further. "I will see you tomorrow, should you stay your course," Epha said to Jasto, before walking past them and back to her home.

They stared after her for a moment before Dad spoke, his tone slightly colder in what Jasto knew was genuine anger. Only some of it was directed outwards. "I misread Sir Suncage," he began. "She knew bringing mercenaries into the Palace would lower our odds, but did not mention that fact." His eyes narrowed down to dark slits as he watched Epha leave. "I had believed her honor would be sufficient to prevent any sort of...back-handedness of this nature. And I put you at risk through that assumption."

"Dad..." Jasto said, his voice quiet and nervous, and his father blinked as if he'd forgotten where he was.

"You're right, son," he said, his voice back to its usual flat cadence. "Bitterness is useless. Give me a moment to compose myself."

Jasto turned away quickly, both to give Dad his moment and because, if he was honest with himself, he needed one too. It was, well, scary to see his father get like this. Even during the year they'd spent in hiding Dad hadn't shown this side once. The last time it had come out was also on Jasto's behalf, when he argued against his son's expulsion from the Valor Academy.

Jasto calmed himself, looking at the slowly eroding ruins of the Truesword Palace, until Dad spoke up again. "Now we have options to discuss," he said, any hint of the anger gone, and Jasto turned back to him. "Given that Epha is more capable of duplicity than I had realized, attending this duel was the correct decision. However, we now know that defeating her with our forces is untenable, and thus we must abandon Plan B completely."

Jasto nodded slowly. "The only path forward," Dad continued. "Is to use the method she proposed, of just you and her entering the Palace. We know that she outclasses our mercenaries in combat effectiveness. Add that to the apparent friendliness of Ralica to Epha, despite her corruption…"

"…And it could work," Jasto finished. "But it depends completely on trusting Epha."

"Correct," Dad said. "There are other Palaces out there, Jasto. With their own difficulties, yes, but in some ways safer than this one."

Jasto thought about it, both what Dad was outright saying and the hint to take a slower-paced, less dangerous course that he was implying. Hints like that had been a constant since they'd set off.

In the aftermath of Nilis' fate, he considered them deeply for the first time in a while. Her course carried some similarities to Jasto's, and it had ended with unceremonious corruption followed by death at the hands of a more typical crystal knight. The fact that she'd been a merc-Crest especially had him thinking, considering his future plans.

It was worth figuring out how it had all gone wrong for her. "Dad, about Truesword. Why do you think she misplayed so badly? If she hadn't tossed that insult, and hadn't been wearing obvious corporate gear, this could have gone way differently."

Dad wasn't jarred by the topic change. "Ah, that conundrum. Though we can't be certain without a detailed inquiry at Bastion Solutions, which they would never allow us to conduct, I suspect that Nilis was acting without her employer's consent."

"Wait, really?" Jasto frowned. "Wasn't she getting this Crest for them?"

"I believe she was, but not in the way you're thinking. When Epha removed part of her armor, while you noticed the vythex weave, I noticed the state of Nilis' clothing. Though her tabard was clean, which I suspect is a testament to her ingenuity, the rest was dirty. As though it had not been washed for days."

Dad paused there, to give Jasto a chance to figure it out on his own. Unwashed clothing…even if Nilis hadn't been sent here on Bastion Solutions dime, she wouldn't have had trouble affording a hotel and must have owned plenty of clothes. Merc-Crests were always well paid. Had she been on some assignment on the other side of Andalon? No, even if she was, transportation couldn't have been that prohibitively expensive…

Jasto's eyes narrowed. Transportation. How had Nilis gotten here? This wasn't the easiest part of Andalon to reach; most of it was arid scrubland, and the closest town, Dry Quarry, had been uninhabited since the end of the War. But he hadn't seen a car, a motorcycle, or anything on their trip to the crater that Nilis could have used to reach the Palace. Had she walked? Why would she do that?

He flipped the thought around. If she had walked, what would make her need to do that? What would prevent her from using her own vehicle or some other transportation?

The same thing that had prevented her from changing her clothes. Something that both Jasto and his family had experience with. "Wait, she was on the run?" he asked, his hand dropping away from his chin. "Then why come here? She should have gone into hiding, not put herself in the crosshairs of someone like Suncage."

"To buy her way to safety," Dad said, nodding towards the Palace. "As you know, the Round Table cannot go after mercenary Crestbearers as strictly as they'd like to, and Bastion Solutions is a decently powerful corporation. For something like the Seafall Crest, they'd be both willing and able to shield her from the consequences of her crime." he blinked in a slightly reptilian way. "Or perhaps she would have purchased their forgiveness with it. Whether Nilis' crimes were against Andalon or her company is something we can no longer find out."

"She did seem…unstable." Jasto pictured it in his head: Nilis made some big mistake, probably without fully meaning to, and instead of talking it out with the authorities gave into her fear and ran. That fit with how quickly she'd dropped her act after its exposure. Then she went into hiding for a while, which wore down on her further, and at some point the idea of this all-or-nothing gamble popped into her head. She might have worn the incriminating body armor out of paranoia, and insulting Seafall had probably just been a mistake she'd made while on the edge.

And now that he knew how Nilis had gotten to this point, and why, Jasto was sure of his own path. "Alright. About what we were saying earlier, Dad," he began. "You're right, there are Palaces out there that would be safer than this one." His father dipped his head in acknowledgement.

"Only in some ways, though. In others they're a lot more dangerous. The main risk here is Epha, and whether she can be trusted, but now we know more about her. And I think I get why she didn't say the mercenaries might be a problem."

"You believe the reason is other than that spite she mentioned?"

"Oh, that's definitely part of it. The other part is that she takes honor so Star-damned seriously. And because we—" Jasto paused, seeing Dad's look. "—Because *I* don't, she was willing to let me reap what I sowed with 'dishonorable' actions."

Dad tilted his head slightly, considering the angle. "She mentioned the mentorship thing at the Valor Academy," Jasto continued. "No one gets a mentor until their second year there, but we learn about the history of Crests during the first. Mentorship is one of their oldest traditions, goes all the way back to the first Crestbearers to call themselves knights. It's probably the most honorable thing Epha can think of."

"And due to that, you say that she can be trusted," Dad said slowly. "Not because of her goodwill to us, but because of her own values."

Jasto nodded, and waited for his father's response. A big part of his theory was the slight repackaging of Dad's own previous conclusions, but that was no guarantee it would sway his father. He'd be worried about the stability of Ralica, since they were apparently more dependent on the corrupted knight's goodwill than they'd realized. It was one more thing that Jasto had no control over, but was still fully capable of deciding his fate.

"Do you still wish to do this, Jasto?"

His heart punched up and back down even as he did his best to answer calmly. "Yes, I still do."

Dad sighed, a strangely resigned look on his face. "So be it. Your injuries will be treated, and afterwards you'll go to sleep immediately. No staying up to study combat footage; however tomorrow goes, you'll need to be well rested."

Jasto nodded along, then called the mercenaries they'd hired for a pickup. As they waited, he glanced back at the crystalline debris now scattered around the crater, each piece slowly but surely eroding away.

There were similarities between Jasto and Nilis, he wouldn't deny that. But after talking it through with his father, he understood how different they were. And those differences were a relief; Nilis had been a merc-Crest under a corporate umbrella, unbound by the expectations that followed crystal knights everywhere. She'd been free in both the obvious way of choosing her work and the more subtle one, of not having her options decided by the Round Table. But she'd squandered that freedom, making one poor judgment after another today, and he was sure there was an even bigger trail of mistakes leading to this moment.

When Jasto became a merc-Crest, he wouldn't waste his freedom. He hadn't told Dad that this was his goal, and it hurt to keep his real intentions a secret, but if his father knew it was a certainty that he'd stop Jasto. Mercenary Crestbearers worked in a gray area and were disliked by the general public, not to mention the much more numerous crystal knights had it out for them. They faced many obstacles and challenges, but then freedom always seemed to come packaged with some dangers. Jasto could accept that.

Because with the Seafall Crest, he'd finally be strong enough to face them.

Chapter 4

"As I thought, you can project some kind of skating device," Epha said as Jasto came to a halt, using the brake pads set over his toes to control the stop. He'd made a full recovery yesterday, thanks to the combat-grade medical tech Dad's mercenaries had been carrying, and the full night of sleep had him feeling alert and ready for one of the most dangerous things he'd ever attempted.

Once more they were right in front of the shadowy blue Palace. No bands of crystal knaves were pouring out of its entry tunnel, so Jasto was forced to concede it was remaining latent for the time being. Maybe there really was something to Sir Seafall's ability to restrain herself.

Regardless, Jasto wasn't surprised to find Epha down at the Palace entrance and already armored, even though she hadn't specified. He'd arrived in his own kit for the same reason, and hadn't bothered to hide his preferred armor form this time. He'd need it for the Palace, and besides that Epha was observant enough to have figured out the basics of it yesterday.

Jasto still had trouble projecting hexagonal mail photothyst, so the base layer of his armor was scales instead. Over that were rounded plates focused on the outsides of his limbs and torso, designed as much to take the impact of bad falls as they were to intercept weapon attacks. Most unique of all were the wheels on Jasto's back, chest, and each of his joints that would allow him to slide along the ground in a variety of positions. His boots carried two of his Lanterns, the others in his axe and the one light flechette that followed him, and his boot wheels could be retracted if he moved their Lanterns the right way.

His helmet was reminiscent of a motorcyclist's, like Epha's had been, and bore shallow grooves on the sides to match the racing stripes in his hair. His brother had insisted, and if Jasto was honest he liked the look too.

But his helmet also made concessions that Epha's hadn't needed to. Jasto wasn't experienced enough with photothyst projections to get small pieces to form translucently, so he'd had to make his visor wide and curved instead. It stretched over the whole front half of his helmet, revealing the inner protective layers and the opening for Jasto's eyes, while Epha's smaller visor left more room for defensive plating. Jasto hadn't learned the trick to making smaller pieces at the Valor Academy, but he planned to. It would just take time, and he'd have that once he was done here.

Though incidentally, Epha wasn't wearing her visor at the moment or any of her more mobile armor form. She'd gone back to her heavier cavalier plate, partially concealed by her black tabard, and her Lanterns were nested in thick flechettes that formed a half-circle behind her.

"Are we getting started?" he asked, keeping his tone businesslike.

"Chaston, is your father not going to see you off?" Epha had apparently shortened her usual way of addressing him since Dad wasn't here. She also sounded a little concerned, but Jasto swallowed the irritation that bubbled up at that and answered without changing his tone.

"He did, Sir Suncage, before I came to this ravine. Is there an issue?"

"No, there is not."

Jasto nodded, and put his annoyance aside. He didn't appreciate the implication that Dad was cold-hearted, it was more complex than that, but with a task to complete he wasn't about to make a scene. "Then let's get—"

"Hold."

Jasto frowned. "What?" Epha was squinting at him. "Is there some problem?"

"I remember you had a firearm yesterday. Is it still with you?"

Jasto stopped and just stared. He'd said himself that Epha was a traditionalist. But that didn't mean he'd expected a move like this. Was she really about to insist on what he thought she was?

"That would be a yes, then," Epha said. "This is a part of your mentorship, Chaston, and I can assure you it is necessary. You will leave the ammunition for your firearm here, then we will proceed."

It wasn't a good look to just stand there silently in response to the demand, but Jasto wasn't sure he could speak calmly right then. Be like Dad, he reminded himself. Be detached and be efficient. Appeal to what Epha respected.

"Guns existed before the Crestbearers did, before they even started calling themselves crystal knights," Jasto said, forcibly stabilizing his tone. "And I know they were used in the Drone War. Aren't they a traditional part of combat?"

"You use the word 'they' instead of 'us' when referring to Crestbearers," Epha said. "That is a poor way of thinking, Chaston. To answer your question, it is because of the Drone War that knights begin their training without firearms. As I suspect you know, our filament kills are the most useful tool we bring to the table against drones," she continued, flaring those in her armor brighter for emphasis. "Crystal knights are therefore trained to deliver finishing strikes, not to participate in firing squads. I am not imposing this restriction simply to be difficult."

Was that really true? Jasto tried to read Epha through the small eyeholes of her helmet, then realized it didn't matter. Epha was insisting on it, that was what mattered.

Maybe she thought his fundamentals were lacking after seeing how he'd fought against Nilis. Jasto hadn't done much in that fight besides evading and shooting, but part of the reason he'd been holding back was to get a look at Epha's Crest Ability. But he couldn't say that right now without lowering himself even further in the old knight's eyes. And like he'd discussed with Dad, Jasto was in no position to push back on any demands Epha made. For all that yesterday had been a disaster, he'd at least learned that much.

So be it. Jasto didn't like having terms dictated to him this way, or that he'd have to proceed without his ammo, but he was still on a path he'd chosen and that was something. To steady himself he went through a calming technique, picturing his indignation within his head as a fire fueled by dry leaves. First it sparked, a single leaf catching and quickly beginning to disintegrate into flame. Then it spread, flaring up with light and heat far beyond its kindling. Then it died, becoming inert ash just as quickly as it had first caught fire.

"I understand, Sir Suncage," Jasto said, meeting her eyes and impressing himself with how calm he sounded. Without any more delay he dismissed his waist armor, revealing the carry bag where he'd stashed both his Redtail and a high-grade medical kit, and drew out the former. Despite his armored fingers he smoothly ejected the magazine, cleared the handgun's chamber, then reached back for his spare magazines and knelt to place them on the ground.

To his surprise, Epha bent down to inspect the round he'd ejected from his Redtail. "This is a custom load," she said, pinching it between her armored fingers and holding it up to the light. "The explosive within is standard, but the shell has been shaped. To direct the shrapnel spread?"

Jasto was surprised Epha had picked up on that. "Yeah, that shape means the shrapnel goes in a tighter forward spread. It's better for getting through photothyst," he said. He was about to mention that he'd designed the custom shape himself, but held back from doing so. Epha might be someone he needed to work with, but she wasn't someone he would be opening up to.

The old knight nodded thoughtfully. "Piercing rounds would still be more effective at penetration, but the photothyst-grade ones can't be housed in a gun as compact as the Redtail. Moreover, this modification is cheaper than piercing rounds in the long run. I assume you had lightness and affordability in mind when choosing this loadout, yes?"

It had been a while since someone other than Dad had read Jasto so thoroughly. He untensed his hands and nodded, since Epha had been right on the mark. Too much weight would slow down his skating movements in combat, and he'd had to pick his gear on a budget. The public-sector bounties he'd claimed, available to all Crestbearers along with a host of security postings, had been mostly spent hiring the now-useless mercenaries that had come along on this trip.

He expected Epha to make some additional comment on his weapon choice, but instead she produced an environmentally sealable bag and dropped the bullet into it, along with his other magazines, before setting it down near the entrance to the Palace. "You can bury that if you wish, but it should be unnecessary," she said. "We are within my defenses, and the only one out here besides your people is me. I checked my receiving area this time."

"...No need for that," Jasto said, feeling a little surprised. Epha had clearly intended to have him do this without firearm use right from the start, but she'd also come prepared with the means to protect his hardware from the elements. She was showing respect for his equipment, even while insisting he do things her way. Strange. "Is there anything else before we go in there?"

"There is not, Chaston." Epha dusted off the ends of her tabard and turned away from him, her flechettes rotating with her as she faced the Palace.

Jasto's confusion at Epha faded, as once more he was reminded why he'd been a little intimidated just by the sight of this structure. The shadows around it still pulsed like a heartbeat, obscuring his view of anything a few feet past the entrance corridor. It reminded him of that one carnivorous plant he'd heard of, the kind with roots that allowed insects in but had inward-facing hairs that prevented them from turning around. Living traps.

"Let us begin."

Swallowing, Jasto stowed his empty gun. White filaments filled his hand with a faint tingle, then solidified into a vivid green axe as he followed Epha into the darkness.

Their footsteps clinked against the perfectly flat floor of the corridor. Perfect ground for Jasto's wheels, though he stayed off them for now and instead focused on suppressing a shiver. Corrupted photothyst actively absorbed heat, rather than just maintaining a steady temperature like his armor, and in a structure made entirely out of it he was already feeling colder.

Light shone brighter around Epha's tabard as she walked forward confidently, brightest near her Lanterns and tracing the veinlike filaments within her armor. Jasto leaned on his Crest to flare his armor too, pushing back some of the unnatural darkness that he knew could hamper both night vision and thermal imaging tech. The desert's heat faded quickly as they advanced.

He quickly realized this corridor wasn't as long as he'd thought. Just ahead of them it opened up into a hexagonal chamber, three hallways identical to the one they'd just come through splitting off from it and twisting in downward directions that prevented Jasto from seeing too far down each. Corrupted filaments sticking out of the photothyst swayed in each of them, like kelp strands inside a wave, and once more Jasto thought of carnivorous plants.

"Ralica always did like her puzzles. It didn't surprise me to see that reflected in this place," Epha said. Her demeanor was strange here, shifted from the stern knight she'd been when confronting Nilis. This place had been projected by Ralica Seafall, a woman Epha had fought under before her corruption, so Jasto supposed it made sense.

He felt a brief urge to ask how Ralica had fallen. It was public knowledge that she and most of her contingent had, in a mission to reclaim a large chunk of Andalon from drone control, gotten surrounded by drone forces. Almost all of them had died, but they'd taken so many drones with them that the balance of the war itself had shifted in humanity's favor. Little else was clear, though, given that so many details about the Drone War were sealed by Round Table edicts.

But he let the urge pass by. It was the wrong time to ask, and in the end it didn't matter. The past was gone.

"Which way do we go?" he asked instead, eyeing the corrupted filaments.

"Down."

"They all lead down."

"Straight down," Epha said, and Jasto turned to her in confusion. The old knight had extended a bundle of golden filaments out of her own hand and seemed to be weaving them over each other to form a thicker cord. "Wait and see."

Epha plunged her hand down, and golden light pierced through the sapphire-blue photothyst beneath his feet. It was like dropping a tiny sun into the ocean, lighting up the floor beneath them both to reveal both shadowy filaments and facets within the photothyst that glimmered in the new light.

The beauty distracted Jasto for a moment, and by the time he focused back on Epha's filament he saw it burrow down to an intersection of corrupt filaments and connect with them.

"What are you—" Jasto started forward, but several flechettes slid around like a curtain being extended to block his advance.

"I know what I am doing," Epha said smoothly. Her filament stayed connected, still glowing just as brightly. "Corrupt filaments must reach the Crest itself to turn a knight, as I'm certain you know. This is part of a process."

"What process?!"

"Communicating with Ralica."

That quieted Jasto down, alright. "Your education on filaments must have been lacking. Though even in my days we focused too much on their killing function," Epha continued, her voice drifting a little. "But that is only one application, only the basis of what the Crystal Star intended. Like only ever using a wrench to strike at others, and never to tighten bolts."

Jasto ignored the lecture and clutched his axe tighter, spinning away from Epha to face the corridors as the filaments within all three of them suddenly shivered, then straightened themselves out.

"Ah. It seems she does not feel especially welcoming today. Perhaps that is fitting."

Darkness bled into photothyst walls set over all three of the corridors, and as Jasto whirled in a panic another formed over the path they had entered through. The temperature plunged immediately.

"Suncage!"

"You may relax, Jasto. This is a good thing."

Instead of relaxing, Jasto flared the light from his filaments out so that they blazed white instead of just glowing. Doing so revealed both the craggy surfaces of the cave system the Palace was built into, and the small, wiggling shapes passing over those rocks. Just like he'd thought. "She's sending knaves at us!"

"And it will be much easier to defeat the trial they impose and earn our advance then it will be to wander through her shifting labyrinth instead, assaulted on all sides as we do so."

Once again Jasto was forced to go quiet. Was he being too twitchy? No, he was just being cautious. As comfortable as Epha was in this place Jasto was still a stranger, someone Ralica might not take kindly to, so he had every reason to stay alert. Following that line of thought, Jasto shook himself and then moved to cover Epha's back. She was still kneeling, her concentration on the filaments below, and the knaves could appear from any direction to backstab her.

As he watched for signs of where their bodies would be projected, he caught sight of something forming around a cluster of filaments within the wall. Immediately Jasto clicked his wheels back out, though he leaned on the brake pads for now to keep his position. What was this thing? Knaves had their bodies projected out of photothyst walls, they weren't formed inside the wall itself.

White light was shining from his armor intensely enough for him to make out a process that would normally be invisible. Facets formed at right angles, indicating that a cube-shaped housing was forming in what had previously been a featureless chunk of photothyst, and within that filaments coalesced into something like a ball of twine. The shadow they generated was dense, but unlike the shadows that had surrounded the Palace or even those that Nilis had given off yesterday, these were edged in faint silver light. Almost immediately Jasto remembered: that had been the color of Ralica Seafall's filaments before she fell.

"She's looking at us," Jasto said, his legs tensing. That had to be some kind of eye.

"Indeed," the old knight said, not turning. It was clear she trusted her communications with Ralica to work out.

That left it on Jasto to prepare for the worst. This battlefield was smaller than he would've liked, as he could only reach his top speed in open spaces, but every surface here was smooth enough that he'd be able to maneuver quickly and even wall-ride in short bursts. He'd have to be careful, though. Latent Palaces couldn't threaten anyone outside of their territory, but within that territory they were far more malleable than active ones. He didn't know all the tricks Ralica could pull, but bringing out corrupted filaments and projecting spikes were some of the most common ones. He'd have to be ready to slice filaments or change directions in an instant with these close quarters.

Fortunately, Jasto knew breathing techniques to help with the G-force of all the turns he'd be making. He shifted the rhythm of his breaths in anticipation of the fight, watching the rising knave cores, and that was when Epha finally spoke up.

"You do not have to be so tense, Chaston. Ralica might be compelled to attack by the Crest that has sunk into her, but she has the strength of will to do so on her own terms. She will not do so until I stand and we are both ready." Her tone was so calm it almost seemed insolent.

"You'll have to excuse me if I'm a little skeptical of—" Jasto reply came to a halt as he picked up on the full implication of her words. "Wait, what do you mean, 'we,' Suncage? You agreed to escort me down."

The knaves swam higher, splitting up their approach so that at least two closed on each wall of the entry chamber. Then the floor beneath them suddenly became an irregular lattice of gold shooting through the blue photothyst, and they stopped in place.

Epha sighed and after a moment pushed herself to her feet, both hands on one knee to support her rise. The filament extending from her hand lengthened, so she remained connected to the Palace even while standing. "Your confusion is on me, I should have been clearer about the details of this excursion yesterday. You will not be given a fight that you cannot win, Chaston. But you will need to fight. Ralica's Crest compels her to attack anyone that enters the Palace."

"I thought you were on good terms with her."

"I am, and that is why she will make the fight balanced. However…" Jasto turned, hearing the frown in Epha's voice, and saw the old knight in a slightly unsettled posture. "She seemed so reluctant today. Worse than usual…"

There was a lot Jasto could say about that, and all of it very much deserved. But of course the moment that thought entered his mind, so did one of Dad's favorite sayings. Something he'd said again and again during their year on the run, and even before that.

"Don't focus on what other people deserve, Jasto," it went. "Your priority, always, is what you and those close to you need."

The young squire-errant exhaled slowly, and relaxed his posture a little. He needed to be strong, so that other people couldn't warp him to their own ends. He needed to work with Epha to get that strength, so he would. It was as simple as that.

"So Seafall did agree to fair terms, right?" he confirmed, and Epha nodded. "Then what do we need to do?"

"I am finding out." Epha tilted her head, and the web of gold filaments beneath her feet dimmed a little before returning to its previous glow. "Hm. Take a step that way."

He did so, moving a bit closer to the now-sealed exit, and the knaves shifted.

Three swam right up to the photothyst wall before him, and at this range Jasto could see that they were far more complex than Nilis' knaves had been. The muscle tails stretching back from their Lanterns were twice as long and bore structures like fins along their length, only these were woven from corrupt filaments and pale, fleshy ligaments.

"There." Epha cut the cord extending from her wrist, and the whole room darkened as the web of gold beneath them went out. Jasto's armor, though, was still bright enough that he could see a thick ribbon of filaments shoot out from one of the hexagonal room's corners. It tunneled beneath the floor to mark off a diamond-shaped chunk of space that he stood in the center of.

He almost bolted but managed to stop himself. Epha hadn't reacted, and as much as he doubted the old knight's assurances it was clear she knew far more about this than Jasto did.

He still kept his axe up, and only clutched it tighter as a body projected itself out of the photothyst before one of the knaves.

The knave swam in, spreading its ability to liquefy photothyst to key joints around the body to give it life, and the armored form pulled itself away from the wall. It didn't have a weapon, and unlike Nilis' knaves this one was far more refined. The head in particular, hidden by a helmet with a t-shaped opening, was remarkably well sculpted and two pinpricks of silver glinted within it.

"Lesson one: the enemy is reasonable," the knave said, and Jasto jumped. It could talk? Just how advanced had Ralica become after her corruption?

"How could it not be reasonable?" the knave continued. Its voice was disturbingly normal, gruff and attention-grabbing like that of a seasoned drill instructor, but also male. That was strange, since Ralica had been a woman. "How could a drone, made by AIs that slipped our leash more than a century ago, not be capable of thought and rationality far beyond our own? Well?"

The knave paused, and Epha let out a faint chuckle. "She still remembers it. Perfectly. Ralica, you…"

"Remembers what?" Jasto asked, his voice tense.

"The speech we heard at initiation. We were both so young…"

"Exactly," the knave said, picking up its speech as if it hadn't heard them. "The Pandora Gate's drones aren't just reasonable, squires. They're more reasonable and thoughtful than you or I will ever be. Which leads us to lesson two: The enemy does not reason with us."

Jasto had plenty of questions, but as he listened he found himself thinking they could wait.

"Note the word choice there: I didn't say they *cannot* reason with us, because they can. It would be easy for them. But they *do not* reason with us. They don't feel the need to be polite, or give us terms, or impose rules and regulations, any more than you feel the need to do all that with a bug you've decided to squash."

The speaker-knave crossed its arms. "That is exactly what you've all been chosen to face. The third lesson tells you how you'll face it: The enemy only listens to violence. So violence is all you'll give them. Violence, delivered via means of your Crests, your will, and any other tool that you deem necessary for the job." It paused for a moment, swept its head like it was looking over a much larger space, a much larger crowd.

"Make no mistake, though: In this war, your Crest is just as dangerous to you as any drone. We use violence on our terms for the defense of Andalon. Your Crest wants you to use violence on its terms, forever. So! All of you will learn to control yourselves, control your violence, and thus control your Crest." For a moment the knave seemed to stare at Jasto.

"This control is the most important thing you'll ever learn. Your education in it starts today: each squire will be tested separately, but the test is the same for everyone. A diamond will be marked on the ground, and you'll fight our training bots within it. Step out of the diamond, even accidentally, and you fail. Maintain control as you fight, and you succeed."

A diamond formed around Epha as well, spaced out from Jasto's like the marks on a playing card, and she sighed contentedly while projecting a halberd. The old knight also called a few of her Lanterns forward, adding photothyst to make them more like floating shields than flechettes and leaving the rest unaltered. Jasto rapidly did the same with his one floating flechette as more knave bodies began to form, these carrying weapons and looming from the walls like statues.

"I've never seen her pull this memory before, but few could be more fitting for today," Epha said. "Obey those instructions to the letter, Chaston, and not only because Ralica will retaliate if you do not. A lesson in self-discipline will do you some good."

"I learned self-discipline from the best of the best," Jasto snapped. It was one thing for the old knight to make a dig at him, as she'd done during their earlier negotiations. But what she'd said was an insult to the training Dad had given him. "You think I could have made this armor without it?" he added, gesturing at his complex protective gear and the wheels spread over it. He'd had to design it from the ground up, and that had been anything but easy.

Epha, though, wasn't fazed. "I can see you neglected your groundwork to develop that armor form, young man. Otherwise your helmet would have a much smaller piece of glass in place."

Jasto grimaced. "With that in mind, I believe this lesson will be a valuable experience." Epha turned towards her diamond, lowering her halberd as two knaves approached. "Especially inside this diamond. It is intended to be a horrible place to fight."

Conceding, Jasto turned away from Epha as a knave swam into one of the waiting bodies, which then raised its head to stare at him. He quickly claimed the center of his diamond as it began to pull itself away from the wall, raising the long spear growing from one of its hands.

Epha was right. This diamond shape would be horrible to fight in. The knave hadn't even entered yet and Jasto already felt like he was being sucked into the tight corner behind him, where a single misstep would have him failing the test and having to deal with who-knew-what from Ralica as punishment.

Should he dismiss his wheels? Jasto was used to wider battlefields, he could honestly admit, and to using the space they provided to evade and charge the opponent on his own terms. This diamond was about five of his body-lengths long and three wide, making it tiny in comparison.

His eyes found the speech-giving knave once again. Control, that was what this was all about, and he was here to take control of his future in the first place. He'd show that best when fighting in the style he was familiar with, even in an otherwise bad environment.

Jasto kept his wheels, but made some other changes. He raised the size of his brake pads a little, making it easier to plant his footing, and quickly sketched out and projected a rectangular shield for his off-hand. He'd be slower like this, but that was actually an advantage since he had to avoid slipping out of the diamond.

The knave stopped just outside of Jasto's diamond, coming to a halt at the same time as Epha's two. It raised its spear until the grip was just in front of its face, then presented the weapon up and outward in a salute. This one looked like a mannequin fused to a set of armor, with ball joints on its limbs and an open-faced helmet revealing nothing but smooth, rounded photothyst in a slightly lighter sapphire than the walls.

The knave waited for a moment. Jasto didn't bother returning the salute, and moments later it stepped forward and the fight was on.

The knave's spear snapped down the moment it entered the diamond, and if Jasto had dashed forward on his wheels outright he would've been impaled immediately. Fortunately he hadn't, and instead used the brief moment when the knave stood still to rapidly shuffle forward, hook its spear with his axe, and yank it to the side so he could bash it with his shield.

Had Ralica, or whatever part of her was left, thought Jasto would go for a quick kill because of the wheels? Her mistake. Jasto might be more combative than Dad, but he'd learned to be just as methodical.

The knave reeled from the blow, but not nearly as much as a human would have, and as Jasto brought his shield forward for a second bash it was caught with one hand. The knave turned back towards him, prying his shield off to the side, and although its mannequin face now bore impact fractures Jasto wasn't feeling much comfort.

It took a step forward, leveraging Jasto with unnatural strength as it tried to free its spear. He gave it what it wanted, sliding his axe up to free the haft and start his own blow, and the reaction was immediate. The pressure on his shield arm relaxed as the knave focused its strength on wielding the spear one-handed, drawing it back for a thrust that would almost certainly get through Jasto's light armor as it kept him pinned with a hand on his shield.

But before that blow could arrive Jasto's flechette smacked down from above, redirecting the tip of the spear into the ground. His axe was already descending in a log-splitter chop, embedding itself in the crown of the knave's head, and Jasto left it there as he continued to move.

The knave put its focus back on wrestling Jasto through its grip on his shield, and it would've been easy to let go of but he didn't want to make any more projections than he had to, surrounded by all this corruption. It started to yank hard on him, clearly wanting to unbalance Jasto so it had time to free its spear.

That was when he engaged his wheels, catching the knave by surprise as he suddenly moved with the shield instead of just being unbalanced. With a nimble mix of his Crest ability and Lantern control he stopped short of the edge of the diamond, then leveraged those same assets to twist himself from the side of the knave to completely behind it. A chunk of his shield snapped off under its iron grip as he completed the maneuver.

Jasto wasted no time in exploiting the position, shifting off his wheels as he simultaneously pushed at the knave's legs and pulled hard on its shoulders to topple it to the ground. Even that maneuver was dubious against the strength of a knave, or at least it was until Jasto mentally tugged on the Lantern in his axe.

It glowed bright white, embedded in the head of the knave, and for a surreal millisecond Jasto thought of those lightbulb moments in cartoons. Then his order to the Lantern to fly down was processed, and as it did it dragged the knave to the ground as well.

Photothyst rang against photothyst, spraying multicolored sparks as Jasto raised one Lantern-augmented boot and stomped hard on both of the knave's ball-joint elbows. Bits of photothyst were sent flying out of the diamond by the impact, but the knave would have its mass shifted to repair those joints in moments. So Jasto wasted no time dropping to his knees over the thing, and preparing for a filament kill.

He reached into his Diagram and drew a line, only this one touched no stars and went straight to the edge of the sky. There was a slight jolt as it entered reality, emerging from his Crest as a filament. He guided it outward, straining to extend the reach of his mental stylus.

But the knave chose that moment to shift its weight beneath him, and as his concentration broke the filament dissipated into nothing. Hissing in a breath, Jasto shield-punched the knave and started again.

It was the transition into reality that made things difficult. Keeping a mental image lined up with a real object, which was necessary in order to extend the filament, took focus. And that was a scarce resource in the heat of combat.

This time he managed. There was a slight prickling in his collarbone, then a brightly glowing filament started to snake through his armor and down to his arm. The knave began to twist so Jasto paused, tugged his axe out of its head to hack at it further, and finally got his filament all the way to his palm, where it extruded from the armor there.

It had only taken a few seconds, but in combat that was far too long. Jasto was about to get his hand in position when the knave took full advantage of the ball joints in its legs and kicked him in the back, in a way that would have been impossible for a human. He lurched forward, nearly losing his lock on the knave, and realized he didn't have time to break its legs too.

So instead he commanded his shield flechette to whirl back around, covering him like a turtle shell, and plunged his filament into the knave's chest. One more twist of mental will, and it reached the corrupted Lantern within.

Jasto clenched his teeth as a foreign Diagram unfolded in his head. The feeling didn't compare to those flickers of the Crystal Star that he got, nothing did.

But he could still tell that Seafall's Diagram was vast, far larger than his own. It took the form of an ocean, textured by crumb-like islands in brown and green and the foamy ridges of waves. Spread across it were dense, swirling hurricanes that he instinctively knew represented Lanterns. One of them spun at the center of his view, whirling with increasing fury as it detected his approach, but despite the urgency Jasto couldn't help but come to a stop.

Because the ocean was split in two. One half, the larger one, was a primal blue that seemed to stretch to an unknowable depth. The smaller half was a muddy red, its waves choppy and crashing against the islands it contained with what Jasto could have sworn was hunger. The divide between the two halves was pure turmoil, a battle line of crashing waves.

Distantly he heard the knave try another kick, and made himself focus. His view zoomed in as he did, until the hurricane and its sunken center filled his Diagram-vision completely.

Questions could wait. Jasto bit his lip, focused on the central hurricane that represented this knave's Lantern, and brought the weight of his mind down on it. The action was similar to using his Crest ability, the flexing of an intangible muscle, but made more personal by the connection. There was contact and for a moment he was the Crystal Star, his thoughts bearing down on another mind to overwhelm it. The hurricane shuddered, resisted for an instant as it tried to stay intact, but the Lantern didn't stop him any more than flesh stopped a knife.

The connection broke and Jasto swallowed on reflex, drawing any bile that tried to well up back down before it could foul his helmet. Beneath him the knave went limp, then cracked into uneven chunks. Smoke from the fried knave core coiled up from it.

It was followed by the smell of burning meat, from where the muscle tissue around the Lantern had been roasted, and Jasto clambered to his feet to escape it.

Only to curse and backpedal as he saw two knaves step up to the edge of the diamond. "Suncage!" he yelled. "Something's wrong, I stayed inside the diamond but Ralica's still—"

There was a popping noise, and half of a photothyst head thunked against Jasto's shield. He turned in surprise despite the waiting knaves, and for a moment thought he was seeing some kind of giant gray sea urchin wrestling seven people at once.

Then he realized it was Epha. Several of the knaves were outside of the diamond due to how packed it was but that hadn't stopped them from trying, and mostly failing, to find some weakness in the shifting chaos of flechettes around the old knight.

"Your trial hasn't ended yet, Chaston," Epha said, her voice strained, then as another knave probed too close she snapped out her halberd, stuck its hook in a divot on the back of the knave's neck, and sandwiched it against the corner of one of her shield flechettes until the pressure decapitated it. "Remember to stay in control the whole way through," she added as the knave teetered blindly and she turned her attention to the others.

"I already told you, that's not an issue for me!" Jasto shouted back. The fact that he'd said that out loud basically disproved it, but he couldn't help himself. This trip was supposed to be straightforward, a middle step where he strengthened his Crest before the hard work of actually learning how to use it as a mercenary. But now he faced a restrictive, infuriating trial that could've been ripped straight from the Valor Academy's curriculum, except with his life in actual danger. And on top of all that, if he'd understood Ralica's Diagram right, then she wasn't nearly as stable as Epha was implying.

But the knaves came forward regardless of Jasto's frustration, one holding a poleaxe while the other had short, flanged maces growing out of each hand, and all he could do was fight.

He only just had time to kick the previous knave's body out of the diamond before Poleaxe rushed in. Jasto remembered to angle his shield to take the blow instead of just meeting it head on at the last second, and the heavy axehead careened off instead of biting into the photothyst.

But before he could ready a counterattack Maces was at his partner's side, the two knaves occupying the widest part of the diamond as one of its flanged weapons came down in a diagonal strike.

Jasto ordered his shield flechette up to intercept and almost stepped back, but remembered how close he was to the edge and halted. His hesitation still cost him as Poleaxe swung a horizontal chop, and Jasto augmented his own axe so it had the force needed to intercept the blow.

But with that move both his shield and axe arm were on the same side of his body, and Maces was still in play. With one arm the knave shoved Jasto's shield flechette to the side, raising the other—

Jasto grit his teeth and gunned his boot Lanterns, darting towards Maces before he could complete the attack. The unnatural strength of the knave worked to his advantage this once. If it had only been as strong as a normal person they both would have fallen out of the diamond, even though Jasto hadn't used as much force as he would in a normal ramming maneuver.

Instead Jasto hit the knave like he was a wall, and quickly shifted his weight back to his brake pads as he tried to step around to the other side of the diamond.

Only for Poleaxe to drive the butt of his weapon into Jasto's side mid-maneuver. He gasped weakly and went down to his knees, then nearly rolled out of the diamond thanks to the wheels there. He stopped himself with a hand and sent his shield flechette and axe whirling behind him in a panic, feeling faint shocks through his Lanterns as they collided with the knaves.

It brought Jasto the second he needed to turn around, but not enough time to get his shield up as Maces blocked one of the flechettes and hit him squarely in the chest. The plate there cracked, and Jasto only kept himself inside the diamond by ordering his boot Lanterns to stay in place.

With a wild cry of frustration he put his shield up, bracing it with his other hand, and once again boosted himself forward to ram Maces. This time he mustered his full force and pushed the knave back a step, but he hadn't been thinking. He'd just been focusing on the knave that had hit him, giving Poleaxe a clear shot.

Maces wrapped an arm around Jasto as the other knave drew its long weapon back. Jasto struggled to get back but the grip on him was too strong, so he desperately tugged on his shield flechette to get it in the way.

The emerald chunk of photothyst slid into place just before impact, cracking with the force of the blow, and as Poleaxe readied another blow Jasto desperately stuck out a hand for his axe. It flew into place and he hacked at Maces' arm, then kicked at the knave with an augmented foot before it finally let him loose.

Jasto was drowning. He stumbled back into the narrow corner of the diamond, his shield flechette worn down to a jagged chunk the size of a dinner plate. The head of Poleaxe's weapon had been damaged too, but he could already see photothyst flowing from elsewhere in the knave's body to repair it as Maces fixed its own shoulder.

Bruises throbbed under Jasto's armor. Sweat dripped from the stripes he'd shaved in his hair, distracting him slightly. He grit his teeth and reformed his shield flechette first, calling it closer to project new photothyst over it. The Crystal Star pressed down on his mind in response, almost disrupting Jasto as the knaves closed back in.

No room to retreat, and even worse they seemed to be positioning themselves to block Jasto from slipping past them like he had before. He'd been on the back foot this whole fight, and now it was about to be even worse.

Maces took the lead and once more Jasto planted his boot Lanterns in place, taking the knave's blows on his shield as Poleaxe also chopped down, not at him but at his shield flechette. It slammed into the ground, and the knave hammered at it again as Jasto called up a filament in a desperate attempt to turn the tide. But the move was slow enough that Maces saw it coming, pulled back as Jasto lunged, and stopped him dead with a kick to his cracked chest plate.

It felt like a leaden blanket dropping from thirty feet up onto his lungs. Jasto gasped, only just managing to replant his boot Lanterns so he didn't fall, as Maces, instead of raising his weapons for an attack, hooked them under Jasto's axe and dragged it down. What?

He understood a second later when Poleaxe slammed his weapon down one last time, biting through Jasto's ailing shield flechette and cracking the Lantern within.

They were setting him up for a killing blow, he realized, as the blue photothyst poleaxe came up and the knave that held it widened its stance. He tried to get free of Maces but it was practically locked onto his axe and stuck one of its arms out to pin his shield down too, and he couldn't maneuver in this corner, he didn't have time to think or project something that could help, all he could do was awkwardly shove his intact armor around to try and intercept the blow headed his way—

—But it didn't arrive. Jasto blinked a little in confusion, trying to understand he hadn't just had something broken, and looked down to see that the poleaxe had stopped just a few inches away from his side, and an impact that could've easily taken him out.

"Huh?" he asked shakily. Ignoring him, Poleaxe stepped back from the diamond and straightened its weapon out, while Maces untangled itself from him and did the same.

"Well done, Ralica," someone said, and Jasto winced as he slowly turned towards the voice.

It was the speaking knave again, and the bits of silver light peeking out from its dark helmet seemed approving.

"The truth is, those robots we put you up against didn't go haywire at all," it said. "They followed our programming the whole time. We ordered them to set up a situation where you could either step out of the diamond or take a potentially lethal blow. You, even under the risk of death, didn't step out of the diamond. You put control first, so we know we can trust you with further training. And on your first try, too, which is rare."

The knave paused for a moment. "Then you would repeat this test until you passed. You'd be surprised how many attempts some need even knowing the trick. Ralica, corruption occurs when a knight reaches for more power than they have. When is that most likely to occur?"

Another pause, presumably where Ralica would've given her answer in the memory. "Exactly. When they're on the verge of death, grasping for some way to preserve themselves no matter the cost, almost anyone will fall into that temptation. In corruption they'll form a Palace, and Palaces make critical supply lines or defensible points completely unusable, which in turn means the drones make headway. The more we can prevent the formation of, the better. That starts right here. By learning to have control even in the face of death."

The silver light vanished abruptly, and the knave's core swam down one of its legs into the photothyst below.

The abandoned body was reabsorbed by the Palace. The eye Ralica had projected to watch them vanished a moment later.

"What…" Jasto stared at nothing. The thought of stepping out of the diamond hadn't even occurred to him in the heat of the moment. All that for…He could've died for…

"For a fucking lesson?!" he spun, looking for something to break, but Maces and Poleaxe had already dissipated.

"It seems I had misread you. My apologies, Chaston," someone said, and he whirled towards the voice. Epha. He'd forgotten Epha was there.

The old knight looked insultingly uninjured. Her plate was damaged in several places, most prominently over her left thigh, but even then the hexmail beneath hadn't been breached. A quick count confirmed that all sixteen of her Lanterns were intact as well, and she was standing too straight to have taken any real blows.

"As you said, your self-control was more than sufficient," Epha continued. "Ralica was one of only five in our class to beat the diamond trial on her first attempt. I needed two attempts, myself."

"You…knew that was going to happen. That I'd be tricked like that," Jasto said, trying to make it sound accusatory, but Epha's unexpected compliments had taken the wind out of his anger. Hadn't she been looking down on him this whole time? It was just too surprising.

Epha nodded. "And I suspect you know why I said nothing."

Did he? Jasto frowned, thought about what had happened for a moment, and realized she was right.

The fact of the matter was, the drill-instructor knave had a point. He objected to having his life toyed with on principle, yes, but he could also imagine what Dad would say about the diamond trial: That with the tactical threat corruption posed, it was necessary to minimize the risk of it. And doing so through a training exercise, where no one was in any real danger, would make it a no-brainer to him.

Jasto found it strange that he hadn't gotten this lesson or anything similar in his time at the Valor Academy, but he could speculate on that later. He knew how Dad would feel about this experience, and it was pretty clear Epha approved of it too. What did he think of it?

Jasto's eyes went down to the translucent floor. Epha had mentioned, during their negotiations, that Seafall Palace's origin point was underground rather than at the surface. It had grown upwards through the large caves it was built in over the years, plugging a massive tear in the earth.

And this was just a latent Palace. When they went active they grew more rapidly, spawned offshoots, and sent hunting parties of knaves out to gather metal, silicon, and associated materials as fuel. They always preferred manmade machines to drones. And almost as often, they killed whatever people they came across in their hunts. But more than all the large-scale concerns, Jasto found himself letting it go for a different reason.

Everything he was trying to become relied on self-control. Without it, he'd end up where Nilis had.

But there was still one issue to bring up. "Let's say I do see the logic there," Jasto said. "Ralica could still have gone rogue during the test. What if she'd broken her own rules and skipped the trial to try and kill me?"

"Then I would have intervened."

"And you would've been fast enough? Surrounded by all those knaves?" Jasto asked. He needed to work with Epha, but if she kept treating his life so lightly then any sort of cooperation was already doomed.

"Do you not know already how fast I am, Chaston?" Epha asked instead of budging. "Do you need another demonstration?" The old knight raised a hand to touch one of her flechettes, and golden fire lit up at the back end of it.

"We're inside Seafall's Palace, and she's latent. This is where she's at her strongest." It was true that only active Palaces grew aggressively, but the interiors of latent ones could be changed more easily. "And you might know her tricks but she knows all of yours, Suncage, and there's more than one way to teach a lesson like this. So answer me: what if it hadn't been enough? What if I'd died because you insisted on doing things 'the traditional way?'"

The fire of Epha's Crest ability winked out, and she paused for a moment before answering. "Then I would have failed in my agreement...and both my family and Sir Seafall's family would remain in their current states. That may not have been a risk I enjoyed taking, Chaston, but it was a necessary one due to both the constraints of this Palace and to ensure you possessed self-control."

"Huh. Alright." Jasto was a touch surprised by that answer. By Epha's acknowledgement of the risk. "And then you'd just tell my Dad to leave?"

"After presenting him with your remains and the Seafall Crest, yes."

And there was another, much larger, surprise. "Wait, you'd still kill Seafall? Why wouldn't you just start your trial back up?" Jasto asked, his irritation temporarily muted.

Epha tilted her head. "I believe you already know the answer. After all, you killed the first knave Ralica sent through a filament connection."

The first knave. Jasto realized almost immediately what Epha was referring to: the state of Ralica Seafall's Diagram, almost half of it taken over by furious, red-and-purple waves. He'd seen corrupted Diagrams before, but none had ever been structured like that.

"The wave colors, what do they mean?" he asked.

Epha inclined her head. "The blue ones represent latency, Ralica's humanity. The others represent activity, the will of her Crest."

"And...there wasn't always that much activity?" Jasto guessed.

"Exactly, Chaston. Your father's offer was not the only reason I consented to abandon my trial."

So Ralica Seafall was, after years of holding out, on the verge of giving into her Crest and going active. That put Epha on a timer, and it also helped explain why she'd given Nilis a chance. "How long until she's active?" he asked.

"Approximately two weeks, at the current rate," Epha replied. "She'll still be somewhat restrained at first, until her latency is fully gone, but it will not come to that." she looked down, a morose resignation to the movement. "One way or another, it will not come to that."

Because Epha would kill her old friend before then, even if Jasto died.

The silence lingered until the old knight looked up once more. "In any case, dismiss the armor above your injuries. I will see to them," she said, her waist armor dissipating with a golden flash so she could draw out combat-grade medical supplies.

"...No need for that," Jasto said. He dismissed what remained of his own waist armor to get at the supplies he'd brought, and went down to a knee. "I've got my own stuff, and I'd rather treat my own wounds. Won't take long."

"Very well. Though you don't need to be in a rush to tend your wounds, as our descent will take some time."

"What do you mean? You're not having us walk while I do this, right?"

"No," Epha said, and Jasto was sure he could hear a faint smirk in her voice. "No, of course not."

Then the whole entry chamber shuddered, and Jasto's heart nearly jumped out of his now-unarmored chest as it began to slowly descend. The entire hexagonal platform was an elevator, he realized, made completely out of photothyst. And if Epha hadn't put them through that trial, they would've been wandering through a twisted labyrinth of tunnels instead of taking this way down.

Though just as she'd said, it was going rather slowly. "Well, okay then," Jasto muttered before getting to work.

"I will stand guard as you work, no need to worry," Epha told him, before moving her Lanterns to do just that.

Jasto kept his eyes on his injuries. He'd thought of Epha as stuck in her ways, looking only at the past and blind to the consequences of the here and now. But that didn't match at all with the careful watch she'd kept on Ralica's latency levels, or the thought-out and rational explanation she'd given for her actions. The 'control in the face of death' mentality was something he saw just as much logic behind, and he wondered again why it hadn't been taught at the Valor Academy.

Whatever the reason, he was forced to admit it: there was a lot more to Epha, and to the crystal knights, than he'd thought.

Chapter 5

"Wait, straight down? And that's it? She's just going to be there?" Jasto asked skeptically half an hour later.

Epha just looked at him like nothing was strange about that as the elevator continued its slow descent. "As I told you, you passed her trial. Ralica is honorable. Before we enter her chamber, I will communicate once more to request a fair duel." The old knight held his gaze. "Ralica remains a true knight even now, so she will accept. After her agreement, all that will be left is…putting her to rest…and claiming the Crest."

Jasto shook his head. It felt strange to be benefiting from Ralica's apparent adherence to her ways, when Epha had caused him so many problems with a similar mentality. The coming duel would be a massive challenge, of course, and Epha was sure to make him participate somehow. Still, this almost seemed easier than he'd expected.

But wait, hadn't he been thinking earlier that this was supposed to be easy? That Epha was supposed to make this whole excursion just become a cakewalk?

Why was he hesitating now?

The Palace gave no answers, just continued to lower the hexagonal platform they stood on at a slow pace. The air had become colder and slightly humid as they'd gone down, and the cave around them had opened up into a wider space packed with photothyst tunnels. Once more Jasto was glad they'd been able to avoid going through Ralica's labyrinth. It was clearly expansive, and he couldn't even see all of it since some Palace walls were frosted to be nearly opaque, or just inundated with so many corrupt filaments that they couldn't be seen through.

The reminder of the danger had Jasto checking his armor again. Fully repaired, of course, and he'd applied med-patches to the bruises from the previous fight. Photothyst really was something else. Even though it couldn't resist impacts from other pieces of photothyst as well as it could from normal material, it had still saved him a lot of pain.

"What moved you to use wheels?"

Jasto looked up at the abrupt question. "For my armor, you mean?"

96

Epha nodded. "Your Crest ability is rotational force, correct? Most knights with that power would think of chainsaw weapons, drills, or possibly a drum spinner of some kind."

"A drum spinner?"

She waved the question away. "A possible offensive application. Rather than the evasive focus you have settled on."

Jasto felt a bit surprised by the casual conversation, especially after their stilted talk earlier. Maybe this was Epha's attempt at reconciliation.

If that was the case, it couldn't hurt to play along. "So I can move fast, obviously," he began. "Most Crestbearers focus on standing their ground when they fight, like...well, like knightly defenders or something."

He shook his head. "They're not using their Crests right at all. It's crazy how fast I can go and how hard I can hit when I let my Lanterns build up some momentum. I only figured them out a little while before I...left the Valor Academy, but when I used them to spar most people just didn't have an answer once I was moving fast enough. They had to trip me up, or wait for me to come to them."

Or wait for him to slip, Jasto admitted to himself, which had been common in the earlier days. There was a pause as Epha looked at him and the Palace slowly crawled by. Screw it, he decided. It wasn't like he was ever going to see this old knight again.

"And I wanted to fight differently than everyone else," he admitted. "To have something they couldn't predict so easily." Sometimes surprising people could be a substitute for strength, as Jasto had learned. His plan to get expelled would've been shut down immediately, if he'd fought like a normal crystal knight.

Epha nodded like she had expected this. "There is always a personal reason for more unique innovations like yours. I developed the jet propulsion aspect of my Lantern-fire because I wanted to be the strongest," she told Jasto. "I nearly killed myself when I was still learning to use it."

"How? Did you set yourself on fire?"

"No. Lantern-fire burns photothyst and drones strongly, but does little to anything else. At least in terms of heat, though it still provides plenty of thrusting force." Epha shook her head. "What I did was commit too many Lanterns to fire generation and not enough to stabilizing my movement and providing downforce during an…unauthorized test run. I ended up flying into the side of a rocky hill at an obscene speed." she chuckled. "Ralica had to dig me out, and I spent a week hospitalized. Then several more facing disciplinary action, for my recklessness."

It was weird to think that the veteran before Jasto had once been a much younger soldier, one apparently prone to joyriding. Not to mention that she'd apparently wanted to 'be the strongest,' which seemed completely out of place with the hermit-like lifestyle she'd taken.

"Was that…before or after the Ascension?" Jasto asked after a hesitant moment. Epha stiffened a little.

The Crystal Ascension. The twelfth year of the war, when the knights had apparently had enough of taking orders instead of giving them and had replaced the General's Council, Andalon's military branch, with the Round Table. The move that had forced Jasto's family to go into hiding for a year, and had given the crystal knights the political power to do all that they had done.

Which, of course, included Jasto's mandatory enrollment at the Valor Academy. He'd had years to think about it and, for better or worse, he was sure he would've preferred military service under the General's Council to that.

"Before," Epha said eventually. "Before the Drone War even started, in fact. There were fewer Crestbearers but fewer drones, back then." She sighed. "And we were all young enough to believe they would be our only opponents."

Epha had shown a side Jasto hadn't expected earlier, both by genuinely complimenting him and with her clear-headed justification of her actions. Still, he didn't care at all for her nostalgic recollections of a time before the coup Epha herself had supported.

"Could've kept it that way," Jasto said. "If you'd all just stayed in line, you wouldn't have had to fight people. But I guess you couldn't help yourselves."

Epha's flechettes, which had been bobbing up and down gently, went still on either side of her. "You have no idea what you speak of," she said, voice low.

"I know Seafall was one of the leaders of that coup. Wasn't she?" Jasto challenged. This was stupid, Dad would be glaring if he was here, but how could he just say nothing? "You and her, and all the knights, picked that fight and made the rules afterwards. Don't act like you're somehow the victims here."

Something in Epha's eyes flickered. "Stop."

"What, you can't—"

"—Chaston, stop talking and re-summon your fourth Lantern *now*." The old knight's voice was urgent, even a little concerned, and it stopped Jasto dead in the middle of his rant. Something was wrong.

He spun, putting his back to Epha as her gray flechettes formed a cordon around them both. Not sure what was about to happen, Jasto dismissed his upper chest armor and plunged into his Diagram as quickly as he ever had.

When Lanterns were destroyed, new ones would eventually form to replace them at the collarbone of the knight they belonged to, where the Crest was closest to the surface. The process took time and absorbed some calories and nutrients from the Crest host, but it could be accelerated.

Just not easily.

The green crystal that stretched across Jasto's collarbone, shaped vaguely like a headless upper torso and moving like skin, began to glow with threads of white light as he reached out to his Diagram. The stars forming it all had a brighter glow than usual, and that light seemed to be tipping forward in some way. It was like the glow had been placed on top of several layers of glass, which had then been placed over the stars.

Jasto spread his mental will as wide as he could to grab it, and began to force the excess light to condense. He felt needles wiggle beneath the skin that surrounded his Crest, then had to adjust his footing as they took their due and a wave of tiredness washed over him. He'd eaten a nutrient supplement bar specially designed for knights earlier, but might need another one later.

Still, he pressed down on the glow of the stars like he was forcing dough into a very small container, clenching his jaw with the mental effort, and it began to condense into a form that he recognized.

That of a satellite, the same way his other Lanterns appeared inside his mind.

Jasto gasped from exertion as the transparent Lantern floated up before his head. He hadn't seen or felt it appear, with all his focus on the mental space where his Crest was. Still, the work was done.

Jasto forced himself to stand straight, re-projected his armor, and readied a shield, axe, and defensive flechette before finally speaking.

"What's going on?" he demanded of Epha as his skin prickled from the projections.

"Interference. Interference from…whose are those?" he followed the old knight's worried gaze down, until it landed on murky shapes just past the walls of their elevator.

A tunnel passed through the photothyst near one hexagonal side of the column they were descending through, sloping down and away from it further below. It was carved without stairs and the sides of the tunnel were wickedly sharp, as if machine-cut, but Jasto's attention wasn't on that.

There were knaves moving around inside of the tunnel, but nothing like the ones he'd fought earlier. While those had been reminiscent of mannequins these knaves were emaciated, their bodies seeming to have been stretched thin by some sort of torture device before irregular, serrated pieces of armor were nailed into them, and their heads were concealed by thick strands of corrupt filaments that fell down like rough curtains to chest level.

And not only that, but the photothyst of their bodies was red. Jasto knew they would have just shown up as black if the blue barrier between them hadn't been photothyst, but that material had always had strange interactions with light. It was one of the reasons the filaments within a piece of photothyst could glow in a color distinct from the surrounding material.

And thanks to that he could see very clearly as several of the red knaves raised mauling weapons, and began to beat at the photothyst wall between them and the elevator shaft.

Jasto stiffened a little as he saw them work. He knew that appearance had little to do with the strength a knave could exert, at least on a mental level. But in the more primal part of his mind, seeing something that looked as sickly as those knaves did tear through the photothyst wall like berserk, starving wolves made him want to run.

That sort of thought was weakness, the kind that could take control of you. Jasto dismissed it as quickly as he could. "What do we do? Do we stop them?" he asked.

"I...why isn't the wall repairing?" Epha asked, sounding concerned. "And that color. By the Crystal Star..."

There was a screeching above their heads, and Jasto's gaze snapped up to it. More crimson shapes were sliding down the shaft, leaving trails of technicolor sparks where their serrated plate bit into the sides of it for traction. All but one of the red knaves dropped to the platform around them, shadowy filaments concealing their faces, as the group below broke through to the elevator shaft beneath them all. The knave that hadn't dropped to the ground held itself twenty feet up with a single clawed hand, leaning out to look down on the knights beneath. Unlike the others, its gaze was not concealed by hairlike filaments.

It wasn't a knave at all, Jasto realized. It was the corrupted knight that had made them, one that had been enthralled by Ralica the same way Nilis had been trying to enthrall Epha yesterday. And from the way Epha was standing, Jasto could tell she was just as surprised as him.

"This part of the trial is meant to be individual, Epha. Isn't it? I knew you'd break your own rules eventually."

The crystal thrall wasn't even looking at Jasto, but he could honestly admit that was a relief. It was a terror, lanky and covered with serrated armor like its knaves, but more organized than them. Its plates were symmetrical and overlapped each other like demonic snake scales, crimson at the base and fading up to a pale red. Where Nilis had been threaded with chunks of muscle tissue, bones seemed to be more prominent in this knight and it contained far more of them than a human would need. The torso especially was packed with a tight corset of ribs, and the photothyst head above was covered by a visor made entirely of vertical, filament-wrapped bones.

In the slits between those bones, Jasto could make out nothing but shadow edged with a faint, purple glint. Red and purple. He'd seen those colors before.

"You...Lenno? When?!" Epha cried out, and Jasto tensed. Did she know this thrall? The person he'd been, before his corruption?

"Right from the start," Lenno replied. *"Because a good soldier doesn't abandon his leader, even when she orders him to. But you went*

beyond that failure, didn't you?" the thrall shook his head, a surprisingly human motion. *"Leaving Ralica was one thing, but this trial...you handpicked knights to kill her for you. You'll answer for that today."*

Epha's flechettes stopped dead, then turned as one to orient on Lenno. "It was you?" she asked. "You killed everyone who passed my trial? You're the one who dragged this out for *years*?!"

"If you'd just been the type to understand, this could have been over in months," Lenno replied, leaning out from the wall. *"The Round Table still hasn't answered for what they've done. Your lack of stomach is responsible for that."* Behind his visor, shadows pulsed like liquid. *"But you finally did one thing right, at least. You brought me the piece I need—"* the thrall waved to Jasto with the hand that wasn't embedded in the wall, and he grit his teeth, *"—to get things moving. He will serve, where all your other picks couldn't."*

"You—Ralica would never want this!" Ralica yelled. "Not mindless vengeance, and not for it to have that price!" Gray flechettes settled back into a cordon around her and Jasto, and Epha raised her halberd as gold threads wormed their way through her armor, from her chest out to her hands. Despite the danger they were in, Jasto blinked at the sight. Was that how Epha was so fast with her filaments? Had she been making them preemptively this whole time?

"You've worn on Ralica for years and still fallen short, Lenno!" Epha continued, snapping him back to the crisis they were in. "That activity within her Diagram...it was you, not her weakness. I won't let you corrupt her another moment!"

"It's not corruption, it's consensus," Lenno snapped, fire entering his voice. *"Ralica supports this. Don't believe me? Look around."*

There was a titanic screeching noise from beneath their feet, and Jasto looked down on instinct. Where there had once been a pack of knaves that had broken into the elevator column, there was now some structure like a mix of scaffolding and a spiderweb, groaning as it forced the elevator to a stop before settling down. Jasto had thought the knaves were just trying to attack them as they descended. Instead they'd reconfigured their bodies to a structure that had stopped the elevator entirely. Jasto felt pressure build in his chest, the primal fear of having nowhere to run.

"Look around, and tell me," Lenno said, *"what exactly it is that Ralica wants."* He released his grip on the shaft and dropped the rest of

the distance to the platform below, landing in a crouch that reminded Jasto more of a tiger than a human.

The knaves that surrounded them raised their weapons, all polearms. A dangerous-looking maul projected into one of Lenno's hands while a mess of spikes covered the other.

"Still no answer? Then I'll show you."

"Stay close!" Epha yelled, just before the knaves charged and hell broke loose.

Jasto was at least equipped to handle it. Seeing the tight quarters, the knaves surrounding them, and the cordon of flechettes Epha had put around them both, he'd known his wheels would have no place in this fight. He'd dismissed all of them, except for those on his boots, but even those had been retracted as he'd covered himself with additional defensive plating and had his boot Lanterns reassigned to the shield flechettes he'd projected. He was about as durable as he could make himself.

It still didn't feel like enough. The knaves—were there eleven of them? Twelve? He wasn't sure—rushed in as one, their corrupted hair blowing back as they brought their weapons up. The flechettes around Jasto and Epha blurred into motion, leaving faint tails of light. Jasto saw a warhammer draw back and rammed one of his shield flechettes into the arms of the knave that held it, ruining the blow before it could start.

Then all coherence vanished from the melee. It was only Jasto's training that saved him, the hours spent intercepting drones meant to emulate flechettes as part of the simulated combat program Dad had put him through after his expulsion. Thanks to it, he had enough experience to react to most of what came his way without thinking.

That was a necessity, because there was no time for thinking in this fight. There wasn't even *room* for thinking, during those moments when Jasto was crushed between one knave and another, or a stray flechette, and the only thing he could focus on was pushing the blade at his neck back until the lock was broken and it was back to fast-paced chaos.

Sparks sprayed a buckshot of white spots across his vision as a knave was impaled by three of Epha's flechettes at once. Jasto made out a red blur, coming from somewhere on his left, and saw it stop as his shield got in the way. More flashes of the battle passed through his head, forgotten as quickly as they arrived. He couldn't think. All he could do was move.

Then he felt something start to worm through the side of his armor. Not a blade. A filament.

Faster than he'd ever managed to before, Jasto drew a constellation line out of his Crest and yanked it towards the intrusion. Time nearly froze as his filament made contact with the invading, corrupted one, and Jasto's Diagram came to the forefront.

The Lanterns of Epha's knaves had seemed like hurricanes to Jasto. His own looked like satellites on a starry backdrop, inside his Diagram. The Lantern within Lenno's knave appeared to him as a bright yellow hornet. One that he could vaguely sense was hovering amid the leaves of a much larger tree. It bore down on Jasto, looming larger in his head, and brought forward its stinger: a mental representation of the filament.

Jasto slammed his will against the knave's. While Epha had told him he'd neglected the fundamentals with photothyst, Jasto knew filament usage was where he really struggled. It was just too esoteric for him to really wrap his head around. He'd taken after his father and focused his life on solid things, real losses and real gains, not this strange mental battlefield.

And now he was paying for it as he struggled against this knave, not letting it intrude any closer to his Crest but not pushing it back either. Slowly but surely he could feel time starting to move by outside his Diagram, and knew that if he didn't deal with this soon it would cost him dearly.

With a shout, Jasto brought his axe down in the real world while doing his best to keep the deadlock in the mental one. In the instant where his defenses were relaxed the knave pushed forward, nearly touching its stinger to one of his stars, but then he cut the filament and it vanished from his Diagram.

A split second later Epha was next to him, driving a fist into the knave's chest as a golden filament shot out from her arm like it had been spring-loaded.

"By my—"

Jasto turned and sent a shield flechette to stop the spear headed for Epha's back. He hadn't had time to angle it properly, though, so while he stopped the thrust the Lantern inside the flechette was punctured. A faint shudder went through his Diagram as one of its satellites exploded.

"—command!"

The knave crumbled as Epha pivoted smoothly back to her side of the fight. Jasto held his own against two of the knaves, keeping his shield flechettes up and ready but not daring to risk a serious counterattack.

They exchanged another dozen blows before the fight slowed down, the knaves withdrawing to their creator, Lenno, as Jasto and Epha panted next to each other.

The crystal thrall straightened as much as the damage he'd taken allowed and twisted his head from side to side, like he was popping it. His spike-coated arm hung downward, missing a chunk at the shoulder, and many of the bones within his photothyst body had been broken. Even his pale visor was chipped at one corner. *"You're still just as much of a monster in combat, Suncage,"* he said.

Epha didn't respond, but Jasto found himself agreeing. There were only three knaves left under Lenno's control, and each one had taken heavy damage. They could all still move, thanks to the resilience every knave came with, but all had rearranged themselves so much to compensate for the damage that none were capable of standing straight.

Jasto shelved his exhaustion, checked his own armor, and nearly yelped in panic. Even with his reinforcements it had been whittled down to nearly scrap in several places, most worryingly right above his heart, and his axe looked like it had been through a bad surgery job.

He started repairing everything, armor first, only to freeze as Lenno turned towards him, the uneven vertical slits of the thrall's visor facing him dead-on.

Epha stepped between them and Lenno sighed. *"You always were obsessed with defending. Your Crest didn't give you Lantern-fire so you could be a shield, Epha."*

"Dead wrong, Lenno. That was always what you struggled with, no? You never question a single thing yourself, even when you *badly* need to." Epha's tone was acidic and her voice remained steady, but at the sight of her Jasto grew worried. Her tabard was ragged, and while her gray armor was already being repaired there was plenty to fix, enough that it might tax her Crest to do so. Even worse, she'd lost Lanterns.

Jasto didn't know how many of them were inside her armor for augmentation, didn't want to take a closer look when enemies were still right in front of him, but she was clearly wielding a much smaller number of flechettes. Not good, especially since she and Jasto were the only ones that could get tired in this fight.

So, letting Lenno talk while they recovered was a good thing.

"I need to question myself more? Really?" The purple glint behind Lenno's helmet glowed brighter, and the shadows surrounding the rest of him seemed to deepen. *"How many 'worthy knights' did you send down here, again? How many years did you spend just assuming Ralica was unsatisfied with all your picks?"* Lenno's spike arm finished repairing, and he raised it to point at the old knight that he'd apparently once fought beside. *"If one of us is unthinking, Epha, it's definitely you."*

"Wrong once more," Epha scoffed. "I delved into this place again and again, spoke with Ralica several times…" she stiffened. "The Crest restrictions. She was prevented from telling me!"

"And hiding from you was easy enough, in this labyrinth," Lenno agreed. *"It's almost like Ralica wanted this to happen. Don't you think?"* Jasto was too winded to keep up with the exchange. Crest restrictions?

But regardless of his confusion, Epha let out a brief, rapid exhalation like she was clearing her lungs of gunk. Something about her posture shifted, and Jasto couldn't explain how but it put him on edge. "You did something to Ralica," she declared. "Otherwise she would have interfered by now, either for or against us. And the real you would have sought me out, discussed this openly. You always adhered to that. Only the Crest is left now, it seems: Lenno Haldern Ironskin is dead."

"All I did to Ralica was share my perspective with her," the thrall said, smugness leaking through the vocal distortion. *"And I'm not dead, just wiser. See for yourself."* Lenno pointed his maul upwards, and Jasto risked a brief glance to the top of the hexagonal shaft.

Where more crimson knaves were arriving. "Reinforcements!" he yelled. Reinforcements that had closed in during the conversation Lenno had happily participated in. They'd been tricked.

Epha tensed. "Prepare to run, Jasto!" she shouted, and her remaining flechettes drew close. The Lanterns within ejected themselves, burrowing into the old knight's armor as Lenno and his knaves rushed forward and the reinforcements above began to slide down the shaft.

Once more reality sped up, but this time it was easier to keep track of.

First, golden Lantern-fire leapt up from Epha's armor. This time it wasn't narrowed into jets, but washed widely over her surroundings from points on her shoulders and chest.

Then as the knaves began to engage with Epha, and Jasto sent his shield flechettes to assist, he saw Lenno swing around to Epha's side. She saw him too, and turned two streams of Lantern-fire towards him as his maul came down.

The Lantern-fire should have at least weakened the maul. Messed with its structure enough that it didn't get all the way through Epha's armor. But a shimmering light began to glow along the length of the weapon, locking into tesselating purple diamonds that formed a protective coating over it.

Epha wasn't the only knight with a Crest ability.

The maul finished its trip through the golden flames to collide with Epha's ribs, the full force of a corrupted crystal knight bearing down on the armor, and she cried out as gray photothyst shattered.

"Forget I could do this? Your memory's—"

"—BURN, Lenno!" Epha lunged into the thrall, pointing every source of Lantern-fire she had at his chest, and he leapt back with a horrifying screech and so much force that he slammed into one of the elevator walls. Moving quickly despite her rib injury, Epha dropped two of the knaves with concentrated fire as Jasto rushed forward and, with an augmented and precise blow from his axe, cracked the Lantern of the last one.

But the reinforcements were still descending, and even though they'd all break down with Lenno's death the thrall was keeping his distance, his purple shield now covering his chest, and even seemed ready to climb back up the shaft if they tried to rush him. What was Epha—

The old knight turned her Lantern-fire downward, to the platform they all stood on, and Jasto suddenly realized they were right above the hole Lenno's knaves had made earlier. The hole that hadn't closed at all during their fight, and led back into the labyrinth that was Ralica's Palace.

Relief soared in Jasto's heart as Lenno let loose an indignant, wordless shout, and the sapphire photothyst between them and escape released an ozone stench as it started to melt.

But the knaves above were descending just as quickly, and with Epha making their escape route it was all on Jasto to hold the line. As the first knave dropped towards them from the left, its glaive already pulled back for a devastating chop, he grabbed his axe with two hands and brought it up in an augmented strike. His shield flechettes moved to intercept the glaive in the same moment.

Jasto struck the Lantern cleanly, cracking it, but the knave was still falling and a moment later he was pinned to the floor beneath it. It was corrupted, so it was breaking apart but wouldn't dissipate for a while. He was pinned—

—A hand plated in gray armor seized him, and with augmented strength tugged Jasto out from under the dead knave and down into the hole Epha had melted. The sounds of clanging chunks of photothyst followed Jasto as he hit the support lattice Lenno had made to stop the elevator, and tumbled out into the corridor a second later.

He scrambled to his feet and saw Epha, about to follow him down, only for Lenno to crash into her from the side. The crystal thrall now held a rectangular shield as tall as he was, and the front of it was completely coated with his purple forcefield.

The filaments of Epha's armor went from glowing gold to burning gold as she engaged her Lanterns, augmented strength meeting corrupted strength in a deadlock. Jasto squinted against the light and raised his axe to throw, aiming for Lenno's back.

But the reinforcement knaves had arrived. The first dropped down between Jasto and Lenno, its feet landing perfectly on the bars of the lattice beneath the elevator, and it spun its battleaxe to knock Jasto's weapon aside as he threw it.

He called his axe back to his hand through its Lantern and rushed up to meet the advancing knave, but more of them were dropping from above. Their long filament-hair whipped wildly as they slid down the walls of the shaft, then leapt from their descent one by one to land near Epha.

The old knight tried to slip around Lenno's shield and follow Jasto into the labyrinth, but he read the move and backed up a step before ramming her a second time. His shield was still covered by his

Crest ability and the knaves kept dropping down, all of them aiming directly for Epha. Not even to try and kill her, Jasto realized as the first one landed next to the old knight and lunged for her in a tackle. She managed to kill it as it came in with a rapid, compact whirl of her weapon that sent the halberd's hook directly into its core, but the knave flopped forward and still managed to accomplish its real purpose: restraining her.

Jasto was fighting frantically to get past his knave and back onto the elevator, but it took only seconds for the reinforcements to dogpile Epha and begin amalgamating themselves into some horrifying photothyst lump. Her Lantern-fire flared, painting the elevator gold as Jasto finally managed to drive a flechette into the core of his opponent. It dropped like a puppet with cut strings, then kept dropping as the lattice it had been standing on suddenly folded back at Lenno's command. The dead knave vanished into the shadows beneath the elevator column in moments, dark hair flapping wildly.

Jasto glanced up at the ledge, one he'd now have to jump across an insanely deep pit to reach. Further back on the platform Epha's Lantern-fire died, either due to her limits on using it or to avoid burning through the elevator herself.

And amidst the chaos, Lenno turned to look straight at Jasto. The thrall had said, right at the beginning, that the squire-errant was the 'piece he needed' for whatever his plans were.

And now he dropped his shield to charge across the elevator at his full, corrupted speed. Lenno still had control of the lattice holding up the elevator, Jasto realized. The moment he got into the corridor he could make it drop, taking Epha out of the picture.

Time seemed to slow down for Jasto, his heart thumping like an engine piston as he frantically considered his options. Would he be able to climb back onto the elevator platform before the crystal thrall reached him? Even if he did make it back, could he beat Lenno and his knaves?

Or was Jasto still too weak to matter, after all this time? The wheels and fighting style he'd developed, his own proof of independence, had done absolutely nothing in this close-quarters battle. He'd probably just worsen things further if he didn't run, but Epha was still here. He couldn't just...

Locked in his internal conflict, Jasto made the worst mistake he could: he froze up mid-combat, doing nothing as Lenno rushed straight for him. In seconds the thrall would enter the tunnel, his knaves right behind.

"DO YOUR DUTY, FALLINGSTAR!" Epha yelled, and golden filaments shot through the elevator platform in a flash.

The Palace reacted. Light-drinking filaments tore themselves loose from the corridor walls and Jasto lurched back on instinct, but they paid no attention to him. Instead they quickly wove themselves together, forming a lattice over the broken wall of the elevator shaft.

"*NO!*" Lenno yelled, diving forward frantically as photothyst started to project over the hole his knaves had carved. His spiked, red hand made it through the forming wall, grasping frantically for Jasto, only for the projection to finish and seal the rest of him outside the labyrinth corridor. Lenno was stuck with his arm in the shaft wall.

But Ralica wasn't done. A heavy shuddering sound filled the air, working its way through Jasto's bones as the elevator pressed downward against the lattice that restrained it. Lenno paused his efforts to free himself as multicolored sparks began to spray from the edges of the hexagonal platform.

Jasto was still reeling. Epha, pinned under Lenno's knaves, had managed to sneak out a filament and communicate with Ralica. The old knight had been confused right at the start by the labyrinth walls not repairing immediately, and by Ralica allowing Lenno's actions.

Apparently, she'd done something about it.

The elevator screeched again and Jasto instinctively backed up. "*Ralica, no!*" Lenno yelled, tugging fiercely at his trapped arm. "*Don't listen to her! I'm this close—*"

Jasto bent and pressed his hands against the side of his helmet as the screeching turned cataclysmic in volume, rainbow sparks spraying furiously against the shaft walls as the elevator shot straight down. Lenno's lattice was crushed beneath it, but the thrall himself remained pinned with an arm inside the wall.

Jasto shook his head, his ears still ringing, and frantically moved up to the corridor wall to look down the shaft.

Just in time to see a faint, golden light vanish into the waiting darkness.

He felt his jaw lock shut from fear. That had been Epha's filament-light. Was she still pinned under all those knaves? What if they tried to corrupt her? Her Lantern-fire could burn through them, but if Epha was at the limits of her Crest then just using it would turn her corrupt anyway.

Jasto swallowed, feeling every drop of the sweat drenching his body. But she wasn't at her limits, right? She was a veteran crystal knight. She knew how to conserve her strength. He tried desperately not to think about how she'd been pushing herself towards the end of this fight.

Epha would survive, he told himself. She would survive.

The noise of a punch, photothyst on photothyst, interrupted his attempts to reassure himself. Jasto scrambled back, his jaw unlocking at the sight of Lenno, still embedded in the wall by one hand and punching furiously at it with the other.

"You will not—" spikes projected over Lenno's fist, and he thrust it forward again. *"—escape—"* More knaves slid down the walls of the elevator shaft, braking and digging themselves in with their uneven armor, and began to join Lenno in his efforts. *"—after all I've sacrificed!"*

The wall started to crack. Jasto sucked in a breath, looking down the elevator shaft again. It burned like white-hot fire that he could only see one thing to do now, only one way to salvage any of this. His wheels had been useless in this fight, but they could still do something.

"I'm sorry," Jasto whispered, ashamed that this was the best move he could make, but he wasted no more time. Two of his flechettes were dismissed, and the Lanterns within sent down to his boots. He leaned hard on his Crest ability, flooding them with rotational force, and turned down the corridor as white light gleamed from his legs.

Jasto sped into the labyrinth, leaving Epha behind as the first knave broke into the corridor.

He faintly heard Lenno curse as he sped away, suggesting the thrall was somehow being hindered by the Palace, but that first knave was already reabsorbing its weapons to chase after Jasto on all fours. The young squire-errant frantically shed the extra armor he'd projected, knowing it would be speed that saved him now, and reached for his Diagram.

111

It flickered into something unknowable, reformed uncomfortably close to his mind. The threat of corruption loomed, along with everything else.

As economically as possible Jasto projected his usual arrangement of wheels over his armor, just in time to kneel and stick an arm out for drag as a sharp turn came up. He pivoted, the wheels on his arm and knee skidding across the photothyst, and returned to a standing position smoothly as the corridor continued down and further away from the elevator shaft. Jasto saw a dense patch of corrupted filaments filling the corridor up ahead, swaying in a way that seemed far too gentle for the violence he'd just been through.

He didn't need to do anything about them, actually. Like he'd told Epha earlier, now that he had some momentum there really wasn't much the filaments could do to him. Even if one did burrow into his armor as he sped by, it wouldn't be there for long. The speed he was moving at would tear it out before it got near his Crest.

Dad would have just sped right on through if he was here, Jasto knew. In almost every lecture he gave, that was the recurring theme: the importance of picking your battles, of not taking action unless that action had a real chance of accomplishing something.

But with all the dreck Jasto had just seen, he discarded those lessons for a moment.

Right now he needed to cut something.

He didn't let his momentum drop, but as he moved Jasto raised his axe and swung it down, then across, then in a weird sort of uppercut he would almost never use in a real fight. The filaments were ripped apart like stalks of wheat beneath his blade, each cut making a noise like tearing paper. There was barely any relief in the motion, but Jasto still breathed a little easier by the time he lowered his axe. Then he emerged from the shadowy gauntlet only to be faced with a much more difficult challenge: a split in the path.

He'd left the slanted corridor for some sort of triangular landing with a low ceiling, emerging from an opening at one of the corners. Two more corridors branched off from the other corners of the triangle, one leading up and one leading down.

Jasto knew he'd gained some ground on his pursuers, and that was the only reason he allowed himself to stop and consider. As confusing as this Palace might be, going up would eventually lead out of the cave system it was built into. Back to the surface, away from this botched mission, and back to Dad. His father wouldn't mind his failure here, would still help him find a place and probably be relieved by how things had turned out.

But did Jasto mind? If he left now he'd have nothing to show for it except another loss brought about by his weakness. He'd come here to get strong, strong enough to really have a choice in who he was. And he didn't want to be someone who could only run from danger.

That thought, strangely, had him recalling the trial he'd been faced with earlier, before the elevator had started descending. It had been about staying on task, not falling to temptation, even when faced with the possibility of death. It sort of applied here.

Before he could contemplate further, the filaments in the wall ahead of him began to shift. Jasto tensed, ready to bolt in any direction if seals started projecting over the exits, but instead they condensed into a sphere at eye level with him inside the wall.

And at the center of the sphere, shrouded in corrupted shadow, a bit of silver light began to glint. Ralica was looking right at him, just as she'd done during the memory trial.

Jasto would've slapped himself if he wasn't armored and inside a Palace. What had he been thinking, standing still on open grounds in a combat zone? He'd already wasted too much time, and now the master of this Palace was watching him. The shock had gotten to his head.

With no more delay, Jasto gunned his boots and sped towards the downward corridor on the left of the triangle. He'd been leaning that way, honestly, despite everything. Just abandoning Epha completely hadn't sat right with him.

But then he screeched to a halt just inside the corridor as the corrupted filaments it held retreated into the walls to form…arrows. Giant arrows on every surface, pointing back the way he'd come.

If Ralica hadn't wanted him to use this route, she could've plugged it as easily as thinking. Jasto frowned at that, and thought back to the events he'd seen in their earlier fight.

Lenno hadn't been prevented from reaching Jasto and Epha with his small army of knaves, but he hadn't been helped along either. He'd needed to break through the elevator shaft wall, then direct some of his knaves to form that stopping lattice instead of the elevator halting on its own.

And during the fight, Epha had accused Lenno of doing something to Ralica to put her out of action. What had Lenno said in response? That he'd just made them 'share perspectives?' That sounded like confirmation to Jasto. And then, immediately after Epha's filament connection, Ralica had made the Palace react. She'd repaired the labyrinth wall and dropped the elevator, both moves aimed to get Lenno away from Jasto. All of that contradicted Lenno's insinuation that their encounter had been part of Ralica's plans. It lined up with the idea that Ralica's latency meant she was still in control.

Jasto spent a moment more in thought. Then he pivoted and sped back up the corridor to the triangular landing.

Sure enough, the arrows continued through the room and pointed to the upwards corridor. But by now the first red knave had arrived, long-legged and swinging a two-handed mace at Jasto as he arrived at the landing.

Jasto dropped to his knees without hesitation, the wheels there jerking as he stuck out his axe at knee level. It lodged in place as he sped past, cutting almost completely through the knave's leg. Jasto left the weapon as he moved on, only to stretch a hand back when he reached the upwards corridor.

The Lantern inside his axe activated, and he heard it pull the knave off its feet with a clatter as it freed itself and slapped into his hand.

Then he accelerated, pouring on the speed as he climbed up and away towards wherever Ralica was directing him.

Chapter 6

Surprisingly, Jasto was only going upwards for a short time. Then he came to another landing, and this time both of the corridors leading away from it pointed down.

"Suncage did say she loved puzzles..." Jasto murmured. Maybe the downwards corridor would have eventually led him back to the surface. Tricky.

"Which way now?" he called out. "Seafall?" he glanced around, expecting another eye to form more than he really expected an audible answer, but all he saw was that the entry behind him had sealed. That was for the best with Lenno after him, Jasto knew. He quickly glanced down both of the other corridors without stepping in and saw that they were long, dark, and completely identical. No clues of any kind.

"Do you have split personalities or something?" Jasto tried. He wasn't about to try a filament connection like Epha, but maybe words would get a rise out of whatever was left of the corrupted knight. He knew they retained their personalities to some extent, and that they weren't just completely bound to what their Crests wanted. Even though Nilis had been corrupted she'd still told Jasto to leave instead of trying to enthrall him, after all.

But then again, Jasto didn't know how much of a person could stick around with a Crest invading their head and corroding their thoughts bit by bit. Having his mind supplanted like that was terrifying, and one of the reasons he'd escaped the Valor Academy. Had he made a mistake trying to trust Ralica?

Maybe. But maybe not, now that there was a bulwark between him and Lenno's knaves. It was confusing, trying to make sense of what the seemingly aloof knight in charge of this Palace actually wanted, but Jasto could already hear Dad telling him his frustration wouldn't be helpful here. He exhaled slowly.

Ralica was apparently a tricky person, so she probably knew that old rule about mazes that said you were supposed to hug the right-side wall. With that in mind Jasto went down the leftmost path instead, coasting down the corridor at a brisk pace and pushing his armor filaments to flare as brightly as possible. He didn't want to get surprised by anything.

In the enhanced light he could somewhat see through the photothyst walls, and it quickly became clear that there was a large room to the right of and below him.

It was hexagonal, which seemed to be a running theme in this Palace, and the tops of its walls converged like a six-sided pyramid. From the look of it, Jasto's corridor would take him right to one of the corners of the large space. And…if he was looking at the angle of things correctly…the right corridor would've taken him to a corner on the other side of the pyramid.

A false choice? Was Ralica just screwing with him?

It didn't matter, Jasto decided. As wild and intricate as they could be, the Round Table had never discovered a Palace without at least one path leading down to the corrupted knight that ruled it. Some final limitation imposed by the Crests, Jasto was pretty sure. He'd find that path, whether or not Ralica was as honorable as Epha claimed.

He touched down just outside the pyramid, as he'd expected, and saw that there was a sort of preparatory room just before the entrance to it. It even had a bench. The room didn't react to his entrance in any visible way.

Jasto didn't sit down, but he did pause to eat another nutrient supplement bar and check on his Crest. It was still some time away from forming his next Lantern, and he knew from experience that if he tried forcing it this early he'd be on the verge of passing out.

He couldn't take that risk, not when a fight was so obviously waiting for him just ahead, and he couldn't sit still for a long time with Lenno still after him, even if Ralica had raised some bulwarks. That meant he'd be going in with only three Lanterns instead of his usual four, and with one in each boot that also meant he'd just have his axe to work with as a potential flechette.

What would Ralica throw at him in that massive room? Jasto figured it was pointless to waste time thinking about why he'd probably have to fight, with how opaque the corrupted knight was. So instead he just focused on how to ensure a victory.

With a space that large Jasto wouldn't be surprised if he had to face multiple knaves at once, but unlike the cramped fight he'd been through at Epha's back earlier he liked his odds much better here. There was plenty of room for him to maneuver in a space this large. Even if a bunch of obstacles suddenly formed throughout the space the moment he stepped in, Jasto was still confident. He'd mastered the wheeled form of his armor, whatever other deficiencies he might have had, and he'd learned and practiced plenty of useful maneuvers for getting around obstacles with roller-skating videos as his reference.

Jasto had already dismissed part of his helmet to eat the nutrient bar, but now he removed the rest of it and pulled a towelette from his medkit to clean the sweat off his face. Then he reformed the helmet and did a once-over of his armor, correcting some small burrs he'd made when flash-projecting it, and checked the spin of his wheels. He even did some warm-up exercises. He frowned afterwards. Was that really all he could think to do? It seemed like a waste of a valuable opportunity.

What did Epha do, before her battles? He'd seen the old knight prepare herself for three, now, and there was no denying her skill. Her photothyst projections really were a level above his, with not only hexmail but also a photothyst weave gambeson beneath it for even more protection. The precision needed to project cloth was something else. Not to mention how quickly she could shift to her faster armor form, and her precise control of photothyst translucency. Unfortunately Jasto wasn't about to develop those skills just from having seen Epha project her armor, and during the start of the elevator fight she hadn't even done that—

Jasto paused. But she had made another preparation, hadn't she? She'd threaded filaments along her arms preemptively, to make her Lantern kills faster.

He could do that.

Without the heat of battle surrounding him, it was much easier to both draw constellation-lines and keep his mental stylus aligned with their position in reality. He threaded one along the underside of his arm all the way to his palm, then dropped his concentration and just let it remain there. Experimentally, Jasto thrust out his hand and lengthened the filament another few inches at the same moment. It took only a flash of concentration, not the multiple seconds he usually needed to get this result. Jasto made another filament, threading this one along his other arm, and felt no additional strain on his mind.

He shook his head in disbelief. Using filaments this way removed nearly every issue he had with them. He just hadn't known this method at all.

Jasto wondered if other Crestbearers knew it. Maybe it would've been part of his later education, if he'd stayed at the Valor Academy? Or maybe he'd been meant to figure it out himself, by picking up on subtle hints from the instructors. The Academy loved that sort of indirect method of teaching, but Jasto did his best learning with direct instructions.

He made several more filaments immediately, some only going down to his shoulders in case his arms were damaged. Jasto considered, looking out over the hexagonal room ahead. Epha had also shouted that catchphrase every time she made a filament-kill. He knew most knights did the same, and he'd assumed it was just some kind of flourish.

But Epha had continued to say 'by my command' with each filament kill even during that high-tension battle against Lenno. Maybe there was some benefit to speaking as you mentally focused. Jasto supposed it might help with focusing through the mental strain of willing something to break.

But what phrase to use, though? There was no way he was shouting the same thing as Epha.

He thought for a moment. The answer that came up was corny, no doubt about that. But it was also his without a doubt, and he wasn't going to let embarrassment rob him of a potential advantage.

Jasto practiced saying the phrase a few times, took one last moment, then stepped forward into the pyramid.

Just as he'd expected a door immediately formed over both entrances. He was putting distance between himself and his door before its projection even finished, flexing his boot Lanterns as hard as he could in case something tried to hit him right at the start.

But nothing seemed to. Jasto slowed as he came up to one of the other corners of the pyramid, looking around for a threat and seeing nothing present itself.

Then, he heard a man's voice.

"Sir. We've got drone footprints up ahead, but we're not sure how old they are. No direct drone sightings yet, either." Ian couldn't tell where it was coming from, something was weird about the acoustics of this space. And more than that, the voice sounded…familiar. From where?

Then a different voice, this one female, spoke up, beginning her words with a light chuckle. "Didn't I tell you already, Lenno? At least at times like this, it's Ralica. Or 'Seafall,' if you're insisting on some formality."

Jasto paused in his search. *That* was why the first voice sounded familiar. He'd heard Lenno's corrupted voice earlier, under circumstances that would be hard for anyone to forget.

This voice sounded much more human, suggesting someone bookish and a little stiff in their manners. This had to be one of Ralica's memories, like the diamond trial earlier, and the other voice was apparently that of Ralica Seafall herself.

Why was this being shown to Jasto?

"Well, Sir, what you specifically said was to be less formal during 'non-combat stuff,' and I am following that request."

"Then what could it be? You said there were no drones nearby. And arguing about the best armor projections with Epha doesn't count, remember?" Ralica didn't sound like Jasto had expected either. As one of the main leaders of the Crystal Ascension he'd expected her to be a severe or at least commanding sort of person. This Ralica sounded far more…sarcastic than charismatic leaders were supposed to.

"Something about our human enemies, Sir," Lenno said quietly. "Almost the entirety of your circle is on this mission, and that's how they wanted it. It's a life-or-death situation until we've returned, and even then…"

Ralica sighed, and when she next spoke her tone was much more serious. "I know, Lenno. If a man had told me six years ago I'd have legitimate reasons to doubt the rest of the Round Table, I'd have punched him. But now? Not a single meeting goes by without them trying to freeze any Crestless out of our leadership or divert relief funds to some senatorial bribe…I knew the Ascension would be tempting for us, power always is, but I didn't think they'd be so *weak*. So greedy."

Jasto blinked. He'd known the Crystal Ascension had been 'intended' as a temporary measure, a way for Crestbearers to regain their autonomy and ensure their safety through the end of the Drone War. But he hadn't expected one of the people behind it to have meant that sincerely, to actually be willing to set down the power she'd claimed. He hadn't expected tension between the knight-commanders of the Round Table, either. In his mind they'd always been a monolith, Ralica included.

"Don't get me wrong: I remember how bad the General's Council was, and all the dreck we were put through, but seeing us become like them is its own horror," Ralica sighed. Jasto was surprised she was being so open about her troubles with those she led. In someone else it might have seemed weak, but here it felt...honest. "Thank the Star I insisted we stop at the military when we rose up. Just that has already corroded us so much."

"The Ascension wasn't a mistake, Sir," Lenno said. "And I wish you didn't say 'us' when you talk about the Table, because you're nothing like them. Or the General's Council, or any of those *cretins* pretending to be good leaders that the world is filled with. They all let themselves go filthy. You stayed clean in a world full of scum." His tone had grown manic with the words, and Lenno seemed to realize because he cleared his throat before speaking again. "That is why I'm here, following you, and why I'm concerned. They haven't done anything outright to you yet, but this is their best, and possibly last, opportunity to get you during this war."

"We're taking a risk, I admit that," Ralica said. "But it's an important one. With the gains we've made by striking out, instead of turtling, the other knight-commanders will be forced to start doing the same soon. To send more than the token forces we had to bully them into giving us for this mission. Then we'll be able to end this, Lenno." There was real conviction in Ralica's voice, and even excitement.

"Once we've reached that tipping point, it won't be long before all of our home is cleaned up. And as soon as it is, the Table can be dismantled too."

Once more Jasto was confused by the memory, and he had to force his gaze down to keep checking for threats. Ralica had been aiming to reclaim all of Andalon? That was a far cry from its current, Palace-ridden state, and he knew some of that damage had come from before the War ended. It must have gotten screwed up with her death, for all that she'd taken so many drones with her.

"Be that as it may, Sir, we can only reach that point if we survive this risk," Lenno noted.

"I know. And that's why I've prepared contingencies for exactly what you're worried about."

"You have, Sir?"

"I have. Our group might not have many allies in the Round Table, but no one else wants them to be the ruling caste of Andalon. So it wasn't hard for me to get some disgraced generals to…did you feel that?"

"Feel what?"

"Drones!" Ralica shouted. "Underground!"

Jasto was already near the edge of the pyramid, so he was well in the clear when a monster carved from photothyst burst out from the center of the hexagonal space. That didn't stop him from immediately firing his boot Lanterns and darting to the side, though, and he stayed in motion as he surveyed the threat.

Six silvery blue legs tapering to insanely fine points touched down on the photothyst floor, each one ringing like an oversized sword. They led up to a blocky body, about the size of two cars stacked on top of each other and bulbous at the back end. The structure reminded Jasto of a spider, except this spider bore two tails that resembled dragon heads and the space where there should have been a mouth was more like some sort of industrial drill. It had seven round eyes made entirely of corrupted filaments, set above the construct's rotating mouthparts, and as the floor repaired itself beneath the monstrosity they drank in the dim light Jasto was shedding from his armor.

He flared it brighter, and saw four dark octahedral shapes set along the spider's body like they were tracing out a spine. The construct was a knave, technically speaking, but a knave that contained multiple Lanterns. That allowed it to surpass the normal size of a knave by miles. Jasto was amazed that Ralica could make things like this without going active.

And this shape it was taking had to be that of a Pandora Gate drone, straight from the days of the Drone War. Jasto had seen pictures, and the Pandora drones always took on mythical, monstrous forms with futuristic weapons built in. This one looked to be no exception with its dragon-head tails and drill-like mouth, though it was made of photothyst instead of the metal that comprised drones.

121

There was no more dialogue from Lenno or Ralica, no more time to process what that memory meant. The construct began to turn towards Jasto, revving up its mouth-drill.

No other threats that he could see. Just one big, slow opponent and plenty of open space.

Jasto smirked.

The drone hunkered forward and charged at him, faster than its size would have suggested but still too slow. Jasto increased his speed and curved forward, sketching out and projecting another axe for his left hand. There was no Lantern set within this one, but it still wouldn't dissipate as long as he kept a grip on it.

The drone tilted its head down and shoved its whirring drill into the floor without losing speed. Chunks of photothyst flew wildly, and since they were corrupted they didn't dissipate the moment they were separated from the ground. That meant Jasto was about to be caught by the edge of a spray of buckshot.

He threw himself flat without hesitation, the wheels on his back taking his weight as chunks of debris flew over his head, and leaned into the curve he'd started. It tightened even further, pulling him around the buckshot and then smoothly under the drone itself.

He stuck both axes out as he passed beneath it, feeling his arms jerk from the force of the collisions, and pulled himself back up to a standing position on the other side of the drone as he continued to move.

No complete cuts, he saw with a frown, and the damage he'd done wouldn't last. The heads of both axes were chipped, and he quickly repaired them as he curved to the left and the spider drone whirled on him.

He'd probably have to aim for the joints of its legs. The drone returned to a standing position as he closed back in, fixing itself, but this time it stood still as he approached and raised two of its legs to try and skewer him. Not only that but it actually screeched, grinding a few of its mouthparts against each other to make an ugly noise.

A leg came forward like an oversized spear and Jasto juked to the right, inhaling as G-forces pressed down and engaging his Lanterns to keep steady. He dropped to a knee as the other leg passed over his head, but as he turned to cut the joint of the extended limb the drone suddenly shifted its weight to try and side-check him.

Jasto threw himself backwards, lessening the impact somewhat, and he landed on his back wheels to skid away instead of just hitting the ground, but there was only so much you could do when what had to be at least six tons of photothyst hit you, even in a glancing blow.

There was a thunk, then darkness pulsed over his vision as he spun out. Breathing was like prying open a can with nothing but his fingers. The faceted ceiling above seemed to bend and twist, and he wasn't sure if that was from the concussion he'd just gotten or from how much he was spinning.

Either way he could still hear the metallic clink of photothyst against photothyst, so Jasto forced himself to sit up and stabilize his momentum as the drone came nearer. Strangely it hadn't charged him outright like he'd been expecting, but he didn't let that stop him from getting to his feet and distancing himself.

His head cleared further and his breath came a little easier as he reached the edge of the pyramid once again, but the drone stopped in the center. Its drill remained inactive, too, instead of spinning up to toss more debris at him.

Jasto looked at the two dragon-head tails of the construct and got a bad feeling. Immediately he abandoned his circling path around the pyramid to instead shoot straight for the center, dropping to lay flat on his chest-mounted wheels and leaning on his Crest ability so hard that it hurt.

Just as he'd feared the mouth of one of the dragon-heads opened, and out came a bullet of compressed photothyst debris moving too fast for Jasto to track. But just as he'd hoped, his sudden acceleration had caught the drone off guard. It hadn't curved its tail downward enough to catch him with the bullet, and in the next split second Jasto was within striking distance of the drone.

He'd aim higher than a leg this time. Like a gust of wind kicking up into a tornado, Jasto let his momentum pull him into a tight spiral as he rose beneath the titan of silvery-blue photothyst that had thought it could kill him. He swung his left-hand axe up, and it bit deep into the belly of the drone with a fierce screech. Jasto came to a nearly complete halt beneath it, and he was injured but this wasn't his first time dealing with heavy changes in momentum.

So there was only an instant's delay before he shot his arm filament up through the axe and into the body of the drone, where its Lanterns were hiding.

Reality doubled as he perceived both the hexagonal arena in the real world and the hurricane he'd connected to in the mental world, Ralica's Diagram. It was more jarring than the momentum shift for Jasto, but he'd still made the connection in moments instead of seconds and he was ready with another of Epha's tricks. Assuming it worked.

"Open—" he began, centering himself for the Lantern-kill. He felt the lines of his Diagram stretching down into reality and then back into unreality to connect with the Lantern, but having something to say grounded him. Made it easier to focus his mind to a point, even while perceiving so much. He'd thought of filaments as the realm of the esoteric. The solidity of his words suggested otherwise.

"—your eyes!" Jasto finished, bringing down the full force of his will on the storm. He felt the connection break and immediately tugged himself away from the drone, leaving his axe in place to dissipate.

And he'd gotten out just in time, because a moment later the two central legs of the drone broke into pieces and it crashed to the floor.

Jasto couldn't help but suck his teeth a little at how the phrase he'd chosen sounded. He didn't regret the choice, as 'open your eyes' was as much of a reminder to himself as it was a battle cry to throw at his enemies. Dad was always telling him to watch his resentment, to avoid getting blinded, and this was his way of honoring that.

It still made him cringe a bit. Oh well. If 'by my command' was the standard for these phrases, he'd probably fit right in.

Jasto shook his head to clear his thoughts—he might need to take one of his mental repair nanotabs after this, if his mind was wandering that much from the concussion—and put his attention back on the drone. It was on its pointed legs again, only now part of its interior was cloudy with the trapped smoke of the Lantern he'd killed. Not only that, the drone now stood much lower to the ground and even seemed to be straining to move. Only its central legs had been destroyed with Jasto's Lantern-kill, as far as he'd seen, but maybe those were load-bearing legs for this drone? It had used only its front pair to try and stab him, even though one of his maneuvers had brought him in range of the middle pair.

"In that case," Jasto murmured, closing back in smoothly. One of the dragon-guns opened to fire but he'd read the timing from the last shot and changed directions just in time. The bullet lodged itself in the ground with a bang as the drone dug its drill into the floor again, spinning it both to gather new ammunition and to spray chunks of rock at Jasto.

Or at least it tried to, but now that its load-bearing legs were gone the construct's turn speed was absolutely abysmal. Its other gun turned towards him anyway, pivoting at a faster speed than the drone's main body, but Jasto threw his remaining axe and guided it using the Lantern within.

It lodged inside the dragon-mouth just as it opened. There was momentary hesitation where the drone chose not to fire, and that was all Jasto needed to swoop behind it and slide a filament into the Lantern at the base of its tails.

"Open your eyes!" he yelled, the hurricane and the weight of his constellation flashing through his mind as the former spun out into disordered wisps of wind. There was a *crack* like a stone breaking against the ground and both of the tails began to come apart above Jasto.

His axe dropped from one of them, and he caught it as the drone screeched. For a moment Jasto thought about pulling back before he engaged further, but he dismissed the idea. Lenno was still out there, and the drone before him had been all but neutered without its load-bearing legs and cannons.

So instead of shooting backwards Jasto pivoted as the drone attempted to side-check him once again, the movement much more telegraphed now that it only had four legs. The photothyst monstrosity passed by him, trailing acrid smoke in its wake, and he moved smoothly with the drone to end up right next to one of its vulnerable joints.

Hefting his axe in two hands, Jasto engaged the Lantern within and brought it down in unison with his arms. This time he cut straight through the photothyst, the augmented force he'd put behind the blow and the weaker target sufficient to cleave straight through the joint of the drone's front right limb.

It snapped off to crack further as the drone slumped down, and Jasto frowned as he hopped on top of it, shifting to his brake pads as he did so and planting his axe in its thick abdomen for stability. Was this really an accurate representation of a drone? Jasto knew he didn't fight like other knights, but this one had seemed too easy to kill.

Regardless of that he extended one of his shoulder filaments outward, preparing to end this, when a familiar voice interrupted his attack. It was younger than when he'd last heard it, and less weary, but he still recognized it.

"Pull back! They're adapting!" a younger Epha yelled, and even though he knew it was the Palace talking Jasto still obeyed on instinct, dislodging his axe and throwing himself off of the drone.

Moments after he did so, it began to contort violently. All three of the construct's remaining legs were pulled into its body even as it lengthened into a bulky cylinder, and the drill-like mouth of the drone turned itself inside out and began to stretch backwards over the rest of its form. It continued spinning as it did so, chewing up the floor and spewing so much debris that Jasto could only see the silhouette of the writhing thing the drone was becoming.

He circled the debris cloud at a distance, finding himself more nervous than he'd expected. This was still his fight, the environment wasn't changing and he had plenty of space to move.

But he'd heard about these adaptations. Not as much as he'd heard about the drone's regenerative capabilities, or how they cannibalized human machines to keep fighting and build more of themselves. But enough to be worried.

What would Ralica remake the knave into with the express purpose of killing Jasto?

As if to answer, the debris cloud suddenly moved. As it powered along the floor towards Jasto the angle of the spew shifted, becoming more like a slanted geyser than a cloud and continuing to obscure the actual form of the drone.

Jasto raised his speed, staying close to the hexagonal edge of the space and leaning so that his path made a wide circle along the inside of it. The drone, in its new form, wasn't left in the dust as he did so.

In fact, it even seemed to be gaining on him. Its exterior had to be moving at dangerous speeds to create all that debris, so if it did manage to touch him he wasn't sure his body would survive. What could he do?

He had just three Lanterns to work with. Not only that, but his ability to use his Crest was still somewhat strained by the earlier battle. He couldn't win like this.

Not unless he changed his fighting style, Jasto realized. His earlier conversation with Epha came back to his mind.

Just like he'd told the old knight, he'd developed his wheel armor and its associated fighting style because he wanted to be different from the other crystal knights. To feel like he actually was in control of his future, and not just fated to become the latest iteration of them.

But those feelings wouldn't be enough to get him through this fight.

Jasto exhaled, doing his best to accept the necessity. He'd shown control in the face of death, he could show control in the face of something unpleasant. Focusing on that, he made a hard turn to the left and braked to let the drone shoot by.

It didn't slow, but the curving path it began to take back to him was far wider than Jasto would have needed. Like he'd thought, it was faster in this form but much worse at turning. That gave him time.

He clicked his wheels up, then ejected his boot Lanterns and brought them to chest level. He flipped his axe to hold it upside-down, moved both his free Lanterns into the head, and began to project photothyst. The usual prickling feeling began at his hands, then sunk deeper into him as more and more filaments rose up to form a massive, drill-like flechette with all three of his Lanterns set in the base. A tool meant only to maximize the damage his Crest ability could do, the kind of weapon a typical crystal knight would make.

He felt his Diagram thump against his mind as he worked, fritzing to reveal the Star and reappearing closer than he usually let it get, but focused on the coming clash. The construct only had two Lanterns, his weapon would have three. It would be enough, Jasto hoped. It would have to be, because his Crest was too strained to do something like this twice.

He moved next to his flechette as the construct came back around, bearing down on him, but it didn't seem to react at all. Maybe it had sacrificed perceptive abilities by entering this form?

Either way, he projected an axe in one hand and placed his other at the base of his drill. The drone grew closer, its spray of debris filling more and more of his vision. Jasto grit his teeth, every muscle in his body tensing as he flexed his Crest ability at full force. His oversized flechette spun like a hurricane, and he shoved it forward.

First was the earsplitting crash of the collision. Then a sound like grinding gears as the two photothyst drills locked against each other. Then the spray of debris diverted, revealing a photothyst body shaped like a worm blended with a drill, its back segments continuing to spin at full speed even as the frontal ones locked up.

The knave listed to the side, tearing away from him with the drill-flechette, and Jasto dropped to his knees as thoughts too intricate and cryptic for any human to come up with shoved their way into his head. He blinked, saw nothing but a starry sky with the right half of his vision. Putting so much force into his Crest ability, in a way he almost never used, had consequences.

Jasto breathed in and out, focusing on the simple but very human act of respiration. The sky evaporated out of his vision first, and after a few more breaths the Crystal Star also receded. Jasto knew, though, that any major use of his Crest would bring them both roaring back.

Still, as messed up as his mind might have been, Jasto's body was fine. He'd even kept a hold on his axe. He pushed himself up and ran after the drone, now locked into contact with his drill, and wedged in a corner of the arena. The two photothyst projections bled sparks where they ground against each other, and their ozone-like scent entered Jasto's helmet as he drew closer.

He'd stopped the construct, mostly, but its back segments were still spinning and he knew that the rest of it wouldn't be locked up by his flechette forever. Already he could see his drill was starting to crack.

The construct thrashed as he drew closer and Jasto slowed. He couldn't use his wheels in this state. One wrong move as he approached...

But he shook the fear away. There were things Jasto struggled with, but this he was strong enough to handle. Tentatively, the squire-errant extended one of his filaments just a little and braced his mind.

It barely registered as a strain on his Crest. He could do this.

Jasto advanced, and whether by chance or because it sensed him the drone suddenly slammed its tail into the ground, the spinning segments there launching a spray of debris at him. Jasto had no shield but he still turtled behind his arms, and the barrage of photothyst knocked him back a step but that was all.

He charged with his arms up, more debris clanging off his shield, and as he saw the drill segments of the construct creak against his flechette he realized this new form did have a weakness. Each cylindrical segment of it was heavy, and capable of rotating with massive power.

But the joints between those segments were far thinner. Jasto grabbed his axe with two hands, then slammed it down on a joint just below one of the Lanterns near the drone's head. He cut deep but not deep enough without augmentation, wrenched his axe out for a second blow—

—And the drone tore itself loose from his drill-flechette.

He brought his axe down anyway, snapping the drone in half even as it dislodged a chunk of the photothyst floor.

It collided with Jasto and he was tumbling across the ravaged ground, his axe lost and dissipating into nonexistence. He completed one full, bumpy revolution across the arena before his chest wheels managed to catch him and lessen the impact of the fall somewhat. Half of his helmet pane was completely gone, meaning he saw the ground pass beneath him in a strange, two-toned way until he slowed himself down with his hands and managed to look up.

That hadn't been how Jasto had planned for this to go, but it had worked. The top half of the drone had apparently contained the Lantern responsible for rotating the drill-like segments but not the one for control, as he saw it ricochet across the arena before hitting a wall at a bad angle. That impact must have broken the Lantern Jasto had exposed, because it crumbled inertly to the floor a moment later.

Meanwhile the other half still twisted and turned its segmented form, but now the spinning outer parts of those segments weren't moving. It was all but neutralized, as long as it didn't adapt again.

Jasto got to his feet slowly, feeling pain flare from his injuries with every other movement, but focused his attention on going forward. One step, then two, then more.

It couldn't have taken him more than a minute to reach the twisting drone but it felt like far longer. It seemed to become aware of him as he stepped closer, and went still.

Jasto readied his filament, drawing it out to his palm. Since he didn't want to risk projecting another weapon, there was only one way to end this. The construct turned its severed end towards him, rearing up like a snake.

They lunged for each other at the same time. The drone was low to the ground but Jasto dropped lower on his wheels, snaking his arms around its trunk before twisting to hook it with a leg. He sent his filament in as it bucked against him.

"Open—"

A hurricane. He latched onto it eagerly.

"Your—"

His body left the ground. Jasto didn't stop.

"EYES!"

The drone cracked in midair and he dropped straight down, landing hard on a piece of it with another crack. Blearily, Jasto rolled himself off of the chunk to lay on his back, staring at the pyramid's ceiling as Lantern smoke curled lazily up towards it.

He glanced over at his drill-flechette some time later, when his breathing was even once more, and saw that it had been chewed up so badly that two of the Lanterns were exposed.

Jasto supposed that was why most knights only placed one Lantern in a flechette. But his mind quickly returned to the fight he'd just survived.

When he'd first seen the drone and the arena, he hadn't expected anything difficult. But now he'd been battered far beyond his expectations, and he'd even been forced to leave his comfort zone after the drone had adapted to him. That had been…humbling. And it had only been a representation of a drone. What would the real thing have been like?

"Form back up!" a disembodied voice called, interrupting his thoughts. It was Ralica's. "Knights, link back with your support groups if you got separated. Ironskin, get a cleanup sweep going. Has anyone seen Suncage?"

She continued to give orders in the memory as Jasto pushed himself back up. Was another construct on the way? Somehow he doubted it, Ralica didn't seem like the ambushing type.

"Dreadstone, how's our timetable looking?" she asked in the memory. The question stirred up a vague memory: one of Ralica's earlier followers, who had little historical importance but had stood out to Jasto in class because of his ridiculous Crest name.

"The drones went after vehicles instead of knights on this attack, Sir," Dreadstone replied in a surprisingly deep voice. "Repairs will take time. Unless we leave people behind, it'll take us twice as long to reach Dry Quarry."

Jasto's eyes narrowed, even as the talk shifted to logistical details. Dry Quarry was a name he remembered, not from a history class but from the much more recent experience of driving past it to reach this Palace. The town had been abandoned near the start of the Drone War, and this area was treacherous enough that it was still empty. And Seafall Palace had formed just a few miles from it.

The memory from before this fight had focused on Ralica's goals and plans. It seemed like she wanted Jasto to understand her, what she'd been trying to accomplish during the War.

If his hunch was right, he'd next learn how it had all gone wrong. Many details of the Drone War had been shrouded by the Round Table. And for all that she'd been hailed as a hero, exactly how Ralica had become corrupted was one such veiled topic.

Jasto suspected he was about to gain some clarity on it.

Chapter 7

Ralica finished her talk with Dreadstone in the memory, then the noises shifted to suggest she was walking while giving clipped orders into a radio. That continued for only a short time before she gasped, and the sound of her footsteps picked up.

"Eph, are you okay?" she asked. Then Jasto winced, as a noise like sheet metal toppling onto gravel followed.

"Please, it takes more than a falling roof to stop me. I've had worse during my glory days," Epha's voice replied a moment later. It was still strange to hear the younger, faster-paced version of it.

"What glory days are you talking about?" Ralica replied with mock surprise, sounding relieved beneath it. "All I remember is digging you out of hills—"

"—That was one time! Hill. Singular!" Epha interrupted with a laugh.

Both voices paused, and Jasto could imagine the two knights smiling at each other. Then Epha spoke up again as the memory continued, and this time her voice was more serious.

"I think they're sharing information, Ral," she said. "Or at least getting smarter. Half a year ago it took a major adaptation for the drones to have decentralized systems. Now they all start with it, so every single one needs multiple filament strikes."

"That tracks with what I've seen," Ralica agreed. "It's bad news, but not horrific. We won't need to rework our combat strategies completely. But that's something to talk about tonight, for now go and help Ironskin with the sweep."

"Yes, Sir."

Footsteps followed, and for a moment Jasto thought the recollection would just end right there. Then Ralica spoke up again, asking, "Wait. What's the matter, Eph?"

"I...it's not..." Epha paused, the silence after her words dense with shame. "No, it'll be worse if I just sit on it. Ral, we've endured so much in this war. We've scraped ourselves down to the bone, lost people, even put up with dreck from the other commanders. Are…are we really doing all that, just to give up everything we've built?"

Jasto's head snapped upwards. Epha Suncage, doubting Ralica? Had this memory been tampered with?

Ralica, after a long moment, sighed. When she spoke her tone was gentle and reassuring. "I could point out how we're only giving up control of the Crestless military, Eph, so that knights lead knights and people lead people again once this is over with neither overstepping. But you already know all of that and still feel this way. So I'll just tell you straightforwardly: yes. The Round Table is a temporary measure to deal with a temporary problem, the drone armies and Palaces. When the problem goes away, so will the measure."

"Why? No one else has earned this," Epha protested. "The General's Council, the Crestless military, the senators, the rest of Andalon, they all had their chance to win. They even had us at their command, Ral, and they still couldn't do it. And I know it's not over yet, but the end is in sight now because we took charge."

"The end is near, and we're already flagging," Ralica said. "It's the minority of us on this mission, Eph. Every other knight-commander except me is busy, trying to secure their positions after the war instead of winning it now."

"So we oust them," Epha said. "You're already the most popular commander. How many people would really mind if you kicked all of them off the Table?"

Jasto leaned back, then flinched as the sudden movement disturbed his injuries. He supposed it made sense for Epha, since she seemed to be all about 'proving your worth' and Ralica had clearly done that in the Drone War. But still, hearing her actually argue in favor of a military dictatorship was…something.

"Eph…" Ralica started. "It would all go wrong. All of it. No."

"But the fact that you can say that, that's why it has to be you," Epha pressed. "Think about it. Would anyone from the Council hesitate for a moment to accept that power? Would any of the knight-commanders be even slightly concerned about it going to their head, about failing to be a good leader? No. They'd all seize it without thinking twice. It's because you worry you might be a bad leader that you're qualified to—"

"You think that's what this is about, Eph?" Ralica asked, the gentleness draining from her tone. "You think I'm afraid of being a crooked leader? The drones prioritized our vehicles today. Most of our backliners were in them, Eph. At *least* two hundred and three people are dead, and we're still counting casualties. Because I failed, and didn't see this ambush coming."

"That's part of war," Epha said.

"That was the kill count for a single battle. Not even a day, just a battle. How many years has this war lasted?" Ralica asked, her voice getting louder. "How many people have died because I wasn't fast enough or smart enough to save them? Do you know, Eph?"

Silence, and maybe Epha shaking her head within it. "I do," Ralica said. "I've tracked the records for every battle I've been in, so I know the number. I used to look myself in the mirror every morning and say it, you know? So I wouldn't forget that I made mistakes and they had consequences."

Silence. Jasto held his breath within it.

"You used to?" Epha asked, her voice quiet. "What do you do now?"

"I still look myself in the mirror, Eph," Ralica said, her voice choking up. "And I still know the number, but I...I can't say it anymore. It's too large, I...so many have..."

A quiet sob filled the air. Jasto looked away and to the side, even though there was no clear source for the noise. He felt like he had to do something, at least, for the sake of decency.

A clanking noise filled the air next, confusing Jasto, but when it was followed by several lighter clanks he figured he understood. Epha was probably hugging Ralica in the memory, and patting her on her armored back.

"I..." Ralica began a few minutes later, then cleared her throat and started again. "I've seen too much, Eph. I can make it to the end of this, but I have to know that someday, that number will stop growing. That I can set down this burden." She took an unsteady breath. "As long as I lead, as long as I hold responsibility, it'll keep getting larger. Maybe if the other knight-commanders could be trusted, then the Round Table could stay. But they can't, so it all has to end with me."

"Of course, Ral," Epha said immediately. "I'm sorry, I didn't know you were carrying all this...oh Star, I must have made it worse," she suddenly added. "Every time I said you were just what Andalon needed, did that—"

"Please, Eph, let's not," Ralica said, her voice recovered and even holding a bit of humor now. "At this rate, we'll be acting out one of those dramas Lenno keeps watching in secret."

A startled laugh burst out of Epha. "Right...I can't believe he thinks we don't know. What's the latest one called? Courts of Dusk and Bone?"

"Courts of Dusk and Ink," Ralica corrected, snickering. "It's like he's still a teenager."

"Heh."

After another quiet moment, there was a clattering as Ralica withdrew from the hug.

"There was some bad to it, but mostly good," Ralica said. "The weight of all this is heavy. I didn't like being reminded I had to be the one carrying it, when it was doing this to me."

"Okay," Epha managed to say, her voice dry.

"But—and I want you to remember this part more, Eph—you're also the one who's been with me since the beginning. Since we were kids in the middle of nowhere, all the way up through the drones, the people, to where we are now. The fact that you can keep going after all this time? It's helped me keep going too."

"Ralica...thank you," Epha said in the memory, her voice steadier. "Still, I should've realized the war was getting to you. I've seen what it's doing to others."

"Yeah?"

"Yeah. You don't hear the things Lenno says behind your back...it's like he's starting to worship you, Ral. Gets worse whenever we hear what the rest of the Round Table is up to, and that's not even the weirdest coping mechanism in our ranks. We're all gonna need therapy after this," Epha said, in a vaguely joking tone.

"What about you, Eph?" Ralica asked, her own voice serious. "And don't pretend you're not dealing with something either."

"I wasn't going to," she said. "Just working up to it." She sighed and for a moment sounded like the Epha that Jasto knew, worn down by time and heavy obligations. "I sort of...started pretending I don't have a family, and ignoring the messages they sent me. That's why I never left the base during that one break we had a few months ago, even though they were close by."

A quiet pause. "It feels easier to just focus on this, you know?" Epha continued. "My brother always had mixed feelings about the Ascension. I know I shouldn't be ignoring them, but it's less complicated to just put all my attention on this family, instead of that one."

"You can't be fucking—" Jasto started, then caught himself. He didn't want to interrupt this memory by accident. But Crystal Star, who did that? The whole reason he'd gone against the Valor Academy had been to get back to his family, and Epha had just abandoned hers?

He exhaled and untensed his shoulders. Epha had taken Dad's deal so that her family would be provided for, he reminded himself. She was trying to set it right. And he'd been pushed to his limits just fighting a replica of one drone, while Epha had fought armies of them and lost people along the way. Jasto would probably pick up some flaws himself, if he'd gone through the same thing. Maybe Ralica had wanted him to understand that.

"Hey, dismiss your armor for a second," Ralica said in the memory. There was a faint hiss of air as Epha did so, then a set of quiet sounds that Jasto took for an unarmored hug.

"We'll get through this together, alright?" Ralica said. "And then we'll figure the rest out."

"We will," Epha replied. "I'm with you to the end, sister."

Once again it was quiet, in a slightly more total way that made it clear this was the end of the memory. Jasto glanced around, then knelt and touched a hand to the photothyst floor.

"Thank you," he said, because it felt like he should honor the moment somehow. Then he stood back up, and considered what he'd heard carefully.

Emotional revelations aside, the context clues confirmed his initial thoughts: This exchange had come from Ralica's last days alive. The exact history of the Drone War had been shrouded by the Round Table, but it was clear that Ralica Seafall had been instrumental to its end. She'd led the Circle of Abdication, the crystal knights personally loyal to her, and a large Crestless military contingent in an expeditionary force during the final days of the War. Their goal had been to strike out, in one of the larger and more daring pushes to reclaim Andalon.

That force had been shattered, and trickled back to safe territory in small fragments. Almost all Crestbearers and many soldiers had been lost, along with Ralica. But the drones had taken so many losses from that effort that they were no longer able to fight as a massed military. Andalon's remaining forces had spread themselves back over the nation, destroying the most prominent pockets of resistance while ignoring many of the Palaces, and the Drone War had been declared as over.

It had been shoddily done, in Dad's professional military opinion, and Jasto might have just learned why. The knight-commanders other than Ralica were apparently cowards, with a greater focus on building up political power than actually risking it during the Drone War. No wonder they'd done the bare minimum, then left the rest to independent crystal knights through their system of public bounties and employments.

But the most interesting part of that conversation had been Ralica herself, and the apparent imperfections in Andalon's most beloved war hero. Jasto had kept a dim opinion of the crystal knights for some time now, but he'd still been caught off guard by the idea that Ralica had been tired even though it made sense. It also made the fact that she'd stayed latent so long even more impressive, and Jasto was honestly envious of that kind of mental strength. He sat down on the floor and began tending to his wounds, thinking back to the most prominent thing she'd said.

Ralica had been both high and low on the totem pole in her life. She'd started under the strict command of the General's Council, rising through the ranks beneath them, and had gone from there to champion a coup and become one of the most prominent leaders of the Round Table. She'd seen more than Jasto could imagine, held more authority than he probably ever would, and she'd still called it a burden. The power she'd wielded had not set her free.

Jasto was still contemplating that when a rumble suddenly went through the arena. He did his best to snap to an alert state, but thankfully no threats emerged. Instead the gouges and cracks that had been torn into the photothyst receded, wiping away all evidence of the battle as a hexagonal pane in the center of the space dropped down a few inches.

"Another elevator…" Jasto muttered. He glanced around the arena suspiciously, but the other entryways were still sealed. In truth that was probably for the best, with Lenno and his knaves still hunting him.

And the fact that they hadn't caught up to him yet meant that Ralica really was working against Lenno. But if that was the case, why hadn't she just commanded Lenno to stand down? Weren't thralls supposed to be completely bound to the will of the knight that claimed them?

So many questions. Too many, honestly, and Jasto couldn't afford to waste too much thought on them. Lenno was trying to kill him, Ralica was trying to…well, putting Jasto's life at risk was clearly part of Ralica's plans, but she still seemed more on Jasto's side than Lenno did. That was something he could work with.

Still, Jasto decided he'd finish his first aid and let his Crest recover before going to the elevator. Just in case.

When he stepped onto the hexagonal platform afterwards—time had almost lost all meaning inside this Palace, with the sun out of sight and the temperature a constant cold—two of his Lanterns were back in his boots, the third was in his axe, and his armor was fully repaired with filaments threaded through and ready to use. Best of all, when he checked on his Diagram it was at a greater distance from the rest of his mind. Corruption was further away now and his fourth Lantern was also closer to forming. Even so, he decided not to risk the caloric drain forcing it would give him just yet.

The platform shuddered a little as Jasto walked to its center, then began to descend smoothly and much faster than the previous one. If he did have to fight here, it wouldn't go well. This elevator was smaller than the other, maybe twelve feet across at most, leaving him next to no room to maneuver.

He made a shield preemptively, then raised the brightness of his armor filaments. He took a moment to peer at the photothyst mechanisms around him, making out cables set at each corner of the hexagonal shaft that ran down long tubes set within the walls. The platform he was on seemed to be linked to them by some sort of joiner below his feet. Were actual elevators structured the same way? He had no idea.

But because he was looking at the seamless connection of his platform and the wall, he noticed immediately when it suddenly opened up to reveal a vast, dark space.

Jasto stiffened as the light of his armor played out over damp, jagged rock formations. He was descending below the Palace itself, into the cave system it was built within! His platform continued to lower towards the uneven ground below, the six tubes continuing down to it like unnaturally perfect stalactites.

There were other pillars of photothyst throughout this cave, he saw. Some thicker than others, interspersed in a way that seemed to form an incomplete pattern and beaded with moisture from the cave environment. At the base of one of the widest he saw roots of photothyst, thick with corrupted filaments and beginning to fractal out into the rock.

Though latency had slowed the rate, even now the Palace was still growing.

"Sir," a tense voice began, echoing through the cavern. Lenno's, before his corruption. "We're picking up movement signatures from the front and both of our flanks. And these numbers are beyond all forecasts for drone presence."

"Let me see," Ralica said. The silence this time was filled with tension, thick enough that even though Jasto knew this had all happened already his fingers still clenched and unclenched on his armaments.

"*Dreck,*" Ralica cursed, and although he'd barely heard the knight-commander speak it still sounded jarring to hear her swear. How large a force had it taken to destabilize her that much? "Did every drone in Andalon just happen to gather up here? We need to retreat before this becomes a slaughterhouse."

"We can't, Sir," Lenno said. "Half our remaining vehicles have been sabotaged, along with lots of our most vital equipment."

"Sabotaged...so the knight-commanders really would go this far to deal with us," Ralica said. Even though her life was in danger, she sounded more disappointed than furious at the betrayal.

"Those walking stains did it through the battlegroups they sent with us," Lenno confirmed, his voice tightening. "All of them acted at once, stealing the gear they could and destroying what they couldn't like vindictive little animals."

"Those steaming heaps of dreck," Epha muttered, joining the conversation. "Never should've let them spread out, it just made it easier for them to do this."

"If we hadn't allowed that they'd have done the same anyway, but killed our people on the way out," Ralica countered. "Then the drones would have arrived and we'd be down on both gear and people. I let them spread out because I already have plans for this. Lenno, what's the time frame on those drones?"

A moment as he checked. "Five hours to the first wave's arrival, Sir."

"Not enough to escape, but more than enough for my contingency," Ralica said. "Pass me that, I'll call in my deal with General Hawthorn."

"Your contingency is that slimeball?" Epha asked.

"My contingency is the rapid-response force I had him prepare before we left on this mission," Ralica said. "They'll hit with artillery, then get us out with the last of Andalon's choppers."

"So you were prepared, Sir..." Lenno said, his tone admiring.

"And what was his price?" Epha asked.

"A hefty fee, paid in both money and military assets, along with my public acclamation of him," Ralica replied. "He wants to stay politically relevant. It's unpleasant to indulge him, but necessary."

This was the backup plan Ralica had mentioned, in her earlier memory with Lenno. The strange thing was, Jasto had studied maps of Andalon from before, during, and after the Drone War. He knew how far this location, Dry Quarry, would have been from the closest safe territory during the War. He also had a good idea of artillery ranges and the speed that a rapid-response force could mobilize with, courtesy of Dad.

Putting all those factors together, it *should* have been possible for Ralica and her people to make it back to safer ground with only partial losses, instead of the two-sided slaughter that had actually occurred in the past. A cold suspicion built in his gut.

Then a *ping* went through the elevator as Ralica's call was answered in the memory. "Joint Commander Hallsey, correct?" Ralica began. Presumably, that was the rapid-response force's leader. "Our situation is critical. Prepare artillery strikes at the coordinates I'm sending you, then move to our location at maximum possible speed, prepared for a fighting advance *and* retreat. This is do or die."

Silence answered. Jasto thought...no, he knew it sounded guilty. As surely as he knew what was about to happen.

"Joint Commander?"

"I can offer only my condolences, Ralica," a heavy voice replied, in the formal knight dialect that Epha stuck to religiously and that no ex-General's Council official would be caught dead using. "It would be too egregious of me to apologize for something I believe needs to be done, but my condolences I can and will offer. As soon as we drew our lines in the sand, a clash such as this became unavoidable."

"Dantos Erelian Duskwall." Ralica's voice was emotionless, as she named the knight-commander who would go on to become the most prominent member of the Round Table in the modern day. "You checked my contingency?"

"Your rapid-response force was sealed, yes. No blood was shed, if that provides any consolation; we simply surrounded them and gave orders to stay put. They have complied thus far, and I hope they will continue to."

That was apparently too much for Epha. "Oh, so with *them* you care about sparing lives? That's fucking rich with what you're doing to us."

"Don't bother, Epha," Lenno cut in, his tone venomous. "He's a traitor now, and even before that he was a tumor. Pointing out hypocrisy means nothing to people who embody it."

Ralica clicked her tongue, and they both quieted down. "Dantos, this is senselessly destructive," she said, somehow still calm. "Attempting to assassinate me would be one thing, but what you've done will destroy a major piece of Andalon's military. You're not stupid enough to do that when the war is still…" Ralica sucked in a breath. "This wasn't the only thing you did."

"It was not," Dantos agreed. "It is more than simple misfortune that led to you being swarmed by an excessively large drone army, just as your vehicles were sabotaged. By our estimates, more than 90 percent of the drones remaining in Andalon were corralled towards your location."

"They prioritize Crestbearers, especially large groups of them," Epha murmured. "You used us as bait."

"And the war can be ended in weeks, now that they've all been gathered up," Ralica said. "Dantos, you do not need to kill us to see this through. Patch me through to Hallsey, I'll convince him to allow your men to board and reinforce us."

"He fucking betrayed us!" Lenno protested.

"He has not drawn blood yet," Ralica said. "Equipment has been sabotaged, traps have been laid, but you've held out on the killing, Dantos. You don't want to go through with this, and you do not have to."

"Ralica…"

"Reinforce us," she pressed. "Make this right, come back with me sharing the glory of the greatest military achievement in the Drone War. Whatever pressure the other knight-commanders have put on you will be overcome by that. You haven't gone through with this yet; you don't need to be chained down by any more ugliness today. Please, don't put this weight on your soul."

It was a compelling argument, Jasto thought. Ralica had noticed Dantos' reluctance almost immediately, and while Epha and Lenno had lashed out at him for his betrayal she'd gone in surgically for a way to turn him around. She'd tossed in an incentive, the acclaim that would come with making a victory here, and she'd pushed all this out before giving Dantos a chance to bring up any objections.

But he still knew it would still fail. "Being chained, being weighed down…those things do bother me, Ralica," Dantos said, something in his tone now solid. "That is exactly why this is happening."

Jasto's gut went cold. "The General's Council was the first to chain me, to chain *us*," Dantos continued. "The Ascension happened for a reason. You championed it for a reason. It's as if you've forgotten what petty leaders do, when they have to lead someone they can't take power away from."

"We had cause for the Ascension but we were never slaves, Dantos," Ralica argued. "And if a betrayal like this is the best replacement you can offer, you've lost all right to criticize."

"Who cares, Ralica?!" Dantos snapped, his dialect falling away. "It's always about 'right' with you, like you live in some grand scoreboard of ethics. What about reality? In the real world, my knights chose me to lead them, put their trust in me. In the real world, I need to make sure the Crestless can't leverage my people again."

"You know we have countermeasures—"

"—And if they're not enough? If our lessers try to get the better of us again, because they're afraid?"

"Lessers?" Ralica said, indignant. "Your own Star-damned family is Crestless, Dantos."

"Not what I meant," he ground out. "I have a responsibility to my knights. I'll fulfill it."

"You do carry a responsibility to them," Ralica said. "A responsibility to not be a monster, to not ruin their homes out of fear. Where is this responsibility going to be, when you choose between cleaning up the Palaces and keeping your position secure? Where is it right now, when you're killing not just me but everyone here with me?"

Silence. Then a click, and the call ended without another word from Dantos.

"I thought so," Ralica muttered. "On the back burner."

"...Sir?" Epha asked, sounding weakened. "What do we do?"

"We kill them all," Lenno growled. "Painfully. I'll impale Duskwall myself."

"We do the only thing we can: minimize losses," Ralica said, and Jasto imagined her thinking of her tally. "And they'll be bombarding this location once the drones arrive...Epha, you're our best pathfinder. Do you still have those maps of the cave systems around here?"

"Yes?"

"Good. Tell our Crestless leadership what just happened. And Lenno, gather all our knights as quickly as you can."

"And then, Sir?" Lenno asked, his rage just barely restrained by discipline.

"Then we draw straws, to find out who will be staying behind."

Silence followed. It continued long enough that Jasto was sure the memory had ended.

"Holy dreck," he said into the darkness, as the floor of the cavern continued to approach. He looked up at the hexagonal column he'd descended through, the distant opening at its top, and wondered if Ralica had felt her stomach sinking the way he was now.

No wonder so much of the Drone War had been censored. The remaining knight-commanders had wanted to cover up the rift between themselves and the most popular of them, Ralica Seafall, along with any details that might reveal this betrayal. What they'd done was...disgusting.

At least, that was Jasto's initial thought. On the surface, just after hearing the memory, Jasto felt the same things he figured almost anyone would feel: shock and disdain, abhorrence for Dantos Duskwall.

143

But past that, two voices whispered that it wasn't so simple. The first was his father's, tallying costs and political realities. If Ralica's force had been the only army willing to move before this major event, that suggested a deeper problem: that Andalon itself, both its military leaders and its armies, had been running out of steam towards the end of the Drone War.

If that was true, if one last push had been all that Andalon was willing to give, then Ralica's plan to start a new wave of counterattacks had been doomed. And Duskwall's sacrifice of a rival faction to present an alternative to that plan made a cold-blooded sense: Andalon had been drained by the war, political friction after it was over would only lead to more suffering.

But the second voice demanding further thought was even more personal. Because Duskwall had talked about being chained by the General's Council. He'd set his plans in motion to make sure he never went through that treatment again. He'd planned to ensure his independence by taking power and keeping it.

And why had Jasto entered this Palace, again? To gain enough strength that he couldn't be pushed around. And why had he gotten himself expelled from the Valor Academy? Because he'd felt himself starting to change, under the pressure it had put him through. He'd put his own self-determination first.

And when Duskwall had turned on Ralica, the knight-commander who had clearly cared the most for Andalon as a whole, he'd done the same. And then his choices had rippled past that moment, to create the Academy that Jasto would one day turn against.

The elevator touched down on the floor of the cavern with a slight jolt. His axe nearly fell from his limp grip on it.

And Jasto dismissed his helmet and shield, putting a hand to his face as he hunched forward. What had he been doing this whole time? Had he thought he understood the world, that he knew what was wrong with it? Nothing could have been further from the truth. He opened his mouth, but only a jagged and wordless exhalation came out.

A clanking noise interrupted his moping, and Jasto cursed himself again for dropping his guard. He looked up, resummoning his shield, as a knave stepped away from one of the photothyst pillars spread through the cavern. He clocked two other knave cores swimming down their own pillars, along with a small filament-formed eyes set in others. Ralica was watching.

Jasto split his attention, half on re-projecting his helmet and exchanging his wheels for treads while the other half watched the knaves as they emerged.

It immediately became clear that these were special in some way. The one that had emerged first was humanoid and wearing heavy armor, similar to Epha's cavalier plate, but topped with a strange teardrop-shaped helmet bearing a thin eyeslit. A long-handled warhammer rested on its shoulder.

The second was in lighter kit, overlapping rectangular plates of metal covering its entire body like the skin of a reptile. It detached from the photothyst pillar it had emerged from with a bounce in its step, strangely, and spun a scimitar in each hand.

The third wasn't immediately visible to Jasto, his first glimpse of it blocked by the tower shield that emerged ahead of its body. That shifted to the side as the rest of the knave followed it out, its body a light shade of turquoise that stood out from the dark cave and photothyst. It marched forward stiffly, a straight one-handed sword at its hip.

Not one of them resembled the mannequins Jasto had been tested against earlier, or the emaciated knaves that Lenno used. Instead they were studies in uniqueness, not just in appearance but even in the ways they moved, like they somehow had different personalities. The knaves came to a stop in a line, still a decent distance from the elevator Jasto hadn't left, and that was when another memory began.

"I have failed you all, and I have no excuse," Ralica said, her tone sober. "Right now there is a drone army bearing down on us that is too large to fight and cannot be outrun. Not only that, both it and us are going to be drowned in artillery fire by our own people. We've been betrayed by those I made the mistake of thinking better of."

She took a slow, steady breath. "Even so, my obligations remain," Ralica continued, "And they include doing everything in my power to save your lives, even if I must break taboos that we all hold as inviolable. Those of you I manage to save, my final order is this: make your survival matter. Do not let the Round Table muzzle the truth."

Her tone shifted, becoming more businesslike. "More immediately, your orders are as follows. Epha has already taken a group

145

of Crestless pathfinders underground. They're scouting an evacuation route through the cave systems below us, and the bulk of our forces will follow the moment a path has been laid out.

"As for us Crestbearers…all those who draw a short straw in a moment will be staying behind with me. We will remain here until the drones have drawn closer. There's more than one entrance to the caves and we can't guard them all, but Crestbearers are priority targets for drones. They'll go after us, the obvious and less well-defended group, first.

"Once they're…" Ralica's voice halted. "Once they're nearly on top of us, we will descend into the caves ourselves and force our Crests to be corrupted."

Jasto inhaled sharply, and was joined by dozens of other voices from the memory as he did so. He'd anticipated Ralica's order somewhat, from the current state of things. But actually hearing it said was something else. 'Death before corruption' was the very idea that the crystal knights had been founded on.

"The military won't start its bombardment of this site until the drones are concentrated on this location, densely enough that they'll have already sent a group to the caves," Ralica continued. "That means intentional corruption is the only way we can buy time. The Palaces we form will become blockades in the narrow caves, and the knaves we produce our main fighting force. The drones like to ignore Palaces if they can, but if they want to get at our people they'll be forced to go through us. Some of the burrowing types might slip around, but that's a newer and less common adaptation. The bulk of their force will be stopped."

Her tone softened. "Under normal circumstances, I would never ask you to shame yourselves like this," Ralica said. "But I've discussed it with our best tacticians and considered everything else. We're in a deathtrap, and this strategy gets as many people as we can out of it. If what happened here is ever going to be made right, it will be through their survival."

Ralica paused for a moment, letting her words sink in, then continued with a more commanding voice. "Now, let's start the drawing. For those who will be staying with me, remember: Latency comes from your humanity, and activity comes from your Crest. If a Palace goes active, it'll attack the back of our retreating forces. So even after corruption, hold on to your humanity at all costs. Control your violence, as you were taught to at the very beginning of your knighthood. I'll be right there with you, doing the same."

The memory ended. Jasto looked slowly at the knaves once more, the careful detail that had gone into each of them.

Was this...Ralica's memorial? Her recollection of the crystal knights that had held the line beside her? Jasto knew there must have been more than three that had stayed, but maybe these were the only ones Ralica could remember after being corrupted for so long. And he knew there were no other Palaces in the area, which meant Ralica was the only one that hadn't been destroyed while covering the retreat.

There was no other memorial of those knights, except this.

Sorrow filled Jasto's throat all at once. It felt wrong, more than it had when he'd learned of the betrayal, to see such a tiny remembrance of people that had sacrificed themselves so completely.

It seemed clear what would happen next. Jasto would step off the platform, and once he did the fight would be on. He wasn't trapped in a diamond this time, either, and while the cave floor might be less even than he would've liked, that wasn't a major issue. Jasto removed some burrs that had come from the flash-projection of his treads, ensured they spun correctly, and threaded his arms with plenty of new filaments before contemplating further.

He didn't see the knaves posing a major threat, no matter how he thought about it. But just ripping through them and trotting on to wherever Ralica sent him next didn't seem right, somehow.

Jasto frowned at himself at the direction his thoughts were taking. Didn't he want to be free? Stopping to think about dreck like this, getting tied up in the invisible strings people called honor, was what he'd come here to escape. And yet he still felt a genuine urge to do so, after all he'd gone through here.

That thought brought him back to the diamond trial, his introduction to Seafall Palace. The knave he'd beaten in the first round had saluted him, before the start of the fight. Jasto hadn't, because he'd seen no reason to, but things had changed.

Standing straight, he raised his axe and held it just in front of his face, his grip on it at eye level and the head of the weapon turned to the side. Then he stretched his arm out, pointing it towards the ceiling at an angle. It was the same form of salute that knave had used.

As one, the three knaves standing before him now mimicked the salute with their respective weapons. Like they'd been waiting for it. Then, to Jasto's total surprise, they stepped to the side, lowered their weapons, and pointed towards one of the thicker pillars in the distance. A panel at ground level recessed into it and slid to the side, revealing a staircase.

"Are…" Jasto glanced around, feeling suddenly awkward, and his gaze landed on a silver glint within one of the thinner pillars. Through one of her filament-made eyes, Ralica stared out at him.

"Are you sure?" he asked the corrupted knight. Was Ralica really going to let him walk past this, just because he'd been polite? Then again, this was a memorial to the knights that had fought with Ralica, even taking on the existential terror of corruption at her order. Maybe showing respect was the point for her.

Jasto took a step off the platform, ready to dart away just in case. The knight-knaves remained still, continuing to point the way towards whatever was next. He took another step, then another, and found the confidence to walk at a calm pace. The moment seemed to hold a very real importance to him, despite all of his other feelings on the crystal knights.

Dad wouldn't have agreed at all, Jasto knew. He wouldn't have registered this as anything more than a convenient stroke of luck, and certainly wouldn't have slowed his pace in respect to the moment. Conversations he'd had a long time ago with Mom, about how his father didn't feel things the same way as most people but still loved Jasto just as much as all the other parents loved their children, came back to him.

He hadn't quite understood the importance of those talks back then. Now he was grateful for them.

One armored footstep echoed across the ground, then another. Jasto was level with the knaves now, and while it didn't quite feel right to watch them as he passed he still kept his ears open for any sound of movement.

Then he heard photothyst breaking, behind and above him.

"How could you do this, Ralica?"

Jasto's treads were spinning before the first word had finished. The armor around his Lanterns flared bright white as he shot left on a diagonal, twisting his trajectory to hook around a pillar and use it for cover.

He turned back to face the knight-knaves just in time to see that they had broken from their frozen stances, but they weren't dashing after Jasto. Instead, all three of them looked up and raised their weapons as a crimson meteor crashed into the central knave.

Not a meteor, Jasto realized as it stood and unfolded limbs covered in serrated red armor. That was a crystal thrall.

Lenno.

Chapter 8

The knave that had carried two scimitars was already broken beneath his feet, but the shield-bearing and hammer-wielding ones still turned and began to attack the corrupted knight without hesitation. Lenno pivoted out smoothly from between them, slapping the hammer down with his maul as he caught the short sword of the other knave in the spikes covering his off-hand.

Jasto froze behind the pillar. Should he break for the stairway? There was no real reason to stay. The knight-knaves and even their cores could be reformed by Ralica with little effort. And moreover, Jasto had come here for the purpose of bringing this Palace down, memorial included. He glanced at the stairway, found his gaze pulled back to the fight Lenno was clearly on the verge of winning, tore it loose again—

—And saw a knave emerge from the pillar that was meant to be his exit, as another stayed in the threshold leading to the staircase and molded itself into a barricade. Lenno must have had them split up to cover more ground, and to encircle Jasto.

That meant he had no choice, again. The thought had him gritting his teeth as swung back around the pillar, his treads kicking up to maximum speed as he shot towards Lenno.

The thrall was prying the tower shield off one of the knaves as the other recovered from a shattered leg when Jasto's axe, thrown and guided by the Lantern it held, sailed straight towards his head. Lenno grunted but didn't look up as a small forcefield of purple, crystallized energy condensed over his helmet, and the axe collided with it and rapidly careened off into the distance.

Jasto had forgotten he could do that. Lenno's shield migrated over his plow-like bone visor a moment later, and he lurched down to gore the knave in the chest. The Lantern there cracked and the shield knave's body went limp.

The smell of blood filled the cold air as Jasto recalled his axe and marked Lenno's other knaves in his periphery. One was still serving as a barricade while the other was running towards the fight but it moved slowly, like it had already been damaged. If Epha had caused that back in the elevator, he had another thing to thank her for. That damage gave Jasto a chance to end this, before the hostile knave got close.

The warhammer-carrying knave's leg snapped back into place, less armored but still functional, and it stood to attack Lenno as Jasto rushed in. The thrall had already dismissed his Crest ability shield to rise from the fragments of the second knave he'd killed, and was sandwiched between two combatants once more.

Only now one of them was Jasto, moving at speeds more comparable to a flechette than a human, and as Lenno swung his maul out he ducked, swerved left, and drove his axe into the crimson forearm passing above his head.

He heard the bone encased within it snap as momentum jerked his axe free, and pulled around to see the warhammer knave had tied up Lenno's spike arm during the attack. Jasto made a dangerously tight turn, feeling g-forces put his chest in a vice, and charged back in to take advantage of the opening.

"And now you're defending someone like him? Is that how you're able to attack me?!" Lenno roared. He tugged his spike-arm back with corrupted strength, and the knave was pulled into Jasto's trajectory. He did his best to steer clear of the new obstacle but he could only turn so much, and clipped the knave's leg to go flying past Lenno. Jasto collided with the ground and slammed his shield down like it was an anchor, braking as he sent a wide sheet of sparks up, and turned to race back towards the fight.

"He's not worthy, Ralica!" Lenno shouted as he tore into the last knave despite his damaged arm, emotion bleeding through a voice that had seemed empty of it. *"You know what we need to do! That the Round Table needs to answer! How will any of that happen if he takes your—"*

Lenno wasn't distracted enough to ignore Jasto's rush, unfortunately, but he did respond to it in a predictable way. Jasto had very deliberately drawn his weapon back as he'd approached, making the angle of his attack clear, and just as he'd hoped Lenno formed his forcefield over the damaged forearm in Jasto's path.

That was when he made his real attack. Keeping the axe in line, he brought his other arm up and jumped as he came in, nailing Lenno's bone visor with a high-velocity shield punch.

The thrall lurched but stayed standing as Jasto barreled past but this time he was ready for the fall, landing on his chest wheels and quickly pulling himself up and around to see Lenno reeling and half-blind. The knight-knave was trying to press the advantage, but Lenno's backup was almost on them. The chance to end the thrall quickly seemed to be gone. Still, with his Lenno's damaged Jasto had a clear shot at his knave and he sped towards it.

It saw him coming, tried to bring the halberd it carried up, but Jasto was in his element this time. And just like he'd told Epha, once he got going fast enough, there wasn't much most opponents could do to him.

On his first pass his axe cleaved straight into one of the knave's forearms, carving the outer half off along with a chunk of the elbow. On his next he had a better angle, and his strike completely removed his quarry's other arm right at the shoulder as it tried and failed to parry his rapid attack. On the third pass Jasto stuck his shield arm out, colliding with the knave and injecting a filament into its gangly torso.

"Open your eyes!" he yelled as their minds locked together. Once again Jasto saw a hornet buzzing around a tree as the mental form of the knave. But this time it was him on the attack.

The weight of the stars and the space between them crashed down on the insect, and it ceased to exist as the knave's body broke into chunks. Jasto braked as the fragments scattered, smoke trailing from the fried core, and a chunk of the knave's head rolled up to his feet. He looked down at it, and finally got a glimpse at what hid beneath their thick hair of filaments.

It was a chunk of blood-red photothyst, translucent and molded into the shape of a human skull.

Maybe the mental repair tabs he'd taken earlier hadn't done their job right. Maybe the Palace was just getting to him. But either way Jasto declined the opportunity to close in on Lenno, who had finished the last knight-knave but still hadn't turned to face him. Instead he just looked at the skull for a long moment, then tilted his head back and burst out laughing.

Lenno whirled. His visor was bone rather than photothyst, meaning it would take longer to repair, and only a quarter of the irregular slits covering his head had remained in place. Filaments waved from the breaks, and behind them Jasto saw a wide cluster of eyes made from

152

corrupt filaments. They were packed densely like those of an insect, and edged in a faint purple glow the same shade as his forcefield. Beneath them was a skinless mouth, blending veins and red photothyst so smoothly that Jasto couldn't see where either of them ended.

"Are you going insane, interloper?" Lenno snarled.

Jasto tried to respond immediately but couldn't, as more laughter forced its way up its throat. That was a bad sign, he thought distantly. "Maybe," he replied, once his voice was under control. "But even if I am..." Jasto gestured at the broken knave. "Creepy bodies with armor nailed in? Heads that are actually just shaped like skulls for no practical reason? The vile dreck you say, and this whole 'vengeance is my motive' shtick?" The laughter came back, and Lenno seemed to actually be unsettled by it.

"Seriously," Jasto managed. "Is this a reference to that drama show you liked? Courts of Dusk and Whatever? You're not a knight, Lenno. Not even a thrall. You're a cartoon." He could barely process it. To think Lenno had gone from being a normal person to this, to think he'd been warped and mutated so utterly by his circumstances into something he wasn't...

Well, actually, that wasn't very funny at all.

And on top of that, Lenno was unfazed by the words. He saw the thrall's lip curl as he started pacing to the side, but that was it. *"Even after seeing her memories, you still don't get it. I am righting a disgusting betrayal, Jasto. But it's clear that righteousness means nothing to you."*

The words had been spoken without even a hint of doubt, banishing any lingering urge Jasto had to laugh. Lenno really believed what he said, didn't he? He was chained in that way of thinking, unable to see the pain he caused. Blind, in the exact way Dad had warned him about.

"Speaking of betrayals, I didn't see you in that little 'last stand' memorial," Jasto said casually, pacing in parallel with Lenno. "I guess you weren't important enough for Seafall to keep a space for you?" It was Dad's training that helped him act flippant in spite of how unsettled he was, and the sorrow he felt at the tragedy that had happened here. He needed Lenno riled up and making mistakes, if he was going to survive this fight.

"*I didn't draw a short straw, so Ralica ordered me to leave,*" Lenno said. "*But I doubled back, like a* truly *loyal knight should, to try and take her place. When she was already corrupted by the time I returned, I thought I'd failed. But only at first.*" the thrall stopped, picked up the largest fragment of his visor, and fixed it back in place over his glare.

"*It was an opportunity,*" he said as the bones began to reconnect. "*A little longer and Ralica will understand: she doesn't need Epha or any of the other stragglers to make their survival count. We can make it count ourselves, by killing the knight-commanders.*" His visor cocked slightly to the side. "*They are still alive, aren't they? I'm sure Duskwall is. I haven't left this place in years but I know that human bacterium. It takes someone like me to cleanse him.*"

"Like you'll make it that far," Jasto scoffed. "Seriously, the contents of one Palace against an entire nation. Ego much?"

"*We'll have some assistance. From you…and from Epha. She fled from me but won't get far in this Palace, and besides that I needed to take you first.*"

The former knight raised his maul, pointing it across the cavern at Jasto. "*You've seen Ralica's Diagram, haven't you? You know she's near the tipping point; what you don't know is that her thralls affect that balance. Epha and everyone she allowed down here would've kept her latent if I'd gotten them enthralled. It was a waste to kill so many capable knights, but I finally have the piece I need: you, Jasto. I've been watching. I know that fury in your chest. And I'll be putting it to good use.*"

Jasto's throat had gone arid. Lenno wasn't just going to kill him. He was going to turn him into a crystal thrall, one that would push Ralica over the edge into an active state. And then Ralica's Palace, which had been building up knaves for years, would send its forces straight into the heart of Andalon. That was…

Jasto stopped himself from gulping. He couldn't show weakness. Lenno had already implied that he'd wanted to enthrall Jasto during their last encounter. There was no reason for that realization to hit harder now.

No matter what Lenno said about him being a tool, a puppet, because of the exact same reasons that had made him seek his independence out. "Big talk for someone who hasn't attacked yet," he managed to say, tone forcibly light. "Even if I'm part of your master plan, do I have to get everything done around here?"

"*I already used this trick and you still can't recognize it,*" Lenno said, his tone biting. "*I'm the one who's disappointed.*" He stretched out his spike arm and Jasto tensed, expecting a chain or some long weapon to form, but the movement had been a distraction.

Dark shapes wriggled out from the ribs packed tightly in Lenno's torso and photothyst statues projected into existence behind him, each an emaciated, armored human with a hand resting on the thrall's back.

Knave bodies, Jasto realized a moment too late. And those dark things swimming out of Lenno were freshly formed cores.

"*Whenever I've wasted my breath talking, it was to buy time. And you* still *let me drag you into a conversation.*"

Jasto was accelerating even as Lenno lectured him, but he wasn't going to make it. The thrall had placed his knaves behind himself for a reason, and the moment where Jasto either swung around Lenno or tried to knock him away from the knave bodies would be long enough for their cores to reach them. All he could really do now was choose between bad outcomes for the start of this fight.

Jasto barely needed to think before swinging around to get at the knaves. Lenno was dangerous, and he'd need to be whittled down before a kill could be attempted. That started with his footsoldiers.

Just as he'd predicted he was too slow to destroy the bodies before they were inhabited, and the three knaves that had formed yanked their hands away from Lenno the moment the cores swam into them. Each one turned to put their bodies between Jasto and their vulnerable cores, which hadn't made it up the arms yet, but that much he'd expected.

It wasn't difficult to strafe to the side as he shot past the knaves, sending an arm flying with a backhanded strike at the shoulder. The body it had been attached to crumpled as the arm wriggled in midair, and Jasto circled back as it landed to stomp on the core within, cracking it and spreading dark blood over the cave floor. That would be the only part of this fight anywhere close to easy.

As the other knaves finished moving their cores into the chests and Lenno began to close on him, Jasto turned and retreated into the cluster of pillars he'd marked earlier. His assailants paused, possibly confused about why he'd cut his movement options by entering the pillars, and Jasto took the moment of confusion to prepare more contingency filaments and trade his shield for a second axe. He was more restricted within the photothyst structure, yes, but to actually take advantage of that Lenno would have to commit to doing so.

Jasto grinned as the crystal thrall split his forces, sending one knave circling wide to the left as the other did the same on the right. It was an understandable mistake. Lenno had seen Jasto struggle in close quarters and escape his knaves quickly later on, when he had a more open space to work with. It was true that blocking Jasto's movements would put him at a disadvantage.

But only if the blockade was strong enough to stop him. Two knaves and one thrall rushed forward, but before they could close in on the openings of the cluster Jasto rocketed out, picking the mace-carrying knave as his weak point.

It must have been caught off guard that Jasto was leaving the space he'd chosen as quickly as he'd entered it, but the knave still reacted well. It swung its two-handed mace out wide as he closed in, aiming not to stop Jasto's weapons, but instead to land a crippling blow that would give Lenno and the other knave an opportunity to close in.

Too bad it was fighting Jasto instead of someone slower. In a move he'd privately named the Leg Noose, the young knight threw himself flat against the ground as he came in and let the treads on his back carry him forward. Jasto passed the knave on the left and stuck his axe out as he did, hooking one of its legs as he rushed by.

The strength the knave held was inhuman but Jasto was being pulled forward by the combined force of two Lanterns. It toppled onto its filament-covered face, sliding a few more feet along the ground with Jasto until he'd braked enough to spring up, pounce on the knave, and bury an axe in the center of its back. One of Jasto's filaments slipped in as the knave lurched under him.

"Open your—"

"—*Like hell!*"

Jasto's mental connection with the knave snapped milliseconds after it formed, as he was blown off the knave by a photothyst maul impacting him. Lenno had thrown it, Jasto realized as he landed headfirst and his faceplate cracked. Corrupted photothyst didn't dissipate immediately when separated from its creator, unlike the regular form, so he could get away with that.

It wasn't Jasto's first time maneuvering with helmet cracks obscuring his vision. He got to his feet quickly and gunned his Lanterns to take off, circling away from Lenno. Before Jasto got the cluster of pillars between them, he saw the thrall dismiss some of the spikes on his off-hand and summon two mauls to replace the one he'd lost.

Jasto's course took him near the other knave as he rounded the cluster, but at his speed it wasn't hard to evade. His bigger concern was Lenno, who was obviously switching weapon arrangements so he'd be able to throw more projectiles at Jasto.

He'd sparred against knights commanding a much larger number of flechettes than him, as part of the Valor Academy's training, and hadn't forgotten the lessons from those bouts. Lenno with his functionally limitless supply of throwing weapons had some similarities to those opponents, but those had been one-on-one fights.

And as he'd feared Lenno was recalling his knaves now, playing it safe. He'd have to get them to spread out a little or build up more speed himself in order to pick them off. Should he re-enter the cluster? He and Lenno were on opposite sides of it now, with only partial views of each other. He wasn't sure how the thrall would react if—

Jasto's train of thought cut off as he saw Lenno kneel. And as he moved, his vision still somewhat obscured by the pillars, he glimpsed one of the knaves placing a hand on its creator's back. Then the other did the same.

Somehow Jasto knew he had to interfere with whatever was happening. There was no time to fix his helmet. He just changed course on a dime, clenching his jaw against the sudden momentum shift, and zigzagged between the blue pillars of the cluster at reckless speeds to close in on Lenno.

The thrall hurled one of his weapons as Jasto came in, and with the cracks in his helmet he just barely made out its trajectory and managed to lean out of the way as it passed him. It glanced off one of his shoulder plates and then Jasto was leaning in and accelerating even as he made out Lenno rising to his feet. With the thrall in the middle of trying to stand and the extra weight he'd be carrying, Jasto was sure the Leg Noose would be even more effective. He leaned back as he cleared the last pillar, going quickly to the ground, and stuck his axe out to hook Lenno's leg.

There was a cracking noise as loud as a thunderbolt and Jasto nearly dislocated his shoulder as he slid past the thrall. The head of his axe was missing.

Jasto focused through the pain rolled to the right, landing on his knee treads and backing up as a maul split the ground where he'd just been, and saw that once again he'd been too late.

Between the damage to his helmet and the speed he'd approached at, Jasto hadn't seen how both of Lenno's knaves had somehow merged with him. His legs and the armor around them were thicker, to support the increased weight, but while Lenno's upper body remained thin it now bore *six* arms instead of two, each spiked and clutching a maul. The filaments that had once draped over the heads of the two knaves were now spread wide behind Lenno's own helmet, like a black lion's mane.

That was all Jasto had time to see before two mauls were spinning towards him, one dead center and the other slightly off to his right. Grateful that they at least weren't as fast as flechettes, he wove to the left even as his mind raced for solutions to Lenno's new strategy.

He didn't get to think for very long as his path took him straight into another maul and Jasto was thrown off his feet once again. That one had been thrown even before he'd moved, Jasto realized faintly as it wedged into his chest armor and he hit the ground. Lenno had herded him into it with his first two attacks.

It was difficult to breathe after that last hit, but thankfully Jasto's Lanterns were moved by mental commands rather than his muscles. All he had to do was lurch himself upwards, and he could maneuver.

Jasto did so, wedging the butt of his axe under the maul sticking from his chest, and levered it out before rushing back in. Lenno was already projecting new weapons and throwing them, but this once it was honestly convenient that he was using his treads. He'd won most of his battles just by being too fast to react to, but at the slower pace his treads required he was much more maneuverable.

He veered left, then pivoted to the right, then dropped down as Lenno threw two mauls at once. A third was right behind them, spinning vertically to catch Jasto despite his crouched posture, but this time he brought both his axes forward to knock the blade aside.

The parry rattled his arms, but it took the maul off course and that was all he needed to clear it and swerve behind Lenno. The light from his armor played over the thrall's back, illuminating the red photothyst that formed it, the dense cluster of ribs running up it like a column, and most importantly the two Lanterns nestled behind Lenno's shoulders.

There were already filaments threaded up both of Jasto's axes. Lenno was turning but Jasto was still in motion, matching his speed to the thrall's rotation—

—And then he received a very painful reminder that knaves could contort their forms beyond what humans were capable of. One of Lenno's main arms swung out, and where a human arm would have been forced to stop the limb kept going, purple light crystallizing into a shield around it as it carved a wide arc through the air—

—and crunching into Jasto's axe as he frantically raised it, ruining the Lantern within. The blow forced him into a gut-wrenching spin. He hit the ground hard, his treads carrying him forward at an awkward angle, and Jasto lurched to the side just in time as Lenno closed in and slammed two mauls into the ground.

Chips of stone showered his back, and it was all Jasto could do veer away from the flurry of swung and thrown mauls Lenno sent towards him. He felt like he was in the elevator battle once more, deep in a forest of crimson death and surviving only by instinct. But with the injuries he'd taken and only two Lanterns left, defeat was even closer. Jasto was going to give out, he could feel it.

Swallowing, he drew back to the thickest pillar he could find at top speed, putting it between himself and Lenno, and then dodged further back between pillars to hide from the thrall as he forced his armor to dim.

Even though it meant giving up the initiative he had to do it. Jasto needed to think, and to repair his helmet before the blindspots he'd accumulated caused a lethal mistake. As he drew a curved rectangle in his Diagram and mentally stretched it, so that it thinned into the wide and translucent faceplate of his helmet, Jasto put his mind to work.

What was Lenno in this form? At long range, he was a moving turret that could fire six shots at once and would effectively never run out of ammo. Jasto only had to look at the size of the Palace around him to see how much photothyst a corrupted knight could produce.

And at close range, with six arms and a reinforced form Jasto stood little chance of toppling, Lenno would be an absolute monster. That enhanced body was dependent on the thrall's knave cores, Jasto was sure, and breaking them might give him an advantage, but that was only if he could get behind Lenno and reach them without dying.

"*Hiding from a fight,*" Lenno said. "*Pathetic. If Ralica was in her right mind she wouldn't have bothered showing you anything. Worms can't learn or change.*"

By now at least, Jasto knew better than to respond. His helmet and armor had been fixed, so he turned to his broken axes and quickly reformed their heads, thankful that the pillar he was behind absorbed enough light to hide the projecting process. Aches still gripped his body like massive fingers, the sensation mingled with the prickle of his filaments emerging, but if he lingered too long Lenno was sure to make things even worse somehow.

But even though standing still was no good, what would moving accomplish? He had nothing, no way out and no way to beat an opponent like Lenno. This went beyond simply not having a choice, like he'd experienced before; he was just going to lose. Completely.

Then he'd become a thrall. Then, if he ever saw anyone he knew again, it would be as a monster broken by his Crest and fighting to settle the grudge of a dead man. Suddenly Jasto wished someone was here with him. Epha would have been welcome, or even one of the worst teachers from the Valor Academy, so that at least he wasn't dying alone. But no, it was just him, Lenno, and…

…and the Palace…

Even just half an hour ago, the idea that occurred to Jasto right then would have been tossed into the proverbial landfill without hesitation. If it was just his life on the line and not his potential corruption, he might still have discarded it. But he'd seen it work before. And Lenno was already planning to turn him into a thrall, then break his mind somehow.

So Jasto didn't have much to lose by interfacing directly with Ralica.

Before he could change his mind Jasto spun to face the pillar and bunched up a dense cluster of filaments in his right hand. Lenno was still getting closer and continuing to toss insults, but his steps seemed to be cautious. As experienced as the former knight was, it seemed like that experience was making him overestimate Jasto this time.

How had Epha done this again? Jasto had the dense filament, which he remembered very clearly, and obviously the next step was to slide it into the photothyst…right, to connect with an intersection of corrupt filaments. Epha hadn't unfolded her filaments to cover a wider space within the pillar until after she'd gotten an agreement from Ralica.

Jasto sucked in a breath, then extended his filament into the pillar.

White light pierced through the sapphire depths of it, revealing hexagonal facets within as Jasto guided his filament to the intersection he'd marked, careful to avoid touching any other filaments. He heard Lenno's words and footsteps suddenly cut off, but he couldn't look up. One misstep might ruin his desperate gambit to ask Ralica for help.

His filament wove around one more fence of corruption before reaching the connection, and as it did a vast, two-toned ocean appeared in his mind's eye.

This time, Jasto registered more details. The blue side of the ocean, still larger but perhaps by a little less, flickered with thin strings of silver as waves formed and broke along its surface. And the depths of the red waters, still choppy and furious, were disturbed by shifting motes of purple. Just looking at them Jasto felt a cold fury press against his mind, one that undoubtedly came from Lenno.

Not only that, but the edges of Ralica's Diagram were absolutely packed with hurricanes lined up in neat rows, each one representing a knave. Ralica had an army here.

And if he didn't stop Lenno, that army would be unleashed. Jasto put his focus on the calmer part of the ocean, knowing he'd have to play it by ear now. Epha hadn't needed to speak to communicate and he didn't want to give any clues to Lenno, so he focused his thoughts like he was making a filament attack and aimed them at the water.

I NEED HELP, SEAFALL, Jasto thought.

There was a ripple across the entirety of the ocean, both calm and disturbed, then something invisible rushed up from it. Jasto almost broke the connection right then, but managed to keep a hold on his panic long enough for it to arrive.

It rippled against his Diagram like the Crystal Star did and for a moment he thought Ralica was trying to corrupt him. For the first instant of contact, it felt just like the filament attack one of Lenno's knaves had tried to make on him earlier.

But past that instant, the sensation changed. Grief suddenly formed a lump in Jasto's throat, as he was forced to look his failures dead in the eye. It hadn't been enough to misread the people he'd once called colleagues, to lead everyone who'd trusted his vision into a trap; for years afterward he'd also failed to suppress Lenno, failed to warn Epha about him or do anything for her deeper issues, and just hours ago had even allowed the thrall to neutralize him for a moment. And on top of that this promising young soul, who could have salvaged the failure he'd never be able to fix, was now a pawn in Lenno's wretched, warped crusade to 'set things right.'

He couldn't even bear to think about the deaths that would add to his tally. All he could do now was offer the little help he was able to, despite its cost, and gamble on the small chance it would make a difference in—

A panicked, shapeless noise stuttered out of Jasto's mouth, and he jerked his hand back to break the connection. His white filaments remained within the column, now spiderwebbed out through it but beginning to fade.

That hadn't…that hadn't been him. Those hadn't been his emotions. Had they been Ralica's, felt or mimicked by his brain? Was *that* how she communicated?

And something else had changed too. Jasto glanced at his Diagram and saw that every star in it was glowing much brighter than they had been a moment ago. Enough to reform both his Lanterns immediately, without any kind of drain. Jasto hadn't even known Palaces could do that.

This must have been the 'small help' Ralica was able to offer. Jasto would have reconnected to ask if the corrupted knight was sure that was all she could do, if not for how real Ralica's regret had felt. And he wasn't exactly eager to put his mind through that level of invasion again.

Would the assistance be enough? Ralica didn't seem to think so, and Jasto found himself agreeing. He needed more, but didn't see how he could get it. Maybe Ralica could only control those knaves she'd formed for the memorial here, and all of those had already been destroyed.

Lenno's footsteps picked up once more, and the fear of becoming a monster came back, but Jasto couldn't let it interrupt his thoughts. He'd pushed through the fear of death, not just in Ralica's trial earlier but in entering this Palace in the first place. He couldn't let this other fear stop him.

Jasto kept his cool like Dad had taught him, and reviewed his resources. Lanterns. Medical supplies. A group of mercenaries outside of the Palace, too far away to be of any use.

He focused. What was inside the Palace? The exit from this place, yes, but it was blocked by a knave and more importantly had the form of a staircase. Jasto couldn't outpace Lenno on that. Even if he could, Jasto only knew of three locations where Ralica had summoned knaves that might serve as reinforcements before. He flicked a glance towards the elevator that had taken him here, wondering if it could be used to go back, only to see that the photothyst tubes connecting it to the rest of the Palace were broken near the top. Lenno must have done that, entering the cavern through the same elevator chute Jasto had used and jumping from there. That meant there was no running from this fight.

Was there anything else Jasto could turn to his advantage? His brain felt like it was overclocking as he rapidly considered and dismissed possibilities.

Lenno took another step, just a few feet away now.

Yes.

Yes, Jasto realized, there was something.

Immediately he formed another filament, connecting it to Ralica quickly, and turned every square centimeter of his brain towards making one last request of her.

Then Lenno rounded the pillar at last, and there was no time to hear a response.

Jasto tore himself loose from the pillar in a flash, abandoning his filament there and racing around it before Lenno could crush him. He recalled the axe he'd dropped a second later and immediately dove sideways.

But the maul Jasto had expected to fly through the air where he'd just been didn't arrive. Confused, he turned to look at Lenno.

The thrall hadn't moved from the pillar where Jasto had hidden. His six arms were lowered as he stared mutely at the spot where Jasto's filaments had entered the pillar, and the fading white grid that had spread out from it.

Knowing he might not get another opportunity, Jasto quickly resummoned his third and fourth Lantern and decided a change to his usual style was in order. The Crystal Star brushed against his thoughts as the haft of his axe lengthened, going down to a wide cap at the end, and the head grew wider as he placed a second Lantern within it. He'd be able to make heavier strikes and do so at a longer range with this weapon, both of which seemed necessary against Lenno's current form.

The thrall finally turned at the hiss of the projections forming, and Jasto tensed.

"You...communicated with her?" Lenno asked. *"With Ralica?"*

Jasto realized that the thrall's lowest pair of arms, the ones that were a part of him rather than the knaves, had started to tremble. It wasn't a ruse to buy time. He was genuinely furious with Jasto.

Of course he was. Jasto hadn't had much time to think during this fight, but he remembered that it had started with Lenno targeting the knaves, not Jasto. At that time the thrall had also been ranting at Ralica for favoring someone 'unworthy' like Jasto apparently was. Topping it off was the way Lenno had apparently been trying to influence Ralica, something he'd just witnessed the full extent of.

It painted such a clear picture Jasto was surprised he hadn't seen it sooner. "You're possessive, aren't you, Lenno?" He asked, laughing for the second time in this fight. "Possessive of Ralica, like one of those clingy, dependent lover types. Holy dreck."

"You understand nothing," Lenno hissed. *"You've never been at war. You don't know what it means to fight besides someone."*

"Sure, fine, *I* don't get it," Jasto said easily. It felt amazing that he'd found a chink in the thrall's armor. "But Suncage does, and she's not being all freaky like you are."

"Don't talk about Epha. That bitch *lost her way!"* Lenno was yelling across the cavern now, and hadn't made a single move to approach. *"She even brought you here to kill Ralica, to take her Crest! A complete betrayal, just like what was done to us!"*

"You really think Seafall's got a problem with that? I did communicate with her, Lenno. I got all up in there, mind to mind," Jasto sneered, wanting to rattle the thrall. "And you know what she told me?

That I was a promising candidate. She doesn't care about your revenge. She picked *me* over *you*."

Lenno stampeded across the space between them, and Jasto knew he'd gotten what he wanted.

Now all he had to do was survive it. He'd made his appeal to Ralica, but even if the corrupted knight did accept she would still need time to make it happen. For now he had to deal with Lenno.

It might have seemed sensible to retreat immediately, but if Jasto did that he gave the thrall good odds of calming down again. The advantages to having him unsettled were already obvious, in how he was closing in for melee instead of throwing his mauls. He had to be kept that way as long as possible.

So as Lenno took a running leap Jasto marked his trajectory and, instead of shooting straight back to escape, skated forward to the other side of the thrall's landing zone.

Lenno crunched the stone as he landed, swung two arms further behind his back than a human could to catch Jasto, but he'd already seen that trick. Air whistled against his helmet as the mauls passed just in front of it, and he took a page from Epha's book.

Jasto whirled his poleaxe around, engaging both of its Lanterns as he let go with one hand and allowed momentum to slide the other down to the cap at the bottom. He added some torque to the motion with his boot Lanterns at the same time, the head of his weapon shining like a comet. It whipped forward, the entirety of Jasto's strength behind it, with enough power to remove Lenno's leg at the knee.

"*You little—*" Lenno snarled. Even as the limb broke off he was turning, his other arms coming up as his mane of filaments contorted, and one of his mauls scraped Jasto's back wheels as he recovered his poleaxe from the heavy blow. Jasto got his dreck together and slid back just enough to be out of Lenno's reach, and the thrall was still so enraged that he dropped two of his weapons and hustled forward on three limbs instead of repairing his leg.

There was a temptation to go for a kill on the thrall there, but an actual threat to his life might make him calm down. Jasto would push for more damage instead. He just had to endure.

Maul blows hammered down as Jasto slowly gave ground to Lenno, and he retreated carefully to make sure he wasn't pushed towards any of the already-damaged cavern floor. Lenno's leg re-projected soon enough, more photothyst than bone since he'd done a rush job, and he planted it on the stone to launch himself straight at Jasto.

It was a mistake. He'd put more force into the movement than was necessary, anticipating a backwards retreat that his lunge was set up to intercept. Instead Jasto clicked his wheels up and stepped to the side like a matador, bringing his poleaxe down in an augmented strike that cut straight through Lenno's *other* leg.

Once again the thrall crashed to the ground, crying out in anger, and hurled a maul that went over Jasto's head before actually turning to face him. Jasto brought his wheels back down and pushed his Lanterns to their maximum speed, making a pass at Lenno to keep him off balance and swinging his axe low to cleave the hip. Lenno's energy shield formed over the impact zone and Jasto nearly lost his grip on the weapon as it careened to the side, but he managed to keep it as he blew past Lenno and knocked a thrown maul out of the air. The thrall growled at the miss.

Jasto smelled blood. He still wouldn't go for a kill on Lenno, but in his angered state he was sure he could get one of the crimson behemoth's knave cores. Another mental command to his Lanterns had him turning, shooting back towards Lenno while the thrall was still down on the ground, and he brought his axe up to make it look like he'd attack with it. His real strike would come from the filament he'd just threaded down his leg.

With augmented strength he slapped another maul away and drew his weapon back as he came in. Just as he'd hoped, Lenno's lowest pair of arms came up to defend against the obvious blow and his energy shield coalesced over their mauls. He'd taken the bait.

Jasto activated his poleaxe Lanterns and, instead of having them pull his weapon into the arc of a strike, drove the butt of his poleaxe straight into the ground.

He sailed over Lenno like a pole vaulter, twisting in midair to stomp hard on the thrall's shoulder and sending his filament in as he made contact. A hornet appeared in his mind's eye, flitting through a tree as triumph surged in his chest.

"Open your—"

"—*Order: Breakdown.*"

Suddenly there were two hornets, resisting the weight of Jasto's strike together, and behind them the leaves of the tree turned as one to point needle-sharp tips at Jasto. The knaves and Lenno were all interlinked, he realized, not just physically but through filaments, and their strength together outweighed his.

Even though Jasto was supposed to have an advantage as the attacker, his strike was reversed. Shadow crawled up his leg, and only a panicked kick from his other foot severed it before the corrupted filament reached his Crest.

He was still falling, though, and he tried to fire his Lanterns as he hit the ground only to remember too late that his back wheels had been damaged earlier. Jasto awkwardly slid a foot or so to the left as Lenno turned despite his missing leg, three of his mauls already swinging down like he'd expected Jasto to do this, like he'd known exactly where he'd land afterwards.

The young squire-errant frantically got his arms on the ground, pushing his back up as his forearm wheels took on his weight, and started moving just in time to dodge the attacks. His muscles burned as he forced himself to his feet from the awkward bridge pose, raising his arms to stop a glancing maul blow that cracked the wheels there, and threw himself behind a pillar an instant later. Another maul whistled by as Jasto stuck out a hand and recalled his axe.

He'd been led into making that attack. Lenno had calmed down, and the moment he'd done so he'd nearly ended the fight in one move. Jasto steadied his breathing and abandoned the pillar quickly, ducking behind another as he heard the thrall reattach his severed leg.

"Taunting me to gain an advantage, because you can't handle a straight-up fight," Lenno said, his corrupted voice thick with contempt. *"I realized after the second leg. But unlike the Round Table, you won't get away with your cowardice."*

More mauls came Jasto's way from new angles, and the pillars were sparse enough that he couldn't use any as cover for long before Lenno either repositioned or just broke through the thinner ones. There was no time to repair his armor.

"Nothing to say? You did such a good job of provoking me earlier. It even worked for a second. But everyone runs out of words

when they're losing. You'll see, when I have you crack one of the knight-commanders yourself."

"Dreck, you really are broken," Jasto muttered, and abruptly decided to change his approach. He braked next to a photothyst pillar, seeing Lenno loom behind him in its reflective surface, and suddenly pivoted to shoot towards the thrall. If he couldn't make time to repair his armor, then he'd force Lenno to defend instead.

The thrall reacted, rushing forward and throwing mauls. Jasto's charge became a zigzag immediately, but his advance continued and so did his words.

"I saw Ralica's memories, and the Lenno in them is dead," he hissed as he rounded a pillar so tightly his fingers brushed it. "Just like Suncage said, you're nothing but a *husk* holding his name." Another maul spun through the air, and Jasto could have dodged but split it in half with an augmented swing instead. Both halves clattered to the ground as Jasto finished closing the distance, and Lenno was forced to raise his remaining mauls defensively as his poleaxe came up.

The collision rattled the air and Jasto's arm, but he was past Lenno and swooping back around in seconds with his weapon out again. "No composure! No self-control!" he yelled as he came in. Another clash. "Nothing making choices except your Crest!" he cried out, even as wooziness from the rapid turns began to set in. "I couldn't have gotten to the real Lenno. You're just some asshole!"

"Say whatever you like," Lenno replied, projecting longer handles on two of his mauls. He swung them wide, forcing Jasto to bail out of his next dash, and followed the move with throws from his upper arms. *"You'll serve your purpose anyway."*

Jasto retreated under the renewed assault, nearly getting clipped and doing his best to ignore the sloshing feeling in his brain. What had he been thinking? The only thing those mad dashes had accomplished was draining him, he'd known going in without a plan would get that result. But he'd felt a need to attack Lenno right then. Why?

"But for your information, interloper, I'm the only one who's still in control," Lenno continued, planting his longer mauls in the ground so he could throw with his lowest arms as well. *"Epha let despair take over, and gave up on doing anything to the Round Table. Then she started her Star-damned trial to ritualize Ralica's murder. And just now, she ran from a fight with me. Even Ralica lost her way, bowed down to die like*

Epha wanted! I'm the only one who kept his head up!" Jasto dodged between pillars as Lenno spoke, saw the thrall spread his hands as dark fans of filaments rose from them. Each became a fistful of long, crimson throwing knives.

"And I won't lower it, until I've set things right."

Jasto took cover as the first of the knives began flying. They were smaller, less able to pierce the pillar he was hiding behind, but Lenno could project and throw them faster. They flew by in a storm on either side of the pillar, keeping Jasto pinned as he repaired his armor with a numb feeling in his chest.

It was that last sentence that had made him realize why he hated the thrall so much. Lenno was angry with the Round Table, heavy in both his self-righteousness and his commitment to his goals. He didn't care what he needed to do to achieve them.

He was way, way too similar to Jasto. Was that what his future looked like, even if he got out of this Palace uncorrupted?

More knives flew past him, indifferent to his thoughts. Too many knives, Jasto realized. And all coming from the same place. Why wasn't Lenno repositioning to raise the pressure, or shifting back to heavier projectiles to break the pillar Jasto had taken cover behind?

Because he was buying time, Jasto realized with a chill. When he'd revealed earlier that he brought time by talking, had it been a calculated move? One meant to make Jasto think the thrall would *only* buy time by talking, so he was caught off guard when Lenno did it with knives instead?

There was no time to wonder. Jasto's armor was back, and he quickly projected a tall shield in one hand and held his poleaxe in the other, engaging its Lanterns to keep it light as he whirled around the pillar towards Lenno and whatever he was doing with the time he'd brought.

Knives clattered off the shield as Jasto advanced, and he peered through its eyeslit to see that Lenno was changing his form again. He'd caught the thrall halfway through another reconfiguration. Only one side of his body still bore three arms, while the other half's leg was changing from bulky to a three-jointed form that seemed like it would fit an animal better.

169

"Took you long enough to realize," Lenno said, but Jasto wasn't listening. Not when the thrall's half-transformed state gave him another chance to take a Lantern. He couldn't move as quickly as he liked between his heavy shield and the treads he was forced to use, but he still pushed his Lanterns for all they were worth.

Knives continued to rain against his shield as he approached, each one forcing at least some course correction, but then the one arm remaining on the transformed side of Lenno snatched up an elongated maul. The limb was longer but thinner, its photothyst only a thin casing around the bones that lined it, but that didn't stop Lenno from swinging it down in a blow that could and would get through Jasto's shield.

He brought his poleaxe around, the might of two Lanterns slapping the weapon down and to the side where it wedged in the stone. Jasto kept his momentum, ducking under the outstretched limb to get behind Lenno and strike at his shoulder Lantern once again. This time he wouldn't try a filament attack, just the raw kinetic force he could bring to bear.

Or he would have, if a photothyst limb like a jagged snake skeleton hadn't whipped down from Lenno's shoulder to intercept him. It was massively flexible but not nearly as strong or as fast as the thrall's arms had been, and on instinct Jasto slapped it aside as he passed under Lenno.

He realized the snakelike limb was covered with filaments at the worst possible moment, right as it wrapped around the axehead and several of them began burrowing for the Lanterns it held.

He frantically tugged his axe back but Lenno had anticipated that. All the filaments that had burrowed into his axe had plenty of slack, and the only thing the maneuver had done was entangle his poleaxe even further. His Diagram shuddered in the back corner of his mind, bladelike leaves appearing around two of his satellites.

"Order—"

Moving in pure panic, Jasto wrenched his tall shield around and cleaved through the filaments with its lower edge. The very ends of filaments could pass through photothyst like it was liquid, but the rest was vulnerable to any kind of physical force regardless of what it came from.

The shadowy threads snapped as Jasto shot past Lenno, his heart thumping like a rabbit's.

"—*Breakdown*," Lenno finished even though the connection was broken. "*I've waited years for this and you're still dragging it out. Fine.*" Once again the thrall rose in an altered body, standing much taller than he had a few moments before. "*I wanted to test this anyway.*"

If his previous form had been a brute's, this one was a pursuer's. Like Jasto had seen earlier, Lenno now had triple-jointed legs reminiscent of an ambush predator. They were the main contributors to his new height, starting wide and tapering down to thin, bladelike lengths at the third joint that ended in three-toed claws. The snake-limbs, one on each shoulder, lashed behind him as he turned towards Jasto, lined with bone and almost like some strange parody of wings. His mane of filaments had been reduced to a single tail dangling behind his bone visor, most of them presumably in the snake-limbs, and as Lenno turned he picked up the second lengthened maul.

Jasto assessed the capabilities of the form at a glance and dreaded what he saw. It was built for speed, maneuverability, and the snake-limbs especially were meant for corruption. It countered everything Jasto could do well, all while setting Lenno up to claim him as a thrall without killing him.

He dropped his shield and fled instantaneously, putting both his boot and poleaxe Lanterns to the desperate task of getting away. Maybe if he tried for the exit staircase now, the thrall wouldn't be able to fit—

Lenno closed in with a sound like distant gunshots, each of his steps in his new form breaking stone. Jasto swerved as he came up to a pillar, turning almost eighty degrees on a dime and hoping the thrall would overshoot his own turn and give him some breathing room.

Instead there was a crack as Lenno landed with both feet on the pillar, coiling up as he impacted it only to corkscrew back out towards Jasto a split second later with both mauls up.

Three blows shuddered through his armor as he frantically raised his poleaxe. The first made his weapon shiver and nearly knocked it out of his hand. The second cracked the wheels of his left boot.

And the third came from one of the snake-limbs as its sharp head whipped into the narrow groove between Jasto's chest armor and right shoulder. It didn't break the protective scales there, the limb was too weak for that.

But it was meant to corrupt, not break, and as Lenno landed just past Jasto with the limb stretched to its maximum length dark filaments began to creep up his shoulder.

He lurched back with a frantic cry and tried to cut them but Lenno was latched onto him like a parasite, swinging both of his mauls down to pin Jasto's poleaxe in place. With no other choice he let go of his axe and dismissed his shoulder armor as he frantically dropped backwards.

Without armor to burrow through the dark filaments grasped only at thin air as Jasto fell, his back wheels catching him. He shot away, pulling his poleaxe back to his hands, but Lenno was bounding forward even faster than it could return to him.

Jasto swerved once again, but Lenno's new legs were just as good when absorbing force as they were generating it. Once more Lenno pivoted in midair, planting both feet as he landed and raising plumes of dust from the cavern floor.

A twist of the thrall's fingers had both of his mauls rotating around, their hammerheads going back as the spikes opposite them came forward. Lenno slammed his weapons down, piercing the ground and bracing himself against it as his legs tightened and he hunched down for a charge.

Jasto swerved once again, hoping to avoid the coming lunge. But the thrall had delayed his takeoff by just a moment, just long enough to see which direction Jasto had chosen to dodge.

Lenno's body moved so fast it disappeared, but Jasto somehow got a clear glimpse of his snake-limbs snapping from coiled to completely taut by the sheer speed of the movement. Then the thrall was on top of him, stomping hard on Jasto's chest armor as momentum pushed them both off course.

Jasto's back wheels ground into nothing as Lenno used him as an improvised brake. He'd taken falls before in his training, heavy impacts and cuts when he'd sparred. But he'd never felt like this, like a stone sucked into the teeth of a vacuum cleaner and battered viciously around. He came to a stop—

—And Lenno swung a maul down, driving a spike into his unarmored shoulder.

Jasto's thoughts went through a paper shredder. He screamed, jerking like a fish on a hook, and nearly broke his legs as his boot

Lanterns fired in useless directions. Jagged chunks of photothyst projected out of him randomly, stomped away by Lenno as the Crystal Star pushed his thoughts into further disarray, and he distantly heard his poleaxe crash into something.

As much as he thrashed, he couldn't get his impaled shoulder loose. Jasto's vision cleared a little and he saw Lenno leaning down, one of his snake-limbs curling around Jasto's midsection.

"*This is just the beginning.*" Jasto finally got his poleaxe moving back towards them but Lenno dropped his other maul and caught it, wrapping his second snake-limb around the weapon to hold it still. His slitted visor hadn't moved a millimeter. Jasto could feel the glare behind it, just as solidly as the pain clawing at his insides.

He tried to project more photothyst over his chest, to force the snake-limb there away, but it was already secreting filaments that slid into his armor without resistance. Just projecting more material wouldn't do a thing to stop those.

"*You'll try to kill me, at first,*" Lenno continued. "*Then you won't be able to, once your Crest asserts itself. After that—*"

The thrall stopped, looked up, and bolted sideways as a stalactite suddenly ripped through the space he'd just been occupying, carrying on to embed itself in a nearby pillar.

No, not a stalactite, Jasto realized with relief.

A lance, gray and shot through with lines of gold.

"LENNO!" Epha roared, tearing after the thrall as she recalled her lance, Lantern-fire jetstreams trailing behind.

Jasto remained on the floor, too drained to properly feel the hole in his shoulder, laughing weakly at the fact that he was still alive. "Epha wasn't running from the fight, Lenno," he murmured, not caring if the thrall actually heard him. "She was trying to find me."

And Ralica had decided to show her the way. It was so ridiculous to think trusting the corrupted knight had actually worked that Jasto wanted to lay there for another half hour, laughing at the insanity of it all. Or maybe that was just the shock.

But he could practically hear Dad telling him it was now or never, that he had to get up. And normally that thought would have had Jasto pausing for a moment, to lament his lack of choice in yet another thing.

But that sentiment felt smaller now, after all of this. Jasto carefully sat up, keeping the maul in his shoulder steady so it didn't fall out prematurely. White-hot pain spiked out as he slowly straightened and dismissed the remains of his back armor, pawing awkwardly through his medkit with one hand.

After a few bleary seconds Jasto found a blocker bead and brought it around, sucking in a breath as he quickly pushed the maul out of his shoulder and thumbed the bead in. It immediately began to congeal over the wound, blunting the pain, but he knew the injury would need a lot more than that. Still, Jasto had to reposition before he could treat it further.

Lenno and Epha were darting between pillars in the denser cluster of them that Jasto had used for cover earlier. Putting a pillar between the explosive noise of their fight and himself, he quickly repaired his wheels, then unstrapped his medkit and repaired the armor everywhere except his shoulder. Now safer, Jasto could do more to the wound than just prevent blood loss and immediately started to.

He did all he could for his arm, layering med-patches and ingesting painkillers in almost dangerous levels, but it still wouldn't be usable for weeks. Even the most bleeding-edge medical tech in the world wouldn't have changed that. Jasto did not want to go back out there, didn't want to be anywhere near Lenno, but Epha seemed to be losing steam. They'd both had hard fights, he suspected.

So if they didn't win now, it was over.

Maybe the knight-commanders had once thought the same thing.

Jasto stuck out his good arm, and the haft of his poleaxe slapped into it. Even that slight impact had his shoulder throbbing enough to distract, so he injected another battlefield stimulant to help ignore the pain and projected a splint through his armor to hold the limb still. Jasto ran through his preparations as electricity from the stim surged through his veins and the pain became even more distant.

Wheels down. Poleaxe up. Filaments prepped.

Jasto fired his Lanterns and darted forward as a pillar cracked before him. Lenno was darting between them, rebounding off stone and photothyst rapidly as he fought. He couldn't move faster than Epha, his springlike legs still unable to outpace Lantern-fire jets, but he could change directions much faster than the old knight.

That was where Jasto came in. Lenno kicked sideways as Epha made a pass at him, landing on another pillar and turning to leap after Epha. The thrall raised his weapons, ready to take a chunk out of Epha's armor before she could turn to face him properly.

Then Jasto's poleaxe got in the way. Lenno yelled wordlessly, forced to deal with him instead of pursuing Epha, and Jasto only managed to engage him for two blows before one of the snake-limbs came around and he had to pull the weapon back.

But by then Epha had reversed course. Lenno was caught flat-footed as she rushed in, forcing him to meet Epha with his weapons instead of dodging. The thrall went for mitigation of damage instead of a kill, slamming the point of the lance to the side as it flared with Lantern-fire. The mauls were broken by the heat and force of the impact, but Lenno's main body was spared as Epha rushed by.

Jasto closed in a moment later, holding his poleaxe by its very end and slamming it down on the shoulder Lantern Lenno had exposed during his parry.

Sparks flew like fireworks, and the crack Jasto heard as the Lantern broke was pure euphoria to his ears. A snake-limb lurched out for him even as the other began to crumble but Jasto had barely lost any momentum during the attack, so the filaments it sent towards him were torn loose before they could even form a proper grip.

"Suncage!" Jasto yelled as he repositioned. "I don't think he can put his shield over his knave parts!" Otherwise Jasto's Lantern kill just now should've failed.

"Understood, Chaston!" the old knight yelled, coming around in her high-mobility armor form. "Continue the staggered attacks, we have this!"

Lenno stomped the ground before Jasto could answer, getting his legs back under himself. They were both triple-jointed again, and he no longer had any snake-limbs after the reconfiguration of his remaining knave. The thrall was going for speed over attack options. Jasto would've done the same.

Lenno leapt into action as both he and Epha completed their turns and shot back towards him. Epha was in the lead, flaring her jets as she picked up speed, and Jasto had trailed at a moderate distance behind her. The spacing would stagger their attacks as the old knight had suggested.

When Lenno moved, it was to disrupt this strategy as much as he could. He darted to the side as Epha approached, zigzagging between pillars and hurling a maul at Jasto as he moved.

It was longer than the others had been, so even with just one arm he had little trouble knocking it out of the air.

But as he did Lenno reappeared from behind another pillar, raising his remaining maul. Jasto turned abruptly, raising his poleaxe as fast he could, but between the projectile he'd just intercepted and the strange angle Lenno had chosen to attack from he wouldn't make it.

Then Epha's lance arrived, the three Lanterns it held giving it enough force to pierce the thrall's back. Lenno lurched, his ribs splintering, and sensing an opportunity Jasto swung to the side and hooked his poleaxe under one of his triple-jointed legs. He was faster with them, and taller, but he was also easier to topple.

Jasto pulled his weapon back with augmented strength and Lenno didn't fall but was forced to put a hand on the ground to steady himself. That was enough. Epha closed in a second later even as Lenno tried to spring away and wrapped a hand around her lance, channeling her Crest ability through the Lanterns within.

Golden Lantern-fire bloomed just before the thrall managed to tear himself loose, and his last Lantern overheated. Lenno's attempted escape became an awkward stumble as the terminal thirds of his legs broke apart midleap, sending him sprawling to the ground. He was out of knaves, and a moment later Epha slammed him down using the lance still embedded in his back. Armor cracked.

"*Epha, I—*"

"Lenno only talks to buy time!" Jasto yelled, speeding forward. The crimson thrall whirled with his visor broken once again, revealing the dense eyes and grotesque mouth hidden there, but before he could say anything else Jasto brought his poleaxe down and split Lenno's face in half.

Dark blood sprayed. Jasto could have gone straight for the Crest, but he was a methodical fighter. Better to make sure he didn't disrupt Epha with words somehow than try for a quick kill.

And it paid off a moment later when the old knight joined him, leaving her lance in place and stabbing two concentrated jets of Lantern-fire down like swords. Lenno's left arm melted off at the shoulder, his right spared by his shield going up, but Jasto brought his own weapon up and cut the limb off at the elbow.

"*KaaAArgh...*" was all Lenno managed to get through his ruin of a mouth before Jasto finally shot a filament into his torso. It slid through the photothyst easily, then curved to pass between the bones hiding the thrall's organs and, most importantly, his Crest.

Jasto had gone for it so eagerly that he didn't even notice Epha's filament connecting at the same time.

This time it wasn't just two Diagrams linking, but three. Jasto's night sky unfolded and below it, in a pocket of desert sunlight, was a tree. He'd mostly focused on the hornets, the representations of Lanterns, when he'd seen this place before. He'd only gotten glimpses of it before, and the hornets representing Lenno's Lanterns had taken most of his attention when he had.

In its own way the tree seemed as vicious as a hornet itself. Each of its leaves was a dusty green dagger, connected to branches that stabbed outward from a gnarled trunk and offered little shade to the cracked scrubland surrounding it. Where the edges of Lenno's Diagram met with Jasto's, there was only a shuddering line of static.

And underneath the tree, a space that was underground but somehow still perceptible to Jasto, there stretched a vast and intricate ant colony. It was somehow as large as both the tree and Jasto's sky, cracking the ground in a rough and complex net patrolled by sixteen ants.

That had to be Epha's Diagram.

Rage pushed out from Lenno, washing over Jasto, and he felt it the same way he'd felt Ralica's emotions. A burning insistence that things were not over, that he would not be cowed, that he refused to have all he'd worked for stripped away like this.

Once again it was far too familiar.

"By my command," he heard Epha say, and the ground beneath the tree started to crumble.

"Open your eyes," Jasto muttered, focusing himself on instinct, and the stars descended. Whether or not Lenno counted as alive, he would be the first sentient being Jasto had ever snuffed out. He didn't know how to feel about that. Or how to feel about anything, right then.

Lenno pushed back, the leaves of his tree flaring out in the Diagram as he struggled in the real world, but he was one thrall facing two knights. It was over.

And a moment later, his crimson body broke apart like wet sand. The two knights stood over the fragments in silence as old, burgundy blood spread out from underneath them, sizzling faintly from the overheated Crest.

Then Epha collapsed, her armor rattling as she hit the ground facefirst.

"Dreck!" Jasto swore, dropping to his knees next to the old knight. He could hear her breathing but the noise was thin and discordant. Epha shifted weakly, and in a panic Jasto flipped her over and cut the front of her helmet away.

Beneath it she seemed to have aged five years, the lines of her face cutting far deeper in than they had yesterday. Her curled hair was limp and matted with sweat, her eyes unsteady and half-blind.

This wasn't just physical exhaustion, Jasto realized. Epha had said that she needed a large number of Lanterns to jet around with her Crest ability, in order to properly control her trajectory. And Jasto knew she'd lost several during the elevator fight with Lenno.

In addition to fighting off and escaping the thrall, Epha had drained her body to create more Lanterns.

She'd be on the verge of Crest corruption.

Chapter 9

Jasto moved without thinking, reaching behind himself and dismissing his back armor at the same time. He shoved his good hand into his medkit, groping around for a nutrient supplement, and tore the wrapper off with his teeth before shoving a chunk in Epha's mouth.

"Eat that, quickly!" he yelled, not knowing if she could hear him. "And I'll..."

The words died as Jasto's panic wore off, replaced by analytical thoughts. What exactly could he do? Nothing in his kit would really treat Crest corruption, if it was at the tipping point in the old knight. The nutrient bar might assist with Epha's health, but that didn't really have a bearing on whether she'd reached past the limits of what her Crest was meant to do. It would be a minor help, if it helped at all.

In fact, if he didn't kill Epha now, she'd become corrupted and try to kill Jasto.

A stone sank into his gut at the cold thought. He turned it over again, tried to find some error, and couldn't. And since Jasto was this close, with the damage he'd already taken, he might be killed just by the initial burst of Epha's Palace formation.

But he knew the training Epha had gone through now, the principle that crystal knights were built on. To stay the course even when it meant accepting death, because that was better for Andalon than corruption.

A principle that made sense, that Epha herself had told him she supported, that Dad certainly wouldn't have flinched at. So why did that knowledge make him feel even worse? Why was he hesitating?

He wanted Epha to live. Despite all that she stood for, all the ways she'd made things more difficult, Jasto didn't want this. He'd told Dad, yesterday, that the old knight was the embodiment of mindless adherence. He'd seen her as weak, and he'd been afraid of falling to that same weakness.

And still he was hesitating, at something Epha herself had needed to do. So many of the knights in the Drone War had been here too, forced to kill their friends to protect people like him. How could he have the right to judge their choices, when he was struggling so much just with this one?

"Rali…ca," Epha whispered, her face pale and wretched. "Can't…end it…anymore. I'm…"

"I'm sorry," Jasto muttered, his voice cracking. If only he'd been able to handle Lenno himself, and spare Epha from overdrawing. But no.

He was still too weak.

With jerky, regretful movements, Jasto cleared layers of photothyst armor away from Epha's neck. But even as he leaned back and raised his poleaxe, even as he told himself that there was no other way, he couldn't stop his mind from racing.

The filaments in Epha's armor began to faintly pulse, a warning sign, but Jasto still remained frozen. He would do it by moving his Lanterns instead of his arm, he decided. That felt less…personal. But maybe it was worse in a different way, since Ralica had given him the energy to create those Lanterns—

Jasto dropped his poleaxe like it had turned molten. Ralica had renewed his Crest when they'd connected earlier, making it possible for him to generate more Lanterns.

Could Jasto do something similar for Epha?

Not wasting another moment, he threaded out a filament and connected it to Epha's Crest. Jasto knew it was a risk he couldn't justify taking. He didn't care, right then.

Epha's Diagram began to unfold next to his own, an ant colony carved through packed earth that Jasto was somehow able to see the full layout of. On his second look, he noticed there was a symmetry to the city-like structure: its tunnels were densest at the center, just below the surface of the dark soil, but further from it they began to grow sparse and less connected. The very edges of the Diagram were only reached by single tunnels connected straight to the center, so that it seemed to form a many-pointed star beneath the earth.

Corruption was starting to break that symmetry. Tunnels were twisting into a warped knot down and to the right of the Diagram's center, as if they were strings rather than hollow passageways, and they tangled up the orderly structure as they did. The knot grew like a tumor.

The Diagram—or was it Epha?—grasped for Jasto the way a drowning man would for a life raft, and he instinctively pulled back within the mental space before it could. That had felt dangerous, was she attempting to enthrall him already?

No. Her Palace hadn't attempted to form yet, so she wasn't corrupted. At least for now.

Jasto hesitated as the reality of the gamble he was making loomed over him. Failure equaled corruption, for him and Epha, and in all likelihood would be followed by enthrallment. The same fate Lenno had planned for them.

So be it. He called his poleaxe back up and repositioned it, setting the head just an inch away from his filament in case something went wrong, and carefully allowed Epha's Diagram to link fully with his own.

Pain flared above his ribs immediately and Jasto almost cut his connection, but he realized there was a familiarity to it. It was the same thing he felt when he tried to make a Lantern too early, and his Crest pulled nutrition from his body in order to compensate. Was Epha recovering by draining his energy?

A wooziness sunk into Jasto and he saw the knot in her Diagram start to straighten, but not fast enough. He wouldn't survive if this kept up, not with how close she was to the edge. Not on his own, Jasto realized.

As his vision started to darken from the drain, Jasto swallowed his discomfort and shot out another filament into a nearby pillar of blue photothyst. A junction was close to the surface, and it took barely any concentration to guide his filament into a connection with it. Ralica's Diagram appeared.

EPHA NEEDS—

The two-toned ocean was surging forward before he could even finish the thought, somehow growing closer without swallowing a single island. There was no opportunity to pull back, and Jasto somehow knew he wouldn't have had the mental strength for it even if there was. Against his will, the connection deepened.

Jasto tasted saltwater. Panic seized him by the throat as the connection finished forming, Ralica's and his own blending together to mangle anything that might resemble a complex thought or plan. In the real world, his whole body stiffened and froze.

And inside his head, another emotion began to bleed into him. Jasto's hands began to shake as it took over, his jaw pulling tight and his eyes opening wide. Fury built in his chest, stoked by the indignity of Lenno, someone he was *responsible for*, ruining things again and hurting those he was supposed to help. And the fact that now, just inches from all of this being over, he had to take himself past the brink to clean up the thrall's mess?

It was too much.

"*Too...much,*" Jasto rasped, as the ocean in his mind's eye was devoured by red. His right arm shook so badly that it strained against his splint, and pain flashed out from it to tear away any last scraps of control he'd had.

In the edge of his Diagram, dark red clouds began to bloom.

Then Epha gasped, one of her arms shooting straight up, and the sudden motion cut Jasto's connection with her. Her three-Lantern lance crashed into him as she moved it blindly, knocking Jasto to the side and breaking the filament that connected him to the Palace. The sea vanished in an instant as he flew through the air towards the remnants of Lenno, taking the distortion in his own Diagram with it.

The pain in Jasto's shoulder flared up again as he landed hard, but that was nothing compared to the wringer his mind had just been put through. Jasto still cried out from it, curling up and shifting some of the nearby pieces of the crystal thrall. One of them was a broken rib that fell next to his face, splattering blood and loose corrupted filaments as it landed.

Suddenly he was glad his helmet was still on.

"What?" Epha suddenly rasped, casting her gaze around. She was still on her back, and the chunk of nutrient supplement bar had fallen out of her mouth. "What was...I can't..." She looked from side to side, the movement frantic and somehow incomplete. Jasto stared, too disoriented to speak, as Epha kept trying to look around until she seemed to give up on something. Then her armor Lanterns glowed, hoisting up her torso like she was a puppet on strings.

"Lenno," she rasped. "Where is—"

Epha paused as she saw the remains of the thrall scattered around Jasto. He was concerned by the strange way the old knight was moving, but she of course had questions of her own. They'd have a lot to catch each other up on. And with what Jasto had seen through his connection with Ralica, he wanted to give Epha the full picture as soon as possible.

He was about to sit up and do just that when, for no reason he could discern, the pain in his shoulder tripled. It spiked out from the hole through his shoulder like a physical thing, hotter than metal left in a car at the height of summer.

A strangled, pain-ridden scream tore itself loose from his throat. The cave ceiling blurred into a watercolor painting as tears filled his eyes and he spasmed on the ground. Faintly Jasto heard Epha shout something, but he couldn't process what it was. It was like all the pain he'd blocked out since receiving the injury had suddenly decided to deliver itself in one singular, thought-melting burst.

But it wasn't just that, somehow. Jasto had been physically injured before, both today and previously, and even in his delirious state he could tell there was something different about what he was feeling now. The pain had a chemical edge to it, like acid had been poured into his shoulder instead of the photothyst maul that had actually been placed there. He had no idea what it meant. The fear only added to his agony.

"—Need to administer—" Jasto managed to make out as he twisted, feeling blood start to leak from the bindings he'd placed on his shoulder. Had that been Epha speaking?

He got his answer a moment later, as two gray flechettes darted down to clamp his head in place. Jasto's gaze was forced up just in time to see a photothyst elbow collide with his faceplate.

The translucent pane of his helmet cracked, but since it was a glancing blow Jasto managed to stay conscious. Had Epha gotten corrupted after all? Was she trying to kill him now? The armored elbow swung down again, its movement unnaturally stiff, and his faceplate shattered. As bits of photothyst dissipated and Epha's arm drew back, Jasto somehow noticed that her hand was completely limp.

The agony in his shoulder spiked before he could make sense of that, and this time when Jasto screamed the noise was anything but strangled. Then photothyst prongs shoved themselves between his teeth, forcing his mouth open.

"Swallow this, now!" he heard, and Jasto had already followed Epha's instructions several times today. He did so again, instinctively, as a small pill was dropped into his mouth.

It fizzed into nothing within his throat, and time glitched out.

What could have been minutes or even hours passed Jasto by, long segments of time seeming to blur past his eyes while individual moments stretched out like taffy.

He saw Epha kneeling over his unarmored shoulder. He didn't remember removing the armor, or med-patches of a brand he didn't know being applied to it. He still re-projected the armor at the old knight's command, her words muffled to his ears and the projection sloppy.

Then Epha was gone, and he was staring at the ceiling. A drop of water had condensed at the tip of a stalactite, formed from the slight humidity within the cave. He watched it descend through the air, slow from his warped perception of time. He knew he had to stay still.

Before he could remember why, the ceiling blurred away. Jasto was being carried on a hard photothyst stretcher, looking back the way he'd come. He recognized the spot where he'd been laid down earlier.

Beside it were four blue, cracked, mannequin-like statues, each crumpled to the floor and leaking smoke, and a splatter of blood so bright it had to be human.

The image swept away, and the next thing Jasto remembered was opening his eyes, laying flat on the ground.

He waited for the image to sweep away or slow, but it didn't. Whatever Epha had given him had worn off, and he noticed a cool sensation emanating from his shoulder. Jasto almost screamed just out of instinct, but stopped himself as he realized the pain was gone. There were some aches in his back from laying on a rocky floor in full armor, but that was nothing. He was alright.

Blinking away his confusion, Jasto tried to put together what he'd seen. Epha had treated his shoulder and the strangely excessive pain he'd felt, which still had him flinching just from the memory of it. Then she'd left him, gone off to do something, and afterwards had moved him to this spot.

Somewhere in between those last two events, she'd fought against and killed four of Ralica's knaves. But why had Ralica attacked her?

Jasto thought of what he'd seen during their connection, her Diagram being swallowed by anger and almost enthralling him with it, and felt like he'd swallowed a stone. They might have killed Lenno, but he'd had years to leave his marks before then.

Was he safe here? A quick glance around revealed that he'd been set behind a wide, stone stalactite, and there were no photothyst pillars visible from where he was. Epha did apparently know these caves, it made sense that she'd found a spot for him away from any further action from Ralica.

There was no sign of the old knight herself, though. He couldn't hear anything besides the ambient noise of the cave, either, even when he dismissed the remains of his helmet and strained his ears. Maybe Epha was elsewhere, too far for him to hear.

Or maybe Ralica had killed her.

The thought should have had Jasto sitting up immediately, but the memory of the pain was still enough to make him hesitate. He had no idea if moving would disturb whatever Epha had done, or even make the pain come back. And after the chaos Jasto had been through he wanted to just stay still, to let whatever would happen come to him instead of throwing himself at it like he always did.

He breathed in, out, and tried not to think about anything.

He failed immediately. If Epha was alive, she'd be back eventually. If she was in battle, he'd hear it. If she was dead, he had time.

If she was corrupted...he also had time. Lenno had said that corrupting Epha without a more active thrall as a counterweight would have kept Seafall Palace latent. His actions matched up with that, since he'd never tried to enthrall Epha or any of the knights that had passed her trial. That meant all of them would have kept Ralica in a latent state, unlike him. And, latency and activity aside, he could barely imagine Epha losing to whatever Ralica threw at her.

But maybe he was wrong to think of her as nearly invincible. He'd thought he knew what he was getting into with this Palace, after all. He'd thought he understood Andalon, how the Round Table had come to power, and he'd been wrong.

He'd even thought he'd known himself. But then he'd seen the betrayal that ended the Drone War, heard Duskwall's fear of being controlled if he wasn't wielding absolute military power. He'd met Lenno again, seen the parallels between them, and had nearly been robbed of all choice and all independence by the thrall.

If those were the people Jasto saw himself reflected in, he didn't understand a thing.

His gaze wandered, trying to find some distraction from the bleak thoughts, and landed on his poleaxe. It had been placed flat on the ground near his feet, and he'd somehow missed it in his look around earlier. Its filaments glowed faintly, brightest near the two Lanterns in its head.

Ralica had made it possible for him to form those Lanterns, and they were at least part of the reason he was alive now. He had Dad to thank for that too, for the leverage he'd put on Epha to make her join him, and Epha herself to thank for rushing to his aid. All of them had made sacrifices for him. Had they made a mistake, trusting Jasto with that?

It was a horrible thought, malignant as Crest corruption, and he felt his heartbeat speed up as he turned it over.

An answer emerged: it was still up in the air, wasn't it? It still wasn't decided if they'd been wrong to trust in him. But if he didn't get up, they definitely would be. Jasto breathed in, out. In, out.

Then he made his choice.

The cool sensation in his shoulder began to fade as he sat up, and he tensed. But although the coolness went away, it wasn't suddenly replaced by an overwhelming pain. There was some stiffness and soreness in the arm, still pinned against his chest in the photothyst splint he'd projected, but nothing like the unnatural chemical shock he'd gotten earlier.

Still, Jasto was certain he'd be in a completely new pain if he tried to move his right arm at all. He projected a few more reinforcements to the splint he'd made, reformed his armor to its usual standard, and called his poleaxe up to his good hand. Jasto leaned on it to get to his feet, then stepped around the wide stalactite he'd been laid by.

Epha immediately came into his field of view, having been set up just on the other side of the rough stone column. She was kneeling, her helmet absent and a few hairs liberated from her military bun, but her gray photothyst armor had changed back over to its more durable cavalier plate form. Her eyes were shut tightly, and her face was lit from beneath by a deep golden glow.

That glow came from the longest filament Jasto had ever seen. It stretched out from Epha's limp right hand, dropped to the ground, and coiled into several overlapping circles around her before stretching outwards. The circles passed through a photothyst construct that made

Jasto think of a cigar cutter, two pieces that each held a Lantern forming a circular hole with a guillotine above it. A contingency in case corruption went up the filament, Jasto figured.

Not saying anything just yet, he followed the stretched-out end of the filament across the cave floor. It led to the base of one of the hexagonal, shadowed pillars of the Palace, as he'd expected.

What surprised him was how far away that pillar was. Other pillars could only be seen past the one Epha had connected to, and behind Jasto there was only more rock. In a technical sense, they were outside of Seafall Palace right now. And it must have been straining Epha mentally to create a filament long enough to cross that gap, even if she was a veteran. With that in mind, Jasto decided to stay quiet for now.

Eyes still closed, Epha breathed out and tilted her head forward slightly. In the distance Jasto saw the end of the filament rise up and slide into the pillar, a golden worm burrowing into blue photothyst.

Her eyes were still closed. How would she find a junction? Jasto couldn't even see where the filaments crossed at this distance. He squinted and noticed a severed, ball-jointed photothyst arm on the ground near the pillar. The limb was slowly eroding into nothing, meaning it had been cut some time ago.

Epha had fought knaves at least once more after moving him, then. Was Ralica only attacking if she got close to the pillars? Of course she was; Ralica was still latent, and the pillars marked her Palace's territory.

A quiet hiss drew his gaze back to Epha. Her eyes were still closed, but now she looked like she was going to bolt to her feet any second. The loops of the filament she'd made flexed slightly.

"Damn it, Seafall, you are *better* than this," Epha muttered. "Lenno is gone. By my own hand, he's gone! He was the one distorting you, creating this...this rage." the frown on her face deepened. "Why hasn't it lessened yet?"

Darkness bloomed from the pillar she was connected to as the corrupted filaments within it briefly drank even more light. For a moment the cave seemed to vanish, leaving just Epha, the lone pillar, and the golden line connecting them.

"Is it not only your voice that is gone now?" she asked, her normally clear tone wavering. "Can you communicate at all? I know I should have ended this sooner. I am sorry, Ral. I…I needed time, after what the knight-commanders did. And I needed to know there were still worthy people out there."

Epha's head curled downwards. Her body remained strangely still. "But I am ready, now," she said. "I…will follow the last orders you gave me. So before it's too late, please. Let me send you on, sister. The right way."

Jasto didn't dare to make a sound. The silence stretched, gaining weight.

Then shadows seemed to bunch up where the filament connected to the pillar, and corruption shot down it.

Filament attacks by corrupted knights were supposed to be slower than those done by the uncorrupted. Jasto wouldn't have been able to evade Lenno's attempts otherwise. But Ralica had been in an abnormal state already, staying latent for this long, and perhaps that was why it took little more than a second for shadows to devour the stretched-out part of the golden filament.

But Epha, even in her grief, had been prepared. As the corruption drew close to her it was forced to follow the stack of loops she'd made, passing through the cigar-cutter construct the old knight had formed, and she slammed it shut with four loops to spare. The corrupted filament broke off, leaving the old knight untouched, and her eyes snapped open.

Jasto thought it was over, but then dark fibers uncurled from the severed end of the filament and latched on to the uncorrupted loop leading to her hand. Had Ralica slingshotted them out from her pillar? Was that how the corruption had moved so quickly?

He dashed forward without an answer, moving quickly but not worriedly. After all, this wouldn't be a problem for Epha. She just had to yank out the filament where it connected to her wrist armor and she'd be fine.

But instead of that the old knight lurched back, falling on her side at an awkward angle as the black filament continued to squirm forward. Jasto cursed and lunged forward, dropping to his knees and slamming his hand down on the golden cord where it extended from her wrist.

It snapped, the corrupted side finally going limp, and he kicked it away. Jasto, crouched next to where Epha lay on her side, turned to look at her in disbelief.

"...You're awake," she said after a moment. The Lanterns set in her breastplate glowed, and he stepped back as she lurched onto her feet. The movement reminded him more of a puppet than a person.

"Combat stimulants and painkillers rarely mix well, Chaston," Epha said like everything was normal. "There are some combinations that won't produce the sort of backlash you just received, but those will depend in part on your own physiology. Just purchasing supplies that all have the same brand is not enough to avoid that. Fortunately I had a neutralizing agent in my own kit. It does warp perception for a time, but judging by your gaze that effect seems to be—"

"—You're paralyzed, aren't you," Jasto said, putting it together. "That's why you're only using your Lanterns to move."

Epha's expression locked up. It spoke to the old knight's fine control that she'd managed to treat Jasto, fight off knaves, and move around even in a state like that, especially with the limitations on Lanterns. They could push their creator around horizontally, the same way anyone sitting on a cart could push themselves around with their hands. But if a Lantern tried to lift up its creator, it would be like that same person trying to grab and lift themselves into the air. Even so, she'd maneuvered without issue.

"I am not paralyzed," Epha said, her voice low. "The nerves below my Crest were damaged, a consequence of being so close to corruption, but that is all." One of her arms came up, and to demonstrate Epha made a fist. "This is a temporary state. Once the dendritic repair tablets I took have had time to work, it will be gone."

Even shut into a fist, her fingers still shook visibly and it was a clear effort to keep them closed. Jasto was surprised to see Epha being so defensive about the damage. The old knight had struck him as the type to wear her injuries with pride, but maybe there was some deeper issue there.

"Alright then," he said instead of pressing the matter, glancing at the pillar she'd been connected to.

They had bigger concerns, for better or worse. At the elevator Epha had linked to the Palace with little issue, and had even gotten

Ralica to interfere with Lenno. Now she couldn't connect without Ralica trying to corrupt her.

Not to mention the attack he vaguely remembered. "Did Ralica send knaves after us?" Jasto asked.

Epha nodded grimly. "It was worse than the previous times when her control slipped. Her Crest demands that she attack intruders in some way, and she often does so with restrictions. But this time, the attacks continued until we left the territory of her Palace." Her eyes darkened. "That has not happened before. And when I checked on her mental state just now…only scraps of her Diagram are still blue. It is like she is falling apart all at once."

The resignation in her voice was what got to Jasto, more than anything else. "She cannot even communicate anymore. If only I had ended it sooner…"

"Wait, she can't communicate at all? Not even those emotion transfers?" Jasto asked.

"You have experienced them?" Epha's gaze had shifted to the side as she'd spoken earlier, but now it landed squarely back on him. "That would explain why you've stopped referring to her as Seafall. Did you feel something other than anger when you did?"

"Uh, yes. Though that was definitely there, too."

"Right now anger is all that is being transmitted, overriding any other emotion or memory. I need to know how it came to this. Tell me exactly what has happened since we separated, Chaston."

It was reassuring to see Epha return to her all-business disposition. Jasto briefly discussed the trials he'd faced earlier, intending to give more details on the encounter with Lenno and the events afterward.

But Epha stopped him before he made it to that topic, asking several questions about the trials and the ways Ralica had communicated with him. She saw his confusion at the inquiries, and quickly explained.

"It is strange that Ralica was able to send you messages, and arrange these trials," Epha said. "After our separation at the elevator, I immediately attempted filament connections to try and find you. But although Ralica didn't attempt to corrupt me then, she also didn't respond at all. I had thought she was drained, from the effort of interfering with Lenno, or that her mind had wandered as it sometimes does."

"That is weird," Jasto said. "Maybe all of her attention was on me?"

"Hm, perhaps." Epha looked down in thought. "It has only been me entering this place for years. If Ralica could only focus her attention on one place within the Palace at a time I would not have noticed, on account of only being one person." Her expression became somber. "Then her deterioration has been worse than I thought for a while now."

Jasto imagined moving just one part of his body at a time, or only being able to work one portion of his mind instead of the whole thing at once. It was a scary idea, and apparently not too far off from the state Ralica was in. Or from the state Epha was in, thanks to her paralysis, and the symmetry there had him feeling a little sick.

"What happened after the trials?" she asked, prompting him to continue. He got back on task and outlined his arrival in this memorial section of the Palace, Lenno's ambush, and the assistance Ralica had given him during the battle.

Once more Epha stopped him. "She lent to you, Chaston? Even though she was corrupted?" the lines on the old knight's face pressed together as her brow furrowed. "That is unheard of."

"Lending?" Jasto asked. It was his first time hearing the term. "So every Crestbearer can do that?"

Epha nodded. "Every crystal knight can take some of the Crest burden from another by connecting with them. But again, for a corrupted knight to do so for an uncorrupted one..." a strange expression, prideful but also rueful, came over Epha's face. "But you always were like that, Ralica," she murmured. "And I remained here for years as well. Neither of us ever truly learned how to stop."

"...Anyway," Jasto said, feeling awkward, "Both Ralica and I were pretty sure that wouldn't be enough. That's when I got the idea to have Ralica call you here."

"And then you battled with Lenno until I arrived?"

"Yeah. You know how that part went, and then after Lenno was down...I tried to lend to you, but I was being drained too fast. So I got some help, from Ralica." Jasto quickly explained the strange three-part filament connection he'd managed to form, and the way it had changed Ralica's Diagram.

Whatever pride had been on Epha's face dripped away as he talked. "Then it was preventing my corruption that did it," she said, looking at the pillar she'd connected with. "That drained the last of Ralica's humanity, and pushed her into…that."

"Is she going active?" Jasto asked. If she was, he'd need to make a cart or something for Epha and get them both out of here as fast as possible.

"Ralica is not exhibiting the behavior of an active corrupted," Epha said carefully. "If she was she would be attacking us now, despite the fact we are outside of her Palace. And from what you've told me, it was Lenno pushing her into an active state. Something I had years to realize myself, but failed to." Epha looked down for a moment before continuing. "Regardless, even if Lenno's influence left marks, it would no longer be a constant struggle for Ralica to remain latent."

"But?"

"But she is displaying the maximum possible hostility for a latent Palace. She even attacked me several times, as you saw. For that reason…I believe she will become active in a few days, at most," Epha said.

Jasto stared at her for a moment. Then he practically growled out his next words. "Then why the *hell* didn't you wake me up sooner? Her entire knave army's about to be unleashed! Why aren't we getting ready to attack her right now?!"

"Because we cannot defeat Ralica, let alone all her knaves, in our current state," Epha snapped.

"Are you losing your memory, Suncage? I brought mercenaries with," Jasto pressed. "You've been here before, you know these caves. Chart us a course back to the surface right now, so I can call them and put an end to this dreck!"

In truth, the idea of Ralica having an unceremonious death under a hail of high-penetration rounds didn't quite sit right with him. But personal preference was the last priority on his mind, with her possibly going active so soon. Dad would be in danger if she did, not just him and Epha.

"Do you not understand? Even then it won't be enough," Epha insisted. "I know this Palace, the forces it holds, better than anyone save Ralica herself. Your hired guns will do damage but they won't survive, not all the way to the central chamber. Even in the best case where they have carved a path for us there, the two of us *cannot* win if Ralica uses her full strength and as long as she is in this berserk state, she will."

"I know we're injured, but the mercs brought a full medical suite with them," Jasto pressed. "Your nerves are already healing. Even if my arm can't be repaired in a day, you've seen how I fight with just one. I know it won't be a guaranteed win, but with that and your Crest ability—"

"—My Lantern-fire is gone."

Jasto's naturally wide eyes widened even further, and the old knight sighed. "This sometimes happens to a Crest, when it comes close to corruption," she explained, her tone clinical. "A knight's connection to it can be…damaged, with varying effects. Using my Crest ability is now 'beyond the limits' of what my Crest is meant to be capable of."

"Wait, then I—" Jasto checked his Diagram, giving the tiniest twitch of force to his Crest ability. He'd already made projections without any issue, but quickly moved all his Lanterns back and forth to make sure they still worked.

"I believe your connection with Ralica was too brief to suffer any negative effects," Epha informed him. "Moreover, you mentioned that the clouds you saw disappeared from your Diagram. Corruption will always leave markers there if it is present."

Jasto scanned his night sky, looking for any trace of a cloud, and slumped with relief when he found none. "Wait, does that mean your Diagram is different now?" he asked a second later, looking back up. He hadn't been able to pay much attention to it after starting the connection with Ralica.

Epha hesitated, almost looking away from him. "Actually…sorry," he said as he got it. "You don't have to tell me." She'd had her Crest for the majority of her life and clearly took pride in it, of course this would be a sore spot. One that Jasto, admittedly, might not have felt the urge to step around at the start of the day.

The old knight nodded in thanks, and continued her explanation as if he hadn't interrupted. "My Lantern-fire was not the only loss. These nine Lanterns continue to work, but I cannot make more without my Crest taking over. Each one I lose now, I lose permanently."

Just yesterday Epha had been a force of nature, a knight Jasto was confident he couldn't have beaten even with the team he'd hired.

193

Now, in what felt like an instant, that strength had been stripped away. But maybe that was the wrong way of thinking about it, Jasto considered. Epha had dedicated the last years of her life to this hermit-like way of living, spent herself watching over Ralica, running her trial and trying to find the strength to end her old friend's misery.

Maybe this loss had been in the wings for a long time. "My ability to make projections was untouched, but that is all," Epha said. "I made a promise to Ralica and I failed, Jasto. Completely and utterly. In light of that I must apologize for how I have treated you, for I held you to standards that I myself fell short of."

She looked at him. He'd thought once that her eyes were like layered rock, but now they were twin sinkholes leading to the same dark, dreary pit. "I will offer reparations," Epha said. "I will petition the Round Table regarding your squire-errant status, to see if it can be repealed. Duskwall will be glad to have my attention on something less politically dangerous for him, after all these years, so I suspect I will succeed after some engagement. Now follow me. We will have to briefly cut back into Palace territory, but afterwards we simply keep to the rightmost cave wall to reach the surface."

She turned, the movement jerky since it had to be done with just Lanterns. Jasto barely noticed. He was staring at the pillars of Seafall Palace, unable to make himself move.

It made complete, logical sense to retreat given the damage Epha had taken. Her Lantern-fire was undoubtedly the biggest loss from her near corruption; it was a Crest ability almost tailor-made to deal with photothyst enemies.

Jasto was sure Dad would have come to the same conclusion, if he was here. He might have deliberated with Epha a bit more, ensuring there really was no way to still kill Ralica and take her Crest. But then he would have shook his head at the wasted time and effort, and turned to follow her without any further thought on it.

But Jasto had felt Ralica's desperation, her furious need to stay latent and remain in control of herself. It was so familiar. And unlike with Lenno, the recognition that he had something in common with this corrupted knight didn't burn him.

Could he really deny Ralica an ending on her own terms?

Jasto whirled, plans and arguments forming on his lips as he considered ways to get into the Palace, and to get Epha to agree to help him.

They all spun apart before he could say a thing, as he saw the object encased in her back armor. Epha turned, looking mildly confused.

"Chaston?" she asked. "While we likely have time before this Palace becomes active, it would still be best to leave now."

"Uh, Suncage," he began carefully. "When did Ralica start sending knaves at you?"

She frowned, but perhaps saw the seriousness in his easy-to-read face and answered him straightforwardly. "Not until forty-five minutes or so after Lenno's death. That is why I had time to see to your injuries."

"But that wasn't all you did, right?" After all, he was staring at evidence she had done more than just that.

Epha finally followed his gaze down to the object within her armor, and nodded. "Ah, I forgot to mention earlier that I had claimed this. I will also be giving it to you once we've left, Chaston, as further compensation. I understand that taking it may make you uncomfortable, but it is fully inert now and has no more connection to its previous holder. It cannot harm you."

"That's not—" Crystal fucking Star, she hadn't realized. How could she not have realized? All the facts were right there. Epha was looking at him once more, clearly not understanding how they fit together.

All the messiness within Jasto faded to the background. It could wait, in the face of a problem this obvious. "This is important, Suncage," he began, preparing himself for an unpleasant conversation. He pointed at the red object sealed in her armor.

It was about the size of his hand, crystalline, rectangular, and edged with complex, serrated embellishments like a coat of arms. Set in the object's center was an intricate symbol reminiscent of a wreath of leaves, almost entirely black with only faint tinges of purple at the edges.

"Did Ralica send any knaves to attack you," he asked, "Before you extracted the Ironskin Crest from Lenno?"

Epha frowned at the question, thinking. Then she engaged her Lanterns and pivoted on the spot to face him fully.

"What on earth are you suggesting, Chaston?" she asked, and just from her tone Jasto knew he'd guessed right.

"You can tell," he said. "Ralica probably is at the edge of going active, yeah. But she was still in control, still holding herself back. Until you took that Crest." In other words, Ralica was essentially drunk; her mind had been damaged and filled to bursting with anger, but it was still her making choices rather than her Crest.

Including the choice to send knaves after Epha. "That is...no," the old knight insisted. "No, if she was still that lucid she wouldn't have attacked me. She had other ways to make her intentions clear."

"You said she can't communicate anymore," Jasto replied. "What if it's more than that? What if she can only interact by attacking now?"

"Then she would not have attacked," Epha declared, her voice rising. "Not with this level of killing intent. Ralica has attacked me before, yes, but she was forced to by her Crest restrictions. And yet you are saying she would choose to go after me so lethally if she had a choice in the matter? No. She would *never* be that petty, even in the depths of corruption."

And with those words, it clicked. Epha hadn't been holding this desert vigil in the middle of nowhere alone; she'd been doing so alongside Ralica. One had held the trial, and dealt with the interlopers that tried to disrupt it, while the other had fought to stay latent and in control. Epha had been looking to Ralica for the strength to keep it going. And now he was telling her that Ralica had flinched first.

Jasto understood why Epha couldn't accept that. He understood, and he didn't feel disdain.

"It wasn't just the Crest she had to struggle with," Jasto said, calming his words. "The Crest restrictions prevent corrupted knights from infighting, when one is the thrall of another. Try to picture it, Suncage. Picture being stuck here for years while someone corrupted you more and more every day, unable to do anything to stop them. Picture Lenno killing everyone that was sent down here to potentially help. Being unable to tell your closest friend any of this, because your Crest wouldn't allow you to endanger your thrall."

And dreck, even with Epha here, the isolation Ralica would've felt...it must have been thousands of times worse than what Jasto had been through at the Valor Academy. But she'd held on for so long, remaining latent even in the most horrible of circumstances. He'd barely made it a single year before getting himself expelled.

"No," Epha said, finding her voice again, but it was smaller. "No, Ralica wouldn't do something so…"

"Don't say it's petty," Jasto said quietly. "*I'm* petty. Ralica stayed latent for years with Lenno whispering in her ear. Even now she's still trying to hold on, to point herself at the Crest instead of the knight-commanders and all the innocent people between her and them. Probably all she can do after lending to us."

Ralica was human, he decided. Not petty. Epha looked off to the side, her face cast in golden filament-light. It was hard to read what she was feeling, except that it was horrible.

"Despite how vulnerable of a target you were, Ralica did not send any of her knaves to attack you," Epha said. Every word seemed to face heavy resistance. "I found it odd. A latent knight may not pursue unbound Crests very strongly, depending on their circumstances, but they do tend to seek new thralls."

Jasto was about to say even more, but managed to stop himself. Epha didn't need commentary from him, positive or negative, to open her eyes right now. She just needed to come to terms with Ralica, her oldest friend, leader, and emotional crutch, not being perfect.

He turned away to give her some privacy. Didn't listen too closely to the shaky breathing that came from behind him, the faint almost-sob that followed.

He had to let his own dreck go, didn't he? Even if he didn't end up as the perfectly unbendable Crestbearer he wanted to be, even if the Valor Academy did get into his head a little, he still had to let go of his spite for it. Otherwise he'd end up like Lenno one day, robbing people of their choices and creating tragedies like this because he'd convinced himself he was righteous.

Not that he was planning to do nothing, after what he'd learned about the misery Ralica had gone through. But whatever consequences the Round Table faced would happen because of what they'd done, not Jasto's personal indignation at them.

Photothyst clanked against stone as Epha came up beside him. Her steps were beginning to get smoother, more controlled despite being done only via Lanterns. Similarly, her expression was sorrowful but composed.

"As I said, I had been planning to give this to you," she told him, bringing up the Ironskin Crest. It sat cradled within one of her flechettes now, which had been reshaped into a carrier. "It would not have empowered you as much as the Seafall Crest, but would still have boosted you significantly." She looked at him. "Would you have accepted it?"

"I…don't know," Jasto said. The Crest was just a tool now, no longer carrying any of Lenno's influence. Even so, if he had a choice, he wouldn't pick it.

Epha nodded, then continued looking at him. "Well?"

"Well what?" Jasto said, confused.

Her eyes narrowed. "Are you claiming you said all of that for no reason? Was it not a buildup to suggesting some course of action? If not, then we will still need to retreat."

"Right, right, a course of action. I…" Jasto floundered. He'd been so focused on the moment that he hadn't thought about what would happen if he actually did bring Epha around. "Uh…"

Epha sighed, then actually smiled a little. "I suppose you are still young, Jasto. Some poor planning is to be expected."

"Hey, don't make this about that," he muttered, though it hadn't escaped his notice that she was using his first name now. He decided to do the same. "Just let me think, Epha."

She nodded, and he turned back to the roots of the Palace and put his mind to work. He wanted to end Ralica's suffering, just like she and Epha also wanted. There had to be a way.

The facts first. Ralica, after lending to both Jasto and Epha, was effectively at the end of her rope. The anger Lenno had placed in her had gone wild after her sacrifice, though ironically that rage was now targeted at the thrall's own Crest.

Jasto knew better than to think it would stay there. If Ralica was given the Crest and did get to destroy it, as she probably wanted to, he was sure she'd quickly find a new target for her rage in the knight-commanders. Her shift to an active state would be guaranteed if that happened. That meant letting her destroy the Crest and trying to have a duel immediately afterwards was out.

But for now, somehow, she was still holding herself back. Jasto checked behind himself and flared his filaments to confirm a hunch. Sure enough, this portion of the wide cavern stretched a few more yards away before narrowing down to an impassable crag.

That was probably by design. Ralica, while latent, could only attack people within the Palace. So she'd herded Jasto and Epha into this limited space, where they could only leave by passing through the Palace again. That fact was probably helping Ralica remain stable for now, as uncomfortable as the thought was.

He looked back towards its blue pillars, knowing that Ralica was watching. How could he get her to put this grudge aside? To accept a clean death?

Jasto only considered the thought for a moment before discarding it, shaking his head. This had been building up within Ralica for years, as he'd just explained to Epha, and it couldn't just be dropped.

So how could he work around that grudge instead?

Jasto looked down, remembering the terms Epha had leveled on him yesterday and the only reason he'd agreed to them, and found a surprisingly simple answer. He turned to the old knight, purpose igniting behind his eyes.

"Epha, there are limits to what Ralica can do here, right? Since it's the edge of her Palace?"

She considered his question for a moment. "In the same way that food takes time to be digested after it is eaten, this area of Palace territory is not as integrated as the rest of it. Her projections here would be restricted to barricades and obstacles of a limited volume, yes." Then an arm Lantern glowed as she raised a hand in caution. "However, even food not fully digested is still within the stomach. Both Ralica and her knaves can move however she wishes down here, as long as they do not step past the pillars."

"Okay," Jasto replied. What Epha had said sounded familiar, from his time at the Academy, but he wanted to make sure he had every detail right. "Okay, what if she goes active? Could she plug these caves completely, make giant projections from her Palace until it crushed us?"

Epha squinted at him. "Please," he pressed.

After a moment she sighed, and gave him his answer without asking why he needed it. "There are several reasons that would be unlikely. For one, active Palaces require materials to grow, and even if Ralica harvested appropriate metal deposits from these caves she would still need time to process them. Though if she was truly driven, and began her shift into an active state at the same time that she began to gather materials…"

"Wait," Jasto said. "Her *shift* into an active state? It's not instantaneous?"

Epha frowned at him. "Jasto, what on earth has the Valor Academy come to? Even though you spent only a year there, you know far less than you should."

Jasto looked away, sucking his teeth. "No, that's on me. I had problems there, with…" he paused, frowning. He'd genuinely been about to open up to Epha about his issues with the Valor Academy. Her, of all people, without it feeling like the wrong call.

Lenno had said fighting besides someone changed things. Maybe it was the one point he'd actually been right about. "Well, maybe I'll talk about that if we survive this," he said instead, meaning it. "How long would it take Ralica to go active, if she started right now?"

Epha looked up at the Palace, her weathered eyes narrowing. "Larger sizes correspond to larger transition times," she murmured. "The full volume of Seafall Palace is unknown due to its subterranean structure, but from what I have seen…between two and seven hours. I cannot be more specific, unfortunately."

Jasto breathed out in relief. "No need," he said. "The way out of here is to just hug the right-side walls, yeah?" Epha nodded.

"Good," he said, rubbing at the stripes shaved into his hair. They were crusted with sweat after all he'd been through, and even a little blood. "I need a reactive painkiller."

Epha looked at him like she was about to object. Jasto hadn't said what he was going to try yet, but his uneasiness at the idea of it was written all over him. Just like all his emotions.

"I need it to end this, Epha," he said, before the old knight could speak. "To put her to rest. She needs that."

Pure grief filled Epha's face. "Yes, Jasto," she replied, her voice somehow steady. "Yes she does."

Her forearm plates dissipated, and the Lanterns within floated out. Epha quickly projected blunt hooks over both, and they zipped

200

behind her back to grab her medical kit and present it. "Third pouch from the left, in the top half."

Jasto unzipped the kit and quickly found the right pocket. He withdrew a marble-colored pill wrapped in plastic, indistinguishable from a piece of candy except for the red warning labels printed over its wrapper and on its surface. It looked far too ordinary the price he knew it had.

After a moment, he grabbed another. "Just in case," he said at Epha's look. "I don't want to screw this up."

"And what is it, exactly, that you do not wish to fail at?" Epha asked. "You have yet to reveal your plan."

"Oh, right," Jasto said. "It's like this: When I first came here, I wasn't sure if you'd actually part with the Crest. So in case you didn't, I had…backup plans."

"Which would have involved killing me," Epha replied, her tone flat.

"Yeah. Sorry," Jasto said. Owning up to it might not mean much, but he'd do so anyway. Epha didn't seem overly offended by the revelation, simply shaking her head.

"As if I would refuse to relinquish it," the old knight muttered. "After years of trying to find…" she seemed to remember Jasto was there, and cut off the thought. "But what was the relevance of this?"

"It's that even before I entered this Palace I had to abandon those plans completely." Jasto got to work on his armor as he spoke, dismissing the treads to create wheels, but they were projected differently than his usual. These wheels were covered with small rectangles at irregular heights, an all-terrain form. "You know why?"

Epha tilted her head, figuring it out quickly. "Because you saw my Lantern-fire. You realized you could not defeat me."

"Right. Exactly." It was strange to look back on that moment when he'd had no choice now, after seeing all it had led to. Maybe people needed that sometimes, Jasto supposed, like Epha had said. Especially when someone wanted power, maybe the process of getting it needed to be uncomfortable. Otherwise they'd never question it, just like he wouldn't have questioned himself without Epha's restrictions.

"I couldn't defeat you, so I had to play along. Even though that meant putting up with your sparring match, leaving my mercenaries, and even having to leave my ammo behind," Jasto continued, patches of his skin prickling as he finished the all-terrain wheels. "I would never have done any of that dreck without you leveraging me." He dismissed his poleaxe, slid the two Lanterns it held into his back armor.

"Jasto, even if you adjust your armor you will not have enough strength to leverage Ralica." From Epha's tone, she was worried his memory of that fact was damaged. Instead of taking offense, he just grinned.

"There's more than one kind of leverage, Epha. If I was a typical crystal knight, I'd be stumped here. But I designed these wheels because I wanted to do things differently, remember?"

Then he told her the full extent of his plan, whispering to make sure Ralica didn't pick it up.

When he was done and stepped back, rolling his good shoulder, Epha just stared at him.

"If you've got a better idea, let's hear it," Jasto said as the silence grew. At that, the old knight looked up with a considering expression.

"If your earlier conclusions about Ralica were correct, I believe it could work. And no alternatives occur to me," she said. "But Jasto, are you certain? To take a risk like this, to put to rest a woman you barely know…"

"It's not really about that," Jasto admitted. "I mean, I want to help Ralica. But I think I have to do this anyway."

Because if he didn't, what had even been the point of leaving the Academy? Staying as himself wouldn't mean much, if it didn't actually change how he lived his life.

Epha smirked at his response. "What?" Jasto asked.

"Ralica once gave me the chance to leave her service," Epha replied. "I told her something similar." The old knight engaged her Lanterns, stepping forward before Jasto could even begin to process that. "But regarding your plan, your helmet design is far too much of a liability for it. It would be better for your understanding to learn the trick on your own, but since time is short I'll explain how to make smaller pieces of photothyst translucent…"

Jasto was caught off guard by the lesson, but listened attentively and understood what he needed to do after only a few minutes. Then he popped the first reactive painkiller, tossing the wrapper away, and closed his eyes to focus on his Diagram.

First Jasto projected his helmet, without the visor, and filled in some of the empty spaces with additional protective layers. He waited for the Crystal Star to clear out his mind fully, then stuck a mental stylus into his Diagram and connected several of the stars in an arcing oblong far smaller than his usual visor.

Then he duplicated the shape, drawing lines from it to form another visor that was linked to the first along one edge, but didn't touch any stars. He did this several more times, forming a stack of the curved pieces. The topmost one, furthest from the stars he'd initially connected to, felt less substantive to his mental senses.

Jasto isolated it, projecting just that layer, and it formed in front of his eyes. He opened them to see that his range of vision had only dropped a touch, and in exchange a major weak point was now gone. He clenched a hand shut in triumph, and left the mental construct in his Diagram in case he needed to reproject his new visor.

Epha made a small noise of approval. "A single try? Your talent as a knight is extraordinary, Jasto."

With all his mixed feelings on knighthood, he decided it would be best to ignore that comment completely. "Any other tips before I do this?" he asked instead.

"No, my wisdom has reached its limits here," Epha said, bringing up the Ironskin Crest. It sat cradled within one of her flechettes, which had been reshaped into a carrier. "I am a typical crystal knight, after all. What you intend is very atypical."

Jasto frowned as he took the Crest, sealing it in place above the splint for his bad arm. "I guess that is true, huh."

"I wish I could do more to guide you," Epha said. "But such is the price of my decisions. It is in your hands now."

"Epha, are you…" Jasto paused, realizing this wasn't the time to get bogged down in another talk. Not when his adrenaline was already rising.

"Nevermind," he said instead. "Time to do things my way."

And with a nod from the old knight, he turned to face the Palace.

"RALICA!" Jasto yelled, striding forward. "Maybe you're damaged right now. Maybe your emotions are screwy, maybe your memories are."

He stopped, still clear of her territory, and tapped the Crest nestled to his breastplate. "But I know you recognize this."

Within the pillars, filaments crawled towards each other to form dozens of circular clumps. Faint rings of silver light, which would have been impossible to see without the deep shadow filling the space, formed around each.

Ralica was watching. Jasto took a deep breath, leaned into a stance. "Well, if you want it…" he flexed his Crest ability, feeling raw force conduct from the Star down to his body, from his Lanterns down to his wheels.

"…Then come get it!" he finished, shooting forward.

The cave terrain was rough. His shoulder was still damaged, and any jostling would bring him pain. But he'd prepared for both of those things.

He activated his back-mounted Lanterns as he gained speed, providing downforce like Epha did with her own Lanterns. His wheels bucked, but he kept his course regardless.

And as pain began to spike from his shoulder the reactive painkiller kicked in, responding to the nerve signals his body sent out. It washed over the jolts like cool water, dulling the sensation and freeing him to speed up.

Jasto did exactly that as he passed back into the Palace territory, but Ralica was already reacting. Jasto caught a dark shape swimming to the edge of one of the pillars, at least ten meters off the ground, and a knave tore itself loose as he passed under it. It was leaping through the air a split second later, all its mannequin limbs curled forward like a blue, man-sized spider in order to catch him. The knave had led its leap, aiming for where Jasto was about to be.

He swerved, ignoring the suppressed flare of pain from his arm as he made a rapid turn. The knave hit the ground ahead of him but he was already away, and regaining the little speed he'd lost.

It turned to charge him on four legs without missing a beat, and more knaves began to emerge from the pillars. The first ones formed a cordon between him and the alcove where Epha waited, but that didn't matter right now. Jasto hadn't made his point yet.

"Most knights get corrupted by accident. But not you, Ralica," Jasto said as he changed directions once more. The knaves weren't as fast as him, even on four legs, but they were starting to form a rough circle around him. He broke towards one side of it, holding the course just long enough for the knaves there to tighten ranks. Then he juked sideways, taking advantage of the gap they'd created at the edges.

One got within arm's reach of Jasto, but then he was clear. He straightlined for a bit, putting some distance between himself and the gathering of knaves. "You did this to save your people, as many as you could," Jasto continued, "But then you were stuck, right? The corrupted can't end themselves."

He saw a shadow move inside an oncoming column and turned away from it, then had to redirect again as a spike strip was projected from another column. "And then you had Lenno to deal with, so it all got muddled," he added, ducking a spear one knave had thrown the moment he'd slowed down. He did a quick circle to take in the battlefield, saw filaments beginning to unfurl between two of the pillars, and shot through them before the barricade could finish projecting. "I don't blame you, Ralica, but not just because of all that."

Shocks rippled through his shoulder as he moved, more sensation than pain thanks to the combat drug in his system. "I don't blame you," he said between breaths, "because I'm the same way."

One knave was separated from the others. It rushed to join up with the group until Jasto suddenly came to a dead stop in front of it, giving Ralica a golden opportunity.

Without hesitation the knave lurched back into a two-legged stance, a long hook forming out of one hand as it lunged for Jasto. He reversed his wheels, then twisted and darted to the left as it lunged again.

"I just wanted to get out of the Valor Academy, at first," Jasto said, dodging two more strikes. "But then it started to become something more than that. Something—" the knave managed to hook his leg but he let himself fall, shooting away on his back wheels as the larger group began to close in.

"Something worse," he continued, getting back to his feet and picking up speed. "And I wouldn't have noticed, if I hadn't been forced to play along by Epha here."

The knaves tried for another encirclement, and Jasto knew the trick he'd used last time wouldn't work again. He made it look like he was going for it anyway, speeding up towards one part of the closing circle. Ralica clustered up her knaves, leaving gaps in the formation to bait him this time. He shot towards one, saw the knaves on either side of it suddenly raise a photothyst chain strung at hip level.

Jasto dropped to one knee and leveraged all his Lanterns in a move that would have been impossible with only two. Sparks flared, carving a tight, furious arc around him as he pivoted on a dime to shoot back the way he'd come. A single knave still blocked his path, rushing forward on four legs, and he jumped.

His wheels skidded across its doll-like back and he was clear, hitting the ground hard enough that the painkiller didn't quite block it. Jasto sucked a breath in quietly, blinking the black spots away from his eyes. He couldn't show weakness here. He wouldn't.

Ralica had gotten him off the dark course he'd been stuck to. He'd do the same for her. "The thing is!" he said once his voice had stabilized. "You don't want to stop, just like I didn't, but you'll have to. Watch!"

When he turned back towards the alcove Epha was in, Ralica went berserk. The knaves rushed him, all tactics disregarded, and the pillars suddenly sucked in twice as much light as they normally did while tripwires and spikes projected from every piece of photothyst at once.

Jasto flared his own filaments, white shining against the black and blue of the Palace, and met the gauntlet head-on.

He tucked his shoulder, passing within inches of an outstretched hook, then dropped to both knees as a knave sailed over his head. A moment later he had to balance on his hand and one knee wheel to avoid a spike row, muscles tensing as armored fingertips trailed sparks along the stone, then stand back up just as quickly to swerve around a low barricade.

All that within a handful of seconds. Ralica was reacting well, improvising projections and tactics to stop Jasto with incredible speed, but that was the thing: against him, she *had* to improvise. Because even if she had fought a typical knight who could move like him, they would still have been using that speed to close in on Ralica.

Whereas Jasto was using it to escape her. He was close now, swinging to the side as he cleared another obstacle and immediately threading the needle between two more knaves. He corrected his course as he passed by and almost didn't see the next tripwire, reinforced and almost invisible in the enhanced darkness. He caught it just in time to spin on himself and set up a short hop.

Another knave dropped towards him right after, and Jasto nearly lost his footing as he tried to deal with both it and the suddenly bumpier section of the cave. One barricade was left between him and Epha, twice as tall as he was, made of solid photothyst, and sloped inwards. Ralica's last attempt to stop him.

Jasto slammed himself back on course with his Lanterns, found a pillar made of rock instead of photothyst, and shot towards it as his brain shifted into its highest gear. He danced through his Diagram, sketching out and projecting spikes over his wheels in a cascade of successive commands, his consciousness almost disappearing as it mingled with flickers of the Crystal Star passing over his mind.

But he was Jasto Chaston, *Jasto Chaston*, and he came back to himself just in time to jump.

With any set of materials other than photothyst and stone, he was sure what happened next would have been impossible. But the toothed wheels on his shins and his good arm dug into the pillar, finding just enough purchase as he spun them with his Crest ability, and Jasto climbed several feet up the pillar before turning and kicking off.

Filaments sprung from the barricade as he dropped towards the sloped top of it, but Jasto had momentum and that was all he needed. The wheels on his back caught the top, and a shock went through his system as the painkiller was nearly overtaxed, but he kept his control and slid off the barricade too quickly to be corrupted.

Jasto hit the ground and bled the last of his speed into a wide, sweeping turn that ended right next to Epha, as she immediately raised her flechettes to ward off any pursuers.

It was unnecessary, though, Jasto saw as he peered through the translucent barricade. Even before reaching the edge of the Palace, the knaves had come to a stop. Like they'd realized it was futile.

"Looks like you get it, Ralica," he called. "I'm injured, tired, and one of my arms is completely out. But I can still move like this, and Epha already told me how to get out of these caves." He detached the Ironskin Crest from his chest, held it up like a trump card. "If I take this and run, you can't stop me from absorbing it. Even going active, you won't be fast enough!"

The shadows pulsed, every filament within the cave swallowing all the light it could and plunging the space into darkness. Jasto tensed, but even though he could hardly see the knaves it was enough to tell that they weren't moving. He'd been right, and Ralica did want the Ironskin Crest destroyed at all costs.

That meant he could leverage her, just like Epha had leveraged him. "You want the Crest, but you can't get it. I want *your* Crest, but you're not dead," he pressed. "So I seek to resolve this, because it can't be ignored!"

The formal challenge to a duel echoed through the cave. Jasto's heart jackhammered in his chest.

This was easily the most desperate gamble he'd ever taken. If Ralica wanted the Crest badly enough to accept, Jasto would still have to actually step back into the Palace to duel her. There would be nothing, nothing at all, stopping her from drowning him in knaves the moment he did.

Nothing except her integrity as a knight, and the fear that he might escape despite her best efforts. "And if you accept, we'll duel right here," Jasto said as he pointed at the cave. "Right where we killed Lenno for you." He exhaled, grateful that he'd locked that down before Ralica could try to get him deeper into the Palace.

Only the faint silhouette of the barricade was visible within the darkness of Ralica's pillars. Jasto stabilized his breathing, in through the nose and out through the mouth, and waited for a response.

If Ralica was too far gone, like Epha had initially assumed, then Jasto's stunt wouldn't have meant anything. Ralica would just be too far gone to accept a duel, even when leveraged. But if she was still in there, and could still make choices, then there was a chance this would work.

"Is there a way we can check?" Jasto asked after a minute had gone by. "You said she can't communicate anymore."

"Not through the filaments, in any case," Epha said. "And her knight body lost the ability to speak some time ago." She frowned, then blinked as if suddenly uncovering an old memory. "But perhaps…" One of Epha's flechettes came forward, and she projected a flat striking surface over one end. Then she hammered it against the stone three times, paused, struck twice, then let a shorter interval pass before again striking twice. The clang of photothyst on stone echoed through the dark cave.

Two knocks, then one, then three, then one. Epha looked down, ever so slightly.

"We created that code when we were children," she said. "Her answer means agreement."

"I..." Jasto was about to offer his condolences, but he stopped himself. Epha had grown up with the corrupted knight he was about to duel to the death. Not only that, Ralica had just confirmed, beyond any doubt, that she'd been lucid through her attempts to kill her old friend. Could he really say anything that would match the depth of what she was feeling?

No, he decided. So instead he nodded, and turned towards the cave as the sounds of shifting photothyst began to echo from the darkness. It didn't seem like a follow-up knocking code, but rather like the knaves within were moving things around. He exchanged a glance with Epha, who simply raised her eyebrows at him before summoning her helmet.

"We will see what she intends soon enough," the old knight said, rearranging her Lanterns in case it came to combat.

"Right." Jasto widened his stance and projected a Lanternless axe. Just in case.

He caught a flicker of movement within the shadow, one portion of the barricade seeming to fold down and inwards on itself. A humanoid silhouette stood, carrying the collapsed portion, and other barricade segments began to fold in as well.

"They're moving photothyst around," Jasto said. With the ability of knave cores to liquefy and reshape the material, it was certainly possible. "But why isn't Ralica just projecting whatever she's trying to make?"

"Because of her limitations in this part of the Palace, and to avoid giving her Crest any further inroads," Epha said. "So I suspect, in any case."

Jasto only had a minute or two to ponder that further before the shadows receded. Several pillars had been noticeably thinned, and others outright removed to form the construct that now filled the center of the cave like an oversized gazebo.

It was round, rather than one of the hexagons Jasto had come to expect, and sat atop a raised, staired dais so inundated with filaments it appeared to be a solid black. Almost like the darkness of the deep sea, he thought.

In contrast the flat roof above the dais, along with the pillars supporting it and the gridded panels between them, were all sapphire blue and threaded with almost no filaments. For some reason the inner ceiling of the roof, visible through the open front of the gazebo, was covered by grooves crisscrossing to form a regular triangular pattern. The mannequin knaves that had previously filled the cave were gone, save for one that waited at the base of the stairs with its arms folded behind its back.

And past it, at the center of the black dais, was Ralica herself.

Chapter 10

"Her face is gone. Another toll of the lending..." Epha murmured.

Jasto didn't answer. He was too busy staring at the master of this Palace, half in wonder and half in fear. Some things, some people, evoked a reaction from others just by existing. With all she'd done, it was no question that Ralica had been such a person during her life.

And corrupted, she was no less striking. Ralica's body was all angles and flat planes, like one of her mannequin knaves had been taken and filed down to a bare skeleton. Her legs were faceted, ending in singular points rather than feet, and the rest of her body was similarly tapered down to bladelike edges.

The similarities to a mere knave ended there. Ralica's photothyst was blue as expected but caught the light in a strange way, as if dozens of slightly angled layers had been pressed together to create her thin form. Beneath those layers her limbs were threaded with slivers of muscle, and corrupted filaments that forked like symmetrical lightning bolts down to pointed extremities. The other corrupted knights Jasto had seen all had some way of covering the organs and Crest stored in their main bodies. Lenno had encased his in bone, Nilis had simply made the photothyst around them opaque.

Ralica didn't hide anything. Her heart beat slowly in the dead center of her bladelike photothyst chest, wrapped in a tornado of veins that encased the other sparse organs she still retained. Nothing was arranged the way it was meant to be in a living human. At the top of the tornado, just below the surface of Ralica's body, an arrow-like symbol pointed straight downwards. It was black, with the faintest trace of silver along its edges.

The Seafall Crest, and the first Crest Jasto had seen visibly exposed on a corrupted knight. He raised his eyes from it, saw angled polygons that vaguely formed the shape of an open-front helmet. But where they should have revealed a face, or a warped organ or some kind of identifying structure, there was nothing but corrupted shadow.

The urge to run tripled within Jasto. Ralica didn't want to go active, to become the kind of threat she'd spent her life fighting against. He believed that. But he'd felt something fracture in her during that three-part connection. What if the Crest actually had taken her over, and was faking them out with all this? What if the moment he stepped onto that dais it swallowed him, and Ralica plucked the Crest from his suffocated corpse? She could do that. Knave cores would be easy to hide beneath that solid black surface.

But could he really just run because he'd gotten cold feet? Epha was too damaged to fight, and by the time anyone else got here Ralica would already be active. Moreover, Ralica hadn't offered this duel to anyone else.

She'd made a choice, and so had Jasto. After fighting so hard to make his own choices, he couldn't run away from one now.

And more than that, he wasn't alone. "Epha." the old knight looked over, and he lowered his voice. "There might be knave cores inside that dais."

Epha considered that behind her helmet. "I have the means to check," she said, and he breathed out in relief. "I will need to be next to the dais to use it, however."

Jasto thought for a moment. He still had preparations to make before climbing up that dais, but most of them hinged on Ralica choosing to duel him fairly. This all fell apart without that. And of course, actually approaching the dueling field Ralica had made put them back in Palace territory. There had to be something he could do before then, some preparation before he risked it all.

At the thought, Jasto found himself chuckling. Epha looked at him, confusion obvious behind the cross-shaped eyeholes of her helmet.

"Sorry. I told you about the drone replica, right, Epha? Ralica gave me some time to prepare before I fought it." Jasto shook his head a little. That felt like it had been a month ago. "I wasn't sure if I'd made enough preparations back then. I'm not sure now, either."

"You did win that battle, Jasto," Epha reminded him.

He looked over at Ralica again. "Well, you think I'll win this one?"

The old knight paused. "Actually, don't answer that," he said. "I still have to fight either way." As long as it wasn't a trap, in any case.

Epha nodded at his words, seeming pleased. "Control in the face of death, I see."

"I know, I know. Just like the principle," Jasto said wryly. He let himself smile for a moment, then focused back on the practicals.

"Epha, we need to be ready to run if Ralica is baiting us," he said. "Can you project some wheels on your armor?"

"I can." Epha stepped closer to him, inspecting his setup for a reference point, and nodded to herself. "Attempting to stand on wheels in my state would be a fool's errand. I will set mine up for a sitting position."

She did so, forming large all-terrain wheels on either side of her lower legs, then over her hips and back. Jasto nodded in approval.

"Worst case, I'll tow you out of here like that," he said. "It'll be bumpy, though."

"Have you forgotten how I used my Lantern-fire already?" Epha asked, her tone slightly amused. "'Bumpy' is something I have experience with."

"Heh. Good point," Jasto said. Epha had to be forcing that cheer, so soon after the revelations about Ralica. But the fact that she was making an effort was probably a good sign.

"You said we had to be close to that dais for you to check it?" he asked

"Indeed."

"Then let's go," Jasto said, forcing himself to take a slow breath.

Epha nodded and gathered three of her flechettes, extracting their Lanterns and commanding them to hover in a cluster. One piece at a time she projected reflective slats of photothyst around the three Lanterns, angled out from it like a bouquet. A conical shape began to form, and she sealed the slats into it with a final projection. The cone contained far more filaments than an average construct once she was done, and Jasto doubted he could have made a similar one so perfectly.

Epha left the improvised flashlight to hover by her shoulder and nodded to Jasto. He nodded back, and took the lead.

Checking once more that the Ironskin Crest was secure against his chest, Jasto stepped back into Palace territory.

He hovered at the edge of it for a beat, but nothing happened. Then again, if he was laying a trap, he'd wait for them to get further in too. Jasto continued forward slowly, both to let Epha keep up and to take in the surrounding space.

The pillars were clear of knave cores, at least where he could see. Jasto flared his filaments a bit brighter, then checked for any signs of abnormal light absorption around the natural cave features. None, suggesting that they didn't hide any knaves. He glanced upwards, saw only rocks and the tops of the pillars. It seemed like Ralica had legitimately accepted his challenge.

Then his gaze shot back down as he heard a noise. The knave at the base of the dais had stepped to the side, leaving the stairs open to Jasto. This close, he could see that the gridded walls around Ralica's construct also contained sliding gates that would seal behind him.

The knave left one hand behind its back, and gestured up the black stairs with the other. "That would be Ralica's second," Epha observed. "Very formal. I believe she wants to start as soon as she can."

"Not yet. Check the dais first." Jasto didn't like acting this paranoid, but it would be beyond easy for Ralica to ambush him in these conditions. He had to be careful.

Epha nodded without any nitpicking and brought her flashlight flechette up. It was already beacon-like just from the ambient shine of her filaments, and when she flared them Jasto had to squint his eyes down to slits. Golden light blazed forward in a solid beam, revealing what had seemed like an impenetrable layer of filaments as only a very dense grid.

Epha swept the beam back and forth several times, then let it dim. "Several pillar-connecting lines to prevent this construct from dissipating, but none wide enough to allow knaves in. And no hidden cores," she said. "Though I would be worried more about the ones you can see." She pointed at the roof with her flechette, and Jasto followed her gaze.

Directly above Ralica's head, four fishlike knave cores waited in a square formation.

"Oh. Right, she would match the number of Lanterns I have," Jasto murmured. That should have been obvious. He'd been so focused on the danger of a potential trap that he'd forgotten about the actual danger a fair duel would still pose.

"She will not deploy them as humanoids, either," Epha said. "Of every corrupted knight I have seen, Ralica fights the most like she did while she was alive."

Jasto processed that, looking at the triangular grid on the ceiling. He hadn't understood its purpose until now. "You mean…"

"I do. Are you aware of her Crest ability?"

"Who isn't?" Jasto asked. It was strange to have the old knight effectively serving as his coach, but he knew he'd need every edge he could get. "She can boost gravity, for herself and any of her photothyst."

"Any of her photothyst that she is touching," Epha clarified. "The effect lingers for a short time after she breaks contact."

"Right, and that's why she chose her Crest name." There were still some videos of Ralica in combat floating around, so Jasto had seen the damage a gravity-boosted flechette could deal from above. Paired with the way she'd apparently be using her knaves, that was trouble.

"Do not be fooled by the name," Epha said. "Ralica only emphasized the most obvious use of her ability with it. Her true strength is—"

Clink. Clink. Clink.

Jasto recoiled, grabbing Epha by the shoulder and tugging her back as Ralica stepped out of the dueling circle she'd created. It was the first movement he'd seen the corrupted knight make.

He was about to bolt when he noticed how slowly she was stepping. Her assistant knave hadn't moved either.

Epha regained her footing with careful Lantern movements as Ralica came to a stop, standing just at the edge of the stairs. Her face was still a featureless void, but Jasto could feel himself being looked at.

Fingers like long knives opened, and black filaments speared out from the corrupted knight's hand to project a saber that was wide, straight, single-edged, and lined with thin bones. Swords were rare among crystal knights because of how difficult it was to cut through photothyst plate, but Jasto wasn't fooled into thinking he had the advantage. That was a chopping weapon, and between Ralica's corrupted strength and a little gravity boost it would fracture his armor easily.

He was tense, one hand tight on Epha's back armor to start towing her away, but Ralica made no other moves. Instead she waited at the top of the stairs, her knave just as motionless.

"I do not believe she intends to attack," Epha said. "And I see no knaves moving to encircle us."

Jasto glanced around for himself before letting go of her armor, trying to make sense of this development. Ralica must have known she'd spook him, so why take the risk of moving like that? What did she gain from walking forward a little and summoning a weapon?

He could feel his brain starting to tire as he considered the new puzzle. Jasto had trained at the Valor Academy for a year and been on some milk-run knave bounties in the past, but he'd never been in a field of battle for so long before. Or taken so many combat drugs.

Even the moments when he'd been sitting still and bandaging his wounds now felt draining in retrospect, not to mention the actual challenges he'd faced. The diamond trial, the elevator, the drone construct, the memorial of dead knights, Lenno. He'd nearly died so many times, learned things he'd never expected to. All of it had tested him.

Jasto blinked, running over that last thought again. This was testing him too, obviously, this struggle to figure out if he'd convinced Ralica to duel fairly. What if…

What if that was the point? He'd come at this from the perspective that he needed to determine if Ralica could be trusted. But maybe she was still deciding if she could trust him.

"Jasto?" Epha asked. He raised his good hand, thinking. A knight, armed, standing before him but not moving.

He'd seen that before. Jasto glanced down at his right arm, still splinted against his chest, and grimaced. If this really was a test, he'd have to do things the painful way to be sure.

"Epha," he said. "I think I get it. Don't…panic, at what I'm about to do." He stepped away from her, moving to stand directly before the steps of the dais. As he did he ejected the Lanterns set in his back armor, forming an axe around one and placing the other in his right-arm bracer.

Ralica's head shifted ever so slightly to track him. The feeling of danger coming off her bladelike form was almost physical, but Jasto kept his back straight and faced the corrupted knight squarely. He carefully tested his right arm, finding that he could move his wrist but couldn't close his hand completely.

That was manageable. He placed the haft of his axe against his palm, locking it in place with a small projection. Epha shifted as she realized what he was about to do.

"Jasto, the damage that will cause…"

"Believe me, I know. But I think it's what Ralica wants," he said in reply. "She wanted to go out with a duel, right? I think this is part of that."

"Will you even be able to move after trying it?"

"That's what this is for." Jasto fished out the second reactive painkiller he'd grabbed from Epha's medkit, holding it up with his left hand. With the second military-grade painkiller on top of everything else he'd taken in here, he'd need a full flush of his internal organs after this. That was an intensive surgical procedure even in the modern day, involving a full night of tubes in places Jasto would rather not think about.

Still, if he made it to that, it would mean he'd survived this. He dismissed the chinguard of his helmet, but stopped as looked at the painkiller again and considered all that it meant. All the risk he was about to take, for the sake of doing right by a corrupted knight he'd only met today.

He had the option, Jasto realized, of backing out. Of saying it was too risky and he had no choice but to retreat, despite everything. It was a decision to face this risk head-on.

He looked down at his wheels. Maybe…maybe it had always been, this whole time since he'd left the Valor Academy. A decision in thinking he needed to get stronger, a decision in feeling the way he did about other crystal knights. Maybe Jasto had been telling himself he had no choice so he could keep pushing forward, keep fueling himself with indignation.

That method had gotten him this far, but right now he felt invigorated for the opposite reasons. Because he had chosen this, and he'd stick with it. Jasto popped the painkiller, sealed his helmet back up as he tossed the wrapper away.

Then he engaged his forearm Lantern, and dismissed the splints. His arm stayed in place, suspended by the lifting force of the Lantern. It was time.

Jasto breathed deep, adjusted his tongue so he wouldn't accidentally bite it, then ordered the Lantern on his forearm to move upwards.

Even with all the medical technology of modern times, there was no way for Jasto to comfortably lift his arm with a hole in his shoulder. Pain immediately washed out from the wound like a wave, the kind that sucked someone in and held them under with pure force, except made of searing lava instead of water. But then that wave receded, as the reactive painkiller did its job.

Jasto continued to raise his arm. At sternum level the pain splashed even further, even hotter. He kept his pace anyway, knowing that if he stopped he might not be able to start again.

Then the pain grew searing, white-hot roots through Jasto's upper body as his hand reached chin level. He nearly stumbled, and shuffled a little to keep himself upright. The painkiller surged in response, cooling his nerves, and Jasto ordered his Lantern to stretch his arm upward and outward at an angle.

He cried out. His vision stuttered, living fire erupting from his shoulder as the wound there started to bleed again. The movement must have pinched a nerve, because a small part of his arm stopped feeling anything. But the pain receded once again and Jasto managed to keep his posture.

And with that he completed the salute that he'd seen used throughout this Palace, that Ralica's memorial knaves had let him pass by peacefully after seeing. Slowly Jasto guided his arm back down and sealed it in place again, gasping from the pain. Nothing else moved for a long moment.

Then, in the void of Ralica's face, two dark silver sparks lit up.

Like eyes being opened.

Her pointed legs scraped against the dais as they snapped together, the sound filling the entire cavern. Ralica kept moving, turning her saber to show the flat before bringing it up to her head. Her eyes glowed on either side of the blade as she made the same salute. A salute that only a human would bother making.

Epha sighed with profound relief. "Ral, you are still in there. I am sorry I—"

Ralica stretched her left arm out and the old knight paused. Was there some second stage to the salute? Jasto watched in confusion as she brought her sword arm around, laying the blade atop her left shoulder.

The saber filled with dark silver light and dropped straight down as its weight amplified, cleaving through photothyst easily. Ralica's severed arm clattered off the dais a moment later, and she made no move to create a new one.

She deactivated her Crest ability as dark shapes slithered within the roof of the gazebo, and three of the knave cores that had been waiting there threw themselves from it to flop on the dark edge of the construct. Ralica turned and stomped down three times, impaling them one by one, then kicked to fling their fleshy bodies off the dais.

Apparently satisfied, she glanced at Jasto one last time with silver eyes before striding back into the gazebo.

He realized his mouth had been hanging open a moment later, and closed it. Behind him Epha sighed with sincere joy, dismissing the armor wheels she'd projected and standing taller without their weight.

"Amazing," she said. "Amazing. Jasto, however she was altered by saving me, I believe you snapped her out of it."

"No, uh, that's not it," he replied after a moment. Ralica had...handicapped herself? Out of respect for him? It made sense, given what he'd seen of her character, but still. "She was testing me just now. And I think she was planning to the moment she made that dais." That was why she'd stepped forward and projected a sword, he was sure now.

"I do not mean that you broke the spell just now, but earlier. With your display of agility," Epha clarified. "I thought you had forced her compliance with it. But if Ralica was going along with all of this reluctantly, she would not have removed her arm now, after you had already agreed to the duel."

That made sense. "So what did I do, then?"

"In the elevator, Ralica's mental state was distorted," Epha told him. "It is why I had to connect with her, and remind her of her duty, before she began interfering with Lenno. You managed to remind her without even using a filament. You fought for her to overcome her Crest, and she noticed."

"...Is that so." Jasto looked away, irritated at himself. He'd thought Ralica had the same issues as him, in a way, but apparently she was beyond that. Subject to anger, but capable of dealing with it in better ways than him. Even though that was working in his favor, he still felt ashamed. Immature.

An armored hand landed on his shoulder, and despite her nerve damage Epha managed a squeeze. "I do not say that to diminish what you've done," she told him, dismissing her helmet. Beneath it she still looked drained from the near-corruption, but her eyes were solid with certainty. "It is the opposite. Anyone with the right resources can threaten, but that is all a threat is: a use of materials and conditions. You told me earlier that Ralica saw potential in you. You reminded her of that fact, Jasto, and thus we ended up here."

"Maybe she just wants to act honorable before she dies," Jasto said, knowing it was the most useless kind of pessimism but unable to stop himself.

"Who is here that she should put on a show for? Us?" Epha smiled patiently. "Is it truly acting with such a small audience?"

"Maybe."

"And what acts are you putting on, then?"

That actually made his thoughts slow down. He wasn't helping anyone with his negativity, especially not himself. Was it really a part of him? Or was it some act he'd gotten used to making, an outflow of his issues with the Valor Academy?

"Alright, I get it," he sighed. Act or not, the old knight was telling him he had to shelve his attitude. More important things were on the table.

Epha gave him a quick nod and withdrew her hand. "Then listen closely. As I was saying, Ralica's true strength is in defense. When she increases the weight of her own body, she is nearly impossible to unbalance or disorient. No matter how fast one is moving when they strike her."

His eyes widened. "Wait, then my skillset..."

"Yes. It is a good thing you have picked up a command phrase for your filament kills, Jasto. Even so, your arsenal will be much less effective against her."

Jasto was far from an unstoppable force, but from the sound of it Ralica could become nearly immovable. "Is she stuck in place when she uses it?" he asked, hoping there was a silver lining.

"That is one thing that has changed from when she was alive, and not in your favor," Epha said with a grim look. "Ralica's corrupted form has an extremely low center of gravity. Though she cannot reposition the points of her legs until she cancels the effect, she will be able to bend and lean to a large degree."

"Okay," Jasto said, imagining combat sequences with that in mind. Exploiting Ralica's stillness would be difficult, no doubt about it, but with only one arm she'd definitely have some gaps in her defense. "Okay, I can deal with that."

Epha nodded. "Ralica was trained the same way I was, Jasto, so do not allow her to grapple you. And do not assume you will be able to cut her easily. Ralica weakened her shoulder joint before severing it just now."

"Really? I missed that." Even with her Crest connection damaged, Epha's battle-honed perception still counted for a lot.

"Corrupted knights refine their forms and capabilities the longer they exist," she continued. "For that reason, you should also be cautious with any filament attacks."

"Will she be able to resist them somehow?" Jasto asked, his heart rate picking up a little as he thought of Lenno.

"Her knaves will not, as you have already seen. For Ralica herself, I do not know. I would only have been able to find out by attempting to kill her."

"Right. You've seen other corrupted knights, though. Could they resist filament kills?"

Epha considered. "Some of them. As the attacker my will still had more 'weight,' but the attack took longer than it should have to succeed. The resistant knights had more time to break the connection before it killed them."

Jasto was appreciating Epha's pep talk more and more. Without it he would have just been moping at all this information instead of looking through it for ways to win. And there was a silver lining to what he'd heard: from the sound of it, Ralica wouldn't be able to turn a filament kill around on him like Lenno had. And remembering the thrall gave Jasto an idea, a gambit he might need to win this fight.

"I have told you not to let Ralica grapple you, but it is best I do not tell you more than that about how she fights," Ralica finished. "Too much information might disrupt your instincts. And if I tell you her habits in combat, she will likely recognize that and use it against you."

"Got it," Jasto said. With his unique way of fighting, he wasn't sure how much of the advice would transfer over anyway. The average crystal knight was constantly engaged in a dance of Lanterns, always on offense and defense. He was more of a hit-and-run combatant.

He transferred his axe back to his left hand, then ejected the Lantern from his forearm. The splint didn't shift at that, thankfully. "Anything else?"

"...No, that was all unless you had further questions." Jasto's eyes immediately landed back on the old knight. He'd picked up on that shift in her tone, the reticence. It took him a moment to realize the source of it as he followed her gaze down to his boots.

"I was way off about you, Epha," he said. "Thanks."

"For what?"

"For holding yourself back. You wanted to remind me that Ralica only has one Lantern now, right?" Epha was good at controlling her expressions, but nowhere near Dad's level. He saw that he was right. "You didn't, though, because you knew it might get me killed to use only one Lantern myself in there. I appreciate it. Really."

Jasto had once thought Epha would be too stuck in her ways to not do something like that. He was glad to be wrong. And now, it was time to approach this battle in his own way.

He projected another axe over the Lantern from his forearm, then he drove both it and his first axe into the stone. Jasto was left with only the two Lanterns powering his wheels.

"I'm not being completely fair, doing it like this," he said as he summoned a new axe. "That's just not me, not when this much is on the line. But I'll at least show respect."

He turned before Epha could say anything, and took a moment to calm himself. It might have been easier, mentally, to stick to an extreme. To either keep all of his Lanterns or to discard all but one of them like Ralica had. But he wasn't just some honor-bound knight like Epha, any more than he was just some soulless operator like Lenno. If it felt uncomfortable, it was because he was breaking new ground.

He held the thought for a moment, then refocused and adjusted the projections holding his arm and the Ironskin Crest in place. When he was done his arm and the Crest were a little further out from his chest, giving him room to maneuver and to store one last trick.

With that done, Jasto returned his wheels to their standard form and strode towards the stairs. Ralica's second remained where it was until he passed it, and as he began climbing the stairs of the dais Jasto heard the knave turn and follow. A moment later, he heard Epha do the same on his right.

He reached the top of the stairs and met eyes with Ralica. She'd moved back from the center of her arena, along with her last knave, and was once more completely still. Her left shoulder was now covered by a stump of photothyst layers, and her legs had been cleaned of knave blood. If his retention of two Lanterns bothered her, she gave no sign.

Jasto ran through his battle plans one last time. Between the small area of the dueling circle and the limited number of Lanterns they both carried, this fight would start and end quickly. Every moment and gambit he had would count.

Within the circle, Ralica's eyes burned with a dark silver that seemed almost impatient. Jasto met them head-on and stepped forward.

"I shall call this duel," Epha declared. He heard her stepping to the side, but kept his eyes on the corrupted knight before him.

"Challenger, state your name," Epha called out in a clear voice, and Jasto paused. He had a choice here that he hadn't realized he would, all of a sudden: what name to declare to Ralica.

A simple 'Jasto Chaston' was the first answer that came to mind, of course. He'd almost said it automatically just now. But all the reasons he'd had for not choosing a Crest name, for holding out on what was a relatively petty bit of tradition…well, they seemed less important now, after coming so close to death and corruption. In fact, continuing to hold out now seemed more like something Lenno would do.

So instead he squared his shoulders and gave the name his brother had come up with a few months ago, the moment he'd seen Jasto's photothyst colors.

"Jasto Chaston Grassbone."

"…The defender's name is Ralica Byerson Seafall!" Epha continued after a second, her voice warm. Ralica tapped her blade against the floor, apparently in confirmation.

"Challenger and defender, you have agreed to duel under these terms: Death only, no time limit, Lantern limit variable, all photothyst projections allowed, all Crest abilities allowed," Epha said, extrapolating the conditions Ralica would fight under. "Turn away from your opponent."

Well, turning his back on Ralica wasn't that much more dangerous than simply standing on top of this dais she'd made. Jasto complied, hearing faint *clinks* as Ralica did the same.

He faced the door, where Epha waited in her armor, and could immediately tell she was smirking at him. "I suspected as much."

Jasto sighed. "Yeah, I do have a Crest name. I just…didn't want to jump on the bandwagon that easily, I guess. My brother came up with it," he added, redirecting the subject of the conversation.

"It is a good one," Epha assured him. "Quick to say, while revealing only your photothyst colors and nothing of your abilities. So many Crest names experience that issue these days. Truesword, for example, was a dead giveaway of a sharpening ability. Seafall is not much better."

"Didn't expect you to say that about Ralica," Jasto noted.

"I badgered her for an entire month to choose something else," Epha said wryly. "But she is quite strong-willed."

Jasto nodded. It had definitely been more than sixty seconds, but Ralica was letting them have the moment.

"Anything else you want to say to her?" Jasto asked. Epha shook her head solemnly.

"It has all been said, long before you arrived here. Now face her, and hold nothing back."

Jasto held her gaze. This was it. His last chance to back out.

He made his choice, and turned. Photothyst rattled as the sliding doors of the arena were closed behind him, one by Epha and one by Ralica's second.

"The duel will proceed. Arm and armor yourselves." Jasto had already done that, so he just rolled his good shoulder and took a stance with his wheels down. Ralica didn't move at all, but the knave core above her swam in a quick circle before facing him head-on.

This was it. "Challenger!" Epha called

"Ready!" Jasto yelled back.

"Defender!" Ralica tapped the floor with her saber in confirmation, then brought it forward to point straight at Jasto. She was ready, it was clear.

"Knights at the ready..." Jasto breathed in. He was tired. But he could do this.

"Lay on!"

Jasto burst from his starting position, implementing his first strategy: end the battle fast. Ralica stepped to the side but he corrected his course, dropped to a knee, then hooked his axe around her arm as he passed under it. He meant to push himself back up to a standing position, twisting Ralica's arm out of the way as he did so, then ram his shoulder into her chest and make contact using the filament he'd threaded there.

But before he could stand up, Ralica dropped her sword and slid her thin, bladelike hand down to grab Jasto by the wrist.

Then the whole arena inverted, as she leveraged her corrupted strength to throw him over her hip one-handed.

He slammed hard into the dais, the impact searing his shoulder once again. Jasto groaned and Ralica adjusted her grip, about to kill him, but with the reactive painkiller clearing his head he was just fast enough to dodge. He dismissed the armor over his hand and triggered his wheels in one smooth sequence, slipping free of Ralica's grip and skidding away from her on his back. One split second later, a wedge-shaped photothyst projectile pounded into the space where he'd been laying to crack the dais there.

"I warned you about grappling!" Epha called. Panting, Jasto turned to recover his footing and curved along the arena's edge. He hadn't really expected to end the battle that quickly, but he'd thought he would at least gain an advantage. Instead Ralica had turned the attack around on him and if she'd had both arms Jasto would have died outright instead of just getting close. He'd have to do things the riskier way, then, and whittle Ralica down until he could make a clean kill. She'd have a lot more chances to kill him this way, but it had to be done.

Jasto had lost his axe in the struggle, so he quickly projected a new one along with his hand armor as he took in the projectile that had almost killed him.

It was guided by Ralica's one knave core, and just like Epha had said it didn't possess a humanoid form. Instead it looked more like an insect limb attached to the ceiling, with the wedge-shaped headpiece still stuck in the floor. The knave core was inside the wedge, while at the ceiling the three-jointed limb fit into the triangular grid of grooves he'd seen earlier.

Just like Epha had implied. Ralica had set this arena up not only to create a sealed space for her and Jasto to battle, but also so she could use her knave the same way she'd use a flechette.

The corrupted knight recovered her saber, and her flechette went up and moved to guard her left side. Then she advanced, the sound of her pointed legs hitting the dais almost musical as she rushed Jasto. Not wanting to engage on her terms, he faked left and then swerved to the right before she could trap him against the wall.

Ralica wasn't fooled, but she also wasn't used to fighting someone who moved like Jasto. Her flechette split from her, swinging over his true trajectory in a clothesline as the corrupted knight herself closed in from the left. Jasto kept his course, guiding himself down onto his back so the flechette passed above him, and cleared the pincer maneuver.

The flechette immediately changed directions to pursue him, Ralica following, but there was a gap between the two of them now. Jasto lunged on the opportunity, switching the rotational directions of his wheels so he corkscrewed back up to his feet, then clicked his wheels up as he faced the flechette.

He had a window of just seconds before Ralica closed in, and he took it. The blue photothyst wedge snapped forward like a scorpion's tail, aiming straight for his gut at a low angle. An actual person would need to be lying on the ground to stab at Jasto like that, making it difficult to block with his axe.

So he didn't use his axe. Jasto yelled as the attack came in and engaged his left boot Lantern, knocking the wedge straight upwards with an augmented kick.

He'd caught plenty of opponents off guard with this move, and Ralica was no exception. The head shot upwards, its supporting limb trailing behind, and in a single movement Jasto brought his leg back down while swinging his axe overhead. The core-bearing wedge flew free, skidding to a stop near the edge of the arena, as the now-headless supporting limb flopped inertly over Jasto's shoulder.

Ralica was still closing in, but she'd be just a little too slow. Jasto clicked his wheels back down, already leaning into a retreat, and felt confused as he set his eyes back on Ralica. Instead of trying to close in, she'd stabbed her sword into the ceiling.

Before he could fully comprehend what was happening, dark silver energy raced up the blade. Ralica's Crest ability conducted through the photothyst ceiling at the speed of thought, highlighting the triangular grid within it, and spread down into the remains of the knave's supporting limb.

The supporting limb still draped over Jasto.

It was like the finger of a god was suddenly laid on his shoulder. Jasto was forced towards the ground as the weight of the photothyst limb on him first quadrupled, then multiplied exponentially further with every microsecond. He didn't escape it intentionally. But since his knees hit the ground first as he hunched beneath its weight, the wheels there engaged and sprawled Jasto backwards. Without them, he would have been immobilized beneath the limb.

As it was he still slammed into the floor jaw-first, a blow that would have turned his visor opaque with cracks if Epha hadn't helped him make a smaller one. Jasto felt the ghost of a concussion, one he wouldn't fully appreciate until the reactive painkiller wore off, but with Ralica approaching he had no time to be in pain. His usual chest wheels were gone because of his splinted arm, but he'd just dealt with a very similar situation against Lenno.

Jasto got his left arm wheels beneath him and immediately triggered his Crest ability, shooting backwards in a one-armed plank.

Ralica's saber punched into the space his head had just occupied, but before Jasto could get more distance between himself and the corrupted knight his arm gave out beneath his weight. That was muscle damage, an injury he hadn't noticed between his adrenaline and the reactive painkiller. The fight had barely begun, and he was already breaking apart.

Jasto scrambled back onto his knees and then his feet as he wheeled away from Ralica, heading towards the edge of the circle where her flechette-knave had landed. Ralica chased after him, still slower than he was but not letting up.

Jasto shot a glance back towards the severed wedge of photothyst, saw that it had sprouted little limbs and was trying to carry itself back towards Ralica.

With the gravity boost he'd been treated to earlier, Jasto didn't have time to stop and make a filament attack on it. Ralica seemed to be counting on that. But unfortunately for her, he didn't need to stop.

Jasto dropped his axe, which he somehow hadn't lost in that earlier sequence, and left it to dissipate in midair as he bent his course towards the knave core. It tried to evade him by switching directions, and at the same time Ralica threw her saber like a javelin.

But Jasto was already in motion, and even though he lacked in other areas this was something he'd mastered. All it took was a little acceleration, and the thrown saber passed behind him instead of through him as he dropped to one knee, scooping up his quarry without slowing down.

Even now it tried to stab at him with its little limbs, but as Jasto swerved away from Ralica he was already snaking a filament into the flechette-knave's core. He made contact, and for the first time since the three-way connection he saw Ralica's Diagram again.

Its layout had shifted, dramatically. Large, volcanic islands had torn themselves free of the churning ocean, bleeding smoke over the fractured remnants of older ones, and every edge of the water was crimson now. Red-purple waves crashed with even more fury across the Diagram, covering the majority of its surface and then some.

But Ralica's latency, her humanity, was not gone. A sapphire-blue whirlpool swirled in the center of the ocean, just the sight of it filling Jasto with focus, and whenever the red waves tried to push in they were torn apart by its force. Hurricanes, each representing a knave, were packed within it and under her control.

Ralica's will was far from broken.

"Open your eyes!" Jasto yelled, and the connection fractured along with the knave in his hand. Ralica stopped moving for the first time since the beginning of the fight, staring at him, and a moment later Jasto came to a halt across from her.

She knew he'd seen; maybe she'd even wanted him to see. Epha had checked on Ralica's Diagram earlier and only seen scraps of blue water, disparate and scattered across the ocean. Jasto could barely believe that his actions had somehow changed that, like Epha had said.

But that whirlpool hadn't been there before, and now it was. And as long as it kept spinning, Jasto suspected Ralica would stay in control.

He gave his shoulder a testing roll, feeling out the restrictions damage had put on its movement, then dropped the smoking remnants of the knave and summoned another axe. The stars of his Diagram fritzed out, reformed closer to him in warning. He'd have to be careful with his projections now.

"It's almost over," he told Ralica, and accelerated.

But she'd already adapted. This time, instead of attempting to meet his charge head on, Ralica darted far to the side with her saber up. Jasto could have altered his course to hit her anyway, but that would mean losing some speed. And passing Ralica while going too slow could easily be a death sentence.

He curved away instead, then looped back towards her at a higher speed, but she was already strafing to the side once more. He kept trying to close, but Ralica had started to get a read on how he moved and continued shifting positions to baffle Jasto's charges, leaning heavily into each move with her low center of gravity. She wanted to force him into a slower charge, and her corrupted form was nimble enough that he couldn't ignore the tactic.

But Jasto wasn't out of tricks yet. His next charge started slightly off-target, forming a gentle curve that would lead him to the right of Ralica. She broke left immediately, and if Jasto had been doing a normal charge he would've had to start over.

Instead he leaned into the curve before tilting left, carving a question-mark shaped path that slingshotted him directly to Ralica's new position at full speed. His axe went down, ready to cut one of her legs at the knee as he passed. Ralica didn't manage to dodge, or to get her sword in the way as he rocketed in.

But she did have time to trigger her Crest ability, and in an instant her form disappeared behind dark silver light. Jasto had leveraged his whole body into the strike, both for greater force and to avoid confining all the strain to his shoulder. But even with that, he felt his arm try to tear itself loose from the rest of his skeleton as his axe collided with her gravity-boosted form.

Whatever noise his weapon made as it bit into the layers of Ralica's body was blocked out entirely by the pain, and when the reactive painkiller cleared Jasto's brain enough to think again he saw its edge had become a chipped and pitted mess. More concerningly, one of his fingers and several patches of his arm had gone numb. He was near his limit, pushing closer to it even when he did land a hit.

But he turned to look back at Ralica and saw that it hadn't been for nothing. Blood, far more than he'd expected, poured from the gash passing more than halfway through her right knee to form an irregular pool. If not for those layers, he was sure would've removed the limb completely. She was still glowing dark silver, but as that faded and her gravity effect let up the flow of blood also slowed.

Her stance was steady, but different. She seemed to be putting all her weight on her uninjured leg, but didn't do so in the exact same way a normal human would have. Maybe that was her lower center of gravity at work. Jasto had managed to make one leg unusable, crippling her, but filaments were starting to writhe around the damage. Her layered structure was taking time to repair, clearly, but it would repair.

If Ralica wanted to wait for that, then Jasto wouldn't give her the chance. He turned to face her fully, preparing for another charge, and raised his arm. Or rather, he tried to. His hand managed to get slightly above his ribcage before dropping back down. Jasto caught it before it could flop to a completely limp state, tried to raise it again at a slightly different angle.

Pain spiked and was numbed, but even so he only managed to raise his arm halfway up before it collapsed again. Ralica adjusted her stance slightly, and was able to put a little bit of weight on her damaged leg.

"Come on," he growled, a weird mix of helplessness and anger working its way through his chest. He'd finally landed a blow on Ralica, only for her Crest ability to damage him just as badly in the exchange. Epha had warned him about this too, the defensive power she had. And now, if he didn't somehow press the advantage anyway, this was over.

"Change tactics, Jasto. You can no longer rely on that arm," Epha called. He almost whirled to ask her what he was supposed to do then, if he couldn't even swing an axe, but controlled himself. He knew better, didn't he? Epha had just shown him how much a crystal knight could do, even when their body gave out.

He dismissed the photothyst holding his boot Lanterns in place and levitated them up. One went into his axe, to save on photothyst. For

230

the other he made as narrow of a flechette as he could without compromising its durability.

Epha hadn't been completely right. Jasto couldn't raise his arm more than halfway, but as long as he could do that there was at least one thing he could rely on it for. But he'd save that trick until the last moment.

Not wasting any more time, he sent his flechettes forward. The most dangerous crystal knights could conduct every single one of their Lanterns independently, attacking and defending in a rhythm that was almost impossible to predict. Jasto didn't have much skill at that, especially since his fighting style was so unique.

So he stuck to what he knew. His flechettes shot forward in a pair, floating as if a ghost was holding them. Ralica leaned to the side to dodge one, shifting far more than a normal human would have been able to on a single leg, and turned her blade to deflect the other with the flat.

Jasto let his flechettes carry past her as she recovered, and slowly began to trudge forward. Ralica noticed, of course, and tried to limp away before he could close in. So he called his flechettes back the way they'd come, lower to the ground this time. They moved as if he was holding them, in patterns he was familiar with.

Ralica had to stop immediately to defend herself, and did so. Neither of Jasto's flechettes scored a hit, but that was fine. They didn't need to.

They just needed to occupy Ralica a little bit longer, until he got within striking distance. It was agonizing to walk so slowly when his legs were actually fine, but it was necessary all the same. He'd only have the edge if he surprised her, by suddenly leaping forward once he was close enough. Ralica wanted to buy time for her leg to recover, so she'd wait until the last moment to break this stalemate. But as long as he kept faking, Jasto could make her think she had more time than she really did.

He changed up his pattern, having his flechettes lance towards Ralica and then linger for a few moments to strike down at her injured leg. She swung it away from them, balancing completely on her other leg as she fought them both off, and Jasto pulled both back before she could score a kill.

Just a little further now. Jasto made his breathing louder, and sent his flechettes in for another pass. It couldn't have been more than a minute since he'd made that leg cut, but it felt like half an hour. Still, he was almost in range.

His flechettes came at Ralica from the opposite side of the circle, forcing her attention to split. Her eyes flicked across the void of her face, to land on the incoming projectiles.

Then, without looking back, she hurled her sword straight at Jasto. He dropped in an instant, the motion instinctive after years of riding on his knee wheels, and it passed overhead.

But because of that movement, just for a moment, his attention had been taken off of his flechettes. Without a new order they continued on their rapid course, but that didn't stop Ralica from snatching one out of the air.

"Dreck!" Jasto cursed, rushing out of the crouch as he called his axe flechette back. He tried to call his second, but it didn't even wiggle under Ralica's iron grip. He had to take his chance now, before she—

Reality disappeared, replaced by his Diagram.

PUSH THROUGH, Ralica commanded, and one of its satellites vanished in an explosion of seawater.

Jasto stumbled, back in the dueling circle with the taste of salt in his mouth, and sharpened fingertips pierced his armor like butter. He lurched back, more out of nausea from the Shard-kill than a conscious reaction, and they slipped free of his chest plate with bloodied tips.

Ralica had leaned forward the maximum distance her low center of gravity allowed and thrust her hand out to stab him. If both of her legs had worked, the stab would have been deep enough to kill instead of just drawing blood. Jasto caught his breath, getting back to his feet as Ralica similarly recovered, and pushed down the lingering feeling that he was about to throw up.

Filament kills weren't supposed to do that. They weren't supposed to feel any different than when he lost a Lantern the mundane way, but the words 'push through' were still echoing through his skull regardless. Epha had warned him that old corrupted knights were capable of more.

Only one Lantern left. Jasto kept it close as he made small projections over his chest wounds, his body so damaged that he barely felt it when the Star descended on his mind to make them. And Ralica's leg…it wasn't fully healed, but she'd recovered enough to limp on it. The pool of blood she had shed rippled from her steps.

All he had was one flying axe, and two nearly useless arms. Ralica's damaged leg scraped as she cleared the blood pool, a new saber forming in her hand. Maybe her regeneration had been slow because she'd also had to make more blood, Jasto thought distantly.

He shook himself as he backed up, knowing the end of this short, brutal fight was close. Even though Ralica was moving again, his last strategy was still the same. He'd just be executing it far more dangerously now.

Jasto guided his axe-flechette up, then tucked his left arm behind his splint and the Ironskin Crest, hunching like he was going to ram Ralica with his left shoulder. He'd already threaded a contingency filament there, and moved it a little closer to the edge of his armor as Ralica paused, her balance steady and her sword low to the ground.

Outside the circle, Epha's breath hitched. This was it, they all knew. The last exchange.

Jasto ran forward with a yell. His axe carved a path in front of him, spinning through the air as it headed straight for Ralica's chest. But she didn't shift her guard, didn't move her sword out of position to give him a chance for a filament-kill with his shoulder.

Instead she just triggered her Crest ability. The axe bit through three, maybe four layers of photothyst before it came to a stop left of the Seafall Crest, and that was it. She wasn't even rattled by the impact, amplified as she'd made her own gravity.

Meanwhile her saber came up. It and her arm were the only parts of Ralica's body not glowing silver, so the stab she'd aimed right at Jasto's throat wasn't slowed in the slightest. He'd already committed to his charge, meaning the blade would only pierce him further.

Jasto's focus condensed to a laser point. He was still a saber-length away from Ralica, but he could see how it would happen. The tip of the saber would pierce the meager scales at his neck and skewer him. Blood would fill his throat. He'd die, Ralica would go active, and in all likelihood Dad would be next.

So he turned, as he'd planned to from the beginning, and ripped his left arm free from behind his splint. He still couldn't get it above ribcage level. But he didn't need to.

Because now he held a long photothyst dagger, projected before the start of the duel and hidden behind his damaged arm. Jasto was a master of momentum after so long training at high speeds, so he continued to turn, leveraging the full force of his body behind his damaged arm as he braced it against his side. With his arm at his ribcage, the dagger was just long enough to intercept the saber.

Sparks screamed from the collision of blades, Jasto's own elbow driving his side as his second reactive painkiller started to give out. He yelled once again as horrible sensation returned to his arms, his body. But even so, it was enough to slide past the saber.

With the last of his strength he planted his foot, whirling back around to slam his left shoulder into the axe still planted in Ralica's chest.

Jasto commanded his shoulder filament forward. It slid into his weapon.

Connected with the Lantern waiting there.

And pressed on until it reached the Seafall Crest.

"Open your EYES!" Jasto yelled as the ocean whirled before him, and the stars descended. Not just them, though. One of his satellites was here too, more present than the unconnected ones outside the dueling circle. If Jasto was a missile dropping from the sky, the Lantern he'd connected with was a smaller missile linked to it.

And thus, his attack sped towards Ralica even faster. She pushed back, hard enough that Jasto could feel the strain through their link, but it wasn't enough. Lenno had managed to turn an attack like this, but only while connected with two of his own Lanterns. Jasto had her.

He saw the ocean erupt, throwing waves in both red and blue into the air as it broke apart. Just before the connection snapped one last, faint thing flitted its way into Jasto's Diagram, a single emotion:

Hope.

The real world appeared once more. Jasto saw Ralica's face inches away from his, stripped of its corrupted shadow and completely motionless. There were only vague suggestions of a mouth and nose in the photothyst, with a complex lattice of filaments forming the eyes. Then he noticed something else at the edge of his vision and turned.

Ralica's hand was next to his throat, frozen in place with its needlepoint fingertips extended. If he hadn't connected with his Lantern for that attack, if he'd been just a little slower...

Jasto staggered back, jostling Ralica's body as he did so, and it clattered to the ground like a statue. The heart within it was no longer beating.

"Jasto…you…" Epha began.

"I did it," he mumbled, and collapsed onto his face.

Chapter 11

Jasto dreamed.

He knew he was dreaming, at least, but couldn't make himself think of much else. He just watched, patiently, as signals from his brain and his Crest blended strangely in his unconsciousness.

He saw that cloudless winter night when his Crest had found him once again, the one that had been preserved forever in his Diagram. Once more it hovered exactly four feet in front of him at chest level, remaining there no matter which way he turned or how far he ran, not that he could run far in this dream. The green body of the Crest shifted like liquid as white filaments unspooled from the torso-like symbol in its center, worming through the air towards his collarbone. When this had happened in real life Jasto had thrown bricks and other trash at it, everything phasing through the Crest like it wasn't even real. It had only turned solid when it touched Jasto, binding him to this life despite his efforts.

So this time he stood there instead, watching its progress. Wondering about life without it, for the first time in a while. Even letting himself ask, if he'd been able to choose back then…

A sloshing interrupted his thoughts, and Jasto looked down to realize he was standing on the ocean.

On Ralica's Diagram, right before its destruction. His feet were on either side of the central whirlpool, as if buffering it from the red waves that filled the rest of the ocean.

"Those of you I manage to save, my final order is this," Ralica said. The words were from the speech she'd given, right before her corruption. "Make your survival matter. Do not let the Round Table—"

The Diagram erupted, red and blue waves drowning out the rest of the words as they rose to cover the sky. Jasto felt, or maybe remembered feeling, that faint emotion transfer Ralica had made with her last moments alive. She'd felt hope. For this? That he'd go after the Round Table, knowing what he knew now?

Or for something else?

The blue waves enveloped him completely as the dream began to shift, then solidified into a large blue hexagon looming over his head. It seemed to slowly grow closer as he watched, occasionally rotating a sixth of a circle like some great gear before stopping again. The hexagon was photothyst, and threaded with black filaments, but something was strange about it. No light absorption, Jasto realized. The corrupted filaments were there, but weren't shrouded in their usual darkness.

Not only that, but the hexagon looked familiar. Set around Jasto and leading up to it was a blue, six-sided column, as if he was watching the whole thing from inside a hexagonal straw.

Wait, not a straw, a shaft. An elevator shaft.

This was reality.

"What…" he said, his voice dry and ragged, and the hexagon—the ceiling at the top of the elevator shaft—came to a stop.

"Jasto…you're awake earlier than I expected. Do not try to move," Epha said from his right. Obeying, he shifted his eyes a little to see her.

The old knight had her helmet off once again, revealing a deeply weary expression. Her armor was a lighter set now, and the Lanterns within had all been moved to her legs and spine. She noted the lucidity in Jasto's eyes and nodded to herself.

"You were unconscious for one and a half hours, approximately," Epha told him before he could ask. "I gave you first aid, then began to carry you back to the surface with my Lanterns. We are inside the elevator shaft now. It seems Ralica prepared a staircase within it for us, before her…death." For a moment it had seemed like Epha was going to use a different word, to distance herself from the reality of what had happened. Instead she'd chosen to face it head-on.

Jasto looked around, taking in the floating stretcher Epha had made for him first, then the staircase she had referred to stretching along all six sides of the elevator shaft. "…Thanks," he said, his voice dusty. "Do you have…water?"

"I do." Epha floated him closer, and to Jasto's surprise reached back to her medkit even though her arm carried no Lanterns. "There has been enough dendritic repair that I can move my arms without any shaking," the old knight explained. "Though I still feel some pain when doing so."

Her hand came back out with a watergel pouch, which she placed over Jasto's mouth. It was at that point he realized his helmet had been removed for Epha's treatment, along with most of his armor.

Regardless, he bit down on the end of the pouch and sucked in some watergel. The way he could feel it break down in his mouth, expanding from its condensed state into liquid, was not pleasant. But the cool hydration it brought was. He swallowed and thanked Epha.

She nodded and withdrew the pouch, resuming her climb up the stairs. "Jasto, how much do you remember?"

"I…" he frowned. "We beat Lenno. Then I did that stunt with the Ironskin Crest, to make Ralica duel me." he concentrated as Epha came to a turn in the staircase, and the ceiling above revolved a sixth of the way.

"Then she accepted—" he began, and the rest returned all at once. He gasped as the beats of the duel flickered through his head, at how close he'd come to dying again and again over the span of a few minutes. "Crystal fucking Star," he muttered. "Her hand…it was right next to my throat." He leaned to the right, trying to get away from that phantom sensation, but the stretcher didn't let him go far.

"Yes," Epha said. "The moment you started that connection, Ralica dropped her sword and went to pierce your throat with her hand. Doing so would have been easy with her body's structure, even though you were armored. But you managed to complete the kill just before she could."

"Thought so," Jasto murmured. He wouldn't have even seen it happen, with all his attention on the mental battlefield. "So the linking really did save me."

"The linking?"

"Yeah, something Lenno did to me," Jasto said. "I went to filament-kill one of his Lanterns, but he'd linked it to his other Lantern and himself. So he turned it around."

"He reversed a filament attack? Completely?" Epha asked, stopping.

"Yeah. Wait, you didn't know that could be done?" Jasto asked. "I thought it was just…something I didn't learn before I left the Valor Academy," he finished, skirting around saying he'd gotten himself expelled. It felt like more of a sore spot now.

"No, I have never heard of what you suggest," Epha said. "And Lenno never mentioned such a technique during our campaigns together. He would have, at least to Ralica, if he'd known it at the time. Especially with how revolutionary it could be against the corrupted."

"Wait, what does that mean? That he learned it after he became a thrall?" Jasto was a little surprised by this tangent, and how seriously Epha was taking it, but now he was curious too. "Even if it would be revolutionary, it's kind of a niche technique if you're already corrupted. Why come up with it? Just to deal with whoever passed your trial?"

Epha was silent for a moment, thinking as Jasto did the same. "Crystal Star, Lenno," she cursed abruptly, before resuming her climb. "It would be that."

"You figured it out?" Jasto asked, turning towards her. Epha's expression had gone from simply morose to clear unhappiness, the corners of her mouth drawn down like creased blinds.

"I thought that it was strange how Lenno could 'influence' Ralica so much," Epha said. "Not just in stopping her interference at the elevator, but over the longer term as well. Thralls are supposed to be subordinate to the knight that corrupts them, so it made little sense for Lenno to be the one altering Ralica's state of mind. But as you now know, filaments are not just tools for executing kills. They can also be used to communicate."

"Yeah. Wait, so the Lantern linking, you think it wasn't just for filament kills?"

"Yes, I suspect it would also strengthen communications. Turn a message into a manipulation, or in this case…push a corrupted knight further into an active state."

"So that's why he developed it," Jasto said slowly, and as he looked at Epha's tight frown something else occurred to him. "Does it bother you? That I used his trick at the end?"

The old knight sighed. "Jasto. Do you recall that I did not say anything, when you brought more than one Lantern into your duel?"

"Yeah."

"Similarly, I will not say anything more on this matter."

That was a yes, then. For a few minutes they simply continued on their way, Epha trudging up the staircase as Jasto looked at the ceiling above.

"I used your trick too, though," he offered. "That hidden dagger prepped in advance, like you had in your duel against Nilis. I was at my Crest's limit and you saw how I couldn't lift my arm too high at the end, so without that…"

"Ah, so that is why you did not project another axe," Epha replied. She nodded to herself. "You incorporate tricks and techniques from everyone you see, even if you set yourself against them…that is a good mentality for a warrior."

Jasto could tell she wasn't just talking about the dagger trick. "That's me, I guess," he replied, feeling weirdly defensive at the praise. "I'll learn from someone even if they piss me off. But, uh…I don't think I'm setting myself against you, anymore."

Epha paused, then looked at him very deliberately, making sure he felt her eyes rest both on the stretcher he was physically bound to and the shoulder that, although treated by modern technology, still had a gaping hole in it. "Truly? That is quite the relief to hear. I simply do not know how I would manage being your enemy."

"I was just—gah," Jasto muttered, looking away as he felt his face turn crimson. Had that been sarcasm? From Epha Suncage, the living legend that had once served an even greater legend?

The old knight's laugh was dusty, from both her age and all she'd been through, but still genuine. "I do appreciate that, Jasto," she said. "And for my part, thank you. I could not have put Ralica to rest on my own. Because of your efforts, her last moments were not spent hurting the innocent in an active state. That means much to me, and I know it meant just as much to her."

Jasto felt the weight behind those words, as heavy as all the photothyst in this Palace put together. But before he could reply a ringing sound filled the air, like a hammer hitting a gigantic block of ice. "What was that?" he asked, wincing.

"The consequence of defeating Ralica," Epha replied. "This Palace will not collapse for at least a day, I suspect, but now that I have extracted her Crest it is beginning to break."

"Right. Wait, her Crest—"

"It is stored in my back armor, along with Lenno's," Epha said easily, turning slightly so he could see them. "Do not worry, it is yours. Both due to our agreement and to Round Table law. Your claim on the

Ironskin Crest is murkier, as we fought together, but I will cede it to you in this case."

"Are you sure?" Jasto asked. "Don't know if you remember, since you almost got corrupted right after, but you technically made the filament kill first." He still wasn't sure how much his connection to Lenno had actually done, at the end.

"I remember, and I am sure," Epha replied, her tone firm now. "I...have no claim on it, not anymore."

"Wait, what?" Jasto asked. "What's that supposed to mean?" It occurred to him that he wouldn't have bothered asking before today.

"It means I am retiring," Epha said, keeping her eyes forward as she answered. "The Seafall trial has finally been completed, and the futures of both Ralica's family and mine are secured. Not only that, but my Crest is now too damaged to be used in combat." She took a quiet breath. "I no longer have a reason to remain in the field, or the ability to do so."

"Oh. Right, that all is true," Jasto said slowly.

"And, as you've eagerly reminded me before, I am old," Epha added. "I am certainly due for retirement, after such a long vigil."

"Yeah...that makes sense."

On paper, anyway. But as Epha nodded at him and continued with her climb, Jasto's eyes narrowed.

It was understandable that someone would want to retire after all this, true. But Epha specifically? He wasn't convinced. On top of that, some of the signs were off. Epha's voice had remained steady and clear, as it almost always did, even though Jasto had heard it shift in her more emotional moments before. And maybe it was just him, but she'd seemed to be coming up with reasons to retire as she'd spoken.

Jasto had been pushed to the brink once himself at Valor Academy, so he knew that was wrong. All the problems he'd had with the school had clattered around in his head until they were the only thing he could hear, and he'd snapped. Rather than thinking of reasons to get himself expelled, he hadn't been able to think of anything else. So it seemed like Epha was lying to him.

But why? What was she going to do, if not retire?

Jasto still hadn't found an answer by the time they'd reached the top of the staircase, returning to the Palace entry chamber. But now, instead of the hexagonal floor where Jasto had faced the diamond trial, there was only an empty pit that the staircase they'd climbed spiraled down. The three entryways to Ralica's labyrinth were still sealed, never to be reopened again.

And at the end of the one open corridor, where he could just catch a glimpse of the desert evening outside…

"Jasto!" someone shouted from the end of it.

"Dad," he breathed, heart leaping, and every other consideration dissolved for a moment. His father was here, and that meant he was safe.

Because Dad was practical even in moments like this, it was a squad of mercenaries that came down the corridor to meet them. Their helmet lights bobbed as they formed a protective perimeter around the two, rapidly questioning Epha.

"Jasto's injuries are severe, but nonlethal," she told them. "Attend him immediately, but do so outside. This Palace will not last." She turned to show the Seafall Crest embedded in her back armor, and Jasto saw at least two mercenaries stiffen. Though the entire Palace was no longer absorbing light, he didn't blame them for their surprise. It was one thing to see aftereffects like that, and another to see direct proof.

They were ushered out quickly, Epha reshaping Jasto's stretcher into a cot as they moved and setting it down on the dusty rock of the ravine. Some hired soldiers brought medical supplies forward for Jasto as others cut away at his combat clothes to expose the damage, one cursing at the state of his shoulder.

"Help Epha too," he said, and Dad looked at him with questions in his eyes. Jasto nodded, and after a moment his father confirmed the order. Surprised, Epha thanked him politely before beginning to dismiss her layers of armor. Meanwhile, Jasto's father knelt next to him as the mercenaries began their work.

Dad was worried enough that his urgency did show on his face, but he still made himself wait. Once the medics had confirmed that Jasto and his shoulder were stable, he immediately leaned forward to block out the darkening sky.

"What happened, son? This was only supposed to take two hours at most, wasn't it?"

"Trouble," Jasto said.

"Elaborate."

And he did, explaining Epha's initial guidance through the Palace and the interruptions it had suffered, both from Lenno and the trials Ralica had put Jasto through. For the sensitive details about Ralica's death, he checked how close the mercenaries were and lowered his voice appropriately. For the parts where he'd done something he knew Dad would disapprove of, he clenched his jaw and told the truth anyway.

Jasto finished his rundown and paused to drink water from a mercenary's canteen, warm and slightly metallic but much more palatable than watergel, then watched quietly as the gears turned behind his father's eyes.

"Ralica was an unknown entity," he said. "When Lenno first appeared before you she did not interfere, showing ambivalence to your survival. Even though she provided some assistance to you, linking with her afterwards and opening yourself up to corruption from her Palace was a severe risk."

"It...yeah," Jasto admitted. "I was out of options."

"In that situation, yes," Dad said. "But you chose to do so a second time when Epha was in danger of corruption." Jasto was about to protest the idea of killing Epha like that, but his father kept going. "And even more than that, after Ralica's apparent breaking or at least near-breaking, choices were available to you. And your decision was to reenter the Palace, with the express purpose of putting yourself in danger to prove to Ralica that you could get out of it. Then..." he paused, frowned at himself, and leaned back a little.

"Then you put yourself completely at Ralica's mercy, by accepting that duel," he said in a calmer voice. "Another massive risk."

"I know that," Jasto said. This was Dad's version of worrying, as critical as it might have seemed. "I know that, but I..."

He paused. 'I had to' was what he'd planned to say just now, more out of bitter habit than anything else. But if there was ever a time to reframe things, it was now.

"But I don't regret it," he said instead. Dad tilted his head at the words, eyes narrow and shaded as they always were. Even after years, there were still moments like this one when Jasto had no idea what his father was thinking.

A long second passed, and Dad reached over to put his hand on an uninjured part of Jasto's chest.

"Then I'll trust your judgment," he said.

Jasto blinked. "But…"

"You acted differently than I would have, yes," Dad said. "Far differently. But making your own decisions is important, and it worked out for you. Not only that, but…" Dad glanced away. "Well, never mind."

"No, what is it?"

"Something unimportant, considering that you're alive and made the decisions you did."

"Dad, please," Jasto pressed. "I saw down there how bad things can get when people keep secrets. What is it?"

His father sighed and relented. "I knew you were hiding things when we came here, Jasto," he said, and the squire-errant swore he felt his heart freeze in place for a second. "About the manner of your expulsion for one, as you told the story too cleanly, but it was obvious there was more." He looked back at his son. "Your attitude, towards both Epha and the crystal knights in general, made that even more obvious."

Dreck, Jasto had been stupid to think he'd fooled his parents. "If you knew I was lying, then why'd you go along with all this? Why not stop me?"

"The first part of that was practicality," Dad said. "We can't truly 'make' a Crestbearer do anything, under the laws set by the Round Table, and thus would not have been able to stop you if you'd tried this on your own. Any funds you received from knave bounties and such would be reduced, thanks to your squire-errant status, but they would still go directly to you. Therefore, you could not be stopped from gaining the funds to attempt this yourself."

"But…I would've stopped, if you'd told me to," Jasto said. That had been the fear hanging over his head, ever since he'd first planned to come to Seafall Palace: that his father would cut all of this off. "I would've, Dad."

"Answer honestly, Jasto," Dad said, in his analyst voice. "Would you truly have stopped if I'd told you to, just like that? Would the idea of making this trip independently, using the freedoms the Round Table affords to all Crestbearers, never have occurred to you?"

"I…" this whole time, Jasto had thought he'd been the one with no choice. But in focusing so much on the Round Table, he hadn't realized how little choice he'd given his family.

Jasto wanted to close his eyes forever. "Crystal Star, Dad, I'm sorry."

"No, we chose this less-risky path without consulting you. Perhaps you would have listened if we had talked, but the answer to that question is lost now." Dad tilted his head. "And besides, a large portion of the problem came from the extreme freedoms granted to Crestbearers. You could hardly have altered those conditions."

"But it was a problem because I was too obsessed, right?" Jasto insisted. "All I was thinking about was getting stronger so I could be more free. I didn't stop to consider anyone else." And in that, he'd acted the same way Lenno had.

"Then I will ask you this, son, and discard all biases when you answer," Dad said. "Are you still 'too obsessed?'"

Jasto thought about it, looking up as he did. He hadn't paid much attention to it earlier, but the sky really was beautiful out here, so deep in the desert and distant from artificial light. A molten orange sunset dropped lower and lower in the west, letting streaks of dusty purple creep in. They revealed a night sky, and more stars than you could ever see in a populated area.

The Pandora Gate was out tonight, hovering in front of the full moon like a metallic, ring-shaped blemish. Jasto searched for a moment and found the Crystal Star on the opposite side of the sky.

Its photothyst was silver today.

"No," he said. "No, I choose not to be."

Dad didn't smile, but his eyes gleamed for a brief moment. "And that leads us to the second reason your mother and I did not speak up, son: hope."

Jasto tilted his head, and Dad continued the explanation. "People can make all sorts of choices, at all sorts of times, even if they say they are already committed. Your mother was confident that you would come around before doing something too destructive. I was…less certain, but many knights describe the time when they absorbed their first Crests as a formative experience. Your anger seems to have been reduced, Jasto, so I am glad that this applies to you as well."

Jasto slumped back a little, the fact that he'd been compared to other crystal knights barely even registering. He'd thought he was being so clever, keeping his plans secret, but he hadn't kept his feelings secret and that had given the rest away. And instead of trying to punish or lock Jasto down, his parents had been counting on him to get over himself this whole time.

He owed them the truth. "Dad, I…the reason I did all this was to absorb the Seafall Crest, like I said." He took a second to try and make his voice shake less. "But I was going to use it to become a merc-Crest. That way I wouldn't have to live on the terms the Round Table made, and I'd be strong enough to fight back if they tried to…Dad? What is it?"

His father's jaw had clenched, visibly. His eyes were wide enough that the full circumference of his irises could be seen. Jasto hadn't seen him panic like this in years.

"It…is good…that you've told me this," he managed to say. "Because following that plan, Jasto, would have been suicidal."

"Suicidal? Merc-Crests are in a legal gray area, yeah, but I could get a corporate protector like you did—"

"—Think about what you learned in the Palace, Jasto," Dad said, looking from side to side to make sure the people they'd hired wouldn't hear. "Perhaps an average mercenary Crestbearer would not be in extreme danger. But one who knows what happened to Ralica Seafall?"

Jasto was about to open his mouth and say everyone knew that, but stopped. Everyone knew the official story, yes, but it was a lie. Ralica had been betrayed by the same people that now sat on the Round Table, while in the middle of risking her own people to end the Drone War.

Jasto knew that now. And the Round Table would know that he knew.

"*Dreck*," he swore. "But wait, would they really kill me if I spoke out? They could just say I'm making it up, I've got a bad track record already. The worst it would do is mess up their reputation a little."

Dad shook his head. "You're dangerous to much more than their reputation. The Round Table may have been able to scrub most of the evidence of what they did, and bribe the survivors who might speak out, but they have not been able to destroy the thing that most makes you a threat."

"What's that?"

"The prestige you've just acquired," Dad said. "Ralica Seafall was a war hero, one the Round Table had to continue acclaiming in order to avoid suspicion. The Seafall Trial is a rather legendary challenge itself. And it is common knowledge that Palaces contain personal traces of the knight that forms them. If you say that Ralica was betrayed, people will believe you." The cool recital of the dangers seemed to calm Dad down a little, and when he next looked at Jasto his eyes were narrow once more.

"The Round Table has enemies, especially now that the Drone War is over. And if you speak out, you could easily become the figurehead they rally around, garnering popular support along the way."

Jasto frowned, running through the points his father had made forwards and backwards. The Round Table could just denounce him…but they were a military organization, and had inherited limits to their involvement in other industries from the General's Council. Corporation-owned media would be able to counter them there.

But the corporations didn't have to get involved, and might not want to. Jasto was sure some of them wouldn't mind getting their fingers in the military, but they'd have to fight the Round Table over that. Except that was a risk they clearly didn't mind taking, given how they'd been lobbying for the existence of merc-Crests. The corporations would go against the Round Table even more strongly, if they thought they could get away with it.

Still, even with all that, Jasto could just not speak up about what he'd seen. He could even approach the Round Table after becoming a mercenary to make an agreement to that effect, and simply not become a threat. Live a life they wouldn't have a problem with. Except…he knew better than to believe they'd go for that, didn't he? Jasto had relived the moment of Ralica's betrayal. He'd heard Duskwall rant at her, afraid of ever losing the power he'd snatched and being trod on again.

And Duskwall, along with the rest of the Round Table, had lived in fear. Just like Ralica had foreseen, they hadn't made any concerted efforts against the Palaces that plagued Andalon. They'd created a set of laws that nudged crystal knights towards that, and secured their own position in power, but that was it. They'd be afraid of Jasto too, of the threat he *might* pose even if he didn't *want* to challenge them.

Even with all the Round Table's power, their fear robbed them of choices and then they turned around to rob Jasto of his. "Dreck," he murmured, his head thudding against the back of the stretcher. "I'm a political landmine. Going mercenary would be like declaring war on the Table…they would kill me for it. They might kill me anyway."

"Perhaps, and we'll take appropriate measures for that," Dad said, probably already thinking about the favors he could call on. "But I can tell you that they would have a much weaker pretext for any action they took, as long as you continue to be a crystal knight."

"Are you sure? I may not be a merc-Crest right now but I'm still in terrible standing. Squire-errant, remember?" Jasto said. "And all that only comes into play if they get caught. They already got away with hiding a mass military action during the Drone War."

"True, but that was at a time when drone activity had jammed communications extensively across Andalon," Dad said. "And the acclaim you've just acquired cuts both ways. If you had chosen to become a mercenary, a path Ralica was vocal about opposing before her death, that would not be as much of a consideration. On the other hand, if the inheritor of the Seafall Crest was a crystal knight in good standing, walking the same vaunted path as Ralica herself, was to die mysteriously and there was even a hint the Round Table was connected to it…" Dad paused. "They would face severe backlash. I will not say that you are completely safe, as I would need to analyze the knight-commanders to verify that. But if they attempted to assassinate you unprovoked, they would take on a great risk."

Jasto nodded. That wasn't as reassuring as simply being told he would be safe, but it was far more honest. That had always been Dad's way, and it was a comfort that he stuck with it even now.

Only, something else occurred to him. "But that means I'm in some danger right now, right?" he asked. "I still have squire-errant status. The Valor Academy might have suppressed most of the news of how I got it, but…"

Dad nodded grimly. "If they are afraid enough, the Round Table might risk revealing those details and then going after you, once they learn of all that's happened here."

Jasto sighed. He knew he was taking all this talk of his potential death far better than he normally would. Part of that was all the near-death and near-corruption he'd just been through, leaving his feelings exhausted, and the rest was probably shock.

Still, as long as he had this clarity he'd make full use of it. His squire-errant status was a problem. Actually this whole situation was a problem, Jasto thought. He'd just wanted to get strong enough to ensure his freedom when he'd come here, and instead he'd been bound in even tighter restrictions that might just kill him.

But his squire-errant status was a problem he could focus on, right now. The Round Table didn't want crystal knights thinking they could break the law at will, so their statuses and associated privileges could be lost through infractions, but they also wanted their knights to spend more time defending Andalon than in jail. So there were ways for an errant status to be recovered.

That said, the most expedient ways were only available to full knights that had completed their Valor Academy training. Jasto was not just errant but also a squire, which limited him there.

The best way to deal with that was obviously—

Jasto stiffened, his eyes snapping into line with his father's. "You…led me here," he said, not quite wanting to put it into words. "Led me into thinking I should go back to the Valor Academy."

Dad nodded. "The largest threat to the Round Table is internal: the doubt of the crystal knights that they lead, who have been taught to be guided by honor and disdain assassinations. Therefore, in addition to the other reasons I've discussed, an environment filled with honor-bound knights would be difficult for them to make a move in."

Jasto almost asked why Dad had led him indirectly like that, but he knew why. He was acting in a way that he believed would keep his son safest, just as he had this whole journey.

He sighed. "Dad, can you please…tell me stuff like this? Directly? It would've saved us a lot of trouble. I mean, dreck, I just saw back there how bad things can get when people lie."

"Nothing I said was a lie."

"But it was a deception, right? At least a little," Jasto said. "Please."

Vikor Chaston thought, going silent for the longest period yet since this conversation had started. It seemed absurd that he had to spend more time thinking about this than large-scale Andalonian politics. But then again, it hadn't been easy for Jasto to ask about it either.

"I expect honesty for honesty," Dad eventually said, his face nearly unreadable as always. "The things you kept hidden on this trip could have easily gotten you killed."

"Alright," Jasto said. "Then…I got myself expelled from the Valor Academy, on purpose," he admitted. "Because I was afraid of getting changed by it." His father had already figured that much out, he was sure, but saying it was still important.

"I'll tell you the full story later," he added after a moment, and Dad nodded.

"For my part: I believe that absorbing the Seafall Crest, returning to the Valor Academy, and becoming a crystal knight in good standing would be the safest path for you now," he replied.

Jasto felt relieved to be upfront with his father again, even on a subject like this. "You want me to absorb it, Dad?" he asked.

"You already know what happened due to your time in Seafall Palace," Dad replied. "It would just put you at a greater risk to not have the Seafall Crest's power as well."

"Right," Jasto said, rolling his neck a little. It had gotten stiff from looking to the side for so long. He found himself watching the sky again.

"It actually does make the most sense to go back, huh," he muttered. He knew from experience it was hard to hide things in the Valor Academy, especially a full-on assassination. With so many knights gathered there, it would also be a good place to act on what he'd learned here without plunging Andalon into civil war. And on a more personal level, Jasto wasn't happy that things had ended with him fleeing the Academy instead of facing it head-on.

But still, to willingly return to the place that had almost compromised who he was on the inside…

"You have more strength than you think, son," Dad said, reading his expression. "Your survival of this Palace, the choices you made within it and the choices you've made now all speak to that. Your mother and I trusted you to come around, and you did. We trust you also to remain as yourself, even within the Valor Academy."

"But I'm…" Jasto hesitated before saying 'weak,' but not out of a feeling of shame. It genuinely felt less true, after all of this.

"And if you're still concerned, perhaps bringing a mentor along would help with those worries," Dad said, looking to the side.

Jasto followed his gaze. It landed on Epha, who was politely but firmly dismissing the mercenary that had been treating her. Her black tabard was as ragged as a cobweb now, and beneath it her desert clothes were layered with medical wrappings. Jasto was surprised by the number of injuries her armor had apparently concealed. Maybe nerve damage hadn't been the only thing restricting her at the end.

"Crystal knights of her standing can come and go from the Academy as they like," Dad continued. "With some paperwork, she would even be able to take an advisory role in your education there."

"That'd be great," Jasto said, a little surprised to find that he meant it. Epha was full of knowledge, but more than that he felt a bond with her. Lenno hadn't been wrong, to say that combat forged connections.

But unfortunately… "She's apparently going to retire after this, though," he told his father.

Dad frowned, looked back at him with slightly widened eyes. "She said that to you? In clear terms?" he asked.

"Right? I wasn't really convinced either," Jasto replied, happy that Dad had picked up on the same thing as him. "You think it's a lie?"

"It doesn't seem right. Epha seems to possess a strong sense of duty, based on her actions. To stop while she's capable of giving more?"

"Her Crest connection is damaged, meaning she can't really fight as much," Jasto said, not to contradict Dad but to make sure he had all the information.

"I remember, but I thought that would simply change how she does her duty, not her desire to execute it," Dad replied. Excitement had seeped into his voice. "If it is a lie, why would she need to tell it? What does she gain by hiding her goals from us?"

Epha had successfully gotten the mercenaries to leave her alone, and was now walking back to the Palace for some reason. "Going after the Round Table?" Jasto proposed, only to immediately shake his head. "Actually no, it wouldn't be that."

"Why not? Based on everything you've told me, Epha has several reasons to attempt the murder of every living knight-commander," Dad said.

"She's not the type to take a path like that," Jasto said, remembering how angry she'd gotten when Lenno revealed his own plans for revenge. "I think she'd consider it a desecration of Ralica's memory, or something."

251

"Yes, I see. That would appear to fit," Dad said, a rare light coming into his eyes. "It seems that we are in need of more information, directly from the source." He stood smoothly, dusting off his clothes with quick movements. Puzzle-solving, especially when the puzzle in question was human, always got Dad genuinely excited. "Are you able to stand, son?" he asked.

"I think so," Jasto replied. There was some uncertainty in his voice, and not just because he didn't know if his feet could handle it.

Dad had gotten him this far, had set up the deal with Epha that had made all this possible. He'd even manipulated the old knight for it, and at the time that hadn't bothered Jasto.

But...

"Could you let me take the lead?" he asked as he sat up. "Epha's going to want to talk to you about sealing the deal you made, but still. Could you let me talk to her alone?"

Shadowed eyes set in a near-expressionless face turned to him. Jasto tried not to react.

"It seems I've overstepped," Dad said. "Of course, son."

"Sorry," Jasto mumbled.

"No, I appreciate it. Your mother would have reined me in, too," he replied, his tone just slightly rueful. "Besides, I've already had plenty of opportunities to analyze others on this trip." Both of Jasto's arms were bound in med-sleeves, so Dad helped him get to his feet. "I will create a window for you, during the conversation. Make use of it."

Jasto nodded, and with that father and son approached the old knight together. When they reached Epha she was kneeling on a patch of ravine stone facing towards the Palace, and for a moment Jasto thought she was saying her goodbyes to Ralica. But then she briskly stood up, and turned with a familiar environmentally sealed bag in hand.

"Your timing is good, Jasto. I had only just recovered this for you," she said, holding out the bag she'd made him store his ammunition in. He blinked at it.

"Oh right, thanks. I'd actually forgotten about this, somehow."

"Extreme battles often have that effect. But in your case I suspect you will acclimate quickly," Epha replied. Jasto's arms were out so he called up one of his Lanterns, which Epha had gathered up for him after the duel, and projected a basket around it. She placed the bag within, the magazines it held clinking. Then she reached into a pocket of her clothes and withdrew two more objects, both rectangular and splashed with black. With no ceremony at all, she added the Ironskin and Seafall Crests to the basket he'd made.

Epha exhaled, and it seemed like years came out of her. "I have now fulfilled this promise," she said, and Jasto frowned at the wording. Was there a promise she hadn't fulfilled? "Mr. Chaston, will you honor your side of this agreement?"

"Of course." Dad pulled out a thin tablet, unfolded it to its full size, and began tapping at its screen. "Within the next few weeks your siblings and Ralica's remaining family members will be recommended for quality housing and employment within Silverton." Not the capital of Andalon, but still a major and well-defended city.

Epha nodded in thanks. "Would it be possible for you to provide some sort of receipt to that effect? A way of showing that I had a hand in this?"

"Hm. Dealings of this nature don't tend to have the largest paper trail," Dad replied, his tone convincingly uncertain. "But I believe I can arrange something. Let me step away for a moment."

Epha's eyes went back to Jasto, a faint question in them, before returning to Dad. Jasto gave it good odds that she'd picked up on something being out of place, but she wasn't in a position to do much about it even if she had.

"So be it," Epha said.

Dad nodded, but didn't step away immediately. Instead he lowered his tablet and stepped up to the old knight, his right hand out.

"Sir Suncage, my son tells me you saved his life several times within the Palace. Even risking your own corruption to do so," he said. "If not for your skill and commitment, he would be dead. I'm grateful."

Jasto knew that Dad was being sincere, but still wondered if Epha would actually shake his hand. Despite how she'd been leveraged to get to this point she did, her calloused hand taking his in a firm grip appropriate for a crystal knight.

"He was under my protection," Epha said. "Thus, I did as I should."

Dad nodded once more, then turned and stepped out of hearing distance without looking at Jasto. He'd be 'occupied' getting Epha's receipt, creating a window that she couldn't just walk away from.

It was all on Jasto to figure this out now. He stared at Epha, and after a moment decided he would just be straightforward.

"If I asked you to be my mentor, would you still insist on retiring?"

Epha's eyes widened, but she composed herself quickly. "Are you asking, Jasto? Not even a day ago you had a rather low opinion of me."

"And I was wrong," he admitted. "About that and a bunch of other things. If there's one thing this Palace made clear, it's that I still have a lot to…"

Jasto trailed off, his head tilting to the side. He was the holder of Ralica's Crest now. Epha had said as much herself, and she felt a duty towards Ralica.

So why wasn't she leaping at the chance to teach him? Why wasn't she trying to make sure he grew as a knight both in character and skill? Epha hadn't been shy about pointing out his weaknesses inside the Palace.

"Enough, Jasto," Epha said, startling him. "I refuse this offer. You obviously do not want me to retire, though it is hardly your business, but I have done my duty to you thoroughly and completely. I cannot be guilt-tripped now."

Guilt.

Everything clicked.

"It wasn't a challenge," Jasto blurted. "This whole trial you set up with the Palace, it was never a challenge. It was…a cry for help. You wanted to find another Ralica."

Epha jerked backwards like she'd been slapped. "You wanted someone to follow again, right?" he asked. "Someone you could trust the way you trusted her. That's why you tested everyone who came here…you knew that Ralica would tell them the truth about her death. You wanted someone that would act on that knowledge!"

"I— how did you—" Epha's voice, so often clear and direct, stuttered. Her eyes shifted like she was watching the world turn inside out, and Jasto made himself give her a moment.

Internally, he reeled at the implications. Epha's usual tests were meant to discern people's character, and Epha herself had been strong enough to stop those who resorted to brute force. The Palace fed into that, offering some tests that weren't what they appeared to be: the diamond trial and the memorial that could be passed simply by showing respect were examples of that. It was all set up so that only someone Ralica approved of would have the chance to kill her.

Epha had wanted it all to play out like some grand drama, where a knight came to her trial, proved themselves by passing it, and walked away with both new power and a quest to reveal the truth. A quest she could follow them on, the same way she'd once followed Ralica.

Instead, Lenno had hijacked her plans. Everyone 'worthy' had been killed by him before they could reach Ralica, and with the time that had brought he'd driven her closer to an active state. It was Jasto that had broken the pattern. He'd gotten Epha to come along, and in doing so had forced Lenno out into the open. Then Lenno had tried to kill them both, to keep things going and complete his revenge quest.

No wait, that wasn't quite right. Lenno hadn't been out to kill them both, he'd been planning to corrupt Jasto. Every other knight that had been allowed into the Palace would've pushed Ralica back toward latency, which is why Lenno had killed them.

But Jasto…was unworthy. He would have pushed the scales the other way if he'd been enthralled, making Ralica go active after years of holding on. He sighed, but then frowned at that thought as he remembered Ralica's very last moment. If he was unworthy, then why…?

"It was only supposed to take a year or two, at most," Epha said, interrupting his thoughts. Her eyes were on the Palace, watching fractures grow and fork through its hexagonal structure. "That was how long I was meant to be wearing this tabard."

She removed it as she spoke, though beneath it she was still fully covered by khaki clothes and bandages. "Were you aware that black was once the color of mourning, in Andalon?" she asked. "It changed to gray during the Drone War. Before then, both Crestbearers and drones were much rarer, and thus the color black was less associated with corruption." She shook her head, hands wandering between the rips and holes that populated the old piece of cloth. "Perhaps you have never believed in chivalry, Jasto, but in those days there were many who did. The sin of the knight-commanders belonged only to them and the ones they had misled. I was confident that there would be other knights…others I could trust with Ralica's power."

She pinched one of the tears in the tabard. "Once I had confirmed that, I would be able to end my grieving. Work alongside those believers, and restore the Round Table to what it was meant to be. Yet it ended like this."

"There were other believers," Jasto said. "Remember what Lenno was going for? People who would make Ralica turn active. But he didn't find any until me, so he had to kill everyone that passed your trial."

"Even so, I have still failed." Epha's gaze settled on her reflection in the slowly breaking Palace, and hardened as she said the words. "I checked the Palace itself time after time, concerned that I was missing something, and I never found even a trace of him. All my intentions served only one purpose: to push Ralica closer to the brink. And at the end, even realizing my mistakes, I was not enough to save her. You had to do that instead, Jasto."

The fractures suddenly multiplied, a boom echoing through the ravine and beating against Jasto's ears. The spot where Epha had been staring was filled with cracks now, too opaque for any kind of reflection.

"How can I possibly continue as a knight or a mentor, after failing so badly?" she asked. "It would be irresponsible. I must retire instead, before my mistakes have another opportunity to hurt someone. This is a moment of personal triumph for you, so I did not wish to sully it by discussing my failures, but you have your answers now." She turned away from Seafall Palace. Her tabard was still clenched tightly in her hands. "A sinkhole will form here in a few hours, Jasto. It is time to leave."

Jasto remained in place as Epha began to walk away. The conversation was over, clearly.

But he was still missing something. Hope. Why did Ralica feel that, at the end, when all her accounts were already settled? Lenno had already been killed, Jasto was already killing her, and he supposed the knight-commanders were still in power but Ralica's feelings had seemed more personal than that, especially when he considered the other emotion transfers he'd felt—

Personal. Her people.

The closest of them. A failure she'd never be able to fix…

"Not the Round Table," Jasto murmured. "I couldn't do a thing to them, they'd just kill me if I tried. She'd have no reason to hope I could fix that, so what…"

"What exactly are you speaking of?"

Jasto turned, realized he'd been thinking out loud as he saw Epha staring at him. It wasn't her normal look, either; something about his words had set her on edge, so that an invisible pressure fell on Jasto.

"The emotion transfers," he said slowly. "I told you about them, remember? How Ralica thought I could fix something?" Then he blinked. "Oh, but I didn't have a chance to tell you about the last one she made, as I was killing her..."

Jasto hadn't meant to pause there, but he was forced to stop and swallow as Epha leaned forward, the weight of her full attention sledgehammering into him.

"Ralica communicated something *other* than anger to you, after spending herself to stop my corruption? You are certain?" Epha pressed.

"It was hope," he said quickly. "Sent right before the kill finished. I think she only managed because she was almost gone."

Epha's old eyes narrowed, looking for a moment like sharpened talons. Then she leaned back, and the invisible pressure on Jasto dispersed.

"I have decided to believe you," she said. "Ralica's emotion transfers are generally far more complex than that, but you have not given me the impression of being a good liar."

Jasto almost laughed at how accurate that was, but managed to stop himself. "Right. So, hope. But I don't think she was hoping I'd deal with the knight-commanders. I think it was something smaller-scale. A personal guilt."

Jasto saw Epha's face change at those words, and became certain of his answer. He hovered on the edge of saying it for a moment, knowing it would hurt her to speak the words and make it real.

But even so, he'd made his choice. "Ralica wanted you to leave, didn't she?" he asked gently. "She didn't want you stuck here, grieving forever. That's what she was hoping for, that you would move on."

Epha looked down at the ragged tabard she held, her expression so still that for a moment she somehow appeared faceless. "If you retire now, I don't think that's really moving on," Jasto said. "If you do, then go. But if not...well, you heard my request earlier. But I can't claim I'm going to start spreading the truth and overturning the Round Table, not with the risk it would bring me and my family, so I understand if you won't—"

"—I accept." Jasto stopped midsentence as Epha slowly dragged her gaze up from her tabard and sighed. "Our retreat from the Round Table's setup went terribly. Worse than any of our strategists expected. When I returned to Seafall Palace for the first time and told Ralica what had transpired, how many we'd ended up losing, and asked what the plan was…" Epha blinked rapidly. "She told me that revealing the Table's betrayal now would only start an unwinnable conflict. That the number of deaths she was responsible for had already grown too high, and it was time to cut losses."

Her eyes tightened at those last words. Jasto could guess what they implied, even if Epha didn't say it: killing Ralica, passing on her Crest, and getting on with her life like she'd never tried to fight for a better world or a betrayed leader.

"I could not," Epha said. "I…could not follow the last orders I received from her."

"So you did all this instead," Jasto replied, his voice softening on its own.

He understood, somehow. Epha hadn't done any of this to cling to Ralica, not primarily at least; it was her own identity that she'd been trying to protect. After a lifetime of believing in and fighting for Ralica, even neglecting her own family in the process, throwing her away must have been unimaginable.

Epha had done all this in a desperate attempt to stay true to herself.

Jasto had forced his expulsion from the Valor Academy for the same reason. He'd help her through this last step.

Since his arms were shot, he printed flat prongs over each of his Lanterns. Then he stepped forward slowly, respectfully, and slid them under the tabard in Epha's arms. Her grip on it turned protective.

"Epha," he said, looking the old knight in the eyes. She'd chosen to become his mentor. She wanted to move forward, do what she hadn't been able to before.

So did he.

"Let's get it right this time."

Eventually she nodded, and let Jasto take the tabard from her. He folded it carefully with the prongs, then knelt to set it before Seafall

Palace. Epha knelt next to him, placing a stone from the ravine atop the black cloth.

The two of them stood when they were ready, and Jasto filled his father in on the relevant details. Their departure was delayed a little as the three of them worked out a preliminary mentorship agreement, Epha tentatively accepting the Ironskin Crest as her down payment.

Not long after that, they left Ralica's grave behind.

Acknowledgements

The first person I'd like to acknowledge is you, reader! It means a lot to me that you gave this story your time, allowed it to enter your head and take on its own life there. If you liked it, please consider sharing *Crystal Grave* with others and/or leaving a review for it. Both help.

And now, I'd like to thank some of the people who helped me get these words onto the page and out to the world. The first of those is Joshua Antonio, who gave loads of valuable advice during the development of *Crystal Grave* and was always willing to take a look at my other little bits of writing. A lot of the confidence that helped me make it this far came from having him look over my work.

Next, I thank several mentors: every librarian in my life, especially Mr. Swindle and Ms. Roelle, for all the books you helped me connect with. Mrs. Vaughn, one of my earliest English teachers, for the many creative writing assignments she gave me. And not to repeat the dedication of this book, but I thank my mother, Cindy Castañeda, and my father, David M. Fanning, for raising me and caring for me and for all the little things they've done for me that I may not have even noticed. It all helped me reach this place, become someone who could write and publish a story.

Thank you.

About The Author

Daniel D. Fanning is the author of *Crystal Grave*, a novel he wrote while working on his biology PhD. He's been writing things for a long time, and reading them for even longer, but sharing his work with a larger audience is new ground. He writes about ideas he thinks are cool, in the hope that other people will also think they're cool and start talking about them with him. Maybe even make some fanart. A guy can dream.

To learn more about him and his writing process, check out his website danieldfanning.com.

www.ingramcontent.com/pod-product-compliance
Lightning Source LLC
Chambersburg PA
CBHW060540260626
47161CB00003B/989